CONTENTS

THE OGRE COURTING *by* Juliana Horatia Ewing 306

MIMA (poem) *by* Walter de la Mare 312

NICHOLAS AND THE FAST MOVING DIESEL
by Edward Ardizzone 313

I HAD A LITTLE NUT-TREE (poem, Anon.) 324

THE OWL AND THE PUSSY-CAT (poem) *by* Edward Lear 325

WHENCE IS THIS FRAGRANCE? (carol, Anon., with music) 327

COBWEBS *by* Margaret Gatty 329

FROM A RAILWAY CARRIAGE (poem)
by Robert Louis Stevenson 339

THERE WAS A CROOKED MAN (poem, Anon.) 341

THE CONSTANT TIN SOLDIER *by* Hans Andersen 342

O LITTLE TOWN OF BETHLEHEM (carol, with music)
by Bishop Phillips Brooks 349

SPELLS (poem) *by* James Reeves 351

THE WONDERFUL TAR-BABY *by* Joel Chandler Harris 354

BRER RABBIT, HE'S A GOOD FISHERMAN
by Joel Chandler Harris 357

THE FAIRIES (poem) *by* William Allingham 361

MARY INDOORS (poem) *by* Eleanor Farjeon 364

THE HERO OF HAARLEM *by* Mary Mapes Dodge 365

ROW, ROW, ROW YOUR BOAT (song, Anon., with music) 370

THE TAILOR AND THE CROW (poem, Anon.) 371

LILLIPUT-LAND (poem) *by* William Brighty Rands 372

LONDON SPARROW (poem) *by* Eleanor Farjeon 374

LAZY JACK (Anon.) 375

IF ALL THE SEAS (poem, Anon.) 380

THE FAIRIES OF THE CALDON LOW (poem) *by* Mary Howitt 381

A KITTEN (poem) *by* Eleanor Farjeon 386

THE WELL OF THE WORLD'S END *by* James Reeves 387

WRITTEN IN MARCH (poem) *by* William Wordsworth 396

SIX O'CLOCK BELLS (song, Anon., with music) 398

LA HORMIGUITA AND PEREZ THE MOUSE *by* Ruth Sawyer 399

TURTLE SOUP (poem) *by* Lewis Carroll 403

A NAUGHTY BOY (poem) *by* John Keats 404

THE FOOL OF THE WORLD AND THE FLYING SHIP
by Arthur Ransome 405

CONTENTS

TOPSYTURVEY-WORLD (poem) *by* William Brighty Rands   419
BIRTHDAYS (poem, Anon.)   420
THE SMALL BROWN MOUSE *by* Janet McNeill   421
NICHOLAS NYE (poem) *by* Walter de la Mare   430
A NORWEGIAN CHILDHOOD *by* Björnsterne Björnsen   432
THE FLY (poem) *by* Walter de la Mare   443
RILLOBY-RILL (poem) *by* Henry Newbolt   444
THE OLD WOMAN IN THE BASKET (poem, Anon.)   447
THE CAT THAT WALKED BY HIMSELF
   by Rudyard Kipling   448
NIGHT (poem) *by* William Blake   460
THE FABLE OF THE OLD MAN, THE BOY AND THE
   DONKEY *by* Ian Serraillier   461
HOW STILL THE BELLS (poem) *by* Emily Dickinson   463
POOH AND PIGLET GO HUNTING *by* A. A. Milne   464
BELLS (poem) *by* James Reeves   469
THEN (poem) *by* Walter de la Mare   471
A HYMN FOR SATURDAY (poem) *by* Christopher Smart   471
RAPUNZEL *by* The Brothers Grimm   472
FOO THE POTTER *by* John Pendry   481
A SPELL FOR SLEEPING (poem) *by* Alastair Reid   494

Index of Titles   497

Index of Authors   500

Index of First Lines of Verse   503

Index of Artists   505

The Stories Classified   507

ACKNOWLEDGEMENTS

The Editor and Publishers acknowledge with gratitude their indebtedness to the authors, their publishers, and representatives, for permission to include the following copyright material:

Tim Rabbit from THE ADVENTURES OF NO ORDINARY RABBIT by Alison Uttley (Messrs Faber & Faber Ltd)

The Dutch Cheese from COLLECTED STORIES FOR CHILDREN by Walter de la Mare (Messrs Faber & Faber Ltd, the Literary Trustees and the Society of Authors as their representative)

Prickety Prackety and *A Hole in Your Stocking* from THE TOOTER by Diana Ross (Messrs Faber & Faber Ltd)

Paul, the Hero of the Fire by Edward Ardizzone

The Christmas Tree by Tove Jansson

The Story of Caliph Stork from THE GREEN FAIRY BOOK by Andrew Lang (Messrs Longmans, Green & Co. Ltd)

Johnny Crow's Garden by L. Leslie Brooke (Messrs Frederick Warne & Co. Ltd)

Where Arthur Sleeps from WELSH LEGENDS AND FOLK TALES by Gwyn Jones (Oxford University Press)

The Lory Who Longed for Honey from THE NIGHTINGALE by Leila Berg (Oxford University Press)

Dobbin and the Silver Shoes from THE TALE THAT HAD NO ENDING and *Robin Redbreast's Thanksgiving* and *Father Sparrow's Tug-of-War* from STORIES AND HOW TO TELL THEM by Elizabeth Clark (University of London Press Ltd)

The Kind Visitor by Eve Garnett

The Golden Touch by Honor Wyatt

The Pavilion in the Laurels by Barbara Leonie Picard

The Baker's Daughter from A STREET OF LITTLE SHOPS by Margery Williams Bianco (Messrs Doubleday & Co. Inc.)

My Delight and *Six o'Clock Bells* from the Gavin Greig MSS (Aberdeen University Library)

W and *The Statue* from THE BLACKBIRD IN THE LILAC by James Reeves (Oxford University Press)

Spells and *Bells* from THE WANDERING MOON by James Reeves (Messrs William Heinemann Ltd)

Roddy and the Red Indians by E. H. Lang

ACKNOWLEDGEMENTS

The Boy, A Kitten, Mary Indoors and *London Sparrow* from SILVER SAND AND SNOW by Eleanor Farjeon (Messrs Michael Joseph Ltd and Messrs J. B. Lippincott Co.)

Can Men be Such Fools as All That? from THE OLD NURSE'S STOCKING BASKET by Eleanor Farjeon (University of London Press Ltd and Messrs J. B. Lippincott Co.)

Paul's Tale by Mary Norton

Cripple Creek from NURSERY SONGS FROM THE APPALACHIAN MOUNTAINS collected and arranged by Cecil J. Sharp (Messrs Novello & Co. Ltd)

The Flying Postman by V. H. Drummond

The Six Badgers and *The Pumpkin* by Robert Graves (Messrs A. P. Watt & Son and Messrs William Heinemann Ltd)

The Swallows from SUMMER STORIES by Mrs Molesworth (Mr H. G. Molesworth and Messrs Macmillan & Co. Ltd)

The Thunder, the Elephant and Dorobo by Humphrey Harman

The Magic Ball from TALES FROM SILVER LANDS by Charles J. Finger (Messrs Doubleday & Co. Inc.)

Giacco and His Bean from PICTURE TALES FROM THE ITALIAN by Florence Botsford (Messrs J. B. Lippincott Co.)

Nicholas and the Fast Moving Diesel by Edward Ardizzone (Oxford University Press)

The Well of the World's End from ENGLISH FABLES AND FAIRY TALES by James Reeves (Oxford University Press)

La Hormiguita and Perez the Mouse from PICTURE TALES FROM SPAIN by Ruth Sawyer (Messrs J. B. Lippincott Co.)

The Fool of the World and the Flying Ship from OLD PETER'S RUSSIAN TALES by Arthur Ransome (Messrs Thomas Nelson & Sons Ltd)

The Small Brown Mouse from A LIGHT DOZEN by Janet McNeill, illustrated by Rowel Friers (Messrs Faber & Faber Ltd, and Messrs A. P. Watt & Son)

The Fly, Mima, Shellover, Then and *Nicholas Nye* from COLLECTED POEMS by Walter de la Mare (Messrs Faber & Faber Ltd, the Literary Trustees and the Society of Authors as their representative)

Rilloby-Rill from POEMS NEW AND OLD by Henry Newbolt (the Executors, Messrs John Murray Ltd and Messrs A. P. Watt & Son)

The Cat That Walked by Himself from JUST SO STORIES by Rudyard Kipling (Mrs George Bambridge, Messrs Macmillan & Co. Ltd, the Macmillan Co. of Canada, and Messrs Doubleday & Co. Inc.)

The Fable of the Old Man, the Boy and the Donkey from THE MONSTER HORSE by Ian Serraillier (Oxford University Press)

Pooh and Piglet Go Hunting from WINNIE THE POOH by A. A. Milne, illustrated

ACKNOWLEDGEMENTS

by E. H. Shepard (Messrs Methuen & Co. Ltd, Messrs E. P. Dutton & Co, Inc., and Messrs Curtis Brown Ltd)
A Spell for Sleeping by Alastair Reid

The Editor and Publishers also thank the Trustees of the British Museum for permission to reproduce the drawing by Randolph Caldecott.

INTRODUCTION

PEOPLE, like animals, are born with five senses. But we very quickly acquire more – the sense of pleasure, the sense of curiosity, the sense of wonder. Pleasure and curiosity are felt by at least some animals, who may even communicate their experiences in a kind of language. What is distinctively human is the sense of wonder, which we may call the religious sense, and the desire to record it in words. *In the beginning was the word* is an idea of tremendous significance, whether we choose to interpret it religiously or not. The spoken word – the recollected word – the recorded word: these are the necessary steps towards full human consciousness. Without recorded language the growth and survival of the human spirit is inconceivable.

What is a word? In the first place it is the sound, or the name, by which we recognize an object and so gain power over it. When a child first learns to make a noise which denotes his mother or father, that is an immense step towards the possession of what he most fears to lose; it is also an expression of the satisfaction he feels in his parents' existence. So words acquire a magic of their own, in becoming the means by which we acquire the power to recall what is absent and to regain what is lost. The word *Troy*, for instance, has a magical potency far beyond the sum of all the separate meanings we attach to it. Its meaning, even to people who have never been there, is enormous. Indeed, we can never go there – though we may visit an archaeological site, but we can possess the idea of Troy by knowing what it meant to Homer and Virgil, Aeschylus and Giraudoux, Chaucer and Henryson, Shakespeare and Racine.

Some of the associations of the word Troy are tragic. The

regions to which language transports the adult are often dark and clouded. But to children the land of romance is, or should be, a golden land. To a child, language makes familiar things permanent and unknown things near. He delights to discover a story or a poem which describes what he knows – his home, his pets, the world just outside his window; and curiosity about the world he cannot reach is awakened and fulfilled by stories of the unfamiliar.

But poems and stories are not just a means to an end; they are an end in themselves. A nut-tree is one thing, and a very good thing if you can find it; the poem *I Had a Little Nut-Tree* is something quite different. Why do most children enjoy the poem, even if they are not at all sure what a nut-tree looks like? You might say they simply enjoy the sound of the words: true, but this enjoyment would soon pall if the words were mere nonsense. Their meaning is their magic, their secret: and it is because of the secrets contained in their first rhymes that children prize them. They don't always want to know what the secret is. They simply want the secret to be there, like the kernel in the nut. They also value their first rhymes because they are gifts or secrets communicated by those they first love, their parents.

The first sound of the golden land should come to every child from the lips of an elder person whom he loves and trusts. His first sight of it may be the pictures in a favourite book. His first real entry into that land is when he can read for himself and so travel there at will, independent of others. Just as the spirit of man would be infinitely poorer if it were not for the recorded vision and experience we call literature, so is the life of the individual poorer if he has not the ability and the desire to find his own way to the golden land. Some men have denied the value of literature, but they have usually been literary men.

These truths will be obvious enough to many, but it seems necessary, even urgent, to insist on them because the two all-important occupations of reading and being read to have, within my time, come up against severer competition than ever before. There is no machine which can give children what they can get from their parents' reading. And there is nothing which can take the place of literature in its power to give a growing child permanent possession of a magical character.

This book, then, is first a book for adults to read to those not old enough to read to themselves. Some parents are disturbed if their children are slow to begin reading. This may be because they themselves have been too busy to read to them. To want to be read to is the first step in wanting to read.

Books are of two kinds – those which are read to be forgotten, and those which are read to be remembered. Both kinds have their uses, but I have not here been concerned with the former kind. I have tried to find stories and poems and songs which children will want not only to hear and read, but to hear and read over and over again. The poems have been chosen for what has seemed to me some quality of language which will give pleasure long after the novelty has worn off; the stories are of three kinds – those which have delighted successive generations ever since they were written; those which were once known and have been unjustly forgotten; and those which are new but have the qualities that make for lasting appeal. It would take too long to say what those qualities are. But we may take it that a good story must have suspense and reality: that is, the power of making a reader want to know what happens next, and the power to hold the attention by persuading him that what it describes is, for the time being, more real than anything outside the story. The test of a good story, so far as suspense goes, is that we should want to hear it again, even though we already know what happens all the way through; as for what I have called reality, that is where the magic of the story lies. There may be other things as well –

humour, sadness, the pleasure that comes from a happy ending, the satisfaction of curiosity about people and places, delight in the ways of nature, an interest in animals or the supernatural. But without suspense a story will never be read; and without reality it will never be re-read.

The idea of this book began with a parent who felt that such a collection was needed: one which should contain the old and the new, and should revive forgotten tales as well as draw on the work of some present-day writers. There should be dozens of illustrations, so that the book might also be worth looking at over and over again, a pleasure to the eye as well as the ear and the imagination. It might be thought that there was a wealth of material to be drawn on; certainly I don't claim to have exhausted the possibilities of selection. But many of the best known and loved of children's authors do not happen to have written short tales. Apart from Hans Andersen and the composers of fables and folk-tales, there are comparatively few who have made the short story their special province. I was anxious, as far as possible, to have everything complete in itself, for there is always something unsatisfying about a book of extracts. I have in one or two instances departed from this rule, but there are few good full-length stories from which suitable complete episodes can be extracted.

In conclusion, I hope I may be forgiven for reiterating my entreaty to adults: read to the children as often as you can spare the time. If you find *A Golden Land* rewarding, and children are led to explore it for themselves, our efforts – yours and mine – will not have been wasted. I must also express my gratitude to the many living authors and artists who have contributed so generously to these pages, and to my publishers for their unstinted help and encouragement.

J.R.

Chalfont St Giles
1958

Tim Rabbit

THE wind howled and the rain poured down in torrents. A young rabbit hurried along with his eyes half shut and his head bent as he forced his way against the gale. He tore his trousers on a bramble and left a piece of his coat on a gorse-bush. He bumped his nose and scratched his chin, but he didn't stop to rub himself. He hurried and scurried towards the snug little house on the common where his mother was making bread.

At last he saw the open door, he smelled the warm smell of baking, and in he rushed without wiping his feet on the little brown doormat.

'What's the matter, Tim?' asked Mrs Rabbit, as she shut the oven door. 'Whatever has happened?' She looked anxiously at Tim who lay panting on the floor.

'Something came after me,' cried Tim, breathlessly.

'Something came after you?' echoed Mrs Rabbit. 'What was it like, my son?'

'It was very big and noisy,' replied Tim, with a shiver. 'It ran all round me, and tried to pull the coat off my back, and it snatched at my trousers.' He gave a sob, and his mother stroked his head.

'What did it say?' she asked. 'Did it speak or growl?'

'It called, "Whoo-oo-oo. Whoo-oo-oo. Whoo-oo-oo,"' whimpered the little rabbit.

'That was only the wind, my son,' said Mrs Rabbit, with a laugh. 'Never fear the wind, for he is a friend.' She gave the little rabbit a crust of new bread, and he was comforted.

The next day, when Tim Rabbit was nibbling a morsel of sweet grass under the hedge, the sky darkened, and a hail-storm swept across the sky, with stinging hailstones. They bounced on the small rabbit and frightened him out of his wits. Off he ran, helter-skelter, with his white tail bobbing, and his eyes wide with fear. He lost his pocket handkerchief and left his scarf in a thicket, but he hadn't time to pick them up, he was in such a hurry.

He raced and he tore towards the snug little house on the common, where his mother was tossing pancakes and catching them in her tiny stone frying-pan.

At last he reached the door, and in he raced without stopping to smooth his rough untidy hair.

'What's the matter, Tim?' asked Mrs Rabbit, as she put down her frying-pan. 'Whatever is the matter?'

'Something came after me,' exclaimed Tim, hiding behind her skirts.

'Something came after you?' cried Mrs Rabbit. 'What was it like?'

'It was big and dark,' said Tim. 'It threw hard stones at me, and hit my nose and back and ears. It must have a hundred paws, to throw so many stones, and every time it hit me and hurt me.'

'What did it say?' asked Mrs Rabbit, lifting her son from the floor, and straightening his ruffled hair.

'It shouted, "Whissh-ssh-ssh! Whissh-ssh-ssh!"' sobbed the little rabbit.

'That was only a hailstorm, Tim,' explained Mrs Rabbit. 'Never heed a hailstorm, for it clears the air, and makes all fresh for us rabbits.' She gave the little rabbit a curly yellow pancake with some sugar on the top, and he forgot his troubles.

The next day when Tim was tasting an early primrose, the first he had seen in his short life, he had another fright. A thunderstorm broke out of the sky, with lightning which flashed around him, and peals of roaring thunder which echoed from the hills.

Tim scampered home as fast as his legs could carry him, to the warm little house on the common, where his mother was toasting currant teacakes in front of the wood fire.

At last he came to the door, and the smell of the teacakes made his whiskers twitch. He rushed inside, without stopping to shake the wet from his coat.

'What's the matter, Tim?' cried Mrs Rabbit, as he stumbled into a chair. She dropped her toasting-fork and leaned over him. 'What's the matter, my son?'

'Something came after me,' whispered Tim, shuddering.

'Something came after you?' echoed his mother. 'What was it like?'

'It was very big and high,' cried Tim. 'It stuck bright swords at me, and flashed lights in my eyes.'

'What did it say?' asked Mrs Rabbit softly.

'It roared "Roo-oo-oo-oo-oo-oo-oo!"' wept the little rabbit.

'That was only a thunderstorm, my son,' replied Mrs Rabbit, soothingly. 'Never mind the thunder and lightning. They never harmed a rabbit yet.' She gave him a large teacake, and he sat by the fire munching it, with his troubles forgotten.

But there came a day when Tim Rabbit sat dozing in a clump of ferns, half asleep, and comfortable. A gust of wind brought a queer scent to his nostrils and he awoke suddenly. He stared round and saw a strange animal bounding towards him with joyous leaps. It wasn't a lamb, nor a foal, nor a calf, nor even a pigling. It looked so playful and danced along so merrily on its four hairy legs that Tim wanted to play Catch, and Hide-and-seek.

What a jolly creature it was! How curly was its hair and its long waving tail! It hadn't seen Tim, for the ferns covered him, but he was prepared to run out and meet it. He would have invited it home with him, if a storm hadn't suddenly swept down from a dark cloud which hung in the sky.

'Beware! Beware!' howled the wind fiercely, and it blew Tim's fur the wrong way, until he was uncomfortable and cold.

'Shoo! Shoo!' sighed the trees, waving their branches and crackling their twigs at him, like tiny wooden fingers.

'Run! Run!' cried the bushes, snapping and rustling their spiky boughs, with the prickly thorns.

'Be off! Be off!' roared the thunder, banging its drum inside the black cloud.

The lightning flashed and showed him the sharp teeth of the merry dancing animal. The hailstones rattled down and hit foolish Tim's nose, so that he turned and ran, leaving the creature to play by itself in the wet field.

He scuttled towards the safe little house on the common, where his mother was making crab-apple tart. He ran in at the door, and flopped down on the oak bench.

'What's the matter, Tim?' asked his mother, dropping her rolling-pin and scattering the bowl of crab-apples. 'Whatever is the matter, my son?'

'Mother, I saw an animal. It was not a lamb, nor a foal, nor a calf, nor a pigling, but a lovely jumping animal. I was going to play with it, but the wind blew me, and the hailstones hit me, and the thunder scolded me, and they all drove me home.'

'What was it like, my son?' asked Mrs Rabbit, as she wiped the floor, and picked up her crab-apples.

'It was white, with kind eyes, and long ears and shining teeth, Mother, and its paws danced and pattered.'

'What did it say, Tim?' cried Mrs Rabbit, faintly.

'It said, "Bow-wow! Bow-wow!"'

'That was a dog, Tim,' whispered Mrs Rabbit, in a frightened tone. 'Beware of a dog! He would have killed you with his sharp teeth and pattering paws.'

So the little rabbit sat on his stool in the chimney corner, warming his toes by the fire, while he learned his first lesson:

'Crouch among the heather,
Never mind the weather,
Forget it altogether.
Run from a dog, a man, and a gun,
Or your happy young life will soon be undone.'

ALISON UTTLEY
Illustrated by JENNIFER MILES

The Dutch Cheese

ONCE – once upon a time there lived, with his sister Griselda, in a little cottage near the Great Forest, a young farmer whose name was John. Brother and sister, they lived alone except for their sheepdog, Sly, their flock of sheep, the numberless birds of the forest, and the 'fairies'. John loved his sister beyond telling; he loved Sly; and he delighted to listen to the birds singing at twilight round the darkening margin of the forest. But he feared and hated the fairies. And, having a very stubborn heart, the more he feared, the more he hated them; and the more he hated them, the more they pestered him.

Now these were a tribe of fairies, sly, small, gay-hearted and mischievous, and not of the race of fairies noble, silent, beautiful and remote from man. They were a sort of gipsy-fairies, very nimble and of aery and prankish company, and partly for mischief and partly for love of her they were always trying to charm John's dear sister Griselda away, with their music and fruits and trickery. He more than half believed it was they who years ago had decoyed into the forest not only his poor old father, who had gone out faggot-cutting in his sheepskin hat with his ass; but his mother too, who soon after, had gone out to look for him.

But fairies, even of this small tribe, hate no man. They mocked him and mischiefed him; they spilt his milk, rode astraddle on his rams, garlanded his old ewes with sow-thistle and briony, sprinkled water on his kindling wood, loosed his bucket in the well, and hid his great leather shoes. But all this they did, not for hate – for they came and went like evening moths about Griselda – but because in his fear and fury he shut up his sister from them, and because he was sullen and stupid. Yet he did nothing but fret himself. He set traps for them, and caught starlings; he fired his blunderbuss at them under the moon, and scared his sheep; he set dishes of sour milk in their way, and sticky leaves and brambles where their rings were green in the meadows; but all to no purpose. When at dusk, too, he heard their faint, elfin music, he would sit in the door blowing into his father's great bassoon till the black forest re-echoed with its sad, solemn, wooden voice. But that was of no help either. At last he grew so surly that he made Griselda utterly miserable. Her cheeks lost their scarlet and her eyes their sparkling. Then the fairies began to plague John in earnest – lest their lovely, loved child of man, Griselda, should die.

Now one summer's evening – and most nights are cold in the Great Forest – John, having put away his mournful bassoon and bolted the door, was squatting, moody and gloomy, with Griselda, on his hearth beside the fire. And he leaned back his great hairy head and stared straight up the chimney to where high in the heavens glittered a host of stars. And suddenly, while he lolled there on his stool moodily watching them, there appeared against the dark sky a mischievous elvish head secretly peeping down at him; and busy fingers began sprinkling dew on his wide upturned face. He heard the laughter too of the fairies miching and gambolling on his thatch, and in his rage he started up, seized a round Dutch cheese that lay on a platter, and with all his force threw it clean and straight up the sooty chimney at the faces of mockery clustered above. And after that, though Griselda sighed at her spinning wheel, he heard no more. Even the cricket that had been whistling all through the evening fell silent, and John supped on his black bread and onions alone.

Next day Griselda woke at dawn and put her head out of the little window beneath the thatch, and the day was white with mist.

'Twill be another hot day,' she said to herself, combing her beautiful hair.

But when John went down, so white and dense with mist were the fields, that even the green borders of the forest were invisible, and the whiteness went to the sky. Swathing and wreathing itself, opal and white as milk, all the morning the mist grew thicker and thicker about the little house. When John went out about nine o'clock to peer about him, nothing was to be seen at all. He could hear his sheep bleating, the kettle singing, Griselda sweeping, but straight up above him hung only, like a small round fruit, a little cheese-red beamless sun – straight up above him, though the hands of the clock were not yet come to ten. He clenched his fists and stamped in sheer rage. But no one answered him, no voice mocked him but his own. For when these idle, mischievous fairies have played a trick on an enemy they soon weary of it.

All day long that little sullen lantern burned above the mist, sometimes red, so that the white mist was dyed to amber, and sometimes milky pale. The trees dripped water from every leaf. Every flower asleep in the garden was neckleted with beads; and nothing but a drenched old forest crow visited the lonely cottage that afternoon to cry: 'Kah, Kah, Kah!' and fly away.

But Griselda knew her brother's mood too well to speak of it, or to complain. And she sang on gaily in the house, though she was more sorrowful than ever.

Next day John went out to tend his flocks. And wherever he went the red sun seemed to follow. When at last he found his sheep they were drenched with the clinging mist and were huddled together in dismay. And when they saw him it seemed that they cried out with one unanimous bleating voice:

'O ma-a-a-ster!'

And he stood counting them. And a little apart from the rest stood his old ram Soll, with a face as black as soot; and there, perched on his back, impish and sharp and scarlet, rode and tossed and sang just such another fairy as had mocked John from the chimney-top. A fire seemed to break out in his body, and, picking up a handful of stones, he rushed at Soll through the flock. They scattered, bleating, out into the mist. And the fairy, all-acockahoop on the old ram's back, took its small ears between finger and thumb, and as fast as John ran, so fast jogged Soll, till all the young farmer's stones were thrown, and he found himself alone in a quagmire so sticky and befogged that it took him till afternoon to grope his way out. And only Griselda's singing over her broth-pot guided him at last home.

Next day he sought his sheep far and wide, but not one could he find. To and fro he wandered, shouting and calling and whistling to Sly, till heartsick and thirsty, they were both wearied out. Yet bleatings seemed to fill the air, and a faint, beautiful bell tolled on out of the mist; and John knew the fairies had hidden his sheep, and he hated them more than ever.

After that he went no more into the fields, brightly green beneath the enchanted mist. He sat and sulked, staring out of the door at the dim forests far away, glimmering faintly red beneath the small red sun. Griselda could not sing any more, she was too tired and hungry. And just before twilight she went out and gathered the last few pods of peas from the garden for their supper.

And while she was shelling them, John, within doors in the cottage, heard again the tiny timbrels and the distant horns, and the odd, clear, grasshopper voices calling and calling her, and he knew in his heart that, unless he relented and made friends with the fairies, Griselda would surely one day run away to them and leave him forlorn. He scratched his great head, and gnawed his broad thumb. They had taken his father, they had taken his mother, they might take his sister – but he *wouldn't* give in.

So he shouted, and Griselda in fear and trembling came in out of the garden with her basket and basin and sat down in the gloaming to finish shelling her peas.

And as the shadows thickened and the stars began to shine, the malevolent singing came nearer, and presently there was a groping and stirring in the thatch, a tapping at the window, and John knew the fairies had come – not alone, not one or two or three, but in their company and bands – to plague him, and to entice away Griselda. He shut his mouth and stopped up his ears with his fingers, but when, with great staring eyes, he saw them capering like bubbles in a glass, like flames along straw, on his very doorstep, he could contain himself no longer. He caught up Griselda's bowl and flung it – peas, water and all – full in the snickering faces of the Little Folk! There came a shrill, faint twitter of laughter, a scampering of feet, and then all again was utterly still.

Griselda tried in vain to keep back her tears. She put her arms round John's neck and hid her face in his sleeve.

'Let me go!' she said. 'Let me go, John, just a day and a night, and I'll come back to you. They are angry with us. But they love me; and if I sit on the hillside under the boughs of the trees beside the pool and listen to their music just a little while, they will make the sun shine again and drive back the flocks, and we shall be as happy as ever. Look at poor Sly, John dear, he is hungrier even than I am.' John heard only the mocking laughter and the tap-tapping and the rustling and crying of the fairies, and he wouldn't let his sister go.

And it began to be marvellously dark and still in the cottage. No stars moved across the casement, no waterdrops glittered in the candleshine. John could hear only one low, faint, unceasing stir and rustling all round him. So utterly dark and still it was that even Sly woke from his hungry dreams and gazed up into his mistress's face and whined.

They went to bed; but still, all night long, while John lay tossing on his mattress, the rustling never ceased. The old kitchen clock ticked on and on, but there came no hint of dawn. All was pitch-black and now all was utterly silent. There wasn't a whisper, not a creak, not a sigh of air, not a footfall of mouse, not a flutter of moth, not a settling of dust to be heard at all. Only desolate silence. And John at last could endure his fears and suspicions no longer. He got out of bed and stared from his square casement. He could see nothing. He tried to thrust it open; it would not move. He went downstairs and unbarred the door and looked out. He saw, as it were, a deep, clear, green shade, from behind which the songs of the birds rose faint as in a dream.

And then he sighed like a grampus and sat down, and knew that the fairies had beaten him. Like Jack's beanstalk, in one night had grown up a dense wall of peas. He pushed and pulled and hacked with his axe, and kicked with his shoes, and buffeted with his blunderbuss. But it was all in vain. He sat down once more in his chair beside the hearth and covered his face with his hands. And at last Griselda, too, awoke, and came down with her candle. And she comforted her brother, and told him if he would do what she bade she would soon make all right again. And he promised her.

So with a scarf she bound tight his hands behind him; and with a rope she bound his feet together, so that he could neither run nor throw stones, peas or cheeses. She bound his eyes and ears and mouth with a napkin, so that he could neither see, hear, smell, nor cry out. And, that done, she pushed and pulled him like a great bundle, and at last rolled him out of sight into the chimney-corner against the wall. Then she took a small sharp pair of needlework scissors that her godmother had given her, and snipped and snipped, till at last there came a little hole in the thick green hedge of peas. And putting her mouth there she called softly through the little hole. And the fairies drew near the doorstep and nodded and nodded and listened.

And then and there Griselda made a bargain with them for the forgiveness of John – a lock of her golden hair; seven dishes of ewes' milk; three and thirty bunches of currants, red, white, and black; a bag of thistledown; three handkerchiefs full of lambs' wool; nine jars of honey; a peppercorn of spice. All these (except the hair) John was to bring himself to their secret places as soon as he was able. Above all, the bargain between them was that Griselda would sit one full hour each evening of summer on the hillside in the shadow and greenness that slope down from the great forest towards the valley, where the fairies' mounds are, and where their tiny brindled cattle graze.

Her brother lay blind and deaf and dumb as a log of wood. She promised everything.

And then, instead of a rustling and a creeping, there came a rending and a crashing. Instead of green shade, light of amber; then white. And as the thick hedge withered and shrank, and the merry and furious dancing sun scorched and scorched and scorched, there came, above the singing of the birds, the bleatings of sheep – and behold sooty Soll and hungry Sly met square upon the doorstep; and all John's sheep shone white as hoarfrost on his pastures; and every lamb was garlanded with pimpernel and eyebright; and the old fat ewes stood still, with saddles of moss; and their laughing riders sat and saw Griselda standing in the doorway in her beautiful yellow hair.

As for John, tied up like a sack in the chimney-corner, down came his cheese again crash upon his head, and, not being able to say anything, he said nothing.

WALTER DE LA MARE
Illustrated by IRENE HAWKINS

The Old Grey Goose

Go and tell Aunt Nancy,
Go and tell Aunt Nancy,
Go and tell Aunt Nancy,
    The old grey goose is dead.

The one that she was saving,
The one that she was saving,
The one that she was saving,
    To make a feather bed.

I saw her a-dying,
I saw her a-dying,
I saw her a-dying,
    With her wing tucked over her head.

She died on Friday,
She died on Friday,
She died on Friday,
    Behind the old barn shed.

She left nine little goslings,
She left nine little goslings,
She left nine little goslings,
    To scratch for their own bread.

Prickety Prackety

THERE was once a hen called Prickety Prackety. She was a little golden brown bantam hen, and she walked about the garden on the tips of her toes – and she pecked here and pecked there and was busy and gay the whole day long.

And once a day she felt like laying an egg.

Away she went to the hen-house: 'Cluck, Cluck, Cluck!' And she'd climb into the nesting box and fluff herself out and make gentle noises in her throat as soft as her own pretty feathers, and she'd sit, and she'd blink her eyes and go into a dozy-cosy and then: 'Cluck, Cluck, Cluck-a-Cluck-a-Cluck!'

What a surprise! What a joy! An egg! A pretty brown speckeldy egg! Away she would go, not a thought in her head, peck here, peck there, on the tips of her toes.

And Anne would come at tea-time to collect the eggs, and when she saw the brown egg she would say:

'Oh! You good Mrs Prickety Prackety, you good little hen.' Because Prickety Prackety was the only hen to lay brown eggs, so Anne knew that it was hers. And she would throw her out an extra handful of corn. One good turn deserves another.

But one day Prickety Prackety felt different. She felt like laying an egg. Oh, yes! But somehow not in the hen-house. So away she went by herself.

'Where are you going to, Prickety Prackety?' called Chanticleer the golden cock.

'I am going to mind my own business,' she said and tossed her head. Chanticleer ran and gave her a little peck, not a hard peck, but enough of a peck to show that although he loved her dearly he wouldn't let her answer him so rudely.

But Prickety Prackety paid no attention to him. She fluttered her feathers and cried 'Cloak!' because she knew he would expect it, and then she ran away, her head in the air.

'Prickety Prackety, where are you going?'

It was good sister Partlet, the old black hen, wanting her to share a dustbath near the cinder-pit.

'I am going to mind my own business,' said Prickety Prackety nodding pleasantly to Partlet, and Partlet ruffled the dust in her feathers and smiled to herself.

Prickety Prackety left the garden and came to the orchard. The grass was very green underneath the apple trees and the blossom was just coming out.

'Prickety Prackety, where are you going?' cried the white ducks rootling in the grass.

'I am going to mind my own business,' she said.

Beside the privet hedge was an old rusty drum.

It had been used last year to cover up the rhubarb, but now it was lying on its side and a jungle of nettles had grown up all round it.

And Prickety Prackety crept through the jungle of nettles, into the oil drum and clucked contentedly to find a few wisps of straw and dried grass. The geese and ducks smiled at each other and went on nibbling the grass in the orchard.

'Prickety Prackety has stolen a nest. I wonder if they will find it?' they thought to themselves.

Every day for twelve days Prickety Prackety disappeared into the oil drum.

Every day Chanticleer said, 'Prickety Prackety, where are you going?'

Every day Partlet said, 'Prickety Prackety, where are you going?'

Every day the geese and ducks said, 'Prickety Prackety, where are you going?'

And every day Prickety Prackety gave the same answer with a toss of the head. 'I am going to mind my own business.'

And every day at tea-time Anne would come in shaking her head.

'No eggs from Prickety Prackety. She's gone right off. And just when she was doing so well too.'

But worse was to come.

On the thirteenth day Prickety Prackety took a long drink and ate as much as she could when Anne put out the hot mash. And then she walked away looking *very* important.

'Where are you going, Prickety Prackety?' said Chanticleer.

'Where are you going, Prickety Prackety?' said Partlet.

'Where are you going, Prickety Prackety?' said the white ducks.

'Where are you going to, Prickety Prackety?' said the geese, following after her as if she were a procession.

But Prickety Prackety didn't even answer. She pranced along, her eyes shining.

That evening Anne came into the kitchen and said:

'Now I know why Prickety Prackety seemed to go off laying. She has stolen a nest. I shall have to go and find it.'

So next day after she had put out the chicken food Anne began to look for Prickety Prackety.

She looked in the shrubbery. She looked in the vegetable garden. She looked in the sheds and outhouses. She looked along the hedges, looked in the orchard, but she didn't see Prickety Prackety, although Prickety Prackety saw her.

And every morning when it was first light and the other hens were still asleep shut up in the hen-house, Prickety Prackety would creep out of her jungle of nettles.

'Where are you going to, Prickety Prackety?' asked the little wild birds, the sparrows, and finches, the blackbirds and the thrushes. But Prickety Prackety seemed not to hear, but would peck here and peck there, gorging herself on grubs and grass and any remains of chicken food overlooked by the others. She would drink and drink from the bowl of water by the back door, and as she lifted her head the rising sun would shine into her eyes, and then back she would go through her jungle of nettles into the oil drum, and not the least glimpse of her was to be seen when the rest of the world were about.

A week went by, and another, and the blossom on the apple trees was falling so that when the soft wind blew it looked like drifting snow. And still Prickety Prackety hid in her nest.

'Have you seen Prickety Prackety?' said Chanticleer to Partlet.

'Oh! She's around somewhere,' said Partlet, flaunting her feathers.

'Have you seen Prickety Prackety?' said Partlet to the ducks.

'Oh! I expect she's around somewhere,' they said.

'Have you seen Prickety Prackety?' asked the ducks of the geese.

'We mind our own businessssss,' hissed the geese.

And Anne, in the kitchen yard, said: 'Now, let me see. It's gone all of two weeks since Prickety Prackety stole her nest. She ought to be out come Friday. I wonder how many will hatch?'

On Friday when the sun rose the sky was quiet and clear.

Prickety Prackety crept out into the orchard shaking the dew from the nettles as she passed, so she looked like a golden hen set with diamonds.

She pecked and pranced and pecked and drank, and cocked her eye at the sun, and then she went back to her eggs, her twelve brown eggs lying on the straw in the cool green shadow of the oil drum and nettles.

She stood, her head on one side, and listened.

Tap-tap, and the smooth round surface of the nearest egg was broken and a tiny jag of shell moved and was still.

'Cluck, Cluck, Cluck, Cluck!' crooned Prickety Prackety, deep in her throat and, very satisfied, she settled on her eggs.

That evening Anne went out at tea-time.

'Coop, Coop, Coop!' she cried, the corn measure in her hand, and from every side the hens came running.

'Coop, Coop, Coop!' cried Anne.

Then who should creep out of the nettles but Prickety Prackety. 'Cluck, Cluck, Cluck,' she said. And out of the nettles crept, one, two, three, four, five, six, seven, eight, nine, ten, eleven, twelve little tiny, tiny chicks, so small, so tiny, so quick, so golden, so yellow – Oh, what a pretty sight!

'Well, you got them at last, Prickety Prackety,' said the geese.

'And very nice too,' said the ducks.

And Prickety Prackety led her family out of the orchard towards the yard. 'Coop, Coop, Coop, Coop,' cried Anne, scattering the corn.

But when she saw Prickety Prackety tripping towards her with one, two, three, four, five, six, seven, eight, nine, ten, eleven, twelve – yes, with twelve – tiny chicks, like little yellow clouds all about her:

'Oh!' she cried, and ran to the house.

'Caroline, Johnny, William, come quick. Prickety Prackety has hatched her chicks.'

And everyone came running.

'Oh! Prickety Prackety, you *good* little hen!' And how they scattered the corn for her. But Anne was busy getting ready the special coop they kept for hens who had chicks; and they called it the Nursery Coop, for here the chicks would be safe from the cats and dogs and crows.

Very gently they lifted Prickety Prackety, and all the chicks came running as she cried to them: 'Cluck, Cluck, Cluck!'

'I reckon you don't run that fast when your Mum calls you,' said Anne – and the children laughed. And they all helped to carry the coop into the orchard, where the trees would shade it. And when at last Anne and the children were gone Partlet came busily by.

'A lot of trouble, but worth it. They're a fine lot, Prickety Prackety.' And she nodded her head with approval.

And as for Chanticleer, he came stalking up glowing in the evening sun, and stood high on his toes, head cocked, looking at Prickety Prackety and the tiny heads poking in and out of her feathers. And then:

'Cock-a-Doooooodle Doooooooooo. Just look at my good wife, Prickety Prackety, and all our sons and daughters. Cock-a-Doooooodle Doooooooo.'

It was like a fanfare of trumpets.

And Prickety Prackety blinked her eyes and smiled.

DIANA ROSS
Illustrated by JENNIFER MILES

Poor Old Horse

My clothing was once of the linsey woolsey fine,
My tail it grew at length, my coat did likewise shine;
But now I'm growing old; my beauty does decay,
My master frowns upon me; one day I heard him say,
Poor old horse: poor old horse.

Once I was kept in the stable snug and warm,
To keep my tender limbs from any cold or harm;
But now, in open fields, I am forced for to go,
In all sorts of weather, let it be hail, rain, freeze, or snow.
Poor old horse: poor old horse.

Once I was fed on the very best corn and hay
That ever grew in yon fields, or in yon meadows gay;
But now there's no such doing can I find at all,
I'm glad to pick the green sprouts that grow behind yon wall.
Poor old horse: poor old horse.

'You are old, you are cold, you are deaf, dull, dumb and slow.
You are not fit for anything, or in my team to draw.
You have eaten all my hay, you have spoiled all my straw,
So hang him, whip, stick him, to the huntsman let him go.'
Poor old horse: poor old horse.

My hide unto the tanners then I would freely give,
My body to the hound dogs, I would rather die than live,
Likewise my poor old bones that have carried you many a mile,
Over hedges, ditches, brooks, bridges, likewise gates and stiles.
Poor old horse: poor old horse.

Paul, the Hero of the Fire

ONCE upon a time there was a small boy called Paul who lived with his mother and father in a pretty house with a large garden.

He had a dog called Fido and a cat called Blacky, and as it was holiday time he should have been very happy, but instead of being happy he was bored and worried. He was bored because he was tired of playing with his toys by himself and worried because his mother seemed so sad and his father so cross.

One day, when he was sitting as quiet as a mouse, trying to

read a book, he heard his father say to his mother in the next room, 'Darling, it is no use. We can't go on as before. The market has gone all to pieces. We have hardly any money left. I'm afraid we must sell the house.'

Then he heard his mother sobbing and sobbing.

This made Paul feel very sad. He loved the house and hated the idea of having to leave it and going to some smaller place.

'Oh, Blacky and Fido, what shall we do?' said Paul. 'We must make some money or we shall have to go away.' But Blacky only miaowed and Fido only wagged his tail, which did not help much.

Then Paul went out and met his friends, Alf the Coalman and Tom the Butcher's boy, and asked them for their advice. They both said, 'You must get a job.'

Tom said, 'Why don't you become a butcher's boy like me?'

Alf said, 'Come and help me with my coals.'

But Paul did not want to do either. He felt sadder and sadder. Then suddenly on the way home he had a great idea. He would get a job at the Fair.

Next morning Paul got up very early while his mother and father were still asleep. He dressed quickly and put in a small suitcase a shirt, two vests, one pair of pyjamas, two pairs of socks, a spare pair of shoes, soap, tooth-brush, toothpaste, and towel.

Then he wrote a letter to his mother and father and said good-bye to Fido and Blacky, and off he went.

Fido was rather a nuisance, as he wanted to go with Paul and had to be ordered home. Blacky was very good and only miaowed sadly.

Paul felt sad too and just a little lonely and frightened. It was such a big adventure and he was only a little boy.

By hard walking Paul soon arrived at the Fair. 'Your money to come in,' said the man at the gate.

'Oh, please, sir,' said Paul, 'I have come to get a job. Must I pay?'

'Ho! That's a nice story, that is! Trying to get in for nothing, are you, you young rascal!' said the man. 'Pay your money, or outside you stay!'

So poor Paul had to give him all the money he had.

It was still very early and the Fair was almost empty, which made Paul feel even lonelier and smaller than before. The first person he saw was a rough-looking man at the coconut shy.

'Oh, please, sir,' said Paul very politely, 'I want a job. Can you give me one?'

26

'Job?' said the man in a loud voice: 'A little snippet like you? Why, dang my eyes, you are so small and pink I could eat you! Haw, haw, haw!' and he roared with laughter.

'Oh dear, oh dear; this will never do,' said Paul to himself as he hurried away. He tried not to cry, but could not help one large tear which trickled down the side of his nose.

He saw some more men but was too frightened to speak to them. Then he saw an enormous woman. She was so big she was quite frightening. However, she had a kind face, and Paul plucked up enough courage to say to her, 'Oh, please, can you give me a job?'

'Why, dash my wig,' said the Fat Woman: 'A little boy like you want a job? Go home to your mother like a good boy.'

Then Paul really began to cry, and between his sobs he told her the whole sad story, which made the Fat Woman feel sorry for him.

'Come with me, child,' she said. 'I will take you to see the Manager.'

Then she took him by the hand and led him through the Fair to a very smart caravan with a real door and knocker.

She knocked on the door, and out came a big man in his shirt-sleeves. It was the Manager.

The Fat Woman told the Manager Paul's story.

'Humph!' said the Manager. 'You are a bit small, aren't you? One of my boys has gone sick and I want a boy to help turn the children's merry-go-round, but I don't think you are nearly strong enough.'

'I know I am small, but I am strong,' said Paul, bending his arm to show his muscles.

'All right,' said the Manager: 'I will give you a trial. Hey, Mike!' he called, and a boy ran up. 'Here's a new boy to help you. Take him away and put him to work.'

Paul did not forget to say 'Thank you' very nicely to the Fat Woman and the Manager.

Mike was a tall, thin boy. He seemed very cross.

'I'm tired to death,' he said, 'of turning that horrid merry-go-round. Now you have come you are just going to turn it all day

while I have a good rest and collect the money. Hurry up and get started. Here come the children.'

Paul turned and turned the merry-go-round all day long till his arms ached and his back ached and he felt so tired that he could hardly stand, but he refused to give in and went on turning and turning. At the end of the day Mike said to Paul, 'I say, you do look tired, but you are a sport, aren't you? You haven't complained a bit. Well, it is time to stop now, so come along with me. I will get you some food and show you where to sleep. Tomorrow I will share the turning with you and you can collect the money, but be sure and give the right change.'

Mike took Paul to a large tent in which were stabled a number of beautiful little ponies. He showed Paul where he slept on a heap of straw in a corner. Mike told Paul there was room for him there, too. He gave Paul a blanket and then got two large mugs of cocoa and two hunks of bread.

Paul felt much better after his supper, but very sleepy, so he put on his pyjamas and went to bed. Mike was surprised when he saw the pyjamas. 'I always sleep in my clothes,' he said.

Paul found his straw bed very warm and comfortable and was soon fast asleep.

Paul and Mike became fast friends. Every morning they got up early and washed in buckets of cold water. During the day they turned the merry-go-round or collected the money, and in the evening they lay on the straw drinking their cocoa and talking or listening to the quiet munching of the ponies.

Mike had been in a Fair all his life and had many adventures to tell Paul. On Sunday the Fair was shut and Paul and Mike had the day off. Paul wrote a letter to his mother and father saying that he had a job and would send them some money soon. Mike brushed his hair and polished his boots. Then they both went off to church looking very tidy.

After church they had a grand dinner with the other people of the Fair. There were lots of good things to eat. The table was laid with a white cloth and set out between the tents. The Manager sat at one end, while the Fat Woman sat at the other. Paul sat between the Lion Tamer and the Dwarf. The two clowns would insist on doing tricks which made everybody laugh.

Now the Lion Tamer looked very ferocious, but he was really a very mild man who was fond of his animals and of children.

He introduced Paul to the animals and after that, Paul, on his off day, would help him feed them and clean out the cages.

Paul would often go into the cages himself and play with the

animals. Though they roared horribly, it was only a trick to thrill the people who came to see them, and they were like their master, very mild.

The really ferocious person was the Lion Tamer's wife. The Lion Tamer was afraid of her and so were the animals.

She used to poke them with her umbrella and say, 'Out of my way, you horrid things.'

The Dwarf was very small and very ugly and very vain. On

Sundays he dressed up in the height of fashion and wore high-heeled shoes to make himself look taller.

He hated small boys because he thought they laughed at him, but when he found that Paul did not laugh at him and was always polite, he liked him so much that he wished to make him his best friend. He would spend hours teaching Paul all sorts of tricks such as standing on his head or jumping through hoops.

He said Paul was a most promising pupil and ought to make the Circus his profession.

Now one day something important happened.

Paul was collecting the fares when he heard one small boy say to another that he never paid any money to come into the Fair as he had found a hole in the fence behind the swings and came in that way without having to pay.

Paul was shocked, but he remembered what the boy had said and it was very lucky that he did so; for, on the very next day while he was collecting the money, he heard a terrible cry of 'Fire! Fire!' and saw clouds of smoke and hundreds of people rushing to the gates in a great panic.

Mike was terrified and so were some of the children. They started to run away. But Paul remembered what he had once been told; that is, never to panic when there is a fire, but to keep your head and be brave.

'Stop, Mike, stop, children,' he shouted. 'Don't run to the gates. If you do you will be squashed in the crowd trying to get out and you will probably be hurt or even killed. I know another way out of the Fair, so stay with me and I will lead you to safety.'

Paul shouted so loudly that Mike and the frightened children came back. Then he formed them up in a long column, two by two, with Mike at the end to see that none of the children became too frightened and tried to run away again.

Putting himself at the head of the column, Paul shouted, 'Forward', and marched them through the burning Fair.

Now a curious thing happened. Though the fire was getting fiercer and fiercer and the flames roared horribly, Mike, who

was terrified of fire, was so busy looking after the children that
he quite forgot to be frightened. He even remembered the ponies.

'Paul,' he shouted, 'the poor ponies will be burnt.'

'Yes,' shouted back Paul, 'and there are the lions and tigers, too. We must save them. Quick, children, after me.' And they all dashed to the pony tent and loosed the ponies, then they hurried to the cages and let out the animals.

By this time the fire was terrible and the smoke was so thick that they coughed and coughed and their eyes smarted so much that they could hardly see. Even Paul could not help feeling very frightened. He wondered if he had done the right thing. Would he be able to save the children?

However, at last, coughing and choking, they reached the fence and found the hole and crept out to safety, just in time.

There was a great crowd of people outside the Fair, and when they saw the children they gave a tremendous shout.

'The children, the children are saved,' they cried.

You can just imagine how the mothers and fathers of the children hugged and kissed them. They thought they had all been burnt up in the fire.

Paul's mother and father were there too and of course they gave him a great hug.

Poor Mike, who had no mother and father, felt rather out of it, but they gave him a hug as well and invited him to come back to the house and stay with them.

The next morning Paul read that the fire had been put out at last and was surprised to see big headlines in the newspaper and the story of how he had saved the children.

He felt very proud.

A little later there was a knock on the door and in came the Manager, the Fat Woman, the Lion Tamer and the Dwarf.

The Manager gave Paul a large sum of money and thanked him for saving the animals; they had all jumped over the fence to safety. The Fat Woman kissed him, the Lion Tamer shook him

by the hand, and the Dwarf gave him a big bunch of flowers, which made Paul blush a lot.

Paul told them how brave Mike had been, so they all shook Mike by the hand and the Manager promised to pay him much more money when he came back.

Before they left they all gave Paul and Mike three cheers, and the Lion Tamer said, 'Brave fellows! Brave fellows!' with a tear in his eye.

This made Paul very happy, but he was even happier still

when his father told him that with the help of the money Paul had won and with the market better, there was now no need to sell the house.

Written and illustrated by EDWARD ARDIZZONE

Robin Goodfellow

From Oberon in Fairyland
   The king of ghosts and shadows there
Mad Robin I, at his command,
   Am sent to view the night-sports here.
   What revel rout
   Is kept about
In every corner where I go.
     I will o'er sea
     And merry be,
And make good sport with Ho, ho, ho!

More swift than lightning can I fly
   About this airy welkin soon,
And in a minute's space descry
   Each thing that's done below the moon.
     There's not a hag
     Or ghost shall wag,

Or cry 'Ware goblins' where I go;
    But Robin I
    Their feats will spy
And send them home with Ho, ho, ho!

Whene'er such wanderers I meet,
    As from their night-sports they trudge home,
With counterfeiting voice I greet
    And call them on with me to roam
        Through woods, through lakes,
        Through bogs, through brakes;
    Or else unseen with them I go,
        All in the nick
        To play some trick
And frolic it with Ho, ho, ho!

Sometimes I meet them like a man;
    Sometimes an ox, sometimes a hound;
And to a horse I turn me can;
    To trip and trot about them round.
        But if to ride
        My back they stride,
More swift than wind away I go,
        O'er hedge and lands,
        Through pools and ponds,
I whirry, laughing Ho, ho, ho!

Yet now and then, the maids to please,
    At midnight I card up their wool;
And when they sleep and take their ease,
    With wheel to thread their flax I pull.

I grind at mill
Their malt up still;
I dress their hemp, I spin their tow,
If any wake,
And would me take,
I wend me, laughing Ho, ho, ho!

By wells and rills, in meadows green,
We nightly dance our heyday guise;
And to our fairy King and Queen
We chant our moonlight minstrelsies.
When larks 'gin sing,
Away we fling;
And babes new-born steal as we go,
And elf in bed
We leave instead,
And wend us, laughing Ho, ho, ho!

From hag-bred Merlin's time have I
Thus nightly revelled to and fro;
And from my pranks men call me by
The name of Robin Goodfellow,
Friends, ghosts, and sprites
Who haunt the nights,
The hags and goblins do we know,
And beldames old
My feats have told,
So Valé, valé! Ho, ho, ho!

BEN JONSON
Illustrated by PEGGY FORTNUM

Hopping Frog

Hopping frog, hop here and be seen,
    I'll not pelt you with stick or stone:
Your cap is laced and your coat is green;
    Good-bye, we'll let each other alone.

CHRISTINA ROSSETTI

The Christmas Tree

In the words of Moominmamma, real trolls are small, shy and hairy, and there are lots and lots of them in the Finnish forests. Moomintrolls, however, are smooth and, whereas the common troll pops up only in the dark, they love the sunshine. The Moomins go to sleep in the winter, as they do not particularly care for the cold. They are proud of the house which they built themselves and, although alarming and extraordinary things often happen there, life is never boring and that is a good thing.

They have many curious but likeable friends in Moominland, not least the Hemulens, who are a larger and somewhat thinner kind of Moomintroll. They are addicted to wearing a lot of clothes. Hemulen aunts are apt to be rather solid characters who say 'Please be sensible,' or 'Wash your hands,' so you see how Hemulen was easily put out.

I

HEMULEN scratched and scratched in the snow. He was wearing yellow woollen gloves and, of course, before long they became very wet and uncomfortable. So he took them off and carefully placed them on the chimney stack, sighed, and went on scratching; then at last he uncovered the attic window.

'Ah, here it is,' said Hemulen. 'And down there they're lying asleep. Sleeping and sleeping and sleeping. And others have to work themselves to death, all because it's nearly Christmas. By my tail!'

He stepped on to the skylight, trying to remember if it opened inwards or outwards. He stamped on it, and, it immediately opened inwards. Down Hemulen tumbled into the snow and darkness, falling on to all those things which the Moomin family had stowed in the attic – to use later.

By now, he was very much annoyed, and besides, he could not quite remember where he had put the yellow woollen gloves that he was so fond of. So he stamped down the stairs and shouted in an angry voice:

'It's going to be Christmas. I'm vexed with you, and your sleeping, and it's going to be Christmas any minute now.'

Down below all the Moomin family lay in their snug winter retreat. They had slept for several months and intended to go on sleeping until spring – the Moomins love to forget about winter in this way. They slept as softly and comfortably as on a long warm summer afternoon. Now sudden anxiety, or perhaps it was cold air, broke in upon Moomin's dreams. Someone was pulling the quilt off him and was shouting that it was vexed with him, and that it was going to be Christmas.

'Is it spring already?' murmured Moomin.

'Spring?' exclaimed Hemulen irritably. 'It's Christmas, don't you know? – Christmas. And I haven't got anything, and nothing's arranged; and then in the middle of it all, they send me to dig you out. I've lost my yellow gloves, I expect, and everyone's running round in circles, and nothing's ready . . .'

And Hemulen stamped up the stairs again and climbed out of the attic skylight.

'Mamma! Wake up!' called Moomin, frightened. 'Something awful's happened. They call it Christmas.'

'What do you mean?' said Moominmamma and put out her nose.

'I don't know really,' said her son. 'But nothing's arranged, and someone's lost and everyone's running round in circles. Perhaps it's the water rising again.'

He shook the Snorkmaiden gently and whispered:

'Don't be frightened, but something awful's happened.'

'Calm!' said Moominpappa. 'Calm above all!'

And he went to wind up the clock which had read a quarter to nine since sometime in October.

They followed Hemulen's wet footsteps up to the attic and stepped out on the roof of Moominhouse. The sky was beautifully blue, so there was evidently no question of another volcanic eruption.

But the entire valley was covered in wet cotton wool – the hills, the trees, the river and the whole house. And it was cold – colder even than in April.

'Is this what they call Christmas?' asked Moominmamma surprised. She picked up a pawful of the cotton wool and looked at it. 'I wonder if it's grown out of the ground,' she said, 'or fallen from the sky. If this all came down at once, how very uncomfortable it must have been!'

The Mymble went past with a tree across her toboggan chair.

'So you've awakened at last,' she said casually. 'Be sure you find a tree before it gets dark.'

'But why . . . ?' began Moominpappa.

'Too busy to stop now,' shouted the Mymble over her shoulder and hurried on.

'Evidently you need a tree to be safe,' Moominpappa said thoughtfully. 'And the peril is coming tonight. She didn't even have time to say hallo . . . It baffles me what it's all about.'

'I can't understand it either,' said Moominmamma thoughtfully, 'but do put on your warm socks and scarves when you go to fetch that tree, and I'll try to get a little fire going in the stove meanwhile.'

They walked off cautiously with stiff legs, keeping a close watch on the sky. You could not be sure that another load of cotton wool would not come tumbling down.

Moominpappa decided that, in spite of the threatening catastrophe, he would not cut down one of his own trees – they were

too precious. Instead, the family climbed over Mrs Fillyjonk's
fence and selected a big tree that they decided would be of no
further use to her, anyway.

'Do you think we're meant to hide in it?' asked Moomin.

'I don't know,' said Moominpappa and continued chopping.
'I don't understand it at all.'

They had nearly reached the river with their tree, when Mrs
Fillyjonk came rushing towards them with her arms full of bags
and parcels. She was red in the face, and thanks be, too hurried
and flurried to recognize her own tree.

'Oh! bother!' cried Mrs Fillyjonk. 'Ill-bred hedgehogs simply
shouldn't be *allowed* to . . . As I was saying to Gaffsie just now,
it's an absolute disgrace . . .'

'The tree,' said Moominpappa, clinging desperately to Mrs
Fillyjonk's fur collar, 'what *are* we supposed to do with our tree?'

'The tree,' repeated Mrs Fillyjonk bewildered, 'the tree? Oh, how dreadful! What an awful bore ... It's got to be dressed, of course ... How on earth shall I get it done in time ...'

She dropped her parcels in the snow, her bonnet slipped forward over her nose and she nearly burst into tears in her agitation.

Moominpappa shook his head and picked up the tree again.

2

At home Moominmamma had cleared the snow from the verandah, got out the life-belt, the aspirin and Moominpappa's rifle, and had made hot fomentations. You never could tell ...

A little Squeak was sitting on the very edge of the sofa, drinking tea. It had sat in the snow under the verandah, looking so miserable that Moominmamma had asked it in.

'Well, here's the tree,' said Moominpappa. 'I only wish we knew what it's going to be used for. Mrs Fillyjonk said it's supposed to be dressed.'

'We haven't got such big clothes,' said Moominmamma worried. 'What could she have meant?'

'Isn't it beautiful!' exclaimed the little Squeak, swallowing its tea the wrong way from sheer nervousness, and was instantly sorry it had dared to raise its voice.

'Do *you* know how to dress a tree?' asked the Snorkmaiden.

The Squeak went as red as a beetroot and whispered: 'With

pretty things. As prettily as you can. That's what I've heard.'
Then it was overwhelmed by shyness, threw its paws over its
face, upsetting the teacup at the same time, and rushed to dis-
appear through the verandah door.

'Now you must all be quiet, because I'm thinking,' said
Moominpappa. 'If the tree is to be made as beautiful as possible
we can't be meant to hide in it, but it's to *pacify* the peril. I'm
beginning to understand what it's all about.'

They immediately carried the tree into the garden, planted it
firmly in the snow, and began to dress it from top to bottom
with all the most beautiful things they could think of. They
decorated it with the shells from the summer flower beds and
with the Snorkmaiden's pearl necklace. They took down the
crystals from the drawing-room chandelier and hung them on
the branches, and at the top they put a red silk rose which
Moominpappa had given to Moominmamma. Everyone brought
the most beautiful things they could think of to appease the mysterious powers of the winter season.

When the tree was ready the Mymble came past again with
her toboggan. This time she was going in the opposite direction
and was, if possible, in an even greater hurry.

'Have you seen our Christmas tree?' Moomin called out.

'Heaven preserve us!' said the Mymble . . . 'But then you've
always been oddities . . . I've got to be off . . . must cook some
food for Christmas.'

'Food for Christmas,' repeated Moomin astonished. 'Does it
have to be fed, too?'

The Mymble hardly listened. 'Do you think one can do
without food for Christmas?' she said impatiently and kicked
off with her toboggan down the slope.

Moominmamma spent all afternoon bustling round, and just
before twilight the Christmas's food was ready and arranged in

small cups round the tree. There was fruit juice, yoghourt, bilberry pie, eggs and various other things that the Moomin family liked.

'Do you think the Christmas is *very* hungry?' asked Moomin-mamma anxiously.

'He could hardly be hungrier than I am,' said Moominpappa, looking at the food longingly; but little creatures must always be very polite to the great powers of nature. He sat shivering in the snow with the quilt drawn right up over his ears.

In the valley below, lights were appearing in all the windows. They shone under the trees and on the branches, and flickering beams darted here and there across the snow.

Moomin looked at his pappa meaningly.

'All right,' said Moominpappa, 'to be on the safe side.'

So Moomin went into the house and collected up all the candles he could find. He pushed them into the snow round the tree and lit them carefully, one by one, until they were all burning – to pacify the darkness and the Christmas.

Little by little, silence fell on the valley – maybe everyone had returned home to sit and wait for the coming peril.

Only one solitary shadowy figure was still to be seen, running among the trees – it was Hemulen.

'Hallo,' called Moomin softly. 'Is it coming soon?'

'Don't distract me,' said Hemulen gruffly. His nose was deep in a long list of things with nearly everything crossed out. He sat down by one of the candles and began to work through it. 'Mamma, Pappa, Gaffsie,' he murmured. 'All the cousins . . . the eldest hedgehog . . . the little ones don't need anything . . . and Sniff didn't give me anything last year . . . Misable and Whomper and Auntie . . . this is driving me crazy.'

'What's the matter?' asked the Snorkmaiden anxiously.

'Presents,' exclaimed Hemulen. 'More and more presents every Christmas.'

In a great hurry, he crossed something off his list and rushed away.

'Wait!' called Moomin. 'Explain . . . and your gloves . . .'

But Hemulen disappeared into the darkness, in a hurry like everyone else, and flustered because Christmas was coming.

The Moomin family went quietly into the house to look for presents.

Moominpappa chose his best trolling-spoon for pike, which lay in a very pretty box. On it he wrote 'To Christmas', and then he put it out in the snow. The Snorkmaiden pulled off her anklet, and with a sigh she wrapped it up in tissue-paper.

And Moominmamma opened her most secret drawer and brought out the book with pictures – the only picture book in the whole valley.

What Moomin wrapped up was so precious and so private

that no one was allowed to see it – and not even later, in the spring, did he disclose what he had given away. Then they all sat down in the snow and waited for the catastrophe.

Time went by, but nothing happened.

Only the little Squeak, who had been drinking tea, appeared from behind the woodshed. It had brought all its relations and their friends; and they were all just as small and grey and shrivelled and cold as he was.

'Happy Christmas,' whispered the Squeak shyly.

'You're the first one to think that Christmas is happy,' said Moominpappa. 'Aren't you afraid of what's going to happen when it comes?'

'But it's here,' murmured the Squeak and settled down in the snow with its relations. 'May we have a look? You've got such a wonderful tree!'

'And look at all the food!' said one of the relations longingly.

'And real presents!' said another relation.

'All my life I've been dreaming of seeing this close to,' added the Squeak with a sigh.

Moominmamma moved closer to Moominpappa:

'Don't you think . . .?' she whispered.

'Yes, but supposing . . .' objected Moominpappa.

'Never mind,' said Moomin. 'If the Christmas is angry, perhaps we can escape to the verandah.'

And he turned to the Squeak and said:

'Please help yourselves; it's all yours.'

The Squeak could not believe its ears. Slowly it advanced towards the tree, and the long line of relations followed, their whiskers trembling with awe.

They had never had a Christmas of their own before.

'I think we'd better be off,' said Moominpappa anxiously.

Quickly they padded off to the verandah and hid under the

table. Nothing happened. Cautiously they began to look out through the window.

Little Squeaks were sitting out there, eating and drinking, and opening presents and having more fun than they had ever had in their lives before. Finally they climbed up into the tree and fixed the lighted candles on all the branches.

'But I think there ought to be a big star at the top,' said the Squeak's paternal aunt.

'Do you?' said the Squeak, looking thoughtfully at Moomin-mamma's red silk rose. 'Does it really matter, so long as the intention's good?'

'Yes, we *ought* to have got a star,' whispered Moomin-mamma. 'But, of course, it's impossible.'

They looked up at the sky, so black and distant, but incredibly full of stars – a thousand times more full than in the summer. And the biggest of them all stood right above the top of their tree.

'I'm rather sleepy,' said Moominmamma. 'And I'm too tired to think any more about the meaning of all this; but it seems to be turning out all right.'

'In any case, I'm not afraid of Christmas now,' said Moomin. 'I think Hemulen and the Mymble and Mrs Fillyjonk must have got things mixed up, somehow.'

And they put Hemulen's yellow gloves on the verandah railing to make sure that he would find them, and went inside to continue their long sleep while they waited for spring to come again.

Written and illustrated by TOVE JANSSON
Translated by MARIANNE TURNER

The Frog and the Crow

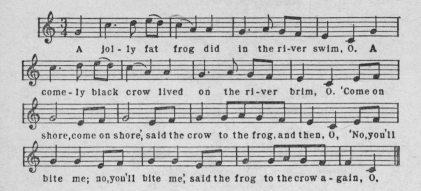

A jolly fat frog did in the river swim, O.
A comely black crow lived on the river brim, O.
'Come on shore, come on shore,' said the crow to the frog,
    and then, O,
'No, you'll bite me; no, you'll bite me,' said the frog to the
    crow again, O.

'Oh, there is sweet music on yonder green hill, O,
And you shall be a dancer, a dancer in yellow.
All in yellow, all in yellow,' said the crow to the frog, and
    then, O,
'All in yellow, all in yellow,' said the frog to the crow again, O.

'Farewell, ye little fishes, that in the river swim, O.
I go to be a dancer, a dancer in yellow.'
'Oh, beware; oh, beware,' said the fish to the frog and then, O.
'I'll take care, I'll take care,' said the frog to the fish again, O.

The frog began a-swimming, a-swimming to land, O.
The crow began a-hopping to give him his hand, O.
'Sir, you're welcome; sir, you're welcome,' said the crow to
the frog, and then, O,
'Sir, I thank you; sir, I thank you,' said the frog to the crow
again, O.

'But where is the music on yonder green hill, O?
And where are all the dancers, the dancers in yellow?
All in yellow, all in yellow,' said the frog to the crow, and
then, O –
But he chuckled, oh he chuckled, and then, O, and then, O!

The Grand Panjandrum

So she went into the garden to cut a cabbage-leaf to make an
apple-pie; and at the same time a great she-bear, coming up the
street, pops its head into the shop. 'What! no soap?' So he died,
and she very imprudently married the barber; and there were
present the Picninnies, and the Joblillies, and the Garyalies, and
the grand Panjandrum himself, with the little round button at
top, and they all fell to playing the game of catch as catch can,
till the gunpowder ran out at the heels of their boots.

SAMUEL FOOTE

The Story of Caliph Stork

CALIPH CHASID, of Bagdad, was resting comfortably on his divan one fine afternoon. He was smoking a long pipe, and from time to time he sipped a little coffee which a slave handed to him, and after each sip he stroked his long beard with an air of enjoyment. This was, in fact, the best time of day in which to approach the Caliph, for just now he was pretty sure to be both affable and in good spirits, and for this reason the Grand Vizier Mansor always chose this hour in which to pay his daily visit.

He arrived as usual this afternoon, but contrary to his usual custom, with an anxious face. The Caliph withdrew his pipe for a moment from his lips and asked, 'Why do you look so anxious, Grand Vizier?'

The Grand Vizier crossed his arms on his breast and bent low before his master as he answered:

'Oh, my Lord! whether my countenance be anxious or not I know not, but down below, in the court of the palace, is a pedlar with such beautiful things that I cannot help feeling annoyed at having so little money to spare.'

The Caliph, who had wished for some time past to give his Grand Vizier a present, ordered his black slave to bring the pedlar before him at once. The slave soon returned, followed by the pedlar, a short stout man with a swarthy face, and dressed in very ragged clothes. He carried a box containing all manner of wares – strings of pearls, rings, richly mounted pistols, goblets, and combs. The Caliph and his Vizier inspected everything, and the Caliph chose some handsome pistols for himself and

Mansor, and a comb with jewels for the Vizier's wife. Just as the pedlar was about to close his box, the Caliph noticed a small drawer, and asked if there was anything else in it for sale. The pedlar opened the drawer and showed them a box containing a black powder, and a scroll written in strange characters, which neither the Caliph nor the Mansor could read.

'I got these two articles from a merchant who had picked them up in the street at Mecca,' said the pedlar. 'I do not know what they may contain, but as they are of no use to me, you are welcome to have them for a trifle.'

The Caliph, who liked to have old manuscripts in his library, even though he could not read them, purchased the scroll and the box, and dismissed the pedlar. Then, being anxious to know what might be the contents of the scroll, he asked the Vizier if he did not know of anyone who might be able to decipher it.

'Most gracious Lord and Master,' replied the Vizier, 'near the great Mosque lives a man called Selim the learned, who knows every language under the sun. Send for him; it may be that he will be able to interpret these mysterious characters.'

The learned Selim was summoned immediately.

'Selim,' said the Caliph, 'I hear you are a scholar. Look well at this scroll and see whether you can read it. If you can, I will give you a robe of glory; but if you fail, I will order you to receive twelve strokes on your cheeks, and five-and-twenty on the soles of your feet, because you have been falsely called Selim the learned.'

Selim prostrated himself and said, 'Be it according to your will, oh master! Then he gazed long at the scroll. Suddenly he exclaimed: 'May I die, oh, my Lord, if this isn't Latin!'

'Well,' said the Caliph, 'if it is Latin, let us hear what it means.'

So Selim began to translate: 'Thou who mayest find this, praise Allah for his mercy. Whoever shall snuff the powder in this box, and at the same time shall pronounce the word "Mutabor!" can transform himself into any creature he likes, and will understand the language of all animals. When he wishes to resume the human form, he has only to bow three times towards the east, and to repeat the same word. Be careful, however, when wearing the shape of some beast or bird, not to laugh, or thou wilt certainly forget the magic word and remain an animal for ever.'

When Selim the learned had read this, the Caliph was delighted. He made the wise man swear not to tell the matter to anyone, gave him a splendid robe, and dismissed him. Then he said to his Vizier, 'That's what I call a good bargain, Mansor. I am longing for the moment when I can become some animal. Tomorrow morning I shall expect you early; we will go into the country, take some snuff from my box, and then hear what is being said in air, earth, and water.'

2

Next morning Caliph Chasid had barely finished dressing and breakfasting, when the Grand Vizier arrived, according to orders, to accompany him in his expedition. The Caliph stuck the snuff-box in his girdle, and, having desired his servants to remain at home, started off with the Grand Vizier only in attendance. First they walked through the palace gardens, but they looked in vain for some creature which could tempt them to try their magic power. At length the Vizier suggested going further on to a pond which lay beyond the town, and where he had often seen a variety of creatures, especially storks, whose grave, dignified appearance and constant chatter had often attracted his attention.

The Caliph consented, and they went straight to the pond. As soon as they arrived they remarked a stork strutting up and down with a stately air, hunting for frogs, and now and then muttering something to itself. At the same time they saw another stork far above in the sky flying towards the same spot.

'I would wager my beard, most gracious master,' said the Grand Vizier, 'that these two long legs will have a good chat together. How would it be if we turned ourselves into storks?'

'Well said,' replied the Caliph; 'but first let us remember carefully how we are to become men once more. True! Bow three times towards the east and say "Mutabor!" and I shall be Caliph and you my Grand Vizier again. But for Heaven's sake don't laugh or we are lost!'

As the Caliph spoke he saw the second stork circling round his head and gradually flying towards the earth. Quickly he drew the box from his girdle, took a good pinch of the snuff, and offered one to Mansor, who also took one, and both cried together 'Mutabor!'

Instantly their legs grew thin and red; their smart yellow slippers turned to clumsy stork's feet, their arms to wings; their necks began to sprout from between their shoulders and grew a yard long; their beards disappeared, and their bodies were covered with feathers.

'You've got a fine long bill, Sir Vizier,' cried the Caliph, after standing for some time lost in astonishment. 'By the beard of the prophet, I never saw such a thing in all my life.'

'My very humble thanks,' replied the Grand Vizier, as he bent his long neck; 'but, if I may venture to say so, your Highness is even handsomer as a stork than as a Caliph. But come, if it so pleases you, let us go near our comrades there and find out whether we really do understand the language of storks.'

Meantime the second stork had reached the ground. It first scraped its bill with its claw, stroked down its feathers, and then advanced towards the first stork. The two newly made storks lost no time in drawing near, and to their amazement overheard the following conversation:

'Good morning, Dame Longlegs. You are out early this morning!'

'Yes, indeed, dear Chatterbill! I am getting myself a morsel of breakfast. May I offer you a joint of lizard or a frog's thigh?'

'A thousand thanks, but I have really no appetite this morning. I am here for a very different purpose. I am to dance today before my father's guests, and I have come to the meadow for a little quiet practice.'

Thereupon the young stork began to move about with the most wonderful steps. The Caliph and Mansor looked on in surprise for some time; but when at last she balanced herself in a picturesque attitude on one leg, and flapped her wings gracefully up and down, they could hold out no longer; a prolonged peal burst from each of their bills, and it was some time before they could recover their composure. The Caliph was the first to collect himself. 'That was the best joke,' said he, 'I've ever seen. It's a pity the stupid creatures were scared away by our laughter, or no doubt they would have sung next!'

Suddenly, however, the Vizier remembered how strictly they had been warned not to laugh during their transformation. He at once communicated his fears to the Caliph, who exclaimed, 'By Mecca and Medina! it would indeed prove but a poor joke if I had to remain a stork for the remainder of my days! Do just try and remember the stupid word, it has slipped my memory.'

'We must bow three times eastwards and say "Mu ... mu ... mu ..."'

They turned to the east and fell to bowing till their bills touched the ground, but, oh horror – the magic word was quite forgotten, and however often the Caliph bowed and however touchingly his Vizier cried 'Mu ... mu ...' they could not re-call it, and the unhappy Chasid and Mansor remained storks as they were.

3

The two enchanted birds wandered sadly on through the meadows. In their misery they could not think what to do next.

They could not rid themselves of their new forms; there was no use in returning to the town and saying who they were; for who would believe a stork who announced that he was a Caliph; and even if they did believe him, would the people of Bagdad consent to let a stork rule over them?

So they lounged about for several days, supporting themselves on fruits, which, however, they found some difficulty in eating with their long bills. They did not much care to eat frogs and lizards. Their one comfort in their sad plight was the power of flying, and accordingly they often flew over the roofs of Bagdad to see what was going on there.

During the first few days they noticed signs of much disturbance and distress in the streets, but about the fourth day, as they sat on the roof of the palace, they perceived a splendid procession passing below them along the street. Drums and trumpets sounded, a man in a scarlet mantle, embroidered in gold, sat on a splendidly caparisoned horse surrounded by richly dressed slaves; half Bagdad crowded after him, and they all shouted, 'Hail, Mirza, the Lord of Bagdad!'

The two storks on the palace roof looked at each other, and Caliph Chasid said, 'Can you guess now, Grand Vizier, why I have been enchanted? This Mirza is the son of my deadly enemy, the mighty magician Kaschnur, who in an evil moment vowed vengeance on me. Still I will not despair! Come with me, my faithful friend; we will go to the grave of the Prophet, and perhaps at that sacred spot the spell may be loosed.'

They rose from the palace roof, and spread their wings towards Medina.

But flying was not quite an easy matter, for the two storks had had but little practice as yet.

'Oh, my Lord!' gasped the Vizier after a couple of hours, 'I can get on no longer; you really fly too quick for me. Besides, it is nearly evening, and we should do well to find some place in which to spend the night.'

Chasid agreed to his servant's suggestion, and perceiving in the valley beneath them a ruin which seemed to promise shelter, they flew towards it. The building in which they proposed to pass the night had apparently been formerly a castle. Some handsome pillars still stood among the heaps of ruins, and several rooms, which yet remained in fair preservation, gave evidence of former grandeur. Chasid and his companion wandered along the passages seeking a dry spot, when suddenly Mansor stood still.

'My Lord and Master,' he whispered, 'if it were not absurd for a Grand Vizier, and still more for a stork, to be afraid of ghosts, I should feel quite nervous, for someone, or something close by me, has sighed and moaned quite audibly.'

The Caliph stood still and distinctly heard a low weeping sound which seemed to proceed from a human being rather than from any animal. Full of curiosity he was about to rush towards the spot from whence the sounds of woe came, when the Vizier caught him by the wing with his bill, and implored him not to expose himself to fresh and unknown dangers. The Caliph, however, under whose stork's breast a brave heart beat, tore himself away with the loss of a few feathers, and hurried down a dark passage. He saw a door which stood ajar, and through which he distinctly heard sighs, mingled with sobs. He pushed open the door with his bill, but remained on the threshold, astonished at the sight which met his eyes. On the floor of the ruined chamber – which was but scantily lighted by a small barred window – sat a large screech owl. Big tears rolled from its large round eyes, and in a hoarse voice it uttered its complaints through its crooked beak. As soon as it saw the Caliph and his Vizier – who had crept up meanwhile – it gave vent to a joyful cry. It gently wiped the tears from its eyes with its spotted brown wings, and to the great amazement of the two visitors, addressed them in good human Arabic.

'Welcome, ye storks! You are a good sign of my deliverance, for it was foretold me that a piece of good fortune should befall me through a stork.'

When the Caliph had recovered from his surprise, he drew up his feet into a graceful position, bent his long neck, and said: 'Oh, screech owl! from your words I am led to believe that we see in you a companion in misfortune. But, alas! your hope that you may attain your deliverance through us is but a vain one. You will know our helplessness when you have heard our story.'

The screech owl begged him to relate it, and the Caliph accordingly told him what we already know.

4

When the Caliph had ended, the owl thanked him and said: 'You hear my story, and own that I am no less unfortunate than yourselves. My father is the King of the Indies. I, his only daughter, am named Lusa. That magician Kaschnur, who enchanted you, has been the cause of my misfortunes too. He came one day to my father and demanded my hand for his son Mirza. My father – who is rather hasty – ordered him to be thrown downstairs. The wretch not long after managed to approach me under another form; and one day, when I was in the garden, and asked for some refreshment, he brought me – in the disguise of a slave – a draught which changed me at once to this horrid shape. While I was fainting with terror he transported me here, and cried to me with his awful voice: "There shall you remain, lonely and hideous, despised even by the brutes, till the end of your days, or till some one of his own free will asks you to be his wife. Thus do I avenge myself on you and your proud father."

'Since then many months have passed away. Sad and lonely do I live like any hermit within these walls, avoided by the world and a terror even to animals; the beauties of nature are hidden from me, for I am blind by day, and it is only when the moon sheds her pale light on this spot that the veil falls from my eyes and I can see.' The owl paused, and once more wiped her eyes with her wing, for the recital of her woes had drawn fresh tears from her.

The Caliph fell into deep thought on hearing this story of the Princess. 'If I am not much mistaken,' said he, 'there is some mysterious connection between our misfortunes, but how to find the key to the riddle is the question.'

The owl answered: 'Oh, my Lord! I too feel sure of this, for in my earliest youth a wise woman foretold that a stork would bring me some great happiness, and I think I could tell you how we might save ourselves.' The Caliph was much surprised, and asked her what she meant.

'The Magician who has made us both miserable,' said she, 'comes once a month to these ruins. Not far from this room is a large hall where he is in the habit of feasting with his companions. I have often watched them. They tell each other all about their evil deeds, and possibly the magic word which you have forgotten may be mentioned.'

'Oh, dearest Princess!' exclaimed the Caliph, 'say, when does he come, and where is the hall?'

The owl paused a moment and then said: 'Do not think me unkind, but I can only grant your request on one condition.'

'Speak, speak!' cried Chasid; 'command, I will gladly do whatever you wish!'

'Well,' replied the owl, 'I should like to be free too; but this can only be if one of you will offer me his hand in marriage.'

The storks seemed rather taken aback by this suggestion, and the Caliph beckoned to his Vizier to retire and consult with him.

When they were outside the door the Caliph said: 'Grand Vizier, this is a tiresome business. However, you can take her.'

'Indeed!' said the Vizier; 'so that when I go home my wife may scratch my eyes out! Besides, I am an old man, and your Highness is still young and unmarried, and a far more suitable match for a young and lovely Princess.'

'That's just where it is,' sighed the Caliph, whose wings drooped in a dejected manner; 'how do you know she is young and lovely? I call it buying a pig in a poke.'

They argued on for some time, but at length, when the Caliph saw plainly that his Vizier would rather remain a stork to the end of his days than marry the owl, he determined to fulfil the condition himself. The owl was delighted. She owned that they could not have arrived at a better time, as most probably the magicians would meet that very night.

She then proceeded to lead the two storks to the chamber. They passed through a long dark passage till at length a bright ray of light shone before them through the chinks of a half-ruined wall. When they reached it the owl advised them to keep very quiet. Through the gap near which they stood they could with ease survey the whole of the large hall. It was adorned with splendid carved pillars; a number of lamps replaced the light of day. In the middle of the hall stood a round table covered with a variety of dishes, and about the table was a divan on which eight men were seated. In one of these bad men the two recognized the pedlar who had sold the magic powder. The man next him begged him to relate all his latest doings, and among them he told the story of the Caliph and his Vizier.

'And what kind of word did you give them?' asked another old sorcerer.

'A very difficult Latin word; it is "Mutabor".'

5

As soon as the storks heard this they were nearly beside themselves with joy. They ran at such a pace to the door of the ruined castle that the owl could scarcely keep up with them. When they reached it the Caliph turned to the owl, and said with much feeling: 'Deliverer of my friend and myself, as a proof of my eternal gratitude, accept me as your husband.' Then he turned towards the east. Three times the storks bowed their long necks to the sun, which was just rising over the mountains. 'Mutabor!' they both cried, and in an instant they were once more transformed. In the rapture of their newly-given lives master and servant fell laughing and weeping into each other's arms. Who shall describe their surprise when they at last turned round and beheld standing before them a beautiful lady exquisitely dressed!

With a smile she held out her hand to the Caliph, and asked: 'Do you not recognize your screech owl?'

It was she! The Caliph was so enchanted by her grace and beauty, that he declared being turned into a stork had been the best piece of luck which had ever befallen him. The three set out at once for Bagdad. Fortunately, the Caliph found not only the box with the magic powder, but also his purse in his girdle; he was, therefore, able to buy in the nearest village all they required for their journey, and so at last they reached the gates of Bagdad.

Here the Caliph's arrival created the greatest sensation. He had been quite given up for dead, and the people were greatly rejoiced to see their beloved ruler again.

Their rage with the usurper Mirza, however, was great in proportion. They marched in force to the palace and took the old magician and his son prisoners. The Caliph sent the magician to the room where the Princess had lived as an owl, and there had him hanged. As the son, however, knew nothing of his father's acts, the Caliph gave him his choice between death and a pinch of the magic snuff. When he chose the latter, the Grand Vizier handed him the box. One good pinch, and the magic word transformed him to a stork. The Caliph ordered him to be confined in an iron cage, and placed in the palace gardens.

Caliph Chasid lived long and happily with his wife the Princess. His merriest time was when the Grand Vizier visited him in the afternoon; and when the Caliph was in particularly high spirits he would condescend to mimic the Vizier's appearance when he was a stork. He would strut gravely, and with well-stiffened legs, up and down the room, chattering, and showing how he had vainly bowed to the east and cried 'Mu . . . Mu . . .' The Caliphess and her children were always much entertained by this performance; but when the Caliph went on nodding and bowing, and calling 'Mu . . . mu . . .' too long, the Vizier would threaten laughingly to tell the Caliphess the subject of the discussion carried on one night outside the door of Princess Screech Owl.

ANDREW LANG

Old Shellover

'Come!' said Old Shellover.
'What?' says Creep.
'The horny old Gardener's fast asleep;
The fat cock Thrush
To his nest has gone,
And the dew shines bright
In the rising Moon;
Old Sallie Worm from her hole doth peep;
Come!' said old Shellover.
'Ay!' said Creep.

WALTER DE LA MARE

Johnny Crow's Garden

Johnny Crow
Would dig and sow
Till he made a little Garden.

And the Lion
Had a green and yellow Tie on
In Johnny Crow's Garden.

And the Rat
Wore a Feather in his Hat
But the Bear
Had nothing to wear
In Johnny Crow's Garden.

So the Ape
Took his Measure with a Tape
In Johnny Crow's Garden.

Then the Crane
Was caught in the Rain
In Johnny Crow's Garden.

And the Beaver
Was afraid he had a Fever
But the Goat
Said:
'It's nothing but his Throat'
In Johnny Crow's Garden.

And the Pig
Danced a Jig
In Johnny Crow's Garden.

Then the Stork
Gave a Philosophic Talk
Till the Hippopotami
Said: 'Ask no further "What am I"'
While the Elephant
Said something quite irrelevant
In Johnny Crow's Garden.

And the Goose –
Well,
The Goose *was* a Goose
In Johnny Crow's Garden.

And the Mouse
Built himself a little House
Where the Cat
Sat down beside the Mat
In Johnny Crow's Garden.

And the Whale
Told a very long Tale
In Johnny Crow's Garden.

And the Owl
Was a funny old Fowl
And the Fox
Put them all in the Stocks
In Johnny Crow's Garden.

But Johnny Crow
He let them go
And they all sat down
To their dinner in a row
In Johnny Crow's Garden!

Written and illustrated by L. LESLIE BROOKE

Where Arthur Sleeps

THERE was once a young man in west Wales who was the seventh son of a seventh son. All such, it is said, are born to great destinies, for with their forty-nine parts of man there is blended one part of Bendith y Mamau (Blessing of the Mothers, or fairies). It happened one day that he had a quarrel with his father and left home to seek his fortune in England. As he walked through Wales he met a rich farmer who engaged him to take a herd of his cattle to London. 'For to my eyes,' said the farmer, 'you look a likely lad, and a lucky lad too. With a dog at your heels and a staff in your hand you would be a prince among drovers. Now here is a dog, but where in the world is a staff?'

'Leave that to me,' said our Welshman, and stepping aside to a rocky mound he cut himself the finest hazel stick he could find. It had to be fine, for as teeth to a dog so his staff to a drover. It was tall as his shoulder and mottled like a trout, and so hard of grain that when the sticks of his fellow-drovers were ragged as straws it showed neither split nor splinter.

He passed through England without losing a beast and disposed of his herd in London. A little later he was standing on London Bridge, wondering what to do next, when a stranger stopped alongside him and asked him from whence he came.

'From my own country,' he replied; for a Welshman does well to be cautious in England.

'And what is your name?' asked the stranger.

'The one my father gave me.'

'And where did you cut your stick, friend?'

'I cut it from a tree.'

'I approve your closeness,' said the stranger. 'Now what

would you say if I told you that from that stick in your hand I can make you gold and silver?'

'I should say you are a wise man.'

'With Capital Letters at that,' said the stranger, and he went on to explain that his hazel stick had grown over a place where a vast treasure lay hidden. 'If only you can remember where you cut it, and lead me there, that treasure shall be yours.'

'I may well do that,' said the Welshman, 'for why am I here save to seek my fortune?'

Without more ado they set off together for Wales and at last reached Craig-y-Dinas (The Fortress Rock), where he showed the Wise Man (for such he was) the exact spot where he had cut his stick. It had sprung from the root of a large old hazel, and the knife-mark was still to be seen, as yellow as gold and broad as a broad-bean. With bill and mattock they dug this up and found underneath a big flat-stone; and when they lifted the stone they saw a passage and a gleam at the far end of it.

'You first,' said the Wise Man; for an Englishman does well to be cautious in Wales; and they crept carefully down the passage towards the gleam. Hanging from the passage roof was a bronze bell the size of a beehive, with a clanger as long as your arm, and the Wise Man begged the Welshman on no account to touch it, for if he did disaster would surely follow. Soon they reached the main cave, where they were amazed by the extent of it, and still more by what they saw there. For it was filled with armed warriors, all asleep on the floor. There was an outer ring of a thousand men, and an inner ring of a hundred, their heads to the wall and their feet to the centre, each with sword, shield, battle-axe, and spear; and outermost of all lay their horses, un-bitted and unblinkered, with their trappings heaped before their noses. The reason why they could see this so clearly was because of the extreme brilliance of the weapons and the helmets glowing like suns and the hooves of the horses effulgent as autumn's moon. And in the middle of all lay a king and emperor at rest, as they knew by the glory of his array and the jewelled crown beneath his hand and the awe and majesty of his person.

Then the Welshman noticed that the cavern also contained two tall heaps of gold and silver. Gaping with greed he started towards them, but the Wise Man motioned to him to wait a moment first.

'Help yourself,' he warned him, 'from one heap or the other, but on no account from both.'

The Welshman now loaded himself with gold till he could not carry another coin. To his surprise the Wise Man took nothing.

'I have not grown wise,' he said, 'by coveting gold and silver.'

This sounded more wind than wisdom to the Welshman, but he said nothing as they started for the mouth of the cave. Again the Wise Man cautioned him about touching the bell. 'It might well prove fatal to us if one or more of the warriors should awake and lift his head and ask, "Is it day?" Should that happen there is only one thing to do. You must instantly answer: "No, sleep on!" and we must hope that he will lower his head again to rest, by which means we may escape.'

And so it happened. For the Welshman was now so bulging with gold that he could not squeeze past the bell without his elbow touching it. At once a sonorous sound of bronze be-wrangled the passage, and a warrior lifted his head.

'Is it day?' he asked.

'No,' replied the Welshman, 'sleep on.'

At these prompt words the warrior lowered his head and slept, and not without many a backward glance the two companions reached the light of day and replaced the stone and the hazel tree. The Wise Man next took his leave of the Welshman, but gave him this counsel first. 'Use that wealth well,' he told him, 'and it will suffice you for the rest of your life. But if, as I suspect, you come to need more, you may return and help yourself from the silver heap. Try not to touch the bell, but if you do and a warrior awakes, he will ask: "Are the Cymry in danger?" You must then answer: "Not yet, sleep on!" But I should on no account advise you to return to the cave a third time.'

'Who are these warriors?' asked the Welshman. 'And who is their sleeping king?'

'The king is Arthur, and those that surround him are the men of the Island of the Mighty. They sleep with their steeds and their arms because a day will come when land and sky shall cower at the sound of a host, and the bell will tremble and ring, and then those warriors will ride out with Arthur at their head, and drive our foes headlong into the sea, and there shall be justice and peace among men for as long as the world endures.'

'That may be so, indeed,' said the Welshman, waving farewell. 'Meantime I have my gold.'

But the time soon came when his gold was all spent. A second time he entered the cave, and a second time took too great a load, only this time of silver. A second time his elbow touched the bell. Three warriors raised their heads. 'Are the Cymry in danger?' The voice of one was light as a bird's, the voice of another was dark as a bull's, and the voice of the third so menacing that he could hardly gasp out an answer.

'Not yet,' he said, 'sleep on!' Slowly, with sighs and mutterings, they lowered their heads, and their horses snorted and clashed their hooves before silence filled the cave once more.

For a long time after this escape he told himself that he would on no account return to the cave a third time. But in a year or two his silver went the way of his gold, and almost despite himself there he was, standing by the hazel with a mattock in his hand. A third time he entered the cave, and a third time took too great

a load, this time of silver and gold as well. A third time his elbow touched the bell. As it boomed, all those warriors sprang to their feet, and the proud stallions with them, and what with the booming of the bell, the jangling of trappings, and the shrill neighing of the horses, never in the world's history was there more uproar in an enclosed place than that. Then Arthur's voice arose over the din, silencing them, and Cei and the one-handed Bedwyr, Owein, Trystan, and Gwalchmei, moved through the host and brought the horses to a stand.

'The time is not yet,' said Arthur. He pointed to the Welshman, trembling with his gold and silver in the passage. 'Would you march out for him?'

At these words, Cei caught the intruder up by the feet and would have lashed him against the wall, but Arthur forbade it and said to put him outside, and so Cei did, flinging him like a wet rabbit-skin from the passage and closing the stone behind him. So there he was, without a penny to scratch with, blue as a plum with fright and bruises, flat on his back in the eye of the sun.

It was a long time before he could be brought to tell his story, and still longer before he grew well. One day, however, he returned, and some friends with him, to Craig-y-Dinas.

'Where is the hazel tree?' they asked, for it was not to be seen. 'And where is the stone?' they asked, for they could not find it. When he persisted in his story they jeered at him, and because he might not be silenced they beat him, and so it came about that for shame and wrath he left the countryside for ever. And from that day to this no one, though he were seven times over the seventh son of a seventh son, has beheld Arthur sleeping with his host, nor till the day of Britain's greatest danger shall any so behold him. So with the hope that that day is a long way off, we reach the end of our story.

GWYN JONES

John Cook's Mare

John Cook he had a little grey mare;
    Hee, haw, hum!
Her back stood up, and her bones they were bare;
    Hee, haw, hum!

John Cook was riding up Shooter's Bank,
    Hee, haw, hum!
And there his nag did kick and prank;
    Hee, haw, hum!

John Cook was riding up Shooter's Hill;
    Hee, haw, hum!
His mare fell down and she made her will;
    Hee, haw, hum!

The saddle and bridle are laid on the shelf;
    Hee, haw, hum!
If you want any more you may sing it yourself!
    Hee, haw, hum!

The Old Woman and Her Pig

An old woman was sweeping her house, and she found a little crooked sixpence. 'What,' said she, 'shall I do with this little sixpence? I will go to market, and buy a little pig.'

As she was coming home, she came to a stile: but the piggy wouldn't go over the stile.

She went a little further, and she met a dog. So she said to him: 'Dog! dog! bite pig; piggy won't go over the stile; and I shan't get home tonight.' But the dog wouldn't.

She went a little further, and she met a stick. So she said: 'Stick! stick! beat dog! dog won't bite pig; piggy won't get over the stile; and I shan't get home tonight.' But the stick wouldn't.

She went a little further, and she met a fire. So she said: 'Fire! fire! burn stick; stick won't beat dog; dog won't bite pig; piggy won't get over the stile; and I shan't get home tonight.' But the fire wouldn't.

She went a little further, and she met some water. So she said: 'Water! water! quench fire; fire won't burn stick; stick won't beat dog; dog won't bite pig; piggy won't get over the stile; and I shan't get home tonight.' But the water wouldn't.

She went a little further, and she met an ox. So she said: 'Ox! ox! drink water; water won't quench fire; fire won't burn stick; stick won't beat dog; dog won't bite pig; piggy won't get over the stile; and I shan't get home tonight.' But the ox wouldn't.

She went a little further, and she met a butcher. So she said: 'Butcher! butcher! kill ox; ox won't drink water; water won't quench fire; fire won't burn stick; stick won't beat dog; dog won't bite pig; piggy won't get over the stile; and I shan't get home tonight.' But the butcher wouldn't.

She went a little further, and she met a rope. So she said: 'Rope! rope! hang butcher; butcher won't kill ox; ox won't drink water; water won't quench fire; fire won't burn stick; stick won't beat dog; dog won't bite pig; piggy won't get over the stile; and I shan't get home tonight.' But the rope wouldn't.

She went a little further, and she met a rat. So she said: 'Rat! rat! gnaw rope; rope won't hang butcher; butcher won't kill ox; ox won't drink water; water won't quench fire; fire won't burn stick; stick won't beat dog; dog won't bite pig; piggy won't get over the stile; and I shan't get home tonight.' But the rat wouldn't.

She went a little further, and she met a cat. So she said: 'Cat! cat! kill rat; rat won't gnaw rope; rope won't hang butcher; butcher won't kill ox; ox won't drink water; water won't quench fire; fire won't burn stick; stick won't beat dog; dog won't bite pig; piggy won't get over the stile; and I shan't get home tonight.' But the cat said to her: 'If you will go to yonder cow, and fetch me a saucer of milk, I will kill the rat.' So away went the old woman to the cow.

But the cow said to her: 'If you will go to yonder hay-stack, and fetch me a handful of hay, I'll give you the milk.' So away went the old woman to the hay-stack; and she brought the hay to the cow.

As soon as the cow had eaten the hay, she gave the old woman the milk; and away she went with it in a saucer to the cat.

As soon as the cat had lapped up the milk, the cat began to kill the rat; the rat began to gnaw the rope; the rope began to hang the butcher; the butcher began to kill the ox; the ox began to drink the water; the water began to quench the fire; the fire began to burn the stick; the stick began to beat the dog; the dog began to bite the pig; the little pig in a fright jumped over the stile; and so the old woman got home that night.

The Lory Who Longed for Honey

ONCE upon a time, in a hot sunny country, lived a very bright and beautiful parrot. He was red and green and gold and blue, with a dark purple top to his head. His real name was Lory. And he lived on honey.

There were hundreds of flowers growing among the trees, so all he had to do when he was hungry was to fly down and lick the honey out of the flowers. As a matter of fact, he had a tongue that was specially shaped for getting honey out of flowers. So he always had plenty to eat, and managed very well. All day long he flew about in the hot sunshine, while the monkeys chattered and the bright birds screamed. And as long as he had plenty of honey, he was perfectly happy.

Then one day a sailor came to the forest looking for parrots. He found the parrot that liked honey and took him away. He didn't know that this parrot's real name was a Lory. He didn't know that he had a tongue specially shaped for getting honey out of flowers. He didn't even know he liked honey. He only knew he was a very bright and beautiful parrot and he meant to take him to England and sell him. So on board the ship he fed the parrot on sunflower seeds and taught him to say: 'What have you got, what have you got, what have you got for me?' And whenever the Lory said this, the sailor gave him a sunflower seed. Although, as a matter of fact, he would very much sooner have had honey.

When they reached England, the sailor sold the parrot who liked honey to an old lady who lived in a cottage on a hill. She didn't know much about parrots. She didn't know the parrot was a Lory. She didn't know he had a special tongue for licking honey out of flowers. She didn't even know he liked honey.

But she thought his red and green feathers, his gold and blue feathers, and the dark purple feathers on the top of his head were beautiful. She called him Polly, and fed him on bits of bread and biscuit.

Whenever he said, as he often did: 'What have you got, what have you got, what have you got for me?' she would give him a bit of bread or biscuit. But, of course, he would very much sooner have had honey.

Now the old lady lived by herself and had to work very hard to make enough money to buy food. Generally she had just bread and margarine for tea, because she couldn't afford to buy honey even for herself, although she liked it.

Then one day when she wasn't in the least expecting it, the old lady's nephew who lived in South Africa sent her a present. It was a wooden box carefully packed with straw. Some of the straw was already poking between the boards, but it was impossible to tell what was inside.

When the postman brought it, he said: 'Looks like a nice surprise, lady. Maybe some jam or some fruit.'

She carried the box carefully into her sitting-room and unfastened it. It wasn't jam or fruit. It was six jars of honey all wrapped up in straw. Inside was a note which said:

Dear Auntie,

I have managed to get a very nice job in South Africa, and I am making quite a bit of money. I am sure you are not able to buy all the things you need, so I am sending you six jars of honey. If you like them, I will send some more.

Love from your nephew – Robert

When she had read the letter she was tremendously excited and pleased, because it was so long since anyone had sent her a present and today it wasn't even her birthday. She took out the jars very carefully and put them in a row in the larder. Then she cleared up all the straw and paper and string, and said to herself: 'I'll start the first jar at tea-time today.'

When the clock struck half past three, the old lady put the kettle on the gas, and began to cut some bread. It was certainly rather early for tea, but the old lady was so excited about the honey that she couldn't wait any longer. She put the bread and margarine on the table, took a plate and a knife, and a cup and saucer and spoon out of the cupboard, and then she went to the larder.

All this made Polly very excited. He wasn't in his cage, but on a separate perch where he could turn somersaults if he liked. The old lady let him sit here in the afternoons. He could tell it was tea-time, and when the old lady went to the larder he expected she would bring out some cake or fruit.

So he shouted at the top of his voice: 'What have you got, what have you got, what have you got for me?' When the old lady brought out neither cake nor fruit, but only a jar of yellow stuff, Polly was rather puzzled. But as soon as he saw her take some on her knife and spread the sticky stuff on her bread, and eat it with such pleasure, he knew it was honey.

And as soon as he knew it was honey, he knew he absolutely must think of some way of getting it for himself.

The old lady never dreamt of giving the Lory honey. She didn't know much about parrots. She didn't know he was called a Lory. She didn't know he had a tongue specially shaped for getting honey out of flowers. She didn't even know he liked honey.

But all the time the old lady was spreading the honey on her first slice of bread and thinking how wonderfully kind her nephew was to send it, and what an unexpected treat it was, the Lory was working out a plan.

Now parrots, as you know, are very clever at remembering words and also at imitating people, and sometimes when they talk they can make their voice sound as if it is coming from a different part of the house altogether, so that you have no idea it is the parrot talking at all.

While the old lady was eating her bread and honey and enjoying it tremendously, she suddenly heard a *Miaow!* It was really the Lory, but she didn't know that.

'There's a kitten outside,' she said. 'Poor thing, I expect it's lost. I'll let it in so that it can get warm by the fire.' And she went to the door and opened it.

Polly just had time to flutter on to the table and take a mouthful of honey with his special tongue and get on his perch again before she came back.

'How very strange,' she said, 'I'm sure I heard a kitten. Yet I've looked in the street, and there isn't a kitten to be seen.'

Polly winked and shouted: 'What have you got, what have

you got, what have you got for me?' But the old lady still didn't know he was after the honey.

While the lady was spreading her *second* slice of bread, he thought of another plan. This time he made a noise like the kettle boiling over.

'Goodness!' cried the old lady, jumping up. 'That will put the stove out, unless I hurry.'

And while she rushed out into the kitchen, Polly flew down and took his second big mouthful of honey.

'That's very peculiar,' said the old lady, coming back again just as Polly scrambled on to his perch. 'The kettle's perfectly all right, and not boiling over at all.' But she still didn't understand the Lory was after her honey.

Then he had what he thought was his best plan of all. He made a noise like big drops of rain falling on the roof.

'Oh heavens!' said the poor old lady. 'Now I shall have to bring all the washing in.'

And she left her tea with the pot of honey standing on the table, and went outside to fetch in the washing before it got soaked.

She was a long time, because she had washed a table-cloth, two sheets, a pillow-slip, a towel, a frock, a cardigan and the curtains from the sitting-room. And while she was taking them all off the line, the Lory was swallowing honey as fast as he could.

At last, her arms full of washing, the old lady came back into the room. 'That's funny,' she said, as she looked at the window. 'The sun is shining as brightly as ever. I do believe I've brought all the washing in for nothing.'

'And that's funnier still!' she went on with a little scream, looking at the table. 'I do believe someone's been eating my honey!'

She picked up the jar and looked at it. There was just a scrap-

ing left at the bottom. Yet she had only opened the jar a few minutes ago.

'It must be a burglar,' she said, and feeling very brave she began to look under the furniture and inside the cupboards and wherever a burglar might find space to hide.

All the time she was hunting, the Lory was turning somersaults on his perch and shrieking at the top of his voice: 'What have you got, what have you got, what have you got for me?' He felt very pleased with himself, and he didn't care a bit that he had made the old lady go to all the trouble of bringing in her washing, and on top of that had eaten almost the whole of a jar of honey that her nephew had sent from South Africa.

When the old lady had decided there was no burglar in the house, she went back to the tea-table. And then she noticed drips of honey leading over the table-cloth, over the floor, and up to Polly's perch. She reached up and touched his perch, and, sure enough, that was sticky too.

'Why, you rascal!' she said. 'I do believe it was you who stole the honey.'

And that was how the old lady who didn't know much about parrots discovered that Lories like honey better than anything else in the world. After that, she always gave her Lory some honey for his tea, and she managed it quite well because her nephew in South Africa sent her six jars every month.

But do you know, she never found out it was the Lory who played those tricks on her just to get a taste of her honey!

LEILA BERG

Turn Again Whittington

ROUND FOR THREE VOICES

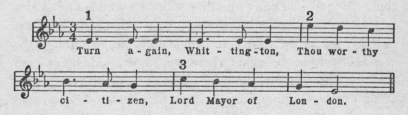

Turn again Whittington,
Thou worthy citizen,
Lord Mayor of London.

Drawing by RANDOLPH CALDECOTT

Blunder

BLUNDER was going to the Wishing-Gate, to wish for a pair of Shetland ponies, and a little coach, like Tom Thumb's. And of course you can have your wish, if you once get there. But the thing is, to find it; for it is not, as you imagine, a great gate, with a tall marble pillar on each side, and a sign over the top, like this, WISHING-GATE – but just an old stile, made of three sticks. Put up two fingers, cross them on the top with another finger, and you have it exactly, – the way it looks, I mean, – a worm-eaten stile, in a meadow; and as there are plenty of old stiles in meadows, how are you to know which is the one?

Blunder's fairy godmother knew, but then she could not tell him, for that was not according to fairy rules and regulations. She could only direct him to follow the road, and ask the way of the first owl he met; and over and over she charged him, for Blunder was a very careless little boy, and seldom found anything, 'Be sure you don't miss him, – be sure you don't pass him by.' And so far Blunder had come on very well, for the road was straight; but at the turn it forked. Should he go through the wood, or turn to the right? There was an owl nodding in a tall oak-tree, the first owl Blunder had seen; but he was a little afraid to wake him up, for Blunder's fairy godmother had told him that this was a great philosopher, who sat up all night to study the habits of frogs and mice, and knew everything but what went on in the daylight, under his nose; and he could think of nothing better to say to this great philosopher than 'Good Mr Owl, will you please show me the way to the Wishing-Gate?'

'Eh! what's that?' cried the owl, starting out of his nap. 'Have you brought me a frog?'

'No,' said Blunder, 'I did not know that you would like one. Can you tell me the way to the Wishing-Gate?'

'Wishing-Gate! Wishing-Gate!' hooted the owl, very angry. 'Winks and naps! how dare you disturb me for such a thing as that? Do you take me for a mile-stone! Follow your nose, sir, follow your nose!' – and, ruffling up his feathers, the owl was asleep again in a moment.

But how could Blunder follow his nose? His nose would turn to the right, or take him through the woods, whichever way his legs went, and 'what was the use of asking the owl,' thought Blunder, 'if this was all?' While he hesitated, a chipmunk came skurrying down the path, and, seeing Blunder, stopped short with a little squeak.

'Good Mrs Chipmunk,' said Blunder, 'can you tell me the way to the Wishing-Gate?'

'I can't, indeed,' answered the chipmunk, politely. 'What with getting in nuts, and the care of a young family, I have so little time to visit anything! But if you will follow the brook, you will find an old water-sprite under a slanting stone, over which the water pours all day with a noise like wabble! wabble! who, I have no doubt, can tell you all about it. You will know him, for he does nothing but grumble about the good old times when a brook would have dried up before it would have turned a mill-wheel.'

So Blunder went on up the brook, and, seeing nothing of the water-sprite, or the slanting stone, was just saying to himself, 'I am sure I don't know where he is, – I can't find it,' when he spied a frog sitting on a wet stone.

'Mr Frog,' asked Blunder, 'can you tell me the way to the Wishing-Gate?'

'I cannot,' said the frog. 'I am very sorry, but the fact is I am an artist. Young as I am, my voice is already remarked at our concerts, and I devote myself so entirely to my profession of music, that I have not time to acquire general information. But in a pine-tree beyond, you will find an old crow, who, I am quite sure, can show you the way, as he is a traveller, and a bird of an inquiring turn of mind.'

'I don't know where the pine is, – I am sure I can never find him,' answered Blunder, discontentedly; but still he went on up the brook, till, hot and tired, and out of patience at seeing neither crow nor pine, he sat down under a great tree to rest. There he heard tiny voices squabbling.

'Get out! Go away, I tell you! It has been knock! knock! knock! at my door all day, till I am tired out. First a wasp, and then a bee, and then another wasp, and then another bee, and now *you*. Go away! I won't let another one in today.'

'But I want my honey.'

'And I want my nap.'

'I will come in.'

'You shall not.'

'You are a miserly old elf.'

'And you are a brute of a bee.'

And looking about him, Blunder spied a bee, quarrelling with a morning-glory elf, who was shutting up the morning-glory in his face.

'Elf, do you know which is the way to the Wishing-Gate?' asked Blunder.

'No,' said the elf, 'I don't know anything about geography. I was always too delicate to study. But if you will keep on in this path, you will meet the Dream-man, coming down from fairy-land, with his bags of dreams on his shoulder; and if anybody can tell you about the Wishing-Gate, he can.'

'But how can I find him?' asked Blunder, more and more impatiently.

'I don't know, I am sure,' answered the elf, 'unless you should look for him.'

So there was no help for it but to go on; and presently Blunder passed the Dream-man, asleep under a witch-hazel, with his bags of good and bad dreams laid over him to keep him from fluttering away. But Blunder had a habit of not using his eyes; for at home, when told to find anything, he always said, 'I don't know where it is,' or, 'I can't find it,' and then his mother or sister went straight and found it for him. So he passed the Dream-man without seeing him, and went on till he stumbled on Jack-o'-Lantern.

'Can you show me the way to the Wishing-Gate?' said Blunder.

'Certainly, with pleasure,' answered Jack, and, catching up his lantern, set out at once.

Blunder followed close, but, in watching the lantern, he forgot to look to his feet, and fell into a hole filled with black mud.

'I say! the Wishing-Gate is not down there,' called out Jack, whisking off among the tree-tops.

'But I can't come up there,' whimpered Blunder.

'That is not my fault, then,' answered Jack, merrily, dancing out of sight.

O, a very angry little boy was Blunder, when he clambered out of the hole. 'I don't know where it is,' he said, crying; 'I can't find it, and I'll go straight home.'

2

Just then he stepped on an old, moss-grown, rotten stump; and it happened, unluckily, that this rotten stump was a wood-goblin's chimney. Blunder fell through, headlong, in among the pots and pans, in which the goblin's cook was cooking the goblin's supper. The old goblin, who was asleep upstairs, started up in a fright at the tremendous clash and clatter, and, finding that his house was not tumbling about his ears, as he thought at first, stumped down to the kitchen to see what was the matter. The cook heard him coming, and looked about her in a fright to hide Blunder.

'Quick!' cried she. 'If my master catches you, he will have you in a pie. In the next room stands a pair of shoes. Jump into them, and they will take you up the chimney.'

Off flew Blunder, burst open the door, and tore frantically about the room, in one corner of which stood the shoes; but of course he could not see them, because he was not in the habit of using his eyes.

'I can't find them! O, I can't find them!' sobbed poor little Blunder, running back to the cook.

'Run into the closet,' said the cook.

Blunder made a dash at the window, but – 'I don't know where it is,' he called out.

Clump! clump! That was the goblin, half-way down the stairs.

'Goodness gracious mercy me!' exclaimed the cook. 'He is coming. The boy will be eaten in spite of me. Jump into the meal-chest.'

'I don't see it,' squeaked Blunder, rushing towards the fire-place. 'Where is it?'

Clump! clump! That was the goblin at the foot of the stairs, and coming towards the kitchen door.

'There is an invisible cloak hanging on that peg. Get into that,' cried cook, quite beside herself.

But Blunder could no more see the cloak than he could see the

94

shoes, the closet, and the meal-chest; and no doubt the goblin, whose hand was on the latch, would have found him prancing around the kitchen, and crying out, 'I can't find it,' but, fortunately for himself, Blunder caught his foot in the invisible cloak, and tumbled down, pulling the cloak over him. There he lay, hardly daring to breathe.

'What was all that noise about?' asked the goblin, gruffly, coming into the kitchen.

'Only my pans, master,' answered the cook; and as he could see nothing amiss, the old goblin went grumbling upstairs again, while the shoes the cook gave him took Blunder up the chimney, and landed him in a meadow, safe enough, but so miserable! He was cross, he was disappointed, he was hungry. It was dark, he did not know the way home, and, seeing an old stile, he climbed up, and sat down on the top of it, for he was too tired to stir. Just then came along the South Wind, with his pockets crammed full of showers, and, as he happened to be going Blunder's way, he took Blunder home; at which the boy was glad enough, only he would have liked it better if the Wind would not have laughed all the way. For what would you think, if you were walking along a road with a fat old gentleman, who went chuckling to himself, and slapping his knees, and poking himself, till he was purple in the face, when he would burst out in a great windy roar of laughter every other minute?

'What *are* you laughing at?' asked Blunder, at last.

'At two things that I saw in my travels,' answered the Wind; – 'a hen, that died of starvation, sitting on an empty peck-measure that stood in front of a bushel of grain; and a little boy who sat on the top of the Wishing-Gate, and came home because he could not find it.'

'What? what's that?' cried Blunder; but just then he found himself at home. There sat his fairy godmother by the fire, her mouse-skin cloak hung up on a peg, and toeing off a spider's-silk stocking an eighth of an inch long; and though everybody else cried, 'What luck?' and, 'Where is the Wishing-Gate?' she sat mum.

'I don't know where it is,' answered Blunder. 'I couldn't find it'; – and thereon told the story of his troubles.

'Poor boy!' said his mother, kissing him, while his sister ran to bring him some bread and milk.

'Yes, that is all very fine,' cried his godmother, pulling out her needles, and rolling up her ball of silk; 'but now hear my story. There was once a little boy who must needs go to the Wishing-Gate, and his fairy godmother showed him the road as far as the turn, and told him to ask the first owl he met what to do then; but this little boy seldom used his eyes, so he passed the first owl, and waked up the wrong owl; so he passed the water-sprite, and found only a frog; so he sat down under the pine-tree, and never saw the crow; so he passed the Dream-man, and ran after Jack-o'-Lantern; so he tumbled down the goblin's chimney, and couldn't find the shoes and the closet and the chest and the cloak; and so he sat on the top of the Wishing-Gate till the South Wind brought him home, and never knew it. Ugh! Bah!' And away went the fairy godmother up the chimney, in such deep disgust that she did not even stop for her mouse-skin cloak.

LOUISE E. CHOLLET

Hare and Tortoise

WHEN Tortoise was very little, his mother said to him, 'You will never be able to go very fast. We Tortoises are a slow-moving family, but we get there in the end. Don't try to run. Remember, "steady and slow" does it.' Tortoise remembered these words.

One day when he was grown up, he was walking quietly round in a field minding his own business; and Hare thought he would have some fun, so he ran round Tortoise in quick circles, just to annoy him. Hare was proud of himself because everyone knew he was one of the swiftest of animals. But Tortoise took no notice, so Hare stopped in front of him and laughed.

'Can't you move faster than *that*?' said Hare. 'You'll *never* get anywhere at that rate! You should take a few lessons from *me*.'

Tortoise lifted his head slowly and said:

'I don't want to get anywhere, thank you. I've no need to go dashing about all over the place. You see, my thick shell protects me from my enemies.'

'But how *dull* life must be for you,' Hare went on. 'Why, it takes you half an hour to cross one field, while I can be away out of sight in half a minute. Besides, you really do look silly, you know! You ought to be ashamed of yourself.'

Well, at this Tortoise was rather annoyed. Hare was really very provoking.

'Look here,' said Tortoise, 'if you want a race I'll give you one; and I don't need any start either.'

Hare laughed till the tears ran down his furry face, and his sides shook so much that he rolled over backwards. Tortoise just waited till Hare had finished, then he said:

'Well, what about it? I'm not joking.'

Several other animals had gathered round, and they all said: 'Go on Hare. It's a challenge. You'll have to race him.'

'Certainly,' said Hare, 'if you want to make a fool of yourself. Where shall we race to?'

Tortoise shaded his eyes with one foot and said:

'See that old windmill on the top of the hill yonder? We'll race to that. We can start from this tree-stump here. Come on, and may the best animal win!'

So as soon as they were both standing beside the tree-stump, Chanticleer the Cock shouted 'Ready – steady – go!' and Tortoise began to crawl towards the far-off windmill. The other animals had hurried on ahead so as to see the finish.

Hare stood beside the tree-stump watching Tortoise waddle away across the field. The day was hot, and just beside the tree-stump was a pleasant, shady place, so he sat down and waited. He guessed it would take him about two and a half minutes to reach the windmill, even without trying very hard, so there was no hurry – no hurry at all. Presently he began to drop off to sleep. Two or three minutes passed, and Hare opened one eye lazily. Tortoise had scarcely crossed the first field. 'Steady and slow,' he said to himself under his breath. 'Steady and slow.

That's what mother said,' And he kept on towards the far-off windmill.

'At that rate,' said Hare to himself sleepily, 'it'll take him just about two hours to get there – if he doesn't drop dead on the way.'

He closed his eye again and fell into a deep sleep.

After a while Tortoise had crossed the first field and was making his way slowly over the second.

'Steady and slow does it,' he muttered to himself.

The sun began to go down, and at last Hare woke up, feeling chilly.

'Where am I?' he thought. 'What's happened? Oh yes, I remember.'

He got to his feet and looked towards the windmill. But where was Tortoise? He was nowhere to be seen. Hare jumped on to the tree-stump and strained his eyes to gaze into the distance. There, half-way across the very last field before the windmill, was a tiny black dot. Tortoise!

'This won't do,' said Hare. 'I must have overslept. I'd better be moving.'

So he sprang from the stump and darted across the first field, then the second, then the third. It was really much farther than he had thought.

At the windmill the other animals were waiting to see the finish. At last Tortoise arrived, rather out of breath and wobbling a little on his legs.

'Come on, Tortoise!' they shouted.

Then Hare appeared at the far side of the last field, streaking along like the wind. How he ran! Not even Stag, when he was being hunted, could go faster. Even Swallow could scarcely fly faster through the blue sky.

'Steady and slow,' said Tortoise to himself, but no one could hear him, for he had very, very little breath left to walk with.

'Come on, Tortoise!' cried some animals, and a few cried, 'Come on, Hare! He's beating you!'

Hare put on extra speed and ran faster than he had ever run before. But it was no good. He had given Tortoise too much start, and he was still twenty yards behind when Tortoise crawled over the last foot of ground and tumbled up against the windmill. He had won the race!

All the animals cheered, and after that Hare never laughed at Tortoise again.

AESOP *adapted by* JAMES REEVES
Illustrated by CONSTANCE MARSHALL

Theseus and the Minotaur

LONG ago there ruled a great king in Athens called Aegeus, and his son, Theseus, was a hero who had done many brave and mighty deeds.

Now the whole country was happy and at peace except for one great sorrow. Minos, king of Crete, had fought against the Athenians and had conquered them; and before returning to Crete he had made a hard and cruel peace. Each year the Athenians were forced to send seven young men and seven maidens to be sacrificed to the Minotaur. This was a monster who lived in the labyrinth, a winding path among rocks and caves. So each spring seven youths and maidens chosen by lot, journeyed in a ship with black sails to the shores of Crete, to be torn to pieces by the savage Minotaur.

One spring, when the herald from King Minos arrived, Theseus determined to make an end of the beast, and rid his father's people of this horrible evil. He went and told Aegeus that when the black-sailed ship set out on the morrow he would go too and slay the Minotaur.

'But how will you slay him, my son?' said Aegeus. 'For you must leave your club and your shield behind, and be cast to the monster, defenceless and naked like the rest.'

And Theseus said, 'Are there no stones in that labyrinth; and have I not fists and teeth?'

Then Aegeus clung to his knees; but he would not hear; and at last he let him go, weeping bitterly, and said only this one word –

'Promise me but this, if you return in peace, though that may hardly be: take down the black sail of the ship (for I shall watch for it all day upon the cliffs), and hoist instead a white sail, that I may know afar off that you are safe.'

And Theseus promised, and went out, and to the market-place where the herald stood, while they drew lots for the youths and maidens, who were to sail in that doleful crew. And the people stood wailing and weeping, as the lot fell on this one and on that; but Theseus strode into the midst, and cried –

'Here is a youth who needs no lot. I myself will be one of the seven.'

And the herald asked in wonder, 'Fair youth, know you whither you are going?'

And Theseus said, 'I know. Let us go down to the black-sailed ship.'

So they went down to the black-sailed ship, seven maidens, and seven youths, and Theseus before them all, and the people following them lamenting. But Theseus whispered to his companions, 'Have hope, for the monster is not immortal.' Then their hearts were comforted a little; but they wept as they went on board, and the cliffs of Sunium rang, and all the isles of the Aegean Sea, with the voice of their lamentation, as they sailed on towards their deaths in Crete.

And at last they came to Crete, and to Cnossus, beneath the peaks of Ida, and to the palace of Minos the great king, to whom Zeus himself taught laws. So he was the wisest of all mortal kings, and conquered all the Aegean isles; and his ships were as many as the sea-gulls, and his palace like a marble hill.

But Theseus stood before Minos, and they looked each other in the face. And Minos bade take them to prison, and cast them to the monster one by one. Then Theseus cried –

'A boon, O Minos! Let me be thrown first to the beast. For I came hither for that very purpose, of my own will, and not by lot.'

'Who art thou, then, brave youth?'

'I am the son of him whom of all men thou hatest most, Aegeus the king of Athens, and I am come here to end this matter.'

And Minos pondered awhile, looking steadfastly at him, and he answered at last mildly –

'Go back in peace, my son. It is a pity that one so brave should die.'

But Theseus said, 'I have sworn that I will not go back till I have seen the monster face to face.'

And at that Minos frowned, and said, 'Then thou shalt see him; take the madman away.'

And they led Theseus away into prison, with the other youths and maidens.

But Ariadne, Minos' daughter, saw him, as she came out of her white stone hall; and she loved him for his courage and his majesty, and said, 'Shame that such a youth should die!' And by night she went down to the prison, and told him all her heart, and said –

'Flee down to your ship at once, for I have bribed the guards before the door. Flee, you and all your friends, and go back in peace to Greece; and take me, take me with you! for I dare not stay after you are gone; for my father will kill me miserably, if he knows what I have done.'

And Theseus stood silent awhile; for he was astonished and confounded by her beauty: but at last he said, 'I cannot go home in peace, till I have seen and slain this Minotaur, and avenged the deaths of the youths and maidens, and put an end to the terrors of my land.'

'And will you kill the Minotaur? How, then?'

'I know not, nor do I care: but he must be strong if he be too strong for me.'

Then she loved him all the more, and said, 'But when you have killed him, how will you find your way out of the labyrinth?'

'I know not, neither do I care; but it must be a strange road, if I do not find it out before I have eaten up the monster's carcase.'

Then she loved him all the more, and said –

'Fair youth, you are too bold; but I can help you, weak as I am. I will give you a sword, and with that perhaps you may slay the beast; and a clue of thread, and by that, perhaps, you may find your way out again. Only promise me that if you escape safe you will take me home with you to Greece; for my father will surely kill me, if he knows what I have done.'

Then Theseus laughed and said, 'Am I not safe enough now?' And he hid the sword in his bosom, and rolled up the clue in his hand; and then he swore to Ariadne, and fell down before her and kissed her hands and her feet; and she wept over him a long while, and then went away; and Theseus lay down and slept sweetly.

2

When the evening came, the guards came in and led him away to the labyrinth.

And he went down into that doleful gulf, through winding paths among the rocks, under caverns, and arches, and galleries, and over heaps of fallen stone. And he turned on the left hand, and on the right hand, and went up and down, till his head was dizzy; but all the while he held his clue. For when he went in he had fastened it to a stone, and left it to unroll out of his hand as he went on; and it lasted him till he met the Minotaur, in a narrow chasm between black cliffs.

And when he saw him he stopped awhile, for he had never seen so strange a beast. His body was a man's; but his head was the head of a bull, and his teeth were the teeth of a lion, and with them he tore his prey. And when he saw Theseus he roared, and put his head down, and rushed right at him.

But Theseus stepped aside nimbly, and as he passed by, cut him in the knee; and ere he could turn in the narrow path, he followed him, and stabbed him again and again from behind, till the monster fled bellowing wildly; for he never before had felt a wound. And Theseus followed him at full speed, holding the clue of thread in his left hand.

Then on, through cavern after cavern, under dark ribs of sounding stone, and up rough glens and torrent-beds, among the sunless roots of Ida, and to the edge of the eternal snow, went they, the hunter and the hunted, while the hills bellowed to the monster's bellow.

And at last Theseus came up with him, where he lay panting

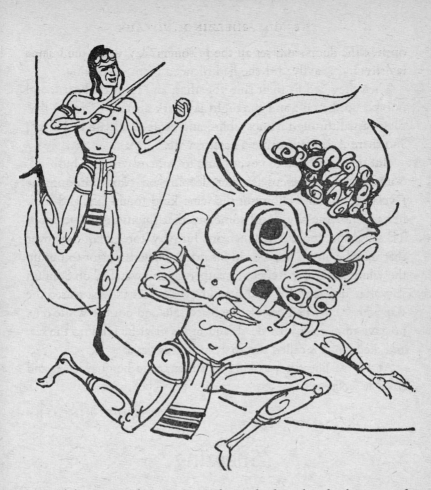

on a slab among the snows, and caught him by the horns, and
forced his head back, and drove the keen sword through his
throat.

Then he turned, and went back limping and weary, feeling
his way down by the clue of thread, till he came to the mouth of
that doleful place; and saw waiting for him, whom but Ariadne!

And he whispered, 'It is done!' and showed her the sword;
and she laid her finger on her lips and led him to the prison, and

opened the doors, and set all the prisoners free, while the guards lay sleeping heavily; for she had silenced them with wine.

Then they fled to their ship together, and leapt on board, and hoisted up the sail; and the night lay dark around them, so that they passed through Minos' ships, and escaped all safe to Naxos; and there Ariadne became Theseus' wife.

But that fair Ariadne never came to Athens with her husband. Some say that Theseus left her sleeping on Naxos among the Cyclades; and that Dionysus the wine-king found her, and took her up into the sky. And some say that Dionysus drove away Theseus, and took Ariadne from him by force; but however that may be, in his haste or in his grief, Theseus forgot to put up the white sail. Now Aegeus his father sat and watched on Sunium day after day, and strained his old eyes across the sea to see the ship afar. And when he saw the black sail, and not the white one, he gave up Theseus for dead, and in his grief he fell into the sea, and died; so it is called the Aegean to this day.

And now Theseus was king of Athens, and he guarded it and ruled it well.

CHARLES KINGSLEY

Sneezing

Sneeze on Monday, sneeze for danger;
Sneeze on Tuesday, miss a stranger;
Sneeze on Wednesday, get a letter;
Sneeze on Thursday, something better;
Sneeze on Friday, sneeze for sorrow,
Sneeze on Saturday, see your sweetheart tomorrow.

Calico Pie

Calico Pie,
The little Birds fly
Down to the calico tree.
Their wings were blue
And they sang 'Tilly-loo' –
Till away they all flew,
And they never came back to me!
They never came back!
They never came back!
They never came back to me!

Calico Jam,
The little Fish swam

Over the syllabub sea,
    He took off his hat,
    To the Sole and the Sprat,
    And the Willeby-wat, –
But he never came back to me!
    He never came back!
    He never came back!
He never came back to me!

Calico Ban
    The little Mice ran,
To be ready in time for tea,
    Flippity Flup,
    They drank it all up,
    And danced in the cup, –
But they never came back to me!

They never came back!
They never came back!
They never came back to me!

Calico Drum,
The Grasshoppers come,
The Butterfly, Beetle, and Bee,
Over the ground,
Around and round,
With a hop and a bound,
But they never came back!
They never came back!
They never came back!
They never came back to me!

Written and illustrated by EDWARD LEAR

The Tale of Dobbin and the Silver Shoes

IT was a very fine day early in June, the sun was shining, the sky was blue, the hedges were full of dog-roses, and the wind blew soft. But Mistress Mary Jane was walking up and down a field of buttercups and grass and clover, looking at the ground and crying as she walked. Big round tears – about two-to-a-tea-spoonful size – were running down her cheeks, and she was saying, 'I can't see one – not one – not even a little one.' She was talking to herself; there was no one else to talk to, except an old white horse standing by the hedge and a stout brown rabbit that was hopping up and down the field, taking no more notice of Mistress Mary Jane than Mistress Mary Jane was taking of him.

Mistress Mary Jane lived in the white cottage just across the road. It had a garden full of flowers in front and a yard full of chickens behind. There was another field with a black and white cow; there was a sty with a nice little pig, and a tabby cat was washing itself on the cottage door-step. Mistress Mary Jane was rosy-cheeked and fat and comfortable. You would have thought she had everything in the world to make her happy that fine sunshiny day; and yet here she was crying, and the old white horse looked just as unhappy as she did.

And now I will tell you what the trouble was. The old white horse had gone lame. He had been all right only the evening before, but when Mistress Mary Jane came into his field on the day this story happened, he could hardly move. His mane and his tail were full of tangles, and he looked as if someone had galloped him far and fast. And next day Mistress Mary Jane was to go to a wedding ten miles away. It was her brother John's wedding, and she had a new bonnet with cherry-red ribbons and a new sprigged muslin gown. There was a pot of honey, three pounds of fresh butter, and some new-laid eggs, all ready to be packed in a basket. And at eight o'clock the next morning Mistress Mary Jane had meant to climb on to Dobbin's broad back and go jogging away, with her basket on her arm, down the green lanes to the wedding.

And now Dobbin was lame, and Mistress Mary Jane was quite sure it was the Fairies who had been galloping him round the field all night. (There was a great fairy ring in the middle of the field so she knew the Good Folk came there.) So she was hunting up and down the field for a four-leaf clover, because as everyone knows, if you can find a four-leaf clover the Fairies cannot play tricks with you. If only she could find one she meant to go to the fairy ring that night to give the Fairies what she called 'a proper good talking to', and to tell them that they must cure Dobbin of his lameness before the next morning.

But for all her searching she could not find a four-leaf clover. It seemed there was not one in the whole green field. Mistress Mary Jane's back ached, her temper ached; she was hot and tired and cross and disappointed, and that was why she was crying. And just at the minute this story begins, a very big tear rolled down her cheek and fell splash! – right in the middle of a clover

leaf. And Mistress Mary Jane looked down and said: 'I do believe that's one!'

But when she stooped and picked it, it was not a four-leaf, but a *five*-leaf clover.

As she stood looking at it, a very odd thing happened. The stout brown rabbit that was hopping up and down the field nibbling at the grass and clover suddenly turned round and came hopping across the field to Mistress Mary Jane. And when he reached her, he sat and looked at her, and there was a four-leaf clover hanging out of his mouth. And then a still more odd thing happened. The stout brown rabbit began to talk!

'At your service, Mum,' he said. 'Please to take the clover.'

Mistress Mary Jane stooped down and took it. 'Wherever did you find it? I couldn't see one,' was the only thing she could find to say. She was so very surprised, and I really don't wonder – do you?

'I've been eating them all the morning,' said the stout brown rabbit. 'I'm caretaker of this field, Mum, and I had my orders to eat every four-leaf clover before you could find it. But the Good Folk,' (he meant the Fairies, you know) 'forgot that it is Leap Year. And if you find a five-leaf clover in Leap Year you can come and go as you like for twenty-four hours by day *or* by night. Elves, Pixies, Fairies, Good Folk, can't stop you. So if I was you, Mum, I should come here after sunset this evening and talk to the Little Folk. Bring both the clovers with you, and you'll get what you want.'

'Thank you. So I will,' said Mistress Mary Jane. She had stopped being surprised, and it seemed quite natural to be talking to a rabbit; perhaps it was because of the five-leaf clover. She went over to the old white horse and patted him comfortably. Then she went back to her cottage and put the clover leaves in water, and had her dinner. And afterwards she finished trimming her bonnet with cherry-red ribbons and packed the butter and eggs and honey. She was quite sure everything was going to be all right now that she had her clover leaves.

The sun does not set till past nine in June-time, as you will see if you look in the calendar. So about half past nine Mistress Mary Jane went across the road to the field with both her clovers safe in her hand. It was still quite light, and she could see old Dobbin standing with his ears pricked watching the fairy ring. Mistress Mary Jane could see nobody, but the stout brown rabbit was waiting for her, and he said: 'Please to come inside, Mum,' and he hopped inside the ring, and Mistress Mary Jane stepped after him. She could still see nobody; but the grass blades all round the ring were shaking and quivering, although there was not a breath of wind. The stout brown rabbit seemed to be listening to something she could not hear. She could see his ears twitching, and presently he said: 'They want to know, Mum, will you have the old horse nimble-and-quick or steady-and-strong?'

'Steady-and-strong,' said Mistress Mary Jane in a great hurry, thinking of the butter and eggs and her own fat, comfortable self.

And as she spoke, it was like throwing a stone into a still pool. You know how the ripples spread and spread. The grass blades quivered and shook, and all round the ring she could hear clear little voices saying, 'Steady-and-strong, steady-and-strong, steady-and-strong, steady-and-strong,' fainter and fainter and fainter, farther and farther away, till all was quiet again.

'*That's* all right, Mum,' said the stout brown rabbit, 'and now, if I was you, I should just go home to bed.' And so she did, and she slept soundly till the birds woke up and began to talk to each other at daybreak.

'Bless me,' said Mistress Mary Jane as she woke, 'it's brother John's wedding day.' And then she remembered about Dobbin and the Fairies, and she jumped out of bed and looked out.

The sun was not up, but the sky was golden in the east and pale, clear blue overhead. She could see Dobbin in his field. He seemed to be standing in the fairy ring. Mistress Mary Jane bustled about and into her lilac print dress. (It was too early to dress for the wedding, of course.) She put on a pair of clogs. 'The meadow will be sopped with dew,' she said. And she picked up her clover leaves and hurried down the garden path and across the road. As she reached the gate of the field, the stout brown rabbit popped out of the hedge to meet her.

'Please to come this way, Mum,' he said, and he hopped across the field in front of her to the fairy ring. And there stood Dobbin most splendid to behold. His mane and his tail were like white silk, so glossy and bright; his coat was like the finest white satin, and he was shod with four brand-new, beautiful, silver-shining shoes.

'There he is, Mum,' said the stout brown rabbit, proudly, 'steady-and-strong and just fit for a wedding.'

And, 'Yes, *indeed*,' said Mistress Mary Jane. And she went and stood by Dobbin in the fairy ring and picked up her lilac print skirts and dropped a very deep curtsey, and said: 'Thank you kindly, all Good Folk, with all my heart.'

'You're very welcome, Mum,' said the stout brown rabbit, and the grass blades round the ring quivered and shook, and Mistress Mary Jane could hear clear little voices saying: 'Welcome, welcome, welcome, welcome,' from farther and farther away, just like spreading ripples on a pond. And then a little wind came rustling across the meadow, and a long ray of sunlight came with it. The sun was up and all the dewdrops sparkled and shone and danced. The sun was up, and Mistress Mary Jane could see her shadow and Dobbin's lying long and dark on the bright green grass.

The stout brown rabbit was nibbling grass and clover with

his little shadow beside him. He did not seem to have any more
to say, so Mistress Mary Jane went back to the gate with Dobbin
following her. His lameness had quite gone and he seemed as
steady and strong as anyone could wish. She patted his shining
coat and went back to her kitchen. And when she had milked
the cow and fed the chickens and the little black pig, and given
the cat a saucer of milk and eaten her own breakfast, Mistress
Mary Jane dressed herself in the sprigged muslin and the bonnet
with cherry-red ribbons, and climbed on to Dobbin's back with
her basket of eggs and honey and butter. And away they went

jogging through the green lanes to the wedding. And when she got there everyone said that Dobbin, with his silver-shining shoes, was the handsomest horse that ever they had seen.

I don't know what the shoes were made of, but they never wore out. For many and many a day Mistress Mary Jane and Dobbin jogged along together, 'Steady-and-strong, steady-and-strong, steady-and-strong,' as the stout brown rabbit had said. As for the rabbit, Mistress Mary Jane often saw him hopping about the field, but he never spoke to her again. The clover-leaf magic only lasted for twenty-four hours, you see. She pressed the leaves in Doctor Johnson's Dictionary, and sometimes when her neighbours came in for a cup of tea she let them have a peep and told them the story of the four-leaf clover and the five-leaf clover, and Dobbin's silver-shining shoes.

ELIZABETH CLARK
Illustrated by ISMENA MURMAGEN

The
Kind Visitor

'I wish, Aunt Emily,' said a little girl with very blue eyes and very yellow hair, whose name was Janet, 'you would make My-Thomas some new clothes – please,' she added after a little pause, and she held up a Teddy Bear that had once had wheaten-yellow silky fur but was now rather grey and showed patches of linen-like thread here and there.

But her Aunt Emily, with whom she was staying, and who was busy cooking the breakfast, said, 'Goodness gracious me! As if I had time to make clothes for Teddy Bears! I've hardly time to make my own! And he looks very nice to me,' she added, taking the bacon out of the frying pan and dishing it up. But Janet shook her head. Aunt Emily couldn't have looked properly at My-Thomas. His knitted striped jumper was torn and coming unravelled. The elastic of his check trousers had 'perished' so that they had to be secured with a safety-pin; and as for his woollen vest – once white, and soft as his own fur, it was white no longer and had shrunk so much from its many washings it was almost impossible to get it over My-Thomas's ears, and when you *did*, it hardly covered his tummy! And soon winter would be coming!

Aunt Emily's house stood in a crooked little road that branched off from the main street of the village. There was only one other house and the road ended in a footpath which led straight on to the Downs – rounded, rolling hills with here and there thickets of hawthorn, gorse and blackberry where birds built their nests, and rabbits burrowed and brought up their families. In spring little lambs ran bleating about them, and great brown hares raced over them, chasing their own shadows on windy mad March days. In summer the larks sang high overhead, the short, sweet, sheep-nibbled turf was carpeted with tiny miniature flowers, and wild raspberries grew among the gorse. In autumn there were mush-rooms and blackberries to pick, and in winter great gales roared inland from the sea, twisting and bending the thorn trees, and making the air taste salt.

Whenever she came to stay with Aunt Emily, Janet played on the Downs. She was allowed to go there by herself for there was no traffic on the little crooked road, and she would walk along, My-Thomas under her arm, and sometimes carrying a basket with a bottle of milk and a packet of biscuits in case she might feel hungry. Today, as soon as possible after breakfast, My-Thomas under her arm as usual, up the crooked little road she went. She was feeling particularly important because, instead of a basket with biscuits and milk, she carried an empty one and on her – anyway partly – depended the pudding for mid-day dinner – stewed blackberries and custard. 'And Real Custard,' Aunt Emily had said, 'made with real eggs; no powder and water stuff at my table!'

The sun was hot but the grass at the road side was wet and sparkling, and every bush jewelled with spider webs, for it was September and the dews were heavy at night. Janet wore gum boots and she wished that My-Thomas had a pair of even papery doll's shoes. He wanted mending, too, she noticed; there was a

slit in one arm and wisps of straw were sticking out of it, while one eye that had been getting loose for a long time seemed to have become looser – even since yesterday. She sighed and wondered why Aunt Emily, who was really very kind, was always too busy to do things. Mummy – who was away having a holiday with Daddy – would have put My-Thomas right in a jiffy – *and* made him a new vest for the winter! She sighed again. But as soon as she reached the end of the crooked little road she forgot her worries for the great business of the day was ahead. Swinging the basket she climbed a little way up the

Downs towards the first clump of blackberry bushes. The turf was short and springy to walk on, and her gum boots made dark foot-prints where the sun had not yet sucked up the dew.

There was another visitor in the village besides Janet. A lady from London was staying with old Mrs Jeans at the Forge. She, too, walked on the Downs but she did not go up the crooked little road; she went along the bridle-path behind the Forge. She walked briskly, with long, swinging strides and Janet never saw her, nor she Janet. Up the old cart tracks she went, right up to the topmost ridges; over them, on and on, to where the Downs ended suddenly, in steep, white cliffs, the home of gulls and jackdaws, and where, far below, the sea broke splashing on a grey, stony beach.

It was not easy, Janet soon discovered, to pick blackberries, hold a basket, and keep My-Thomas out of the wet all at one and the same time. She must find some dry spot in which to leave him while she picked. She walked a little further along to where the gorse and blackberry bushes were thicker and grew more closely together. The ground beneath them was full of rabbit holes, she remembered – dry as dry. Yes; there they were; big, little and middling-sized holes. She walked round a little before she could decide which to choose. At last she selected one, and telling My-Thomas not to be frightened if a rabbit should suddenly pop out, and that she would not be away long, she put him sitting down just inside the opening. Then she ran off, singing gaily.

It was what people called 'a good blackberry year'. What a lot there were! Big, inky-black, and so ripe that you had to be careful how you picked them or they squashed in your fingers and spurted juice all over you! She ran from bush to bush, bush to bush, picking only the very best and biggest. 'Don't eat too many,' Aunt Emily had said, 'or you won't want any of the pudding.' Janet was not sure about that, but she tried at least to pick more than she ate, and it was not long before the basket was full. It was quite heavy and she put it down for a moment to rest her arm.

How tiny the village looked, away down below! The houses were like dolls' houses, and the hay-stacks and cattle like the models out of the toy-farm Aunt Emily had given her last Christmas. Even the church with its tall tower and funny little steeple looked tiny! As she stood gazing, the big clock on its tower began to strike. She counted the strokes carefully. Nine, Ten, Eleven! Eleven! It was still quite early; no need to go back yet. She thought for a moment. It would be nice if she could find a few mushrooms for a surprise for Aunt Emily! Last year she had found a lot; they had been growing all together in one place, somewhere, she was sure, not far from where she was now. She picked up the basket and wandered off in search of it. Several times she saw what she thought was a gleaming white shape, but each time it turned out to be a lump of chalk or a flint glistening in the sun.

The dew had melted right away now. It was very hot, and before long Janet began to feel not only discouraged but tired, and the basket, though she had added nothing to it, to feel suddenly heavier (as baskets are so strangely apt to do when *you* feel tired). She would go home she decided, and turned back.

As she walked along she wondered very much whether any rabbits had come and looked at My-Thomas, and if so what he had thought of them, and how they had behaved. It seemed much further going back than coming, and there was no doubt about the basket being heavier! Once or twice Janet thought perhaps she had passed the bushes where she had left My-Thomas – and yet – she was sure she had not . . . That big clump just ahead – that was the one. But when she looked inside it, although there were rabbit holes in plenty, she was not quite sure if it *was* the one – and most certainly there was no sign of My-Thomas! She went on to the next, and then the next, and the next ... She put down the basket and ran back to the first one of all again, but My-Thomas was definitely not there. She looked in them all again, and then again and again ... Now she was crying. My-Thomas was 'lost' ... Really lost ... A rabbit had taken him into its hole ... a rabbit had perhaps *eaten* him! ... What – oh what, could she do? She had looked everywhere – *every*where! ... It was no use looking any more ... besides, she was now crying so hard that she could not see at all. And then, suddenly, she thought she heard a voice calling, 'Janet! Janet!' She rubbed her knuckles in her eyes and looked towards the village. At the top of the crooked little road waving and calling was Aunt Emily.

Janet picked up the basket, now very heavy indeed, and went slowly towards her.

'Come along! Hurry up!' called Aunt Emily as she came nearer. 'It's after 12 o'clock! I thought you'd got lost,' and then, as Janet came up to her, 'Well you *have* picked some lovely blackberries, but' – seeing the tears, 'what's the matter? What's happened?'

The dreadful story was soon told. Aunt Emily was very kind, consoling and sympathetic. My-Thomas couldn't possibly be really lost she said, and they would both go and have a good hunt for him in the afternoon. As to his having been eaten by a rabbit, that was ridiculous; *quite* ridiculous!

2

Even before they began to eat the stewed blackberries and creamy, real egg custard, the lovely day seemed to be changing; before they had finished, the sky had begun to darken, and no sooner had they set off to look for My-Thomas than great black clouds came rolling up behind the Downs. There was a shivery sort of breeze, and they had hardly reached the end of the crooked little road when, quite suddenly, a miniature whirlwind blew round them, a few hailstones fell, and the next minute, rain mixed with hail, came pouring, drenching down! Neither Janet nor Aunt Emily had coats. They ran as quickly as they could but even so, by the time they reached Aunt Emily's house they were so wet that they had to change almost everything they had on.

'A real cloudburst!' said Aunt Emily, 'and such a lovely morning!'

But Janet thought only of My-Thomas. Where was he? *Where?* For in spite of all Aunt Emily could say she kept imagining the most terrible happenings.

Towards tea-time there were gleams of sunshine but Aunt Emily, looking out, saw what she called 'a weather dog' – a half-rainbow – which she said meant more storms. It seemed, too, she was right. In half an hour it was pouring again, and it rained all night.

And it rained the next day, too, all of it, without stopping once, and the next, and the next! . . . Poor My-Thomas! And poor Janet! She had cried so much she really couldn't cry any more. Aunt Emily had been very kind. She had taken her to the cinema in the near-by town; made toffee with her; read to her, played 'Ludo' and 'Snakes-and-Ladders' with her. She had even suggested buying a new Teddy Bear – one they had seen in a shop near the cinema – bigger, softer, and in every way superior-looking to My-Thomas. But Janet had cried again at the very idea. She had also been rather rude. She wouldn't ever, *ever*, she told Aunt Emily, stamping her foot, have another bear instead of My-Thomas, not *ever*!

So Aunt Emily said no more and only wished the rain would stop and they could have a thorough hunt for My-Thomas, though what, poor dear, she said to herself, he could be like after all this deluge, she trembled to think.

On the day the rain finally stopped Janet and Aunt Emily had an appointment with the hair-dresser, but the lady from London announced to old Mrs Jeans at the Forge that it was such a lovely day she would like to stroll on the Downs and pick blackberries for jam.

Old Mrs Jeans was not at all anxious to make jam for, she said (what she believed), the blackberries would be far too wet – if not washed off the bushes altogether. And she muttered to herself that it was just like someone from London not to know you couldn't make jam with wet fruit. But her visitor took no notice; so hot a sun – shining since before seven o'clock – should dry anything. And old Mrs Jeans, seeing she was determined to go, grudgingly produced a basket which she carefully lined with newspaper lest it should be stained (for she was a fussy old lady), opened the gate for her visitor, said tea would be all ready when she returned, and then muttering 'lovely day or not' went upstairs to lie on her bed for she was getting on in years and felt tired.

The lady from London was late for her tea but she came at last, and carrying the basket straight out to the kitchen she put it down on the table.

'Sakes alive!' exclaimed old Mrs Jeans peering short-sightedly towards it for she had not put on her glasses, 'Whatever have you got there!'

For on top of the blackberries, at one end of the basket, peeping up between pieces of the newspaper with which she had so carefully lined it, were two furry ears, and at the other what looked like two furry pads!

'Sakes alive!' exclaimed old Mrs Jeans again, 'A rabbit! Well I never!'

'No,' said the lady from London, 'though that's exactly what *I* thought when I first saw it – especially as it was lying half in and half out of a rabbit hole. Even the clothes,' she went on, 'didn't surprise me – they seemed natural, somehow; like Peter Rabbit and his cousin Benjamin, and the Flopsy Bunnies – you know Mrs Jeans?'

But Mrs Jeans didn't. She had never heard of Peter Rabbit or his relations. She looked at the lady from London and decided,

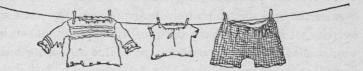

not for the first time, she was what she called A Queer One. Then, taking her glasses from her pocket, she put them on. 'Well I never!' she exclaimed again, removing the top layer of paper, 'if it isn't one o' they what-do-you-call-'em bears! Some child's been missing that I shouldn't wonder!'

'Some child's cried itself to sleep *I* shouldn't wonder,' replied the lady from London.

The what-do-you-call-'em bear stared up at them with his one eye – the other hung now by a thread. It was, of course, My-Thomas. He was sodden with rain and spattered with mud, slugs had crawled over him leaving shiny, silvery trails on his woolly jumper. His check trousers were full of tiny little holes as if something had tried to eat them (and not altogether fancied the taste) and his woolly vest had shrunk more than ever!

'Straightaway, with your permission Mrs Jeans,' said her visitor, 'I'm putting him in the airing cupboard. Tomorrow – well we shall see what we shall see.'

It was many tomorrows since My-Thomas was lost and in two days Janet was going home. She and Aunt Emily had looked for him 'literally under every blackberry bush on the Downs', Aunt Emily had written to Janet's mother, and if this was an exaggeration, they had certainly looked under every one within a mile of where Janet had picked her blackberries. Aunt Emily had torn two hair nets and several pairs of stockings and finally she said it was really no use looking any more and Janet must be brave and try to forget My-Thomas. Janet tried very hard though she was sure she would never forget him – not if she lived to a hundred; and she cried a little every night when she went to bed for that was the time she missed him most. She still played on the Downs on fine days, and every now and then she would stop what she was doing and peep forlornly into bushes and peer hopefully down rabbit holes.

The morning before Janet was to go home Aunt Emily had an important parcel to post and she went off soon after breakfast to the village, leaving her in the garden very busy cutting off the dead roses.

On the way home a notice in the window of the baker's shop attracted her attention.

'Found!' she read, 'A Teddy Bear. Apply Within.' Aunt Emily was in and applying in less time than it takes to write it, and out again and speeding homewards almost as quickly.

'No,' she told Janet, 'I didn't see it because for the life of me I couldn't remember what My-Thomas was wearing – and they won't give that bear to anyone unless they can say just exactly what he was like and what he was dressed in – so you must go yourself.'

Janet stood hesitating a moment. If there was one thing she

hated above all others, and was shy about, it was asking for things in shops. '*You* ask!' she always said to whoever was with her, and usually 'you' kindly did. Now she must go all alone! But – it was for My-Thomas and for him she would go anywhere and ask anyone, anything!

'Keep on the foot-path all the way,' said Aunt Emily as she set off, 'and don't be disappointed if it's not My-Thomas after all. There's lots of Teddy Bears about and some other girl or boy might have lost one besides you.'

Mrs Curley, the baker's wife, was alone in the shop when Janet arrived.

'Please,' said Janet, very shyly – and very out of breath for she had run nearly all the way, 'please I think you've got My-Thomas – my Teddy Bear?'

'Well I wonder,' said Mrs Curley. 'Can you tell me what he was like, and what he was dressed in? You see,' she continued, 'a lady – a visitor to the village like yourself – found him and she wanted him to go to his *real* owner, and the real owner would of course know all about him, and exactly what he was wearing. Take your time,' she went on, 'take your time – there's no hurry.'

But there *was*!

So anxious was Janet to make sure it was My-Thomas, so frightened it might not be, she became more breathless still, falling over her words in her eagerness to describe him. The colour of his fur; his arm with the stuffing sticking out; his eye that was 'coming loose'; his knitted striped jumper, his check cotton trousers, and his vest that had 'washed short'.

Mrs Curley listened very carefully and seriously. 'Just a minute,' she said when Janet came at last to the end of her description, and she went through a door at the back of the shop. Janet's eyes followed her – wide with suspense. In less than a minute she was back – and with her was My-Thomas! She pushed forward a large biscuit tin on the counter and sat him up against it.

'There!' she said.

For a second or two Janet stood staring. It couldn't be true! It couldn't! But it was! There sat My-Thomas as large as life and far, far cleaner and tidier than he had looked for a very, very long time. The slit in his arm had been repaired, and the eye that had got so loose had been sewn firmly in its right place once more. As for his clothes, they had all been washed, and partly mended. His jumper was no longer coming unravelled, and though his check trousers were full of odd little holes that had not been there before, there was new elastic at the waist, while his woolly vest, if still no longer, was white again. Almost more surprising was a green paper parcel, almost as large as himself, tucked under his arm! It was tied up with pink string, and attached to the string was a yellow label of the sort people put on trunks and suitcases when going by train. On it was some writing.

'What does it say?' asked Janet who had not learnt to read properly yet.

'It says,' replied Mrs Curley, ' "From a Friend. To keep you warm and dry". Undo the parcel and see what's inside!'

Janet tore off the pink string and the yellow label; tore off the green paper. Inside was more paper – tissue paper, and there, folded like clothes when they come from a laundry or cleaners – very neatly and all in the right creases, were: First a thick dark blue knitted jumper with green stripes across the chest and round the cuffs. Next, a pair of blue and white checked flannel trousers – just like the old cotton ones except for one thing; they had the dearest little patch pocket on one side, and in it was a blue hand-kerchief with white spots. Last of all was a long, thick woolly vest, snowy white and soft as fur! No, not last – there was some-

thing else – something in a neat little roll all by itself. It was
something black and it was soft and slippery. Wonderingly Janet
unrolled and smoothed it out. As she did so, plop! out fell something on to the floor.

The soft black thing – what *was* it? It was – she could hardly
believe her eyes – a mackintosh! A black, shiny mackintosh such
as sailors wear but with a hood to go over My-Thomas's head.
And the thing that had fallen out plop, was a little pair of black
gum-boots to match!

Janet could say nothing at all. She stood staring, staring, staring.

After a minute or two, her hands on the clothes as if she was
afraid they might vanish, she looked up shyly at Mrs Curley.

'I think,' said Mrs Curley, 'those should keep him dry if he
ever got lost again, though of course,' she added hastily, 'I hope
he never will.'

'Yes!' said Janet softly. '*Oh* aren't they lovely! My-Thomas,
look!' And she held up each garment in turn to him.

My-Thomas stared with all his might. What was he thinking?
That it was worth being lost a while and almost rotted with

rain; worth being frightened by inquisitive rabbits sniffing and
nibbling at one's clothes; being patronized by impertinent birds,
and putting up with big, slimy, black slugs crawling all over one,
to be presented with a trousseau like this? No one would ever
know.

But what Janet was thinking she said.

Lifting My-Thomas from the counter, she gave him a big
kiss. Then she smiled up at Mrs Curley. 'What a *kind* visitor!'
she said.

Written and illustrated by EVE GARNETT

The Golden Touch

LONG ago, when the world was younger than it is now, people believed that there was not one God, but many. They believed that everything had its own special God to look after it. Some were important, like the God of Love and the God of the Harvest; others, who were less important, were half human and half animal, with horns and pointed ears. These haunted the forests, fields, and streams and were known as satyrs.

Many stories are told about the gods and satyrs. This story of the golden touch is one of them:

Once, in the country of Greece, there lived a king called Midas. Midas was the richest man on earth. He collected money as you or I might collect stamps or little glass animals, not because it was useful but because he liked to look at it and play with it. Midas would spend many hours every day with the big chests in which he kept his money, dipping his hands in among the coins. In those days money was made of gold, so that when Midas let it fall through his fingers it glittered in the light. Midas thought that the yellow of gold was the best of all, better than the red of roses, than the blue of the sky, than the green of grass. He thought he loved gold more than anything else in life. But he was to find out that other things were more precious to him, as you shall hear.

One day the king was walking in the forest near his palace, thinking. He was thinking how he could be even richer than he was already. Perhaps he could sell some of the corn from his fields? Perhaps he could make a law saying that all the people he ruled over must give him money? Then suddenly he heard the sound of snoring. It seemed to come from a field of grapes –

a vineyard – on the edge of the forest. Midas went towards it and there, sure enough, fast asleep with a grape-vine trailing over his face, was a very old satyr called Silenus. Midas knew Silenus. He lived with Bacchus, the god of wine, and Bacchus loved him well. The king shook the satyr's shoulder.

'Wake up, Silenus! What are you doing here?'

Silenus opened his eyes and yawned. 'Oh, it's you, Midas! I'm lost.'

'I'm not surprised!' the king told him. 'You are a very long way from home.'

'I know. But I've had such a lovely day wandering in the vineyards eating grapes! I've eaten thousands and thousands of grapes.'

'Very greedy of you!' said Midas sternly.

Silenus grinned and put his hands on his stomach. 'M'm! Grapes are tasty! Wine is made from grapes and wine is the best thing in the world. Bacchus taught me that.'

Midas shook his head. He knew, of course, that it was not wine but gold that was the best thing in the world. But he did not say so. He said –

'Come, I will take you home, Silenus. And as you are so tired you may travel on my back.'

Bacchus lived on a mountain called Olympus, way up above the clouds that covered its top, in a cave as big as a palace. He was overjoyed to see Silenus again and very grateful to Midas for his trouble.

'What would you like as a reward?' he asked the king. 'Wish for anything you like and it shall be yours.'

Midas could hardly believe his good luck. Here at last was a way to become rich beyond his dreams.

'I wish', he said, 'that everything I touch may turn to gold.'

Bacchus looked a little sad. 'Are you sure that's really what you want?'

Midas said he was quite sure, and Bacchus sighed. 'Very well, it shall be as you ask. But I wish you had made a better choice for I fear the Golden Touch will bring you sorrow.'

But Midas felt only joy as he went away through the misty clouds and down the mountain-side. As soon as he came to the woods at the foot of Olympus he decided to try his new power. Could it really be true that whatever he touched would turn to gold? He broke a twig from a small oak tree. And – he could scarcely believe it – it was gold, with golden leaves and a little golden acorn. Enchanted, the king picked up a stone from the ground. And it was a golden stone. Then he walked through a field of corn and every blade he touched stood stiff and golden, flashing in the sun. Back in his Palace garden, Midas picked an apple from a branch to make a golden apple. A little lizard basking on the wall became a golden model of a lizard, and the king thought how it would make a pretty toy for his little daughter.

Still full of happiness Midas entered his Palace, turning the pillars and doorways to gold as he went. And then, feeling hungry after so much excitement, he called for his dinner. His servants brought in a table covered with crisp bread, roast meat, chicken, cakes and fruit. And it was then that the first dreadful thing happened. The king put out his hand to take the bread and . . . horror! the bread was as hard as a brick and as hard as – gold. Trembling with fear he put a piece of meat in his mouth, and his teeth bit on metal. He lifted a glass of wine to his lips, and liquid metal poured into his mouth and nearly choked him. He spat it out in disgust and rose from the table. He knew that not all the food in the world could stop his hunger now, nor all the wine and water quench his thirst. He would sleep and forget his terror. On his way up the wide golden stairway the king paused to look from a window over the evening landscape. In the west the sun was setting in a blaze of golden light, casting its glitter on a distant river and on the tops of the trees. Midas turned sadly away. The brilliance of gold no longer seemed beautiful. His heart felt heavy within him. He thought, 'Perhaps my heart too is turning to gold.'

But there was worse to come. For when Midas lay down to sleep his head was on a pillow of solid gold while a heavy golden counterpane pressed down on his body. He could not sleep a wink but lay listening to the owl in the woods and the sweet song of the nightingale, thinking how much happier were these creatures of nature than he, the richest man in the world.

Dawn glimmered in the room. And the king heard footsteps. By his bed stood a little girl who smiled at him.

'Good morning, Father!'

The king greeted her joyfully. 'Good morning, my daughter!' For the first time in many hours he was happy, for even food and sleep were not so precious to him as his own child. He remembered the golden lizard in the garden, and he said to her:

'Go to the wall that surrounds our garden, and there in the shade of an olive tree you will find a toy I brought for you yesterday!'

The child ran excitedly to do his bidding, and Midas dressed himself. He knew even before he touched his clothes that he would be wearing a heavy golden tunic that day and that the cloak he threw over his shoulders would be shining and stiff. When he was ready his daughter came running back with the lizard in her hand.

'Oh Father, isn't it pretty! It looks so real, except, of course that it's made of gold, so it isn't alive. Thank you! thank you!'

With sudden dread the king saw that she was running to kiss him. He cried out in terror,

'Stop! Don't touch me!'

But it was too late. King Midas held in his arms a little golden girl, as lifeless as a statue.

This was more than he could bear. He knew beyond any doubt that he never wanted to see gold again if only that little statue, with her graceful golden limbs and hair of finest golden thread, could become flesh and blood again.

There was only one thing to be done. He must go to Bacchus and ask to be forgiven for making such a foolish wish. Then perhaps the god would have pity on him and take away the golden touch.

On his way up the mountain to Bacchus's cave, Midas could hardly bear to brush against the corn and trees as he passed, so sickened had he become by the very sight of gold. He found Bacchus and Silenus having a late breakfast of grapes and wine. When the god heard why Midas had come he smiled,

'Ah! So you have enough gold at last, Midas!'

'Too much!' cried the king. 'I know I have been greedy and silly, but I have been cruelly punished. And now I have only one wish – that you will take the golden touch from me.'

Thoughtfully Bacchus helped himself to another grape and ate it while Midas watched him anxiously. At last the god nodded,

'Very well. I will take my terrible gift away from you. I think you have learned for good that gold is of little worth. But if you want to wash the golden touch from your skin you must go to the river called Patroclus which you can see from your Palace, and bathe in its waters . . .'

Bacchus had hardly finished speaking before the king was setting off down the mountain-side. When he reached the river

he was breathless for he had run all the way. In a moment he had laid his golden clothes on the bank and had plunged into the cool water. As he did so he noticed that the river became cloudy with golden dust. When he came out he put his hand on his tunic which lay there, stiff as a statue. And to his joy the stuff turned to linen under his fingers. Hurriedly he put it on, then his cloak of finest wool.

'There you are, Father!' The voice was his daughter's. She did not know that she had been turned to gold, but thought she had slept and had an evil dream, in which she stood, unable to move, staring in front of her. It was such a silly dream that she did not even speak of it. And now here she was by the river, holding a lizard in her palm. 'Look, Father, it isn't gold after all, it's alive! Look at its lovely skin, green and gold and blue. I think he's prettier than if he were all gold.'

'I think so too,' said the king. And he stroked his daughter's silky hair. 'And now,' he went on, 'shall we go back to the Palace? I happen to be very hungry!'

So they went home. And for the rest of his life King Midas never forgot that food and rest were more precious than gold, and that his child was the most precious thing in his life.

But from that day on, the river called Patroclus rolled over golden sands and carried gold dust to the sea. And whenever Midas walked beside it he was reminded of the foolish wish which had nearly taken all happiness from him.

HONOR WYATT

Lion and Mouse

IT was a hot day, and Lion was sleeping under a rock. He was a big Lion, very splendid and noble; in fact, as everyone knows, he was King of All Animals. Now it so happened that Mouse had lost her way. Running hither and thither, she stumbled over Lion's very nose and woke him. Instantly Lion put out a paw and held Mouse fast to the ground. Mice, as everyone knows, are very little animals, and this Mouse was specially little. But she stuck her head out from under Lion's paw and began to squeak piteously.

'Oh, Your Majesty,' she squeaked, 'please forgive me. I didn't mean to trip over Your Majesty's nose and wake Your Majesty, truly I didn't. Of course Your Majesty *could* squash me dead with one squash, but would it be worth it for such a noble and dignified animal as a Lion to squash such a miserable little creature as a Mouse?'

'Stop squeaking!' ordered Lion. 'Tell me why I should be merciful to such an insignificant creature as you.'

'Well,' said Mouse, 'it is a noble act for a King to be merciful. It shows how noble he is. Besides, Your Majesty, perhaps one day even a miserable little creature like me *might* be able to do Your Majesty a good turn. Who knows?'

'Ho, ho, ho!' laughed Lion, King of All Animals, with a great roar that nearly terrified Mouse out of her small wits. 'That's a good one – a Mouse help a Lion! Well, that's a good joke, upon my whiskers.'

And he twiddled his whiskers to show what fine whiskers they were, and also how amused he was.

'Well, I didn't say it *would* happen,' said Mouse, 'I only said it *might*.'

And *she* twiddled *her* whiskers, just to show that she too had whiskers, even though they were such little whiskers.

'Very well,' said Lion. 'Off you go, and leave me to my sleep. And in future mind where you're going.'

'Oh, I will, Your Majesty,' said Mouse. 'Thank you so *very* much for sparing my life.'

But Lion only snored. He was asleep again.

Well, a long time afterwards, Lion was roaming through the jungle, not looking where he was going, because he was King of All Animals and had become just a bit careless. And he fell right into a trap that some hunters had set for him. It was a deep pit covered over with a net, covered over with leaves. Into the pit fell Lion with the net all round him, so that he got tangled up in it and couldn't free himself. So he let out a great roar, and the whole jungle shook with his roaring, and every creature in the jungle stopped what he was doing and trembled with fear.

Not far off the little Mouse put down a corn-stalk she was nibbling and said to herself: 'Now where have I heard *that* noise before? Why, of course, it's King Lion, and it sounds as if he's in trouble.'

So in less than one minute she had run to the place where Lion was caught in the net, and begun to bite through the strings of the net. Soon she had made a hole large enough for Lion to get through, so he was able to escape and wasn't caught by the hunters after all.

But I am sorry to say that he didn't thank Mouse quite so graciously as he ought to have done. But Mouse did not mind. She scampered away to look for the corn-stalk she had put down when she heard King Lion's roar.

AESOP *adapted by* JAMES REEVES
Illustrated by CONSTANCE MARSHALL

Green Broom

There was an old man lived out in the wood,
    His trade was a-cutting of Broom, green Broom;
He had but one son without thrift, without good,
    Who lay in his bed till 'twas noon, bright noon.

The old man awoke, one morning and spoke;
    He swore he would fire the room, that room,
If his John would not rise and open his eyes,
    And away to the wood to cut Broom, green Broom.

So Johnny arose, and he slipped on his clothes,
    And away to the wood to cut Broom, green Broom,
He sharpened his knives, for once he contrives
    To cut a great bundle of Broom, green Broom;

When Johnny passed under a lady's fine house,
    Passed under a lady's fine room, fine room,
She called to her maid, 'Go fetch me,' she said,
    'Go fetch me the boy that sells Broom, green Broom.'

When Johnny came into the lady's fine house,
    And stood in the lady's fine room, fine room,
'Young Johnny,' she said, 'will you give up your trade,
    And marry a lady in bloom, full bloom?'

Johnny gave his consent, and to church they both went,
And he wedded the lady in bloom, full bloom;
At market and fair, all folks do declare,
　　There is none like the Boy that sold Broom, green
　　Broom.

The Pavilion in the Laurels

I

THERE was once an honest merchant who opened a chandler's shop in the lower room of the tall house where he lived in a dark narrow street. He worked so hard, and gave those who traded with him such good service that he prospered and was able to open other shops in more fashionable parts of the city. These shops also brought him success, and he and his wife and daughter were able to move from the tall house in the narrow street to another house, not very large, but in a street that was a little broader and sunnier.

As the years passed, though he still lived simply with his family, he became richer and more and more successful, and eventually he became a city councillor. He was pleased with his new standing, and spent much of his time discussing the city's affairs with his fellow-councillors, leaving the care of his shops to the people who worked for him. He soon made a name for himself as one whose honesty and judgement could be respected, and in time his career was brought to the notice of the king, who was pleased by what he heard, and knighted him.

The merchant, now very rich, was delighted and took his latest station very seriously. 'Now that we are Sir John and Lady Brown,' he said to his wife, 'it is not fitting that we should live so simply and in such a small house.' And he bought a large house with a big garden, and he and his wife and their only daughter went to live there, with servants to do their bidding.

It was a very beautiful house, with wide rooms and large windows and mahogany furniture in the latest fashion; chests-of-drawers with bulging sides, chairs with curved legs ending in feet with claws, little lacquer cabinets, mirrors set in ornate gilded frames, and in each room a fine brass clock.

All these things particularly delighted Sir John's daughter, who ran from room to room excitedly examining everything, until her mother was obliged to remind her, 'Walk slowly, Sarah, and with more dignity. Remember, dear, you are a young lady now, and young ladies are always dignified.'

Sir John's daughter had been known as Sally until her father had been knighted, and then her parents had decided that Sarah would be a more fitting name for the daughter of a knight; but she still thought of herself as Sally.

'Oh, mother, what lovely furniture,' she exclaimed. 'See those pretty chairs and that handsome table. They are so fine that they will be a real pleasure to dust and polish.' For Sally had always helped her mother in their old home.

The knight's lady threw up her hands in horror. 'Sarah, what are you saying? There will be no more housework for you now. You will have nothing to do all day but wear pretty clothes and walk in the garden. And I think, dear,' she added in a lower voice, 'it would be better if you forgot that you had ever polished or dusted. It might give people the wrong impression.'

Sally was so excited by her new home that for the first few days in it she could think of nothing else, and her greatest wish was that she might show it to her sweetheart Tom, who was a sailor, when he came home again. But when she said so to her father, Sir John seemed embarrassed. 'I think, Sarah, that you had best forget about Tom,' he said.

'Forget about Tom!' exclaimed Sally, and then a terrible thought came to her. 'He is not drowned, is he?'

'Why no, I expect he is well and half across the world in the pleasant sunny lands by now. I am sure he is not drowned.'

'Then why should I forget him, father?'

'Because, my dear, it is not fitting that one of your station, the only daughter of a knight, should count among her acquaintances a common sailor.'

'But, father,' protested Sally, 'he is my oldest friend. And you know how he always said that when he had saved a little money he would leave the sea and marry me.'

'Yes, yes, my dear, I know, and that was all very well before our circumstances were altered, but now it is a different matter. Tom is a good lad, and I have nothing against him, but you are a young lady now and must marry a rich gentleman, or perhaps even into society. How would my little girl like to be a baronet's lady, or perhaps even a countess?'

'I should much prefer to be Tom's wife,' said Sally.

But her parents had made up their minds, and though they were kind, they were very firm, and there was nothing Sally could do about it.

'She must have music and dancing lessons, and as soon as she has the accomplishments of a young lady, we must find her a rich young gentleman to marry,' said her mother.

But Sally remembered how she and Tom had played as children in the ugly backyard behind their homes, for Tom had lived in the house next to hers. 'When I am grown up,' he would say, 'I am going to be a sailor. I shall sail and sail over the sea and across the world, and there I shall find a pirate's treasure chest and bring it home and marry you.' And they had played for hours at finding treasure, with a few stones and a halfpenny in an old wooden box.

And she remembered how Tom had done what he wanted and gone to sea, and when her father had moved from the narrow street to the house that was a little larger than the one where she had been born, whenever he was home from his ship,

Tom would come to see them. And her parents would sit and listen with pleasure to his tales of foreign lands, and he was always a welcome guest at their house.

And Sally remembered how she and Tom would sit together and talk, and Tom would say, 'When I have saved enough money, I shall leave the sea and come home and marry you.'

And Sally could not imagine a future without Tom, and she knew that she could never forget him, whatever her father said. But there was nothing she could do about it, and no one she could talk to, for she was living in a strange new house and Tom was at sea.

In order that she might acquire the accomplishments of a young lady, Sir John sent for the best teachers to instruct her in the arts. She had a singing lesson every day with Signor

Belcanto, who sang rather beautifully himself and accompanied
her on the harpsichord with a flourish; and a dancing lesson
twice a week with a tall thin excitable gentleman named Monsieur Pirouette; and her music lessons, which were every afternoon, were given her by a very learned teacher indeed, one
Doctor Hammerklavier. The rest of the time she was free, as her
mother had said, to wear pretty clothes and walk in the garden.

The garden was a very stately one, with carefully trimmed
lawns and tidily cut hedges, well swept stone walks and beds of
orderly flowers; rose bushes pruned into neat little trees, and
rows and rows of tulips standing stiffly like soldiers, each exactly
the same distance apart.

One day when Sally was walking in the garden, wearing a
dress of dimity spotted with pink and green posies, and on her
head a big hat tied on with a broad blue scarf, she noticed a

narrow gap in the hedge that ran all the way round the garden
in front of the trees that peeped over the high garden-wall to the
road. She had never noticed a gap there before, and wondering
if there were anything on the other side of the hedge, between
the trees and the wall, she slipped through. Instead of the wall
which she had expected, she found herself in a part of the garden
where she had never been before, and which the gardeners had
obviously forgotten. Here the roses scrambled everywhere, and
the daisies and buttercups bloomed on the lawn. There were
weeds in the flower-beds, pretty sun-spurge and golden cinque-
foil and purple self-heal. Here the stone paths were covered in
lichen and moss, and tufts of grass grew up through cracks in the
paving. There was a stone seat half-overgrown with honey-
suckle; and the hedges, privet and bay and box, were all in
blossom.

As Sally wandered in this deserted spot, she came upon a little pavilion surrounded by laurel bushes. It was a small round building of grey stone, covered with yellow lichen and pink roses, and it had a very ornamental roof, like a hat with a fern or two hanging down from the brim in place of a jaunty feather. A little verandah with stone pillars ran all the way around the pavilion, and it had a closed wooden door.

Sally went up the steps to the door, but as she put out her hand to open it, something made her change her mind, and for no reason at all, she knocked instead. At once a voice said, 'Come in,' and she opened the door and stepped inside.

2

She found herself in a little room with eight sides. Four of the sides had windows which let in the light, and of the other four, the door was in one, and another was covered with a curtain. In the centre of the room sat an old lady busy at her needlework. She smiled at Sally. 'Come in and close the door,' she said.

Sally closed the door behind her and curtsied to the old lady. 'Good afternoon, ma'am,' she said.

'Come and sit down and rest, child,' said the old lady; and Sally sat on a stool at her feet.

It was very cool and very peaceful in the pavilion, and Sally did not feel as though she were intruding in any way. She sat and watched the old lady as she embroidered in soft delicate shades on white satin. 'What are you making, ma'am?' she asked at last.

'That is a secret, child, which you may not know yet,' replied the old lady; and Sally did not feel the words were a rebuke for her curiosity, because of the kindly smile in the old lady's eyes, and she smiled back.

The old lady went on with her needlework and Sally's eyes strayed to her workbox made of many different woods inlaid in a pattern of flowers and birds and lined with quilted blue taffeta. 'Your skeins of silk are rather tangled, may I sort them for you?' she asked.

'I should be grateful if you would, child.'

So Sally sorted and tidied the skeins, pink, pale peach, periwinkle blue, and duck's egg green, like a sunset seen through a mist, and laid them in neat rows in the workbox. And when she had finished, the old lady said, 'Thank you, my dear. Now perhaps there is something I could do for you in return. Is there anything you would like?'

'Thank you, ma'am, but I think there is nothing that I would like. Except . . .' and Sally hesitated.

'Except what, child?'

'Except to know how Tom fares.'

'Tom?' inquired the old lady.

'Thomas Williams. He is a sailor. His ship is the *Golden Duke* and he sailed in her for the islands where the spices grow with a cargo of woollen cloth two months ago. But I am foolish to trouble you, for he is only a poor sailor lad, and how could you ever have heard of him or know how he fares?'

The old lady put down her work. 'I think perhaps I can help you,' she said. 'Draw aside that curtain there.'

So Sally drew back the curtain that covered one of the eight sides of the room, and behind it was a large mirror. But she noticed at once that it was no ordinary mirror, for she could not see herself in it; it seemed instead as though she were looking at the reflection of a cloud, and as she watched, the cloud cleared away, and she was seeing the blue sea and the bluer sky and, in the foreground, the sandy beach of a little coral isle. And over the sea, the wind filling her sails, came the *Golden Duke*.

But even as Sally watched her, she ran into a hidden rock on the coral reef, and it tore a hole in her side and she began to sink. Sally saw the boats lowered and the sailors jumping overboard, and she wrung her hands in terror. And she watched one sailor who struck out bravely for the shore of the little coral island, and when he left the water and staggered a few steps before he fell senseless on the sand, she saw that it was Tom. 'He is safe,' she thought with joy.

But she did not know how long she had been watching him before she noticed that the tide was coming in. The water reached his feet and then crept upwards over his legs, and he did not move. It was almost to his shoulders, and still he did not stir.

'He will be drowned,' thought Sally in anguish. 'Oh, what can I do?' And though she was not aware that she had spoken out loud, she heard the old lady's voice, very calm and quiet, 'Go and help him, child.'

And without stopping to question how she could do that, Sally picked up her skirts and stepped right into the mirror and found herself standing on the hot sand under a blazing sky. She ran to Tom and dragged him out of the water, and laid him in the shade of a palm tree, beyond the reach of the tide. When she straightened her back from the effort, her head spun from the glare and the dazzle, and she covered her eyes with her hands.

A voice said gently, 'Is it not time for your music lesson, child?'

She looked up and found that she was sitting on the stool before the old lady who smiled at her. 'Doctor Hammerklavier will be waiting for you.'

Sally looked at the wall where the mirror was, but the curtain was drawn across it once again, and she could not tell whether she had been dreaming or not. She looked at the old lady, but when she was about to ask what had been happening to her, the old lady repeated, 'Hurry, child, Doctor Hammerklavier will be waiting for you.'

She rose and dropped a curtsey. 'Good-bye, ma'am,' she said.

'Good-bye, my dear.'

And Sally went out of the pavilion and ran across the deserted garden, through the gap in the hedge, over the well-trimmed lawn between the flower-beds and back to the house, and found it was just time for her music lesson to begin.

Afterwards, playing scales for Doctor Hammerklavier, it was difficult to believe that she had not been dreaming about Tom and the shipwreck; yet later, when she took off her shoes, she found there was sand in them. But she said nothing about it.

A few days after, she slipped through the gap in the hedge again and knocked once more on the door of the pavilion. The old lady was at her embroidery as before, and Sally sat on the stool at her feet and watched her as she laid a fine thread of gold among the flowers and leaves she had worked on the white satin in her delicate shades.

'And how have you spent the morning, child?' she asked.

'I spent most of the time at my singing lesson,' said Sally, with a sigh.

'And do you make good progress?' There was a twinkle in the old lady's eyes.

'My mother thinks my voice is pretty, but Signor Belcanto says that I shall never make a good singer,' Sally replied.

'Perhaps you would sing for me, while I work.'

'My mother is wrong and Signor Belcanto is right,' said Sally hastily. 'I sing very ill.'

'Never mind, child. Sing just one little song for me.'

And Sally found that she felt neither shy nor nervous, so she sang one of the songs that Signor Belcanto had taught her; and though she did not sing it very well, she did not sing it very badly, either. 'I am afraid that was not very good, ma'am,' she apologized, when the song was over.

'It was quite pretty enough, child, and besides, it is a pleasure to find one young person who is not conceited about her accomplishments.' And she and Sally both laughed.

'Is there anything you would like me to do for you in return for the song?' asked the old lady.

'If you could tell me how Tom fares,' said Sally, 'that is all I want.'

'Go and look into the mirror, my dear, and see how he is.'

Sally drew back the curtain over the mirror and looked into it, and when the clouds had cleared she saw the same coral isle that she had seen before, and lying on the beach, tossing in a fever, was Tom.

'He is sick,' she thought to herself, 'and he will die if no one comes to aid him.' And while she was wondering if she could possibly help him, she saw a ship sailing by. 'If only the sailors see him and send a boat to pick him up,' she thought; and then she realized that unless he signalled to the ship they would pass the isle without ever knowing he was there, and Tom was too ill even to see that help was at hand.

'The ship will not save him,' she thought in anguish, and though she was not aware that she had spoken aloud, she heard the old lady say calmly, 'Go and help him, child,' and she picked up her skirts and stepped into the mirror and ran across the sand to a rock, and tearing a strip from her white petticoat, she waved it at the ship. And after what seemed like hours, she saw the sailors lower a boat over the side and row towards the shore.

Sally felt that she could have wept with relief. Tears misted her eyes and she closed them; and when she opened them again she found she was sitting at the old lady's feet in the little pavilion, and the curtain was drawn across the mirror once more.

Before she could ask any questions, the old lady spoke. 'Is it not time for your dancing lesson, child? Monsieur Pirouette will be waiting for you.'

She rose and dropped the old lady a curtsey. 'Good-bye, ma'am,' she said.

'Good-bye, my dear.'

And Sally went out of the pavilion and ran across the deserted garden, through the gap in the hedge, over the well-trimmed lawn between the flower-beds and back to the house, and found that it was indeed time for her dancing lesson.

Afterwards, as she practised dainty steps to the counting of Monsieur Pirouette, it seemed hard to believe that she had not been dreaming of Tom and the rescue; but later she found that there was a great piece torn away from the hem of her white petticoat. Yet she said nothing to anyone else about the pavilion in the laurel bushes.

3

After three or four days she went there again one morning, and the old lady welcomed her kindly, and Sally sat on the stool at her feet and watched her sew tiny pearls among the silken flowers and the golden threads on the white satin. She picked out the pearls one by one from their little enamelled box and slipped them on to the old lady's needle until they were all sewn on.

And when she had finished, the old lady thanked her, and said, 'Perhaps there is something I could do for you in return?'

'Only if you could tell me if there are tidings of Tom.'

'Look into the mirror, child.'

So Sally drew the curtains aside and looked into the mirror, and when the clouds cleared away she saw Tom's new ship in port, and Tom himself, very lonely and thinking of her, walking along the shore. After a time, as she watched him, he lay down under a palm tree and slept, for the sun was hot.

'Poor Tom,' she thought with a sigh, but though she was not aware of having spoken out loud, she heard the old lady say, 'Perhaps it would cheer him, child, if you walked for a moment near him and sent him dreams of you.' And Sally picked up her skirts and stepped into the mirror and found herself on the tropical beach. She walked a while near Tom, and did not wake him, though she longed to do so, and she saw him smile a little in his sleep and she knew that he dreamt of her.

As she walked, a breeze suddenly came up from the sea and caught the little lace cap that she was wearing and whisked it away. She ran after it, and as she ran, she kicked against something that was hidden under the sand. She stopped to look at it, and saw that it was the corner of a wooden chest, and she remembered the games that she and Tom had played in the little yard behind her home when they had been children.

She knelt down and dug in the sand with her hands, heedless of the sharp shells and jagged stones that scratched her; and when she had cleared enough of the sand away, she broke the rusty lock of the chest and opened it. Inside were hundreds of pieces of gold, and necklaces, bracelets, and brooches. 'A pirate's treasure,' she said to herself. And instantly she knew what she had to do with it. She rose and began to drag the chest over the sand towards the sleeping Tom, and though it was not an easy task, for the chest was very heavy, Sally pulled with all her might, and at last the chest lay only a few feet from him. 'He will see it when he wakes,' she thought. But the sun was hot and the chest had been a great weight, and her head spun round and she bent it into her hands.

The next thing she heard was the old lady's voice saying, 'Is it not time for your singing lesson? Signor Belcanto will be waiting for you.' And she found she was back in the pavilion and the curtain was drawn over the mirror.

She rose and dropped a curtsey. 'Good-bye, ma'am.'

'Good-bye, my dear.'

And Sally went out from the pavilion and ran across the deserted garden, through the gap in the hedge, over the well-trimmed lawn between the flower-beds and back to the house, where she found it was indeed time for her lesson. Afterwards, while she sang to Signor Belcanto's accompaniment, it was difficult to believe that she had not been dreaming of Tom and the pirate's treasure. Yet later, when she looked at her hands, she saw that they were scratched. But again she said nothing to anyone about the pavilion in the laurel bushes.

The following day she had hoped to visit the old lady again, but running downstairs to breakfast too quickly, she slipped and sprained her ankle. 'That is what comes of rushing about in a way that no young lady should,' said her mother as she tucked her up in bed, where Sally had to stay for a whole week. Even after that, when she got up, she could only hobble about the house, and for more than a month she had no dancing lessons and could go no further into the garden than to walk on the terrace under the windows, leaning on her father's arm.

But her singing and her music lessons went on as usual, and day by day her ankle grew stronger, until her father said, 'To-morrow I shall send to Monsieur Pirouette to tell him that in three days' time you will be able to dance again.'

But that very day something exciting happened. In the afternoon her mother said to her, 'From whom do you think we had a visit this morning, Sarah?'

'I have no idea, Mother. Who was it?'

'Young Tom Williams, Sarah. He is home from sea and intends never to go back again. It seems he had good luck on his last voyage, and found a buried treasure.'

'Oh, mother, why did you not tell me he was here, so that I could have seen him?' exclaimed Sally.

'You were having your music lesson and I did not want you to be disturbed. But he is coming again tomorrow and you may see him then. Quite the young gentleman he looked in a fine blue coat with a great fortune to spend.'

The next day, when she was having her music lesson, Sally left the door ajar, and it is to be feared that she paid little attention to Doctor Hammerklavier when he corrected the mistakes in her scales. And as soon as she heard Tom's voice in the hall, she jumped up with an 'I beg your pardon, Doctor Hammerklavier,' and ran out of the room, leaving that gentleman very much startled.

Sally saw Tom standing in the hall looking very well and sunburnt, in his fine blue coat with gold buttons, and a three-cornered hat trimmed with gold braid, and she called, 'Tom!'

'Sally!' he cried, and opened his arms and she ran right into them.

'Sarah,' said her mother, 'You must remember that you are a young lady now.'

And because Tom had come by a fortune and was no longer a poor sailor lad, he was considered a suitable husband for Sally, and they were betrothed. And as soon as she could speak to him alone, Sally told Tom about the pavilion in the laurel bushes, and the old lady and the mirror.

'We must go and thank her,' said Tom. And together they went into the garden. But though they searched for a whole morning, they could not find the gap in the hedge.

'It was here, in this very spot,' said Sally. 'I am sure of it.'

'But there is nothing behind the hedge here except the trees, and beyond the trees, the garden-wall,' said Tom. 'There is no room there for a deserted garden or a pavilion.'

And in the end, they gave up the search.

Preparations were made for the wedding, and a very exciting time it was for Sally. 'She must have the best seamstress in the city to make her wedding gown,' said Sir John.

But on the morning of the day when the seamstress was to come to measure her and show her the patterns of silks for the dress, when Sally awoke, she saw, laid carefully over a chair at the foot of her bed, a wedding gown of white satin, finer than any seamstress could make, embroidered with flowers worked in silks of soft delicate shades, entwined with threads of gold and sewn with pearls.

And Sally knew then the answer to that first question she had asked the old lady in the pavilion, and she dropped a curtsey and whispered, 'Thank you, ma'am,' even though she was quite alone.

BARBARA LEONIE PICARD

Ah Poor Bird!

ROUND FOR FOUR VOICES

Ah poor bird!
Take thy flight
Far above the sorrows
Of this sad world.

The Baker's Daughter

O BUT the Baker's Daughter is beautiful!

The Baker's Daughter has yellow hair, and every night it is curled with rags, and every morning it stands out in a frizzy fluff round her head. The Baker's Daughter has blue dresses and pink dresses and spotted dresses, with flounces and flounces on them; she has beads around her neck and jingly bracelets and a ring with a real stone. All the girls in class sigh with envy of the Baker's Daughter.

But the Baker's Daughter is proud. She points her chin and she turns up her nose, and she is very, very superior. You never see her in the Baker's shop. She strolls up and down the sidewalk, sucking her beads.

You all know the Baker's shop, two steps down. It is warm in there, and busy. It smells of hot bread, and every few minutes the Baker, a hot, untidy little man in shirt sleeves, comes up from the basement carrying a big tray of crullers, or shiny rolls, or twisted currant buns. The Baker works hard all day and he never has time to do more than just poke his nose outside the doorway, every hour or so, for a sniff of cool air. It is hard to believe that anything so beautiful as the Baker's Daughter could ever come out of the Baker's shop!

Once I started to write a poem. It began:

> O it is the Baker's Daughter,
> And she is grown so fair, so fair . . .

I thought I would make a very splendid valentine of it, all written out in a fine hand, with pink roses around and lots of crinkly paper lace, and send it to her, secretly. But unfortunately I found out that it was too much like a poem that someone else wrote a long time ago, and so I have never finished it. But still it always comes into my mind whenever I see the Baker's Daughter sucking her beads.

There was only one thing in the Baker's shop that at all came up in magnificence to the Baker's Daughter herself, and that was the big round cake that sat right in the middle of the Baker's window. It was a chocolate cake, with all sorts of twirls and twiddles of lovely icing on it, and the word BIRTHDAY written in pink sugar letters. For some reason or other the Baker would never sell that cake. Perhaps he was afraid he would never be able to make another one quite so beautiful. He would sell you any other cake from his window but that one, and even if you went there very early on a Friday morning, which is cruller day, when there are no cakes at all, and asked him for a nice party cake, he would say:

'I can let you have one by three o'clock!'

And if you then asked: 'But how about the cake in the window?' he would reply:

'That's not for sale. You can have one by three o'clock!'

For though you should offer him dollars and dollars, he would never sell that cake!

I seldom dare to speak to the Baker's Daughter. I am much too humble. But still she has friends. Never little boys; these she points her chin at, from across the street. But there are little girls with whom she is on friendly terms for as much as a week at a time. Naturally they are very proud. If you can't be a princess or a movie star perhaps the next best thing is to be seen walking up to the drug-store soda fountain with the Baker's Daughter, and sitting there beside her on a tall stool eating pineapple sundae.

Now there was one little girl with whom the Baker's Daughter condescended at one time to be friends. Perhaps her name had something to do with it. She was called Carmelita Miggs, and Carmelita is a very romantic and superior name. She had black hair and a pair of bronze slippers, and she was the only little girl ever seen to stroll publicly with the Baker's Daughter, arm in arm. What they talked about no one knew. But Carmelita sometimes wore the Baker's Daughter's beads, and the Baker's Daughter would wear Carmelita's beads, and altogether they were very, very special friends while it lasted.

And it lasted until Carmelita had a birthday party.

The Baker's Daughter of course was invited, and several other of Carmelita's school friends. It was to be a real party, at four in the afternoon, with ice cream. And the Baker's Daughter said, very grandly, that she would bring a cake.

'I will bake you a nice one,' said her father, 'with orange icing on it. Now let me see . . . how many of you will there be?'

But that wasn't at all what the Baker's Daughter wanted. Anyone at all could bring a cake with orange icing. 'I will choose my own cake!' thought the Baker's Daughter.

But all she said was: 'That will be very nice!'

And in the afternoon, while her father was down in the bakeshop kitchen putting the last twiddle on the orange cake (for he wanted to make it something very special), and while her mother was taking forty winks in the back room, and the bakery cat was sound asleep, with her four paws curled under her, behind the counter, the Baker's Daughter crept into the shop on tiptoe, in all her finery, and stole – yes, *stole* – that big magnificent cake from the very middle of the shop window!

You see, she had her eye on it, all along!

She lifted it up – and a nice, light cake it seemed – wooden platter and all, and she covered it over with sheets of waxy paper and carried it round to Carmelita's house.

O but she looked proud, walking down the street with that big cake in her arms! Everyone turned to look at her.

'What a lovely cake!' cried all the little boys and girls when she arrived at Carmelita's house.

And the wrappings were taken off, very carefully, and it was set right in the middle of the table, with candles all around it.

'*What* a nice light cake!' said Carmelita's mother.

'All good cakes are light!' said the Baker's Daughter.

'It was very, very kind of your father to make such a splendid cake,' said Carmelita's mother.

'I chose it myself!' said the Baker's Daughter, tossing her head.

They talked a little, very politely, and Carmelita Miggs showed all her birthday presents. And at last came the moment for the ice cream to be handed round on little glass plates.

'And now,' said Carmelita's mother, 'we'll all have some of that delicious cake!'

Carmelita had to cut it, because it was her birthday. She stood there feeling very shy, for there was a great silence all round; everyone's eyes were fixed on the cake, and all one could hear was Tommy Bates busily sucking his ice-cream spoon, so as to get through first.

Only the Baker's Daughter sat there proudly, with her skirts spread out, looking indifferent, as though cakes like this were quite an everyday affair with her!

Carmelita took the knife and stuck it into the very middle of the pink icing, and pushed. You could have heard a pin drop.

But the knife didn't go in. Carmelita turned very red, and took a long breath and tried again. Still the knife wouldn't go in.

'You must try harder, dear,' said Carmelita's mother, smiling pleasantly. 'I expect the top icing is a little bit stiff! Do you want me to help you?'

Now Carmelita knew that she had been pushing just as hard

as she could. It came upon her, all at once, that there must be something very very queer about that cake! But she took another long breath, again, and this time her mother put *her* hand on the knife, too.

You could have heard *two* pins drop!

And then, suddenly, there was a funny 'plop', and the knife went in. And as it went in the cake slipped and turned a sort of somersault, and there it was, upside down, sticking on the tip of the knife that Carmelita's mother was still holding, and everyone looking most surprised. And that wasn't the worst of it!

It was all hollow inside!

In fact, it was just a big pasteboard shell covered over with icing, and *that* was why the Baker would never sell it to anyone!

Can you imagine how the party felt? How the little boys and girls whispered and giggled, how Carmelita wept and the Baker's Daughter grew redder and redder, and snifflier and snifflier, and how Carmelita's mother tried to smooth everything over and pretend that it was really all very funny, and quite the nicest thing that could happen at any birthday party? And how, at the very last minute, while the ice cream was all melting away, they had to send out and buy a real cake, *somewhere else!*

But Carmelita Miggs didn't think it was a joke. She never, never forgave the Baker's Daughter for spoiling her party. For quite a long time she wouldn't speak to her at all. As for the other boys and girls, whenever they met Carmelita or the Baker's Daughter they would say:

'Now we'll all have some cake!'

You would think, after this, that the Baker's Daughter would have changed her ways. But not a bit of it! I saw her, only the other day, strolling up and down the sidewalk and sucking her beads just as proud as ever.

As I went past her I whispered very softly: 'Now we'll all have some cake!'

And do you know what the Baker's Daughter did? I hate to tell you.

She stuck – out – her – tongue!

There, in the middle of the Baker's window, is another cake. This time it has green icing and pink roses, and two little sugar doves on top. It is even grander than the old one, and will probably last twice as long.

Unless, of course, someone else should have a birthday party!

MARGERY WILLIAMS BIANCO

My Delight

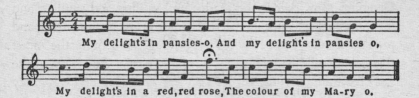

My delight's in pansies-o, And my delight's in pansies o, My delight's in a red, red rose, The colour of my Ma-ry o.

My delight's in pansies-o,
And my delight's in pansies-o,
My delight's in a red, red, rose,
The colour of my Mary-o.

Before the Paling of the Stars

Before the paling of the stars,
Before the winter morn,
Before the earliest cock crow,
    Jesus Christ was born:
Born in a stable,
    Cradled in a manger,
In the world his hands had made
    Born a stranger.

Priest and king lay fast asleep
    In Jerusalem;
Young and old lay fast asleep
    In crowded Bethlehem;
Saint and angel, ox and ass,
    Kept a watch together
Before the Christmas daybreak
    In the winter weather.

Jesus on his mother's breast
In the stable cold,
Spotless lamb of God was he,
Shepherd of the fold:
Let us kneel with Mary maid,
With Joseph bent and hoary,
With saint and angel, ox and ass,
To hail the King of Glory.

CHRISTINA ROSSETTI
Illustrated by PEGGY FORTNUM

Poringer

What is the rhyme for poringer?
The King he had a daughter fair,
And gave the Prince of Orange her!

Simple Simon

Simple Simon met a pieman
    Going to the fair.
Says Simple Simon to the pieman,
    'Let me taste your ware.'

Says the pieman to Simple Simon,
    'Show me first your penny';
Says Simple Simon to the pieman,
    'Indeed I have not any.'

Simple Simon went a-fishing
    For to catch a whale;
All the water he had got
    Was in his mother's pail.

Simple Simon went to look
    If plums grew on a thistle;
He pricked his finger very much,
    Which made poor Simon whistle.

Roddy and the Red Indians

RODDY STUMPER was a little boy with very solemn, round, blue eyes which looked as though they were always wondering about something, a flattish sort of nose which was covered with freckles, and a wide sort of mouth which turned up ridiculously at one corner as if it were always on the point of laughing, and he lived all by himself in a house at the edge of the forest with his Mummy and Daddy and his big sister Anna Belinda. He lived all by himself because, although his Mummy and Daddy and his big sister Anna Belinda lived in the same house too, they were so very grown-up and dull that it really wasn't any good trying to talk to them at all.

One morning after breakfast Roddy walked moodily down the path in the front garden. When he came to the end of the path he climbed up the bars of the gate and hung over the top for a long time watching the people go by. People are funny, he thought curiously . . . I wonder if people ever stop being people, just for a change, when nobody else is looking . . . He saw Miss Quilch coming slowly up the road, waddling a little as she walked because her legs were rather short and stumpy, with a long black dress on with a white thing down the front, and her long sharp nose held very high in the air as if there were a bad smell always a little way ahead. She was exactly like a penguin, he decided. Then he saw Mr Umpleby. Mr Umpleby was a nice woolly sort of old man. He had a mass of woolly hair which tumbled down over his forehead, and thick woolly eyebrows that hung above his eyes. He had woolly whiskers that covered his ears and both sides of his face, and even spread a little on to the bridge of his nose, and he looked, Roddy thought, as he watched him coming shambling up the road, like a great friendly shaggy dog.

'What are *you* doing, Youngster?' inquired Mr Umpleby pleasantly when he had come quite close.

'Nothing,' said Roddy. 'Not at this very minute. But I was just thinking of having an Adventure,' he said.

'Oh,' said Mr Umpleby. 'What sort of adventure?'

'Just an Adventure,' said Roddy airily. 'A Red Indian sort of adventure I think, but I haven't found it yet,' he explained. 'They are a bit difficult to find sometimes.'

'Oh,' said Mr Umpleby again. 'I thought you were usually a Cowboy.'

'As a matter of fact,' said Roddy, 'I am tired of being a cowboy. I would rather be a Red Indian.'

Mr Umpleby shook his head. 'Red Indians are bad. They scalp,' he explained vaguely, 'and shoot people with arrows. Nobody wants to be a Red Indian.'

'*I* do,' said Roddy obstinately. 'So do cowboys shoot people,' he added after a moment's thought.

When Mr Umpleby had gone Roddy trotted quickly along the path, round the end of the house, into the back garden. He crawled round the trunks of all the trees and peered behind all the bushes, but there was nothing there, and at last he came to an old narrow rusty iron gate, and stood with his legs apart and his hands stuck in his pockets staring out into the lane that wound mysteriously past between the forest and the garden wall.

'Have you found any adventures yet?' asked a very husky voice.

Roddy pressed his face close to the bars and, squinting sideways, saw a large shaggy dog sitting against the wall looking up at him with its head on one side and a twinkle of amusement in its soft brown eyes, but when he looked again he saw that it was Mr Umpleby.

'No,' he said. 'I have looked and looked but there isn't one anywhere.'

'I expect it is waiting round the corner,' said Mr Umpleby. 'Adventures usually are, you know, until you find them. But you have to look very carefully in case they see you coming. You have to catch them by surprise.'

'What happens if they see you coming?' asked Roddy with interest.

'They catch *you* by surprise,' said Mr Umpleby.

'Oh,' said Roddy thoughtfully. 'They wouldn't see *me* coming,' he said.

Mr Umpleby got up and shook himself: then he stepped out into the lane and glanced back over his shoulder, wagging his tail invitingly. 'Why don't you come out?' he asked.

'Because this gate won't open,' explained Roddy. He put his hands back into his pockets and leant dejectedly against it, frowning, and instantly the gate swung open, so suddenly that he fell sprawling out into the lane, but when he had picked himself up

Mr Umpleby had gone. There was nobody in the lane except a penguin which was waddling importantly towards him from the opposite direction with its beak held very high in the air in such a superior and comical way that he could not help laughing. When the penguin came quite close it turned its face towards him with a very disapproving expression, and he saw that it was Miss Quilch.

'Have you no manners, Boy,' she said, 'when you meet a lady?'

Roddy stopped laughing at once, feeling very much ashamed. 'Sorry, Miss Quilch,' he stammered in a very small voice. 'But you did look funny.'

'I am never funny!' said Miss Quilch with dignity, and continued on her way with a stiff little bow and an angry little flap of her flippers.

Beside him the trees of the forest rose like a great green wall, standing motionless and silent with their branches twined together, and at his feet the lane ran crookedly for a little way until it vanished round a corner. 'I bet there is a Red Indian round there!' he said to himself, walking forward eagerly, but when he reached the corner he stopped, remembering what Mr Umpleby had said. 'I must be very careful,' he said to himself, 'in case he sees me coming.' He crept stealthily forward, step by step . . .

'Bang, bang!' he cried. 'You are dead!'

The Red Indian looked very surprised. 'Don't shoot me!' he begged.

'It is all right,' said Roddy quickly in case he were too frightened; 'I haven't got any real guns. Besides, there aren't any bullets in them: that is why I have to say "Bang! Bang!" myself.'

'It wasn't fair,' said the Red Indian sulkily. 'You caught me by surprise.'

'Yes, I did, didn't I?' said Roddy proudly.

Roddy stared at the Red Indian with great interest, and the Red Indian stared at Roddy in a very aloof sort of way. 'How!' he said.

'How!' answered Roddy politely, and after that they stood and stared at one another again. 'Can I be a Red Indian too, please?' he asked at last. 'I'm afraid I don't know any more Red Indian language,' he said, 'except How.'

'It doesn't matter,' said the Red Indian, 'Red Indians are very silent people.'

Roddy was just going to ask what they said when they wanted to say something different, when he remembered several other important things that he wanted to know first. 'Have you ever scalped anybody?' he asked.

'Only my enemies,' said the Red Indian. 'Enemies have to be scalped,' he said, 'because otherwise how would anyone know I was a Warrior?'

'Is it an awfully sore thing to be scalped?' asked Roddy curiously.

'*How!*' said the Red Indian.

For several minutes Roddy stood quite still thinking about how sore it would be. 'What else do Red Indians do beside scalping?' he inquired at last.

'They shoot arrows . . .' said the Red Indian.

'So do I shoot arrows,' said Roddy proudly. 'I have got three arrows at home with red feathers in them,' he said, 'only they

don't shoot very far. They are not real arrows, because they haven't got sharp points,' he admitted, 'but only sort of rubber things. I *wish* I could shoot *real* arrows ...'

'... And they hunt bears,' went on the Red Indian, staring intently into the forest.

'I could easily catch a bear,' said Roddy.

'No, you couldn't. The bear would catch you first. It would hug you tight until you were dead, and when you were hugged quite dead it would eat you.'

Roddy stared into the forest too, and at that very moment a twig snapped suddenly. 'I hear it!' he cried in great excitement, and darted in between the trees.

2

The forest was full of little noises: rustling noises and snapping noises and strange murmurs as if a thousand things with very small voices were all whispering at once. And everywhere about him there were trees: some were big and some were little, some were straight and some were crooked, and above his head their branches mingled in a thick canopy of leaves: but one tree was different from all the rest because it had fallen down and was lying almost flat upon the ground in a tangle of broken branches. It must have fallen a long time ago, for when it fell its roots had torn a deep hollow in the ground which was hidden now by tall ferns and twigs and grasses. Roddy stepped close to it and listened: then he parted the ferns with his hands and poked his head inside.

'Are you there, Bear?' he called.

'Hush!' said the bear. 'I am hiding.'

Roddy wriggled further in and stared into the darkness. It was a large hollow, warm and dry and comfortable, and the bear was lying in the darkest corner so that he could not see it clearly. 'There is a Red Indian out in the lane,' he said, 'hunting for you.'

'Yes, I know,' said the bear grumpily. 'I don't like Red Indians.'

'Why don't you?' asked Roddy in surprise.

'How would *you* like to be hunted?' inquired the bear.

'I wouldn't like it at all,' said Roddy. 'He says you hug people until they are dead,' he remarked after a pause.

'I only hug them because I love them so much,' protested the bear, 'and then sometimes they go Squash. I can't help it if they go Squash.'

'I think it is a bit soppy,' said Roddy. 'Hugging people I mean. The Red Indian says you eat them up afterwards,' he went on accusingly.

'Well,' said the bear, 'it would be a pity to waste them. They are no good after they have gone Squash.'

'No,' said Roddy thoughtfully, 'I suppose not. I wouldn't like to go Squash,' he said, moving back a little.

'And besides,' said the bear, 'it isn't true, because I would much rather have honey. Or even nuts and things,' it added gloomily.

It is a very nice bear really, thought Roddy, as he wriggled out through the opening, but dreadfully unhappy; and before he went away he carefully arranged the ferns so that nobody would see where he had been. I won't tell the Red Indian about it, he thought as he walked back to the lane, because it is my own bear and I hunted it myself. I'll tell him I did catch it, he decided when he had walked a little farther, only I let it go again, and then he will let me be a Red Indian too. It is easy catching bears, he thought contentedly, but when he reached the lane the Red Indian was nowhere to be seen. There was no one there except Mr Umpleby who was sitting quietly scratching his right ear with his foot and grunting to himself with satisfaction.

'Where is the Red Indian?' inquired Roddy.

'Gone,' said Mr Umpleby. 'I bit him and he ran away. He tasted beastly,' he said.

'Why did you bite him?' asked Roddy.

'He annoyed me,' explained Mr Umpleby, 'because he kept on being silent and aloof. I wasn't having any adventures at all,' he complained disgustedly, 'so I bit him. I have never bitten anyone before,' he said. 'Where have you been?'

'I was just catching a bear,' said Roddy in a casual sort of voice.

'A *bear*?' exclaimed Mr Umpleby, pricking his ears.

'But afterwards I let it go,' said Roddy.

'A *bear*!' exclaimed Mr Umpleby again. 'I am going to catch one too,' he said, and went bounding into the forest making loud snuffling noises of excitement through his nose.

'Bother!' said Roddy, and started running towards the next corner as fast as he could go without remembering to be careful in the least.

At the other side of the corner Miss Quilch was standing, looking very cross indeed, and Roddy was running so fast that he ran bump into her before he could stop. 'Sorry!' he said breathlessly. 'Have you seen a Red Indian? Because I have lost one.'

'Yes,' said Miss Quilch. 'I gave him a good sharp peck. He had a sore leg too,' she added.

'I know,' said Roddy. 'He got bitten by Mr Umpleby.'

'It serves him right,' said Miss Quilch viciously, 'for bumping me.'

Roddy moved a little further away. 'I expect the Red Indian is jolly angry,' he remarked. 'I expect he has gone to get his thing for scalping with, and then he will come back and scalp you. Scalping hurts awfully badly,' he explained cheerfully.

3

There was a faint movement in the forest, so faint that one could hardly see it, like a wisp of shadow flickering among the trees. 'It must be the Red Indian!' he whispered excitedly, and suddenly the forest was full of movement. 'There are a *lot* of Red Indians!' he cried. Swiftly and silently they came from every side, and as he turned his head to look they stopped and sat cross-legged in a great circle round him, staring at him fiercely.

'How!' they said.

'How!' he answered.

'Cowboy!' they said angrily. 'We don't like cowboys.'

'I am *not* a cowboy,' said Roddy. 'At least I am sometimes,' he explained, 'but I am not one today because I haven't got my cowboy suit on . . . It would serve you right if I *were* a cowboy,' he said as they continued to stare, 'because then I would shoot you all dead with my guns. You wouldn't like *that*,' he said severely, but they went on staring in such a fierce, silent way that he suddenly began to feel rather lost and lonely and almost a little bit frightened. 'I wanted to be a Red Indian,' he gulped. 'I didn't want to be a cowboy at all. I wanted to be a Red Indian, and have fun like Red Indians do, and hunt bears and be a warrior . . . and now you have spoilt it,' he said dejectedly.

Then one of the Red Indians stood up and stretched out his arm. He was very tall and proud and haughty, and Roddy knew he must be the Chief because his head was covered with a circlet of great long eagles' feathers which reached all the way down his back as well, almost to the ground. 'How can you be a Red Indian?' asked the Chief scornfully. 'Are you a warrior?'

'Well . . .' said Roddy doubtfully.

'Are you a hunter?'

'Well . . .' said Roddy again. 'I can shoot arrows,' he said, 'and I can catch bears.'

'*How!*' laughed the Chief.

Roddy stamped his foot in fury. 'I can!' he cried. 'I can!' and as he turned away to hide his tears he saw something large and hairy moving among the trees. The Red Indians saw it too, and jumped to their feet in great alarm. 'It is a bear!' they cried.

He watched it with interest as it came cautiously towards him. 'Do you mind if I catch you, Bear?' he asked when it had come quite close, 'because I said I could, you see.'

'All right,' agreed the bear, 'but don't catch me too hard,' it said, 'because I am dreadfully tired. There has been a great shaggy dog chasing me all day and I have been running and running. It tried to bite me,' it said miserably.

'I expect that was Mr Umpleby,' explained Roddy, 'He is quite gentle really.'

'It kept on snapping its teeth at me,' went on the bear, 'so I know it wanted to bite me. I don't like shaggy dogs.'

'I won't let it bite you,' said Roddy kindly. He stepped close to the bear and gave it a gentle hug, and it lay down at his feet at once and went to sleep. '*Now* can I be a Red Indian, please?' he asked.

'*How!*' shouted the Red Indians. '*Great Chief Mighty Hunter!*'

The Chief took off his circlet of great long eagles' feathers and placed it on Roddy's head, and the feathers stretched down his back as well and trailed upon the ground because it was really much too long. 'Is this for *me?*' cried Roddy in delight.

'You are the Chief,' said the Red Indians.

For a moment he stood perfectly still and silent, and his eyes were like two round shining pools of wonder. 'Oh!' he said, because that was the only word that would fit the roundness of his mouth. He twisted his head over his shoulder to see how fine he looked, but he could not see himself properly, except the bit at the end where the feathers trailed upon the ground. 'Oh!' he said again with a sigh of happiness and pride. '*I am the Chief!*'

Deep in the forest there was a distant yapping sound which seemed to be coming nearer, and presently Mr Umpleby appeared running between the trees. He came bounding into the lane with his head bent down and his nose pointing towards the ground, and at the same moment the bear woke up and sat gazing at him gloomily.

'That is my bear,' said Mr Umpleby as soon as he saw Roddy.

'No,' said Roddy, 'it is mine. I caught it.'

'Well, I have been hunting it all morning,' said Mr Umpleby in an aggrieved voice, 'so I don't see why . . .' He looked at the bear and grinned cheerfully. 'Cheer up!' he said. 'You might have been scalped as well, you know: that would have been much worse!'

'Nobody gets scalped,' explained Roddy, 'except enemies, but I can't think of any enemies, not at this very minute,' he said regretfully. 'You are not enemies, are you, Bear?'

'No,' said the bear. 'I'm friends.'

It was rather disappointing, he thought, that nobody was being scalped, but as he stood looking round at the Red Indians in an aloof sort of way as a Chief always should, he suddenly remembered something else that warriors do. 'I want to shoot arrows,' he commanded. 'I want to shoot *real* arrows, with sharp points.'

He fitted an arrow to the string, and set his legs wide apart, and pulled, but the bow was very long and stiff, and it would not bend at all. Out of the corner of his eye he saw Miss Quilch watching

him in a very superior and scornful way. 'Pah!' she scoffed. '*You* could never be a warrior!' He pulled with all his might, and shut his eyes, and pulled again: 'I *am* a warrior!' he told himself fiercely. '*I am the Chief!*' And suddenly the arrow flew from the bow. Ping! it went . . .

*

Roddy hung over the top of the gate watching the people in the road go by. Mr Umpleby came shambling up like a great friendly shaggy dog and winked as he went past, and after him came Miss Quilch. She held an arrow in her hand and her long sharp nose was crimson with fury. 'You *horrid* little boy!' she said angrily. 'You might have killed me!'

Roddy looked at the arrow with delight. 'I *was* a warrior after all!' he said happily.

E. H. LANG
Illustrated by AUDREY WALKER

Robin Redbreast's Thanksgiving

IT was an autumn morning. The sun was shining brightly, but the wind was cold, and there had been a little frost in the night; quite a shower of yellow leaves had come down and were lying all over the green grass. The dahlias looked pinched and hung their heads, and the robin felt puzzled. What could be going to happen.

He was a country robin, and when his robin papa and mamma had said, 'Now you are grown up, be off and find food for yourself,' he had flown away till he came to a large garden on the edge of a town. There he had stayed, all through July, August, and September. He was a quite grown-up robin, but it was only about five months since he was a baby robin just out of the egg. That means, you see, that he first peeped out in April, and so he had never seen anything but a pleasant world with green leaves and flowers everywhere; plenty of caterpillars and other insects to eat, and warm sunshine to bask in.

An old tortoise lived in the garden, and he and the robin had been good friends, and had often chatted together in the long, sunny days of summer. But the tortoise was cross today. 'Do be quiet,' he said to the robin; 'you sing so loud you make my head ache; and what there is to sing about I don't know, now that summer has gone!'

He had been busy all the morning at something the robin could not understand at all – digging and scratching with his little paws among some dry leaves that lay in a sunny corner, under a high old brick wall. The ground was soft there, and the tortoise had made quite a hole and had crawled in and out again several times. He seemed to want to sleep there. The robin could not think why; always before, the tortoise had pulled his head into his shell and slept soundly just where he was, whenever he needed a nap. But today he never seemed to think of doing that; and as the robin watched with his little bright black eye and listened with his little brown head on one side, he heard the old tortoise talking to himself, as he scratched so busily, about something strange called 'winter'. 'Winter is coming,' said the tortoise, 'cold, cold winter. I must hurry – hurry – hurry!' And you know – and even the robin knew – it takes a great deal to make a tortoise think about hurrying!

'What is *winter*?' said the robin, when the tortoise stopped digging for a minute.

'Don't interrupt me with foolish questions,' said the tortoise. 'You can see for yourself: the fruits and flowers are gone, the leaves are getting tough and dry, there is not a dandelion fit to eat, and the days are getting colder and colder, and damper and damper. There is nothing to sing so loud about, I can tell you!'

'But I am so happy,' said the robin, 'and when I am happy I can't help singing. Look at the sunshine; feel how warm it is, under this old wall. I have plenty to eat, and friends all round me.' Just to think of it made the robin so happy that he flew to the branch of an old apple tree and sang his song all over again, looking like a little red apple himself among the withering leaves.

'Wait and see,' said the tortoise grumpily; 'wait till you wake up one morning and find the ground frozen hard and not a worm to be got. What will you sing about *then*?'

'I don't know,' said the robin; 'I don't know, friend tortoise; but as you say, I will wait and see, and meantime – meantime – meantime –' And the robin was so afraid that he was going to vex the tortoise by singing again that he flew away and sang to the great bushes of Michaelmas daisies, where the bees were still humming in the sunshine.

When he came back, the tortoise was better tempered. He had

finished his digging; there was a snug hole in the soft, dry earth, under the old brick wall. He was feeling so pleased and comfortable (and I think he was sorry he had been cross) that he actually invited the robin to share a corner. 'Come in with me, little friend, and sleep till spring comes – with beautiful juicy green leaves and warm sunny days that grow longer and longer. Only you must promise not to sing, for I cannot be disturbed in my sleep,' said the tortoise.

The robin's black eye twinkled, and he hopped closer to look at the beautiful hole. 'It is very kind of you,' he said politely, 'but I think perhaps I sleep best with my head under my wing, tucked away in the ivy, or in the crook of a bough.'

'Very well – very well,' said the tortoise kindly, 'only take good care of yourself, little friend, and be sure you come and sing to me when I wake up in the spring: that is to say' (he said, with a sad sigh) 'if you do not die of cold and hunger in the winter – dearie me, dearie me!' And he crawled into his hole under the warm, dry leaves, and was soon fast asleep.

The robin missed the tortoise a good deal after that, and certainly the days did get shorter and the nights longer – and both grew colder and colder. Sometimes the sun hardly shone all day; the other birds were very quiet, some of them had gone quite away; there were very few insects to be found, but there were still berries to eat and warm corners in the ivy, and the robin still sang. The berries were so good and the ivy shelter was so cosy; the robin perched on the bare bough of the apple tree and sang his little song, and then flew to where the gardener was digging, and sang it over again. He was so warm and happy, he felt he *had* to sing!

But one morning – it was a little time before Christmas – he woke up and found everything very strange. It seemed dark, and the air was full of something falling, softly without a sound, and something cold and white lay on the ivy leaves. The robin wondered if the tortoise had been right after all, and he cuddled down rather unhappily in his shelter and thought how dreadful it would be if there was never anything to eat any more. Then he went to sleep again, and when he woke it was still very cold; all the garden was white, but the sun was shining; and everything was sparkling. The robin was so glad to see the sun again that he forgot how hungry he was. 'Pr-r-r-t, Pr-r-r-t,' he said, and he flapped his wings and fluffed his feathers to get rid of the snowflakes; and flying on to the old apple tree, he sang his very sweetest that cold, December morning.

Then he flew away to look for food, and just on the edge of a little fir plantation he found a holly tree all covered with bright red berries. He could see them plainly, quite a long way off, against the white snow, and so could a great many other birds. But there were plenty for all, and when he had breakfasted the robin flew to the warm shelter of the fir trees and sang, and then flew back for just another berry or two, and sang once more!

It was very cold – terribly cold – for the next few days; the snow lay thick and the frost held fast. So many birds feasted at the holly tree that some branches were quite bare; and then came such a storm that for a whole night and day and another night the robin could not even put his little brown head out of his ivy shelter. Then the snow stopped and the robin peeped out and shook himself, unfolded his little wings, and flew straight to the holly tree. It was covered with snow, and the robin thought it looked smaller; there was not a sign of a red berry to be seen!

Poor little robin! He hopped anxiously from twig to twig, peeping under the leaves, but there was nothing to be found but cold, white snow and prickly, dark green leaves; and he was so *very* hungry. But on the snow, below the tree, he found one berry – just one. 'Better one than none,' said the robin, and he actually sang a note or two, he was so pleased. There were footmarks in the snow, and in one of them lay another red berry, and further on, two more. The robin hopped along, picking them up; the footmarks led to a large house, and that was the end of the berries. 'Well, I have had some breakfast,' said the robin, 'and breakfast is good.' And he flew on to a rose bush and tidied his feathers and sang – and tidied them some more, and sang again.

Somebody came to a window of the big house and peeped out.

'Oh, look, children!' she said, 'there is a robin, and we have taken all his holly berries for our Christmas decorations. How kind of him to sing! We must give him some crumbs instead for a Christmas feast.' And while the robin watched with his bright eyes, the window was pushed open, the window-ledge cleared of snow, and something sprinkled on it that smelt different from anything the robin knew, but very good indeed. Perhaps another day he might have been shy, but four berries are not much after two nights and a day with nothing to eat, and the robin was too hungry to be afraid! He flew down on to the window-ledge and pecked at what was scattered there; it tasted very good indeed, and he pecked again. 'Crumbs *are* good,' said the robin, and he pecked till his little red waistcoat was quite puffed out, and then flew to the rose bush and sang, and came back and pecked again. Then he flew away, and sat on the branch of the old apple tree, near the tortoise's little hole, and sang very loud indeed to tell the tortoise all about it, just in case he could wake up and listen, on that Christmas morning.

Next day he went back to the window-ledge, and there were more crumbs; and the day after, and the day after that. There were no more hungry days for the robin; and every evening he would go and sing on the apple tree of the wonderful things that were happening – of the crumbs, and the children who scattered them, and the warm little shelter all lined with wool that they had made for him to sleep in, on cold, snowy nights. January came with frost and cold, February with sleet and rain, March with sunshine and stormy winds. The robin sang happily and thankfully through all. And one fine spring day, when the grass was long and green, with beautiful juicy green dandelions growing among it, and the sun was warm and the apple tree was in blossom, the old tortoise really did crawl out of his hole; and there sat the robin – singing.

He sang all the louder when he saw the tortoise, and told him all the wonderful things that had happened that winter. But the tortoise wouldn't believe a word! 'I have been dreaming all manner of fine things myself,' he said, 'and no doubt you have had a nap and dreamed too. Everyone knows that winter is cold and dark, and there is nothing to eat. But I am glad to see you so well, little friend. I can see a very nice dandelion over there.' And he went away and ate it!

I am glad he found something to be pleased about, and he certainly had a snug winter. But I think I would rather be the robin than the tortoise, wouldn't you?

ELIZABETH CLARK

W

The King sent for his wise men all
  To find a rhyme for W;
When they had thought a good long time
But could not think of a single rhyme,
  'I'm sorry,' said he, 'to trouble you.'

JAMES REEVES

The Jumblies

I

They went to sea in a Sieve, they did,
   In a Sieve they went to sea:
In spite of all their friends could say,
On a winter's morn, on a stormy day,
   In a Sieve they went to sea!
And when the Sieve turned round and round,
And every one cried, 'You'll all be drowned!'
They called aloud, 'Our Sieve ain't big,
But we don't care a button! we don't care a fig!
   In a Sieve we'll go to sea!'
    Far and few, far and few,
      Are the lands where the Jumblies live;
      Their heads are green, and their hands are blue,
      And they went to sea in a Sieve.

2

They sailed away in a Sieve, they did,
In a Sieve they sailed so fast,
With only a beautiful pea-green veil
Tied with a riband by way of a sail,
To a small tobacco-pipe mast;
And every one said, who saw them go,
'O won't they be soon upset, you know!
For the sky is dark, and the voyage is long,
And happen what may, it's extremely wrong
In a Sieve to sail so fast!'
Far and few, far and few,
Are the lands where the Jumblies live;
Their heads are green, and their hands are blue,
And they went to sea in a Sieve.

3

The water soon came in, it did,
The water it soon came in;
So to keep them dry, they wrapped their feet
In a pinky paper all folded neat,
And they fastened it down with a pin.
And they passed the night in a crockery-jar,
And each of them said, 'How wise we are!
Though the sky be dark, and the voyage be long,
Yet we never can think we were rash or wrong,
While round in our Sieve we spin!'
Far and few, far and few,
Are the lands where the Jumblies live;
Their heads are green, and their hands are blue,
And they went to sea in a Sieve.

4

And all night long they sailed away;
   And when the sun went down,
They whistled and warbled a moony song
To the echoing sound of a coppery gong,
   In the shade of the mountains brown.
'O Timballo! How happy we are,
When we live in a sieve and a crockery-jar,
And all night long in the moonlight pale,
We sail away with a pea-green sail,
   In the shade of the mountains brown!'
     Far and few, far and few,
      Are the lands where the Jumblies live;
      Their heads are green, and their hands are blue,
      And they went to sea in a Sieve.

5

They sailed to the Western Sea, they did,
   To a land all covered with trees,
And they bought an Owl, and a useful Cart,
And a pound of Rice, and a Cranberry Tart,
   And a hive of silvery Bees.
And they bought a Pig, and some green Jack-daws,
And a lovely Monkey with lollipop paws,
And forty bottles of Ring-Bo-Ree,
   And no end of Stilton Cheese.
     Far and few, far and few,
      Are the lands where the Jumblies live;
      Their heads are green, and their hands are blue,
      And they went to sea in a Sieve.

6

And in twenty years they all came back,
    In twenty years or more,
And every one said, 'How tall they've grown!
For they've been to the Lakes, and the Terrible Zone,
    And the hills of the Chankly Bore';
And they drank their health, and gave them a feast
Of dumplings made of beautiful yeast;
And every one said, 'If we only live,
We too will go to sea in a Sieve, –
    To the hills of the Chankly Bore!'
        Far and few, far and few,
            Are the lands where the Jumblies live;
        Their heads are green, and their hands are blue,
            And they went to sea in a Sieve.

Written and illustrated by EDWARD LEAR

A Needle and Thread

Old Mother Twitchett had but one eye,
And a long tail which she let fly;
And every time she went over a gap,
She left a bit of her tail in a trap.

The Boy

Is it, I wonder, a rum thing,
    Or nothing to wonder upon,
That whenever a man's doing something
    There's always a boy looking on?

If he's mending a road or a motor,
    If he's loading a crane or a van,
If he's tinkering at an old boat or
    A boot, there's a boy near the man.

If he's climbing a tree or a steeple,
    Or shoeing a horse, to the joy
Of a number of on-looking people,
    You'll find at his elbow a boy.

If he's wrecking a house, if he's rubbing
    A window or building a wall,
Unmoving, unmoved, and past snubbing,
    There's a boy in the forefront of all.

If he's doing odd things with the drainpipes,
    If he's pouring hot tar on the street,
Or playing about with the main pipes,
    There's a boy almost under his feet.

He may stand for hours like a dumb thing,
    But this can be counted upon –
Wherever a man's doing something
    There's always a boy looking on.

ELEANOR FARJEON
Illustrated by HOLLY BOURNE

Can Men be Such Fools as All That?

I WAS nurse to the little Duke of Chinon, who lived in the great grim castle on the hill above the town where the Rag-picker's Son lived. The little Duke, of course, had everything that the poor boy hadn't: fine clothes to wear, white bread and chicken to eat, and a pedigree spaniel called Hubert for a play-fellow.

Except for all these differences, the two boys were as like as two peas; when I took the little Duke walking by the river, and we happened to meet the Rag-picker's Son, you could not have told one from the other, if one hadn't worn satin and the other rags, while one had a dirty face and hands and the other was as clean as a new pin. Everybody remarked on it.

The little Duke used to look longingly at the poor boy, though, for he was allowed to splash about in the water of the river as he pleased; and the water of the Loire is more beautiful to splash about in than any water in France, for it is as clear as honey, and has the brightest gold sand-bed you can imagine; and when you get out of the town, it runs between sandy shores, where green willows grow, and flowers of all sorts. But it was against my orders to let the little Duke play in the water, and I had to obey them, though I was sorry for him; for I knew what boys like.

One day as we were out walking, the Duke's spaniel Hubert ran up to the Rag-picker's Son's mongrel, Jacques, and they touched noses and made friends. And the Duke and the poor boy smiled at each other and said, 'Hullo!' After that, when we met, the boys always nodded, or winked, or made some sign of friendship; and one day the Rag-picker's Son jerked his thumb at the river, as much as to say, 'Come in and play with me!' The Duke looked at me, and I shook my head, so the Duke shook his. But he was cross with me for the rest of the day.

The next day I missed him, and there was a great hullabaloo all over the castle. I and his guardian and all his attendants went down to the town to find him, and asked everybody we met if they had seen him; and presently we met the Rag-picker, who said, 'Yes, I saw him an hour ago, going along the river-bank with my son.' And we all ran along the bank, the Rag-picker too, and most of the townsfolk behind us.

A mile along the bank, there they were, the two boys, standing in the middle of the river as bare as when they were born, splashing about and screaming with laughter; and on the shore lay a little heap of clothes, rags and fine linen all thrown down anyhow together. We were all very angry with the boys, and called and shouted to them to come out of the water; and they shouted back that they wouldn't. At last the Rag-picker waded in and fetched them out by the scruffs of their necks. And there they stood before

us, naked and grinning and full of fun, and just as the Duke's guardian was going to scold his charge, and the Rag-picker to scold his son, they suddenly found themselves in a pickle! For without their clothes, washed clean by the river, they were so exactly alike, that we didn't know which was which. And the boys saw that we didn't, and grinned more than ever.

'Now then, my boy!' said the Rag-picker to one of them. But the boy he spoke to did not answer, for he knew if he talked it would give the game away.

And the Duke's guardian said to the other boy, 'Come, monseigneur!' But that boy too shook his head and kept mum.

Then I had a bright idea, and said to the boys, 'Put on your clothes!' for I thought that would settle it. But the two boys picked up the clothes as they came: one of them put on the ragged shirt and the satin coat, and the other put on the fine shirt and the ragged coat. So we were no better off than before.

Then the Rag-picker and the Duke's guardian lost their

tempers, and raised their sticks and gave each of the boys three strokes, thinking that might help; but all it did was to make them squeal, and when a boy squeals it doesn't matter if he's a Duke or a beggar, the sound is just the same.

'This is dreadful,' said the Duke's guardian: 'for all we know,

we shall get the boys mixed for ever, and I shall take the Rag-picker's Son back to the castle, and the Duke will grow up as the Rag-picker's Son. Is there *no* way of telling which is which? Can we all be such fools as that?'

Just as we were scratching our heads and cudgelling our brains, and wondering what on earth to do next, there came a sound of yelps and barks; and out of the willows ran Jacques and Hubert, who had been off on their own, playing together. They came racing towards us joyously, and straight as a die Jacques jumped up and licked the face of the boy in the satin coat, while Hubert licked the boy in the ragged jacket.

So then there was no doubt about it. We made the boys change their coats, and the Rag-picker marched his son home to bed, and the guardian did the same with the Duke. And that night the Duke and the poor boy had exactly the same supper to go to sleep on; in other words, nothing and plenty of it.

But how had the dogs known in the twink of an eye what we hadn't known at all? Can men be such fools as all that?

ELEANOR FARJEON

The Statue

On a stone chair in the market-place
Sits a stone gentleman with a stone face.
He is great, he is good, he is old as old –
How many years I've not been told.
Great things he did a great while ago,
And what they were I do not know.
But solemn and sad is his great square face
As he sits high up on his square stone base.
Day after day he sits just so,
With some words in a foreign tongue below.
Whether the wind blows warm or cold,
His stone clothes alter never a fold.
One stone hand he rests on his knee;
With the other stone hand he points at me.
Oh, why does he look at me in just that way?
I'm afraid to go, and afraid to stay:
Stone gentleman, what have you got to say?

JAMES REEVES

Gather ye Rosebuds

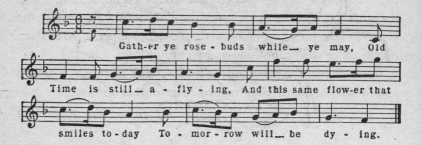

Gath-er ye rose - buds while ye may, Old Time is still a - fly - ing, And this same flow-er that smiles to - day To - mor - row will be dy - ing.

Gather ye rosebuds while ye may,
   Old Time is still a-flying,
And this same flower that smiles today
   Tomorrow will be dying.

The glorious lamp of Heaven, the Sun
   The higher he's a-getting;
The sooner will his race be run,
   And nearer he's to setting.

Then be not coy, but use your time,
   And while ye may, go marry;
For having lost but once your prime,
   You may for every tarry.

ROBERT HERRICK

Paul's Tale

'"Ho! Ho!" said the King, slapping his fat thighs. "Methinks this youth shows promise." But at that moment the Court Magician stepped forward . . . What is the matter, Paul? Don't you like this story?'

'Yes, I like it.'

'Then lie quiet, dear, and listen.'

'It was just a sort of stalk of a feather pushing itself up through the eiderdown.'

'Well, don't help it, dear, it's destructive. Where were we?' Aunt Isobel's short-sighted eyes searched down the page of the book: she looked comfortable and pink, rocking there in the firelight . . . *stepped forward* . . . *You see the Court Magician knew that the witch had taken the magic music-box, and that Colin* . . . Paul, you aren't listening!'

'Yes, I am. I can hear.'

'Of course you can't hear – right under the bed-clothes. What are you doing, dear?'

'I'm seeing what a hot water bottle feels like.'

'Don't you know what a hot water bottle feels like?'

'I know what it feels like to me. I don't know what it feels like to itself.'

'Well, shall I go on or not?'

'Yes, go on,' said Paul. He emerged from the bed-clothes, his hair ruffled.

Aunt Isobel looked at him curiously. He was her godson; he had a bad feverish cold; his mother had gone to London. 'Does it tire you, dear, to be read to?' she said at last.

'No. But I like told stories better than read stories.'

Aunt Isobel got up and put some more coal on the fire. Then she looked at the clock. She sighed. 'Well, dear,' she said brightly, as she sat down once more on the rocking-chair. 'What sort of story would you like?' She unfolded her knitting.

'I'd like a real story.'

'How do you mean, dear?' Aunt Isobel began to cast on. The cord of her pince-nez, anchored to her bosom, rose and fell in gentle undulations.

Paul flung round on his back, staring at the ceiling. 'You know,' he said, 'quite real – so you know it must have happened.'

'Shall I tell you about Grace Darling?'

'No, tell me about a little man.'

'What sort of a little man?'

'A little man just as high –' Paul's eyes searched the room – 'as that candlestick on the mantleshelf, but without the candle.'

'But that's a very small candlestick. It's only about six inches.'

'Well about that big.'

Aunt Isobel began knitting a few stitches. She was disappointed about the fairy story. She had been reading with so much expression, making a deep voice for the king, and a wicked oily voice for the Court Magician, and a fine cheerful boyish voice for Colin, the swineherd. A little man – what could she say about a

little man? 'Ah!' she exclaimed suddenly, and laid down her knitting, smiling at Paul. 'Little men ... of course ...

'Well,' said Aunt Isobel, drawing in her breath, 'Once upon a time, there was a little, tiny man, and he was no bigger than that candlestick – there on the mantleshelf.'

Paul settled down, his cheek on his crook'd arm, his eyes on Aunt Isobel's face. The firelight flickered softly on the walls and ceiling.

'He was the sweetest little man you ever saw, and he wore a little red jerkin and a dear little cap made out of a foxglove. His boots ...'

'He didn't have any,' said Paul.

Aunt Isobel looked startled. 'Yes,' she exclaimed. 'He had boots – little, pointed –'

'He didn't have any clothes,' contradicted Paul. 'He was bare.'

Aunt Isobel looked perturbed. 'But he would have been cold,' she pointed out.

'He had thick skin,' explained Paul. 'Like a twig.'

'Like a twig?'

'Yes. You know that sort of wrinkly, nubbly skin on a twig.'

Aunt Isobel knitted in silence for a second or two. She didn't like the little naked man nearly as much as the little clothed man: she was trying to get used to him. After a while she went on.

'He lived in a bluebell wood, among the roots of a dear old tree. He had a dear little house, tunnelled out of the soft, loamy earth, with a bright blue front door.'

'Why didn't he live in it?' asked Paul.

'He did live in it, dear,' explained Aunt Isobel patiently.

'I thought he lived in the potting-shed.'

'In the potting-shed?'

'Well, perhaps he had two houses. Some people do. I wish I'd seen the one with the blue front door.'

'Did you see the one in the potting-shed?' asked Aunt Isobel, after a moment's silence.

'Not inside. Right inside. I'm too big. I just sort of saw into it with a flashlight.'

'And what was it like?' asked Aunt Isobel, in spite of herself.

'Well, it was clean – in a potting-shed sort of way. He'd made the furniture himself. The floor was just earth but he'd trodden it down so that it was hard. It took him years.'

'Well, dear, you seem to know more about this little man than I do.'

212

Paul snuggled his head more comfortably against his elbow. He half-closed his eyes. 'Go on,' he said dreamily.

Aunt Isobel glanced at him hesitatingly. How beautiful he looked, she thought, lying there in the firelight with one curled hand lying lightly on the counterpane. 'Well,' she went on, 'this little man had a little pipe made of a straw.' She paused, rather pleased with this idea. 'A little hollow straw, through which he played jiggity little tunes. And to which he danced.' She hesitated. 'Among the bluebells,' she added. Really this was quite a pretty story. She knitted hard for a few seconds, breathing heavily, before the next bit would come. 'Now,' she continued brightly, in a changed, higher and more conversational voice, 'up in the tree, there lived a fairy.'

'In the tree?' asked Paul, incredulously.

'Yes,' said Aunt Isobel, 'in the tree.'

Paul raised his head. 'Do you know that for certain?'

'Well, Paul,' began Aunt Isobel. Then she added playfully, 'Well, I suppose I do.'

'Go on,' said Paul.

'Well, this fairy . . .'

Pauled raised his head again. 'Couldn't you go on about the little man?'

'But, dear, we've done the little man – how he lived in the roots, and played a pipe, and all that.'

'You didn't say about his hands and feet.'

'His hands and feet!'

'How sort of big his hands and feet looked, and how he could scuttle along. Like a rat,' Paul added.

'Like a rat!' exclaimed Aunt Isobel.

'And his voice. You didn't say anything about his voice.'

'What sort of a voice,' Aunt Isobel looked almost scared, 'did he have?'

'A croaky sort of voice. Like a frog. And he says, "Will 'ee" and "Do 'ee".'

'Willy and Dooey . . .' repeated Aunt Isobel.

'Instead of "Will you" and "Do you". You know.'

'Has he – got a Sussex accent?'

'Sort of. He isn't used to talking. He is the last one. He's been all alone, for years and years.'

'Did he –' Aunt Isobel swallowed. 'Did he tell you that?'

'Yes. He had an aunt and she died about fifteen years ago. But even when she was alive, he never spoke to her.'

'Why?' asked Aunt Isobel.

'He didn't like her,' said Paul.

There was silence. Paul stared dreamily into the fire. Aunt Isobel sat as if turned to stone, her hands idle in her lap. After a while, she cleared her throat.

'When did you first see this little man, Paul?'

'Oh, ages and ages ago. When did you?'

'I – Where did you find him?'

'Under the chicken house.'

'Did you – did you just speak to him?'

Paul made a little snort. 'No. I just popped a tin over him.'

'You caught him!'

'Yes. There was an old, rusty chicken-food tin near. I just popped it over him.' Paul laughed. 'He scrabbled away inside. Then I popped an old kitchen plate that was there on top of the tin.'

Aunt Isobel sat staring at Paul. 'What – what did you do with him then?'

'I put him in a cake-tin, and made holes in the lid. I gave him a bit of bread and milk.'

'Didn't he – say anything?'

'Well, he was sort of croaking.'

'And then?'

'Well, I sort of forgot I had him.'

'You forgot!'

'I went fishing, you see. Then it was bedtime. And next day I didn't remember him. Then when I went to look for him, he was lying curled up at the bottom of the tin. He'd gone all soft. He just hung over my finger. All soft.'

Aunt Isobel's eyes protruded dully.

'What did you do then?'

'I gave him some cherry cordial in a fountain pen filler.'

'That revived him?'

'Yes, that's when he began to talk. And he told me all about his aunt and everything. I harnessed him up, then, with a bit of string.'

'Oh, Paul,' exclaimed Aunt Isobel, 'how cruel.'

'Well, he'd have got away. It didn't hurt him. Then I tamed him.'

'How did you tame him?'

'Oh, how you tame anything. With food mostly. Chips of gelatine and raw sago he liked best. Cheese, he liked. I'd take him out and let him go down rabbit holes and things, on the string. Then he would come back and tell me what was going on. I put him down all kinds of holes in trees and things.'

'Whatever for?'

'Just to know what was going on. I have all kinds of uses for him.'

'Why,' stammered Aunt Isobel, half-rising from her chair, 'you haven't still got him, have you?'

Paul sat up on his elbows. 'Yes. I've got him. I'm going to keep him till I go to school. I'll need him at school like anything.'

'But it isn't – You wouldn't be allowed –' Aunt Isobel suddenly became extremely grave. 'Where is he now?'

'In the cake-tin.'

'Where is the cake-tin?'

'Over there. In the toy cupboard.'

Aunt Isobel looked fearfully across the shadowed room. She stood up. 'I am going to put the light on, and I shall take that cake-tin out into the garden.'

'It's raining,' Paul reminded her.

'I can't help that,' said Aunt Isobel. 'It is wrong and wicked to keep a little thing like that, shut up in a cake-tin. I shall take it out on to the back porch and open the lid.'

'He can hear you,' said Paul.

'I don't care if he can hear me.' Aunt Isobel walked towards the door. 'I'm thinking of his good, as much as of anyone else's.' She switched on the light. 'Now, which was the cupboard?'

'That one, near the fireplace.'

The door was ajar. Timidly Aunt Isobel pulled it open with one finger. There stood the cake-tin amid a medley of torn cardboard, playing cards, pieces of jig-saw puzzle and an open paint box.

'What a mess, Paul!'

Nervously Aunt Isobel stared at the cake-tin and, falsely innocent, the British Royal Family stared back at her, painted brightly on a background of Allied flags. The holes in the lid were narrow and wedge-shaped made, no doubt, by the big blade of the best cutting-out scissors. Aunt Isobel drew in her breath sharply. 'If you weren't ill, I'd make you do this. I'd make you carry the tin out and watch you open the lid –' She hesitated as if unnerved by the stillness of the rain-darkened room and the sinister quiet within the cake-tin.

Then, bravely, she put out a hand. Paul watched her, absorbed, as she stretched forward the other one and, very gingerly, picked up the cake-tin. His eyes were dark and deep. He saw the lid was not quite on. He saw the corner, in contact with that ample bosom, rise. He saw the sharp edge catch the cord of Aunt Isobel's pince-nez and, fearing for her rimless glasses, he sat up in bed.

Aunt Isobel felt the tension, the pressure of the pince-nez on the bridge of her nose. A pull it was, a little steady pull as if a small dark claw, as wrinkled as a twig, had caught the hanging cord . . .

'Look out!' cried Paul.

Loudly she shrieked and dropped the box. It bounced away and then lay still, gaping emptily on its side. In the horrid hush, they heard the measured planking of the lid as it trundled off beneath the bed.

Paul broke the silence with a croupy cough.

'Did you see him?' he asked, hoarse but interested.

'No,' stammered Aunt Isobel, almost with a sob. 'I didn't. I didn't see him.'

'But you nearly did.'

Aunt Isobel sat down limply in the upholstered chair. Her hand wavered vaguely round her brow and her cheeks looked white and pendulous, as if deflated. 'Yes,' she muttered, shivering slightly, 'Heaven help me – I nearly did.'

Paul gazed at her a moment longer. 'That's what I mean,' he said.

'What?' asked Aunt Isobel weakly but as if she did not really care.

Paul lay down again. Gently, sleepily, he pressed his face into the pillow.

'About stories. Being real . . .'

MARY NORTON
Illustrated by GERALDINE SPENCE

A Cherry

As I went through the garden gap,
Who should I meet but Dick Red-cap!
A stick in his hand, a stone in his throat.
If you'll tell me this riddle, I'll give you a groat.

Elizabeth

Elizabeth, Elspeth, Betty and Bess,
They all went together to seek a bird's nest.
They found a nest with four eggs in it,
They all took one and left three in it!

Cripple Creek

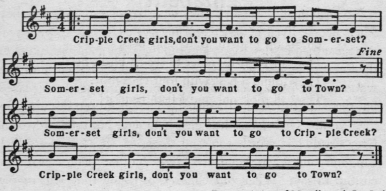

Crip-ple Creek girls, don't you want to go to Som-er-set?

Fine

Som-er-set girls, don't you want to go to Town?

Som-er-set girls, don't you want to go to Crip-ple Creek?

Crip-ple Creek girls, don't you want to go to Town?

By permission of Novello and Co. Ltd

Cripple Creek girls, don't you want to go to Somerset?
Somerset girls, don't you want to go to Town?
Somerset girls, don't you want to go to Cripple Creek?
Cripple Creek girls, don't you want to go to Town?

Collected and arranged by CECIL J. SHARP
Decoration by JOAN MILROY

Lady Greensleeves

I

ONCE upon a time there lived two noble lords in the east country. Their lands lay between a broad river and an old oak forest. In the midst of his land each lord had a stately castle; one was built of white freestone, the other of grey granite. So the one was called Lord of the White Castle, and the other Lord of the Grey.

No lords in all the east country were so noble and kind as they. Their people lived in peace and plenty; all strangers were well treated at their castles. Every autumn they sent men with axes into the forest to hew down the great trees, and chop them into firewood for the poor. Neither hedge nor ditch divided their lands, but these lords never had a quarrel. They had been friends from their youth. Their ladies had died long ago, but the Lord of the Grey Castle had a little son, and the Lord of the White a little daughter; and when they feasted in each other's halls it was their custom to say, 'When our children grow up they will marry, and have our castles and our lands, and keep our friendship in memory.'

So the lords and their little children, and their people, lived happily till one Michaelmas night, as they were all feasting in the hall of the White Castle, there came a traveller to the gate, who was welcomed and feasted as usual. He had seen many strange sights and countries, and he liked to tell of his travels. The lords were delighted with his tales, as they sat round the fire after supper, and at length the Lord of the White Castle, who was always very eager to know all he could about new countries, said:

'Good stranger, what was the greatest wonder you ever saw in all your travels?'

'The most wonderful sight that ever I saw,' replied the traveller, 'was at the end of yonder forest, where in an old wooden house there sits an old woman weaving her own hair into grey cloth on an old worn-out loom. When she wants more yarn she cuts off her own grey hair, and it grows so quickly that though I saw it cut in the morning, it was out of the door before noon. She told me she wished to sell the cloth, but none of all who came that way had yet bought any, she asked so great a price. And, if the way were not so long and dangerous through that wide forest, which is full of bears and wolves, some rich lord like you might buy it for a cloak.'

All who heard this story were greatly surprised; but when the traveller had gone on his way, the Lord of the White Castle could neither eat nor sleep for wishing to see the old woman that wove her own hair. At length he made up his mind to go through the forest in search of her old house, and told the Lord of the Grey Castle what he had made up his mind to do. Being a wise man, this lord replied that travellers' tales were not always to be trusted, and tried to advise him against undertaking such a long and dangerous journey, for few who went far into that forest ever returned.

However, when the curious lord would go in spite of all he said, he vowed to go with him for friendship's sake, and they agreed to set out without letting anyone know, lest the other lords of the land might laugh at them. The Lord of the White Castle had a steward who had served him many years, and his name was Reckoning Robin. To him he said:

'I am going on a journey with my friend. Be careful of my goods, deal justly with my people, and above all things be kind to my little daughter Loveleaves till my return.'

The steward answered: 'Be sure, my lord, I will.'

The Lord of the Grey Castle also had a steward who had served him many years, and his name was Wary Will. To him he said:

'I am going on a journey with my friend. Be careful of my goods, deal justly with my people, and above all be kind to my little son Woodwender till my return.'

His steward answered him: 'Be sure, my lord, I will.'

So these lords kissed their children while they slept, and set out each with his staff and cloak before sunrise through the old oak forest.

The children missed their fathers, and the people missed their lords. None but the stewards could tell what had become of them; but seven months wore away, and they did not come back. The lords had thought their stewards faithful, because they served so well under their eyes; but instead of that, both were proud and cunning, and thinking that some evil had happened to their masters, they set themselves to be lords in their places.

Reckoning Robin had a son called Hardhold, and Wary Will a daughter named Drypenny. There was not a sulkier girl or boy in the country, but their fathers made up their minds to make a young lord and a young lady of them; so they took the silk clothes which Woodwender and Loveleaves used to wear, to dress them, putting on the lords' children their coarse clothes. Their toys were given to Hardhold and Drypenny; and at last the stewards' children sat at the chief tables, and slept in the best rooms, while Woodwender and Loveleaves were sent to herd the swine, and sleep on straw in the granary. The poor children had no one to take their part. Every morning at sunrise they were sent out – each with a barley loaf and a bottle of sour milk, which was to serve them for breakfast, dinner, and supper – to watch a great herd of swine on a wide field near the forest. The grass was scanty, and the swine were always straying into the wood in search of acorns. The children knew that if they were lost the wicked stewards would punish them; and between gathering and keeping their herds in order, they were readier to sleep on the granary straw at night than ever they had been within their own silken curtains.

Still, Woodwender and Loveleaves were a great help and comfort to each other, saying their fathers would come back or God would send them some friends. So, in spite of swine-herding and hard living, they looked as cheerful and handsome as ever; while Hardhold and Drypenny grew crosser and uglier every day, notwithstanding their fine clothes.

The false stewards did not like this. They thought their children ought to look genteel, and Woodwender and Loveleaves like young swineherds. So they sent them to a wilder field, still nearer the forest, and gave them two great black hogs, more unruly than all the rest, to keep. One of these hogs belonged to Hardhold and the other to Drypenny. Every evening when they came home the stewards' children used to come down and feed them, and it was their delight to reckon up what price they would bring when properly fattened.

2

One very hot day, about midsummer, Woodwender and Loveleaves sat down in the shadow of a mossy rock. The swine grazed about them more quietly than usual; and the children plaited rushes and talked to each other, till, as the sun was sloping down the sky, Woodwender saw that the two great hogs were missing.

Thinking they must have gone to the forest, the children ran to search for them. They heard the thrush singing and the wooddoves calling; they saw the squirrels leaping from branch to branch, and the deer bounding by. But though they searched for hours, no trace of the hogs could be seen.

Loveleaves and Woodwender dared not go home without them. Deeper and deeper they ran into the forest, searching and calling, but all in vain. And when the woods began to darken with the fall of evening, the children feared they had lost their way.

It was known that they never feared the forest, nor all the boars and wolves that were in it. But being weary, they wished for some place of shelter, and took a green path through the trees, thinking it might lead to the dwelling of some hermit or forester.

A fairer way Woodwender and Loveleaves had never walked. The grass was soft and mossy, a hedge of wild roses and honey-suckle grew on either side, and the red light of the sunset streamed through the tall trees above. On they went, and it led them straight to a great open dell, bordered with banks of wild strawberries, and all overshadowed by a huge oak, the like of which had never been seen in grove or forest. Its branches were as large as full-grown trees. Its trunk was wider than a country church, and its height like that of a castle.

There were mossy seats at its great root, and when the tired children had gathered as many strawberries as they cared for, they sat down on one, close by a small spring that bubbled up as clear as crystal. The mighty oak was covered with thick ivy, in which thousands of birds had their nests. Woodwender and Loveleaves watched them flying home from all parts of the forest, and at last they saw a lady coming by the same path which led them to the dell. She wore a red gown; her yellow hair was braided and bound with a red band. In her right hand she carried a holly branch; but the strangest part of her dress was a pair of long sleeves, as green as the very grass.

'Who are you,' she said, 'that sit so late beside my well?'

And the children told her their story, how they had first lost the hogs, and then their way, and were afraid to go home to the wicked stewards.

'Well,' said the lady, 'you are the fairest swineherds that ever came this way. Choose whether you will go home and keep hogs for Hardhold and Drypenny, or live in the free forest with me.'

'We will stay with you,' said the children, 'for we do not like keeping swine. Besides, our fathers went through this forest, and we may meet them some day coming home.'

While they spoke, the lady slipped her holly branch through the ivy, as if it had been a key – soon a door opened in the oak, and there was a fairy house. The windows were of rock crystal, but they could not be seen from without. The walls and floors were covered with thick green moss, as soft as velvet. There were low seats and a round table, vessels of carved wood, a hearth inlaid with strange stones, an oven, and a storeroom of food against the winter.

When they stepped in, the lady said: 'A hundred years have I lived here, and my name is Lady Greensleeves. No friend or servant have I except my dwarf Corner, who comes to me at the end of harvest with his handmill, his basket, and his axe. With these he grinds the nuts, and gathers the berries, and splits the firewood; and cheerily we live all the winter. But Corner loves the frost and fears the sun; and when the topmost branches begin to bud, he returns to his country far in the north, so I am lonely in the summertime.'

By these words the children saw how welcome they were. Lady Greensleeves gave them deer's milk and cakes of nut-flour, and soft green moss to sleep on. And they forgot all their troubles, the wicked stewards, and the straying swine.

Early in the morning a troop of does came to be milked, fairies brought flowers, and birds brought berries, to show Lady Greensleeves what had bloomed and ripened. She taught the children to make cheese of the does' milk, and wine of the wood berries. She

showed them the stores of honey which wild bees had made and left in the hollow trees, the rarest plants of the forest, and the herbs that made all the creatures tame.

All that summer Woodwender and Loveleaves lived with her in the greak oak tree, free from toil and care. The children would have been happy, but they could hear no news of their fathers. At last the leaves began to fade, and the flowers to fall. Lady Greensleeves said that Corner was coming. One moonlight night she heaped sticks on the fire, and set her door open, when Woodwender and Loveleaves were going to sleep, saying she expected some friends to tell her the news of the forest.

Loveleaves was not quite so curious as her father, the Lord of the White Castle, but she kept awake to see what would happen, and very much afraid the little girl was when in walked a great brown bear.

'Good evening, lady!' said the bear.

'Good evening, bear!' said Lady Greensleeves. 'What is the news in your part of the forest?'

'Not much,' said the bear; 'only the fawns are growing very cunning – one can't catch above three in a day.'

'That's bad news,' said Lady Greensleeves; and at once in walked a great wild cat.

'Good evening, lady!' said the cat.

'Good evening, cat!' said Lady Greensleeves. 'What is the news in your part of the forest?'

'Not much,' said the cat; 'only the birds are growing very plentiful – it is not worth one's while to catch them.'

'That's good news,' said Lady Greensleeves; and in flew a great black raven.

'Good evening, lady!' said the raven.

'Good evening, raven!' said Lady Greensleeves. 'What is the news in your part of the forest?'

'Not much,' said the raven; 'only in a hundred years or so we shall be very genteel and private, the trees will be so thick.'

'How is that?' said Lady Greensleeves.

'Oh!' said the raven, 'have you not heard how the king of the forest fairies laid a spell on two lords, who were travelling through his kingdom to see the old woman that weaves her own hair? They had thinned his oaks every year, cutting firewood for the poor. So the king met them in the likeness of a hunter, and asked them to drink out of his oaken goblet, because the day was warm. When the two lords drank, they forgot their lands and their people, their castles and their children, and minded nothing in all the world but the planting of acorns which they do day and night, by the power of the spell, in the heart of the forest. They will never stop till someone makes them pause in their work before the sun sets, and then the spell will be broken.'

'Ah!' said Lady Greensleeves, 'he is a great prince, that king of the forest fairies; and there is worse work in the world than planting acorns.'

Soon after, the bear, the cat and the raven bade Lady Greensleeves good night. She closed the door, put out the light, and went to sleep on the soft moss as usual.

In the morning Loveleaves told Woodwender what she had heard, and they went to Lady Greensleeves where she milked the does, and said:

'We heard what the raven told you last night, and we know the two lords are our fathers. Tell us how the spell may be broken.'

'I fear the king of the forest fairies,' said Lady Greensleeves, 'because I live here alone, and have no friend but my dwarf Corner. But I will tell you what you may do. At the end of the path which leads from this dell turn your faces to the north, and you will find a narrow way sprinkled over with black feathers. Keep to that path, no matter how it winds, and it will lead you straight to that part of the forest in which the ravens dwell. There you will find your fathers planting acorns under the forest trees. Watch till the sun is near setting, and tell them the most wonderful things you know to make them forget their work. But be sure to tell nothing but truth, and drink nothing but running water, or you will fall into the power of the fairy king.'

The children thanked her for this good advice. She packed up cakes and cheese for them in a bag of woven grass, and they soon found the narrow way sprinkled over with black feathers. It was very long, and wound through the thick trees in so many circles that the children were often weary, and sat down to rest. When the night came, they found a mossy hollow in the trunk of an old tree, where they laid themselves down, and slept all the summer night – for Woodwender and Loveleaves never feared the forest.

3

So they went, eating their cakes and cheese when they were hungry, drinking from the running stream, and sleeping in the hollow trees, till on the evening of the seventh day they came into that part of the forest where the ravens lived. The tall trees were laden with nests and black with ravens. There was nothing to be heard but cawing.

In a great opening where the oaks grew thinnest, the children saw their own fathers busy planting acorns. Each lord had on the velvet cloak in which he left his castle, but it was worn to rags with rough work in the forest. Their hair and beards had grown long; their hands were soiled with earth; each had an old wooden spade, and on all sides lay heaps of acorns.

The children called their names, and ran to kiss them, each saying: 'Dear father, come back to your castle and your people.'

But the lords replied: 'We know of no castles and no people. There is nothing in all this world but oak leaves and acorns.'

Woodwender and Loveleaves told them of all their former state in vain. Nothing would make them pause for a minute. So the poor children first sat down and cried, and then slept on the cold grass, for the sun set, and the lords worked on.

When they awoke it was broad day. Woodwender cheered up Loveleaves, saying: 'We are hungry, and there are two cakes in the bag, let us share one of them – who knows but something may happen.'

So they divided the cake, and ran to the lords, saying: 'Dear fathers, eat with us.'

But the lords said: 'There is no use for meat or drink. Let us plant our acorns.'

Loveleaves and Woodwender sat down, and ate that cake in great sorrow. When they had finished, both went to a stream that ran close by, and began to drink the clear water with a large acorn shell. And as they drank there came through the oaks a gay young hunter; his mantle was green as the grass, about his neck there hung a crystal bugle, and in his hand he carried a huge oaken goblet, carved with flowers and leaves, and rimmed with crystal.

Up to the brim the cup was filled with milk, on which the rich cream floated. And as the hunter came near, he said: 'Fair children, leave that muddy water, and come and drink with me.'

But Woodwender and Loveleaves answered: 'Thanks, good hunter, but we have promised to drink nothing but running water.'

Still the hunter came nearer with his goblet, saying: 'The water is dirty; it may do for swineherds and woodcutters, but not for such fair children as you. Tell me, are you not the children of mighty kings? Were you not brought up in palaces?'

But the boy and girl answered him: 'No: we were brought up

in castles, and are the children of yonder lords. Tell us how the spell that is upon them may be broken.'

At once the hunter turned from them with an angry look, poured out the milk upon the ground, and went away with his empty goblet.

Loveleaves and Woodwender were sorry to see the rich cream spilled, but they remembered the warning of Lady Greensleeves; and seeing they could do no better, each got a withered branch and began to help the lords, scratching up the ground with the sharp end, and planting acorns. But their fathers took no notice of them, nor of all that they could say. When the sun grew warm at noon, they went again to drink at the running stream.

Then through the oaks came another hunter, older than the first, and clothed in yellow. About his neck there hung a silver bugle, and in his hand he carried an oaken goblet, carved with leaves and fruit, rimmed with silver, and filled with mead to the brim. This hunter also asked them to drink, told them the stream was full of frogs, and asked them if they were not a young prince and princess dwelling in the woods for their pleasure.

But when Woodwender and Loveleaves answered as before: 'We have promised to drink only running water, and are the children of yonder lords; tell us how the spell may be broken,' he turned from them with an angry look, poured out the mead, and went his way.

All that afternoon the children worked beside their fathers, planting acorns with the withered branches. But the lords would mind neither them nor their words. And when the evening drew near they were very hungry. So the children divided their last cake; and since they could not make the lords eat with them, they went to the banks of the stream, and began to eat and drink, though their hearts were very heavy.

The sun was getting low, and the ravens were coming home to

their nests in the high trees. But one, that seemed old and weary, alighted near them to drink at the stream. As they ate, the raven lingered, and picked up the small crumbs that fell.

'Brother,' said Loveleaves, 'this raven is surely hungry. Let us give it a little bit, though it is our last cake.'

Woodwender agreed, and each gave a bit to the raven. But its great bill finished the morsels in a moment, and hopping nearer, it looked them in the face by turns.

'The poor raven is still hungry,' said Woodwender, and he gave it another bit. When that was gobbled, it came to Loveleaves, who gave it a bit too, and so on till the raven had eaten the whole of their last cake.

'Well,' said Woodwender, 'at least we can have a drink.'

But as they stooped to the water, there came through the oaks another hunter, older than the last, and clothed in scarlet. About his neck there hung a golden bugle, and in his hand he carried a huge oaken goblet, carved with ears of corn and clusters of grapes, rimmed with gold, and filled to the brim with wine.

He also said: 'Leave this muddy water, and drink with me. It is full of toads, and not fit for such fair children. Surely you are from fairyland, and were brought up in its queen's palace!'

But the children said: 'We will drink nothing but this water, and yonder lords are our fathers. Tell us how the spell may be broken.'

And the hunter turned from them with an angry look, poured out the wine on the grass, and went his way.

When he was gone, the old raven looked up into their faces, and said: 'I have eaten your last cake, and I will tell you how the spell may be broken. Yonder is the sun, going down behind the western trees. Before it sets, go to the lords, and tell them how their stewards used you, and made you herd hogs for Hardhold and Drypenny. When you see them listening, catch up their wooden spades, and keep them if you can, till the sun goes down.'

Woodwender and Loveleaves thanked the raven, and where it flew they never stopped to see, but running to the lords began to tell as they were bidden. At first the lords would not listen; but as the children told how they had been made to sleep on straw, how they had been sent to herd hogs in the wild pasture, and what trouble they had with the unruly swine, the acorn planting grew slower, and at last the lords dropped their spades.

Then Woodwender, catching up his father's spade, ran to the stream and threw it in. Loveleaves did the same for the Lord of the White Castle. That moment the sun went down behind the western oaks, and the lords stood up, looking, like men just awakened, on the forest, on the sky, and on their children.

So this strange story has ended, for Woodwender and Love-leaves went home rejoicing with their fathers. Each lord returned to his castle, and all their people were merry. The fine toys and the silk clothes, the flower gardens and the best rooms, were taken from Hardhold and Drypenny, and the lords' children got them again. And the wicked stewards, with their cross boy and girl, were sent to herd swine, and live in huts in the wild pasture, which everybody said became them better.

The Lord of the White Castle never again wished to see the old woman that wove her own hair, and the Lord of the Grey Castle continued to be his friend. As for Woodwender and Loveleaves, they met with no more misfortunes, but grew up, and were married, and got the two castles and broad lands of their fathers. Nor did they forget the lonely Lady Greensleeves, for it was known in the east country that she and her dwarf Corner always came to feast with them in the Christmas time, and at midsummer they always went to live with her in the great oak in the forest.

FRANCES BROWNE

A Hole in Your Stocking

ONCE there was a beetle who loved another beetle. Oh, dear me! How he did love her!

So he went to her house to ask her to marry him. He knocked on the door. Bang, Bang! 'May I come in?'

'Oh, dear me, no! I am busy resting this fine afternoon.' And he looked up and, sure enough, the window curtains were tight drawn.

'But listen to me,' he said. 'I have come to ask you to marry me. Open the door so that I can do it properly.'

'Why ever should I marry you?' she asked. But she drew the curtains aside a little to take a good look at him.

'Why should you marry me?' he said. 'Well, there are reasons enough. I am quite the most handsome beetle in all the parish. My

236

fine black armour is smooth and shiny. I hold my pincers bravely. My legs are elegant and my eyes are bright. You will never meet a beetle more beautiful than I.'

'Listen to him,' she said. 'Just listen to him! All he can think of is his own beauty! If he thinks himself so fine he won't think the more of me!'

And she shouted through the door:

'Go away, now, do. I am beginning to feel sleepy.'

But still he knocked and still he cried:

'Open the door, do open the door. Only open it a little. You will see for yourself, so handsome, so strong. There's not a beetle so strong as me in all the parish. My legs are firm, my pincers cruel. Woe betide the enemy who is taken in my jaws. There's not a beetle alive dare face me in mortal combat. How happy you should be to have such a husband.'

'That's all very well!' she said. 'But what about me? You have only to lose your temper with me, and then what price your strength? I'd be lucky to keep my head on my shoulders. No, no. Take it away. I can do well enough without it in my house.'

'Oh, but listen to me! Do listen to me! That is not all, really it isn't. I'm the richest beetle hereabouts, indeed I am. I have more stored away in my little house than you or your Granny ever thought of.'

And he began to tell her all he had.

'I have three pretty boxes all full of threepenny bits. I have seven new packets of glass-headed pins, all different colours, not one the same. A peacock's feather and a piece of red seaweed, a drawerful of postage stamps and new paints in tubes.

'And as for the larder! I have seven shelves of sweeties in big glass jars, a shelf of honeycombs, and another of jellies and pink blancmange. If you had one for dinner every day of the year you would not reach the end of them.'

'Oh, stop it, do!' she said. 'How tired I am. If you have so much already, then you cannot want me. Go away now, do, and let me go to sleep.'

And she slammed the window to, so that she could not hear him any more.

And then how sad he was. He began to cry. He turned round about and was going down the road, the big tears splashing in the dust.

She was looking after him as he went down the road, for after all she was curious to see what he looked like. And she saw two big holes in his stockings, one in either heel. She saw them clearly as he went down the road.

She opened the window and called out after him:

'Hey! You there! You, so rich and strong and beautiful. Here you come out courting with holes in your stockings. Who looks after you at home to allow such a thing?'

'Well, that's how it is,' he said. 'There's no one to look after me. My Granny is so blind she sits all day by the fire. My mother takes in washing and she has no time for me. And as for my sister, she is down at the end of the garden playing cards and talking to her friends. No one bothers about me, and so I get holes in my stockings.'

'Come along back here,' she cried. 'I can't have you going away from my house looking like that.'

And she had him in and took up her needle and thread, and darned up his stockings and sewed on a button, and – oh, well. There you are!

By the time she had done with him she loved him so dearly that when he asked her to marry him she didn't say no.

So when you go out courting, you take it from me – go with a full heart and a hole in your stocking, and then you, too, shall marry a wife.

DIANA ROSS
Illustrated by FAITH JAQUES

Queen Mab

If ye will with Mab find grace,
Set each platter in his place:
Rake the fire up and get
Water in, ere sun be set.

Wash your pails and cleanse your dairies;
Sluts are loathsome to the fairies:
Sweep your house: who doth not so,
Mab will pinch her by the toe.

ROBERT HERRICK

Father Sparrow's Tug-of-War

FATHER SPARROW was perched on a twig, talking very fast and very loud to Mother Sparrow, who was sitting on a nest full of eggs. It was early in the day; the sun was shining brightly, the monkeys were chattering, birds were hopping and chirping – it was a pleasant morning, but Father Sparrow was cross.

He had been down to the river to bathe, in a nice shallow place he knew of, and there was the Crocodile, half in and half out of the water, filling up the whole of the bathing-place! And when Father Sparrow scolded him, he only opened his mouth wide and laughed (it was a *very* wide mouth), and said, lazily, 'I shall stay here just as long as I please.'

So Father Sparrow was very cross, and as I have said, he was telling Mother Sparrow all about it, when suddenly, *bump*, somebody very big crashed against the tree, which rocked and swayed so that Father Sparrow nearly fell off his twig; and if Mother

Sparrow had not sat very tight the eggs would certainly have rolled out of the nest.

'Really, there is no peace in the forest this morning,' said Father Sparrow still more crossly (and I think he had some excuse). 'Now, who can that be?'

He flew down to see, and there was a big grey back and a little grey tail disappearing amongst the trees. It was Brother Elephant taking a walk in the forest.

'Stop, Brother Elephant!' said Father Sparrow with a loud chirp. 'Do you know that you have nearly shaken my wife off her nest?'

'Well,' said Brother Elephant, 'I don't mind if I have.' Which, of course, was very rude of him; he might at least have said he was sorry.

'You don't mind!' twittered Father Sparrow. 'You don't mind! I'll make you mind, Brother Elephant, and if you shake my nest again, *I'll tie you up!*'

Mother Sparrow gave a little chirp of surprise, and Brother Elephant chuckled. 'Tie me up then,' he said, 'you're quite welcome to do it; but you can't keep me tied, Father Sparrow, not even if a thousand sparrows tried!'

'*Wait and see*,' said Father Sparrow. Brother Elephant trumpeted with laughter and went crashing and trampling through the forest, and after a little talk with Mother Sparrow, Father Sparrow flew down to the river. The Crocodile was still there, fast asleep and filling up all the bathing-place. Father Sparrow chirped indignantly, and the Crocodile opened one eye. 'I like this place,' he said.

'You may like it,' said Father Sparrow, 'but I can tell you this, if I find you here tomorrow *I'll tie you up!*'

'You may tie me as much as you like,' said the Crocodile, shutting his eye again, 'but you can't keep me tied, Father Sparrow – not if a thousand sparrows tried.'

'*Wait and see*,' chirped Father Sparrow; but the Crocodile was fast asleep again. So Father Sparrow flew away.

He was very busy all that morning, talking to all his sparrow friends, and next day they were all up very early and working hard. There were quite a thousand of them, and they had a long, long piece of a creeper that grows in the forest, and is nearly as strong as the strongest rope.

Presently Brother Elephant came crashing through the forest. *Bump!* he went against Father Sparrow's tree. (Mother Sparrow was expecting him, so she was not shaken much.) 'Well,' said Brother Elephant, 'here I am! Are you going to tie me up, Father Sparrow?'

'Yes,' chirped Father Sparrow, 'I am going to tie you up and hold you tight.' And he and all the other sparrows pulled, and pecked, and hopped and tugged, and fluttered (you can imagine the noise they made), till the rope – it was really a creeper, of course, but we will call it a rope – was tight round Brother Elephant's big body.

'Now, Brother Elephant,' said Father Sparrow, 'when I say "Pull", *pull.*'

'So I will,' said Brother Elephant, shaking with laughter; and he waited, while Father Sparrow and all the other sparrows flew away with the rope, tugging it through bushes and tall reeds to the riverside. There was the Crocodile, in Father Sparrow's bathing-place, and when he saw them he laughed.

'Have you and your friends come to tie me up, Father Sparrow?' he said.

'Yes,' said Father Sparrow. 'I am going to tie you up and hold you tight.'

'Tie away,' said the Crocodile; and the sparrows pulled, and pecked, and chattered, and tugged, and hopped, till the rope was tight round the Crocodile's long body.

'Now,' said Father Sparrow, 'when I say "Pull", *pull*.'

The Crocodile was too lazy to answer; he only chuckled till the water rippled round him, and the sparrows flew away.

Then Father Sparrow perched himself on the middle of the rope among the bushes, where neither Brother Elephant nor the Crocodile could see him; and of course neither of them could see the other. '*Pull*.' cried Father Sparrow in a very loud chirp, and Brother Elephant gave a great tug.

'That will surprise Father Sparrow,' he said. But it was really Brother Elephant who was surprised, because from the other end of the line came such a jerk that he was nearly pulled off his feet. Of course he thought it was Father Sparrow, but as you know it was the Crocodile, who never meant to trouble to pull at all; he was far too lazy! *He* thought it was Father Sparrow pulling too, and was even more surprised than Brother Elephant.

'What a strong sparrow he is!' said the Crocodile.

'How hard Father Sparrow can pull,' said Brother Elephant, and they both pulled and pulled and pulled and *pulled*.

Sometimes Brother Elephant pulled hardest and the Crocodile was nearly pulled out of the river. Sometimes the Crocodile gave a jerk and Brother Elephant had to twist his trunk round a tree and hold on. They were really just about equal, and neither could move the other an inch. It was a wonderful tug-of-war. The sun rose high in the sky and began to creep down towards the west; they grew hot and thirsty and tired. The sparrows laughed at them when they puffed and grunted and panted. Each of them thought, 'I wish I had not laughed at Father Sparrow.' And still they pulled and pulled and pulled – they were so very ashamed and tired.

At last, just as the sun was beginning to slip out of sight, Brother Elephant said in a very small voice: 'Please tell Father Sparrow that if he will stop pulling and untie me, I will never be rude to him again.'

Just at the same moment the Crocodile said to himself, 'All the animals will be coming to drink, and how they will laugh when they see me tied up here!' and he called, 'Please, Father Sparrow, stop pulling and untie me, and I will never take your bathing-place again.'

'Very well,' chirped Father Sparrow very loud; 'very well, very well,' (which was the same as 'Hip, hip, hurrah!' would be for you and me), and the sparrows hopped, and pecked, and pulled, and chattered till they untied Brother Elephant, and he went away with his head hanging down, terribly ashamed of being beaten by Father Sparrow. They untied the Crocodile too, and he crawled in among the high reeds that grew by the river and hid himself, dreadfully cross because he had been tied up all day.

Neither of them ever knew they had really been pulling each other, and after this Brother Elephant walked quietly, *so* quietly, in the forest, and the Crocodile let Father Sparrow bathe in peace.

As for Father Sparrow, he and all his friends flew away and told their little wives all about the tug-of-war. Then they put their little heads under their wings and all went fast asleep. It had been a very busy day!

ELIZABETH CLARK

Bobby Shaftoe

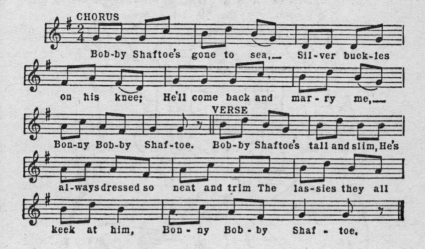

Bobby Shaftoe's gone to sea,
Silver buckles on his knee;
He'll come back and marry me,
    Bonny Bobby Shaftoe.

Bobby Shaftoe's tall and slim,
He's always dressed so neat and trim,
The lassies they all keek at him,
    Bonny Bobby Shaftoe.

Bobby Shaftoe's bright and fair,
Combing down his yellow hair;
He's my ain for ever mair,
    Bonny Bobby Shaftoe.

The Flying Postman

MR MUSGROVE was a Postman in a village called Pagnum Moss.
Mr and Mrs Musgrove lived in a house called Fuchsia Cottage.
It was called Fuchsia Cottage because it had a fuchsia hedge round
it. In the front garden they kept a cow called Nina, and in the back
garden they grew strawberries . . . nothing else but strawberries.
Now Mr Musgrove was no ordinary Postman; for instead of
walking or trundling about on a bicycle, he flew around in a

Helicopter. And instead of pushing letters in through letter-boxes, he tossed them into people's windows, singing as he did so: 'Wake up! Wake up! For morning is here!'

Thus people were able to read their letters quietly in bed without littering them untidily over the breakfast table.

Sometimes to amuse the children, Mr Musgrove tied a radio set to the tail of the Helicopter, and flew about in time to the music. He had a special kind of Helicopter that was able to loop the loop and even fly UPSIDE DOWN!

But one day the Postmaster-General and the Postal Authorities sent for Mr Musgrove and said, 'It is forbidden to do stunts in the sky. You must keep the Helicopter only for delivering letters and parcels, and not for playing about!'

Mr Musgrove felt crestfallen.

After that Mr Musgrove put his Helicopter away when he had

finished work, till one day some of the children came to him and
said: 'Please do a stunt in the sky for us, Mr Musgrove!'

When he told them he would never do any more stunts, the
children felt very sad and some even cried a little. Mr Musgrove
could not bear to see little children sad, so he tied the radio set

to the Helicopter, and jumping into the driving seat flew swiftly into the air, to a burst of loud music.

'I'll do just one trick,' he said to himself, 'a new, and very special one!'

The children stopped crying and jumped gaily up and down.

He flew high, high, high up into the sky till he was almost out of sight, then he came whizzing down and swooped low, low, low over the church steeple and away again.

The children, who had scrambled on to a near-by roof top to get a better view, cried: 'It's a lovely trick! Do it again! PLEASE do it again!'

So Mr Musgrove flew high, high, high into the sky again and came whizzing and swooping down low, low, low . . . But this time he came TOO low and . . . landed with a whizz! Wang! DONC! right on the church steeple.

The Postmaster-General, from his house on the hill, heard the crash and came galloping to the spot on his horse, Black Bertie. The Postal Authorities also heard the crash, and came running to the spot, on foot.

When he got to the church the Postmaster-General dismounted from Black Bertie and, waving his fist at Mr Musgrove, said sternly: 'This is a very serious offence! Come down at once!'

'I can't,' said Mr Musgrove, unhappily, '. . . I'm stuck!'

So the Postal Authorities got a strong ladder and climbed up the steeple and lifted Mr Musgrove and the Helicopter down.

When they got to the ground, they examined Mr Musgrove's arms and legs and saw that nothing was broken. They also noticed that the radio set was intact. But the poor Helicopter was seriously damaged; its tail was drooping, its nose was pushed up, and its whole system was badly upset.

'It will take weeks to mend!' said the Postal Authorities.

The Postmaster-General turned to Mr Musgrove and said: 'For this you will be dismissed from the Postal Service. Hand me your uniform.'

Mr Musgrove sadly handed him his peaked hat and his little jacket that had red cord round the edges.

'Mr Boodle will take your place,' said the Postmaster-General.

Mr Boodle was the Postman from the next village. He did not like the idea of delivering letters for two villages. 'Too much for one man on a bicycle,' he grumbled, but not loud enough for the Postmaster-General to hear.

Mr Musgrove went back to Fuchsia Cottage in his waistcoat.

'I've lost my job, Mrs Musgrove,' he said.

Even Nina looked sad and her ears flopped forward.

'Never mind,' said Mrs Musgrove, 'we will think of a new job for you.'

'I am not very good at doing anything except flying a Helicopter and delivering letters,' said Mr Musgrove.

So they sat down to think and think, and Nina thought too, with her own special cow-like thoughts.

After a while Mrs Musgrove had a Plan.

'We will pick the strawberries from the back garden and with the cream from Nina's milk we will make some Pink Ice Cream and sell it to people passing by,' she cried.

'What a wonderful plan!' shouted Mr Musgrove, dancing happily round. 'You *are* clever, Mrs Musgrove!'

Nina looked as if she thought it was a good idea, too, and said 'Moo-oo!'

The next day Mr Musgrove went gaily into the back garden and picked a basketful of strawberries. He was careful not to eat any himself, but put them *all* into the basket. Mrs Musgrove milked Nina and skimmed off the cream. And together they made some lovely Pink Ice Cream. Then they put up a notice:

PINK ICE CREAM FOR SALE

Nina looked very proud.

When the children saw the notice they ran eagerly in to buy. And even a few grown-ups came, and said, 'Num, Num! What elegant Ice Cream!'

By evening they had sold out, so they turned the board round. Now it said:

PINK ICE CREAM TOMORROW

Every day they made more Pink Ice Cream and every evening they had sold out.

'We are beginning to make quite a lot of lovely money,' said Mr Musgrove.

But though they were so successful with their Pink Ice Cream, Mr Musgrove often thought wistfully of the Helicopter, and his Postman's life. One day as he was exercising Nina in the woods near his home, he met Mr Boodle. Mr Boodle grumbled that he had too much work to do.

'I would rather be a bicycling postman than no postman at all,' sighed Mr Musgrove.

Early one morning before the Musgroves had opened their Ice Cream Stall, Nina saw the Postmaster-General riding along the road on his horse, Black Bertie. Nina liked Black Bertie, so as they passed she thrust her head through the fuchsia hedge and said, 'Moo ooo.'

Black Bertie was so surprised that he shied and reared up in the air ... and tossed the Postmaster-General into the fuchsia hedge.

'Moo,' said Nina, in alarm, and Mr and Mrs Musgrove came running up.

Carefully they carried him into the house. They laid him on a sofa and put smelling salts under his nose, and tried to make him take some strong, sweet tea, and a little brandy.

But nothing would revive him.

They tried practically everything, including chocolate biscuits and fizzy lemonade, but he never stirred, till Mrs Musgrove came towards him carrying a Pink Ice Cream.

'What's that?' he said, opening one eye, 'it smells good.'

So they gave him one.

'It's delicious!' he cried. 'Delicious!'

They gave him another and another and another ...

He ate six!

'I have recovered now,' he said, standing up, 'thanks to your elegant ice creams, which are the best I have ever tasted!'

Then he walked outside and called Black Bertie, who had walked into the garden and was eating the grass with Nina. 'Come on, Black Bertie, we must go home,' he said, and jumped into the saddle and rode away, waving his hand graciously to the Musgroves.

That afternoon, much to the Musgroves' surprise, he re-appeared again. Nina was careful not to moo through the fuchsia hedge at Black Bertie this time.

'I have reappeared', said the Postmaster-General, 'because I am so grateful for your kindness and your ice creams that I have prepared a little surprise for you up at my house. Would you like to come and see it, Mr Musgrove?'

'Why, yes!' cried Mr Musgrove, wondering excitedly what on earth it could be.

'Jump on, then!' cried the Postmaster-General. 'I am afraid there isn't room for Mrs Musgrove too.'

At first Mr Musgrove felt a bit nervous of Black Bertie, but he was too excited to see what the Postmaster-General's surprise was really to care.

When they arrived at the Postmaster-General's house they put Black Bertie away and gave him a piece of sugar. Then the Postmaster-General led Mr Musgrove up the steps of the house into the hall, where stood a large wooden chest. He opened the chest, and drew out . . . Mr Musgrove's peaked cap and little blue jacket with red cord round the edges!

He handed the uniform to Mr Musgrove. 'Please wear this,' he said, 'and become once more the Flying Postman of Pagnum Moss!'

Mr Musgrove was very excited and thanked the Postmaster-General three times. Then the Postmaster-General took him out into the garden. 'Look!' he said, pointing at the lawn, and there stood the Helicopter all beautifully mended!

'Jump in!' cried the Postmaster-General. 'And be on duty to-morrow morning.'

Mr Musgrove raced across the lawn and leapt gleefully in. As he was flying away the Postmaster-General called: 'Will you sell me six of your beautiful Pink Ice Creams every day, and deliver them to me with the letters every morning?'

'Most certainly!' cried Mr Musgrove, leaning out of the Helicopter and saluting.

'Six Pink Ice Creams . . . I'll keep them in my refrigerator. Two for my lunch, two for my tea and two for my dinner!' shouted the Postmaster-General.

Imagine Mrs Musgrove's and Nina's surprise when Mr Musgrove alighted in the front garden, fully dressed in Postman's clothes.

'I'm a Postman again!' he cried. 'Oh, happy day!'

'Moo-oo,' cried Nina, and Mrs Musgrove clapped her hands.

The next morning he set out to deliver letters and to sing his song: 'Wake up! Wake up! For morning is here!' and everyone

woke up and shouted: 'Mr Musgrove, the Flying Postman, is back in the sky again! Hurrah, Hooray!'

Mr Boodle, the grumbling postman, said, 'Hurrah, Hooray!' too, because now he would not have so much work to do. He was so excited that he took his hands off the handlebars, and then he took his feet off the pedals till the Postmaster-General passed by and, pointing at him said, 'That is dangerous and silly.'

So he put his hands back on the handlebars and his feet back on the pedals.

Mr Musgrove never forgot to bring the Postmaster-General the six Pink Ice Creams; two for his lunch, two for his tea and two for his dinner. And every day clever Mrs Musgrove made Pink Ice Cream all by herself, till soon they had enough money to buy a little Helicopter of their very own, which they called FLITTER-MOUSE. They had Flittermouse made with a hollow in the back for Nina to sit in, and on Saturdays they went to the city to shop, and on Sundays they went for a spin.

Often Mr Musgrove did musical sky stunts in Flittermouse for the children, but he was careful never to fly low over the church steeple.

Written and illustrated by V. H. DRUMMOND

York, York for my Money

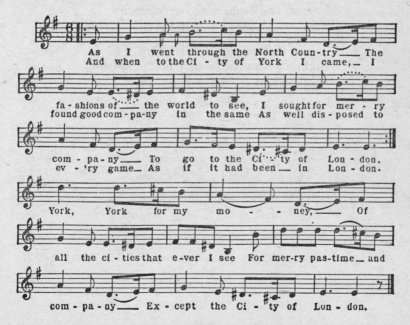

As I went through the North Coun-try___ The fa-shions of___ the world to see, I sought for mer-ry com-pa-ny___ To go to the Ci-ty of Lon-don.

And when to the Ci-ty of York I came,___ I found good com-pa-ny in the same As well dis-posed to ev-'ry game, As if it had been___ in Lon-don.

York, York for my mo___ney,___ Of all the ci-ties that e-ver I see For mer-ry pas-time___ and com-pa-ny___ Ex-cept the Ci-ty of Lon-don.

As I went through the North country,
The fashions of the world to see,
I sought for merry company
    To go to the City of London.
And when to the City of York I came,
I found good company in the same,
As well disposed to every game
    As if it had been at London.

York, York for my money;
Of all the cities that ever I see
For merry pastime and company,
    Except the City of London.

And in that City what saw I then?
Knights and Squires and gentlemen
A-shooting went for matches ten,
    As if it had been at London.
And they shot for twenty pounds a bow,
Besides great cheer they did bestow,
I never saw a gallanter show,
    Except I had been at London.

York, York for my money;
Of all the cities that ever I see
For merry pastime and company
    Except the City of London.

WILLIAM ELDERTON
Decoration by ROBERT HODGSON

The Six Badgers

As I was a-hoeing, a-hoeing my lands
Six badgers came up with white wands in their hands.
They made a ring around me and, bowing, they said:
'Hurry home, Farmer George, for the table is spread!
There's pie in the oven, there's beef on the plate:
Hurry home, Farmer George, if you would not be late!'
So homeward I went, but could not understand
Why six fine dog-badgers with white wands in hand
Should seek me out hoeing and bow in a ring,
And all to inform me so common a thing!

ROBERT GRAVES
Illustrated by CONSTANCE MARSHALL

The Swallows

WINTER showed signs of coming early that year. The summer had been bright and hot, but short. Already there had been discussions among the old and experienced swallows as to the wisdom of fixing a day for the departure to the south, and though the younger members of the colony were not of course admitted to these solemn consultations, yet little birds, as is well known, have quick ears, and it is not easy to keep secrets from them, nor, sometimes, to prevent their telling them again. So though they had not been told so, the young swallows were quite aware that something was in the wind, though the trees had not yet lost their leaves, and the signs of what was coming could not as yet be read by inexperienced eyes.

And many, almost all, of the young birds were full of delight and excitement at the prospect.

'Think of all we shall see – the orange and myrtle groves, the blue waves of the Southern Sea – best of all the glorious sunshine, compared with which this cold English sunshine is not worthy of the name,' exclaimed an enthusiastic and rather self-conceited swallowkin, flapping his wings, and looking as if he were ready to start at once.

'How do *you* know?' said another of a less poetical imagination. 'You have never been there.'

'I have seen it in my dreams. I have breathed the balmy air. I have heard the lapping of the waves far beneath us. Oh, the south, the south, the glorious south for me!' he exclaimed, as he flew off.

The other young birds looked after him admiringly, all except two – the one who had questioned his knowledge, and another who had said nothing.

'He is so exaggerated,' said the former. 'I daresay the south is all well enough. I am very well pleased to go, but I don't see that one need make such a fuss about it.'

'I am very grieved to go,' said the other sadly. 'I love the north. I have been very happy here, and would fain stay.'

'But that is impossible,' said his companion.

'I suppose so.'

'And we shall come back again?'

'So they say, but who knows? It is not all the birds who fly south that come north again. I think it a hard fate to have to leave the home one loves, and the friends one loves even more, uncertain if one will ever see them again,' and the young swallow flew slowly away.

'What a queer bird,' said the other one. 'I wonder who the friends are he makes such a talk about. For my part, I don't hold with exaggeration one way or the other. Take things as they come, and make yourself comfortable, is my doctrine.'

Who were 'the friends'? Shall I show them to you?

It was a long, low, old-fashioned house, with deep-set windows and gable ends. And nothing was more remarkable about it than the depth and roominess of the eaves, formed by its overhanging roof. How many generations of swallows had in these same eaves been hatched and tended by their parents it would be difficult to say. It had seemed impossible to prevent the birds building in them, and though former proprietors had managed to frighten their uninvited guests away from two sides of the house, there remained the south gable, which, more difficult of access for gardeners' ladders, had only been protected at last by running wire netting in front. And by this means for some years there was peace

from the twitter and flutter, and, I suppose, it must be allowed, from the mischief wrought by the feathered lodgers. But in time, an end of the netting had come loose. No one had noticed it when the quaint old house had been prepared for its new owners; no one had thought of swallows in the eaves till one sweet spring morning when two curly heads, whose owners should still have been fast asleep, were stretched far out of the nursery window to inquire into the causes of all the chirping and twittering and piping and fluttering that was going on just outside.

'It's birds,' said one curly head solemnly – as if it could possibly have been anything else! 'It's lovely, darling birds making a nest just at *our* window. Oh, what a beautiful house this is to live in, with birds at the windows!'

'Oh, the sweet little darlings!' agreed curly head number two. 'How *kind* of them to have chosen this corner!'

And the soft, childish chatter inside bid fair to rival the delicate bird-bustle and flutter outside.

Suddenly a new idea struck number one.

'If we make such a noise we'll frighten them, perhaps. We must be quiet and watch them, and then we'll see all they're going to do.'

Number two had great respect for his elder's authority, so they watched quietly, almost holding their breaths with interest and delight, till the maid, coming to wake them, exclaimed, aghast at finding the two small people at the window with nothing on but their night-gowns:

'Miss Mab – Master Clem! you'll catch your death of cold,' she cried. It was true that the mornings were chilly still, notwithstanding the sunshine, for it was only spring. 'Go back to bed and get warm again. I'll leave you ten minutes later on purpose.'

Mab and Clem obeyed. They were ready to obey what their maid told them, for she was kind and gentle. But all the time they were dressing they could talk of nothing but the birds, and whenever they had a leisure moment during the day they were sure to be found at *the* window – the birds' window, they called it. But, alas! no happiness is unalloyed. The gardener, who had been long about the place – long enough to remember the former trouble with the swallows – noticed the curly-heads so constantly at the same place, that he called up to ask what they were watching, for he had not hitherto remarked the feathered new-comers. And in the innocence of their hearts they told him of their delight. He said nothing – he was a man of few words – but that evening when the two went downstairs to say good night, sad tidings were in store for them.

'Swallows are building again in the eaves at the south end of the house, Crabb tells me,' said their father to their mother, 'just by one of the nursery windows. In my old uncle's time they had no end of trouble with them. I have told him to take down the nest tomorrow morning, and to fasten up some more netting where it has come loose.'

'Take down the nest tomorrow morning.' The nest 'by one of the nursery windows'!

The curly-heads looked at each other, and gasped for breath. Could it be *papa* that was speaking so – kind, good papa? They hardly dared look at him. Could some terrible transformation have come over him? Could he be turning into an ogre? They looked at him with much the same expression in their faces that poor Red Riding Hood must have had when first she caught sight of the ears and teeth inside her kind grand-mother's night-cap, but all they said was just –

'Papa!'

Another word and they would have burst into tears. Mamma was the first to see the dismay on the two faces.

'What is the matter, dears?' she said.

'Mamma! *Our* birds, *our* nest! Mamma, we told you about it this morning. You can't have forgotten?'

She had for the moment, but quickly remembered again, and blamed herself for not having paid more attention to what they were chattering about.

'Dears,' she said, 'you don't understand. Swallows in the eaves are very mischievous, and cause a great deal of trouble. It isn't that papa would be unkind to poor little birds, but we must take care of our own nest, you know,' she added playfully.

No, they didn't understand, and they couldn't understand.

'If there were nests all round and round the roof, though it would be *very* nice, perhaps it would be a little dirty and messy,' sobbed Mab, 'but *one* little nest. Oh, papa!'

'But, my darling,' expostulated papa, 'it wouldn't stop at one. They would go on more and more once they found the place, till it would be as bad as in the old times.'

'They *couldn't*, papa. They couldn't get past that nest to make others. It blocks up the end where the wire is loose. Oh, papa, dear papa! do have the wire fastened just at the other side of that nest, so that they couldn't get in any more – we wouldn't mind that – but this nest that's all begun. Oh, do leave *it*!'

And Mab's clasped hands and tearful face, and Clem's echoed 'Oh, do, dear papa – do,' carried the day, notwithstanding Crabb's sour face and very plain though unexpressed disapproval.

2

And it was in this very nest that our friend the young swallow who was so grieved at the thought of leaving his northern home was hatched and reared, and even when he was no longer a nestling, but out and about in the world on his own account, the corner by the eaves was always 'home' to him, and the two curly heads would have known 'our swallow', so they said, among a thousand.

So now you know who were the friends he grieved to leave.

Alas! the cold came on rapidly. Soon the winter flight was decided on, and there was great excitement in swallow-world. Excitement and delight among the young ones, to whom it was all new, who had never seen the broad stretching sea or the deep blue sky of the south. But to *our* swallow it was all regret and no delight.

'What care I for dancing waves or blue skies or brilliant sun?' he said to himself. 'Where in these strange new lands shall I find friends to greet me like these two sweet children – to open their window to call to me as soon as their eyes are open in the morning, to listen to my feeble chirping, which is all I can give them in return, with as much pleasure as if it were the song of the night-ingale or the carol of the lark? Alas, alas! I cannot even tell them of my sorrow – I must leave them – I must seem ungrateful and heartless, though I love them so dearly.'

And thus he was grieving when, in the still soft autumn winds, a murmur seemed to be wafted towards him – whence it came, he could not tell, but he grew strangely comforted, for he felt that it was true.

'Grieve not,' it seemed to say; 'with the spring the swallows shall return,' and for the first time he *trusted*, and the future no longer looked so dark.

'What made our swallow fly about the window so long to-night, I wonder,' said one curly head to the other. 'He has been fluttering and fluttering about as if he couldn't make up his mind to go to sleep.'

And smiling at their little friend, they went to bed as happy as their wont.

But tomorrow brought unexpected grief. Birdie did not come as usual to wish them good morning, and it was with a little anxiety in their hearts that the curly heads went down to breakfast.

'He may have been sleepier than usual this morning; he was up so late last night,' whispered Clem to Mab on the stairs, by way of suggesting an explanation of Birdie's non-appearance. But Mab shook her head. Some vague remembrance came into her mind of remarks she had heard made a few days before by some 'big' person of the early cold this year, and that 'the swallows would be leaving us soon'; and for the first time a fear occurred to her that their pet bird, being, as she knew, a swallow, might be involved in the prediction.

She ate her breakfast gravely. So for that matter did Clem also. Papa and mamma seemed grave too, and were talking now and then about some letter which Mab knew nothing of, but which had evidently made them anxious. She did not listen; her little mind and heart were too full of their own anxiety; but at last some words struck her.

'This sudden, early cold,' papa was saying, 'is most unfortunate.' 'If they really start so soon,' mamma remarked; 'good-byes are so painful in such cases – the hope of returning so uncertain;' and Mab *thought* – she was not quite sure, but she *thought*, there were tears in mamma's eyes. Mab opened hers wider, and stopped eating. Could mamma be thinking of what *she* was thinking of? It was very strange; the words Mab had caught seemed just to suit what was in *her* mind.

'What is it, mamma?' she exclaimed at last; 'is it about the swallows? Are they really gone?'

Mamma stared in her turn.

'The swallows, dear Mab,' she said, 'what do you mean? Who was speaking about the swallows?'

Then Mab broke out with her hidden fears, and Clem listened in sorrowful surprise to what was to him a very unexpected explanation of their bird's absence. Papa and mamma smiled, but rather sadly, at the children's distress.

'I am afraid it is true,' said mamma. 'I am afraid your pet swallow must have gone with his friends. Poor bird; he couldn't help it, you know, Mab. He would have died if he had stayed up here. You must try to look forward to his coming back again in the spring.'

'In the spring, mamma! Not till the spring; and it is so, *so* long to the spring. And perhaps the swallows won't come back here

next year; perhaps they'll find it so nice down there where they've gone.'

'No, not *down*,' corrected Clem; 'it's *up* – up, close to the sun. Birds always fly up when they fly away,' and for some reason of her own, mamma just smiled, without correcting his pretty fancy.

'Mab,' she said, 'you should have more hope and trust. I will give you something to remind you. Do you remember the pictures of different kinds of birds painted on cards that I have in a little case in my room, and that I have shown you sometimes?'

'The pictures with the funny letters at the foot, that Clem and I can't read?' said Mab, and mamma nodded. 'I know,' said the little girl, and she was off in a moment and quickly back again.

Mamma turned over the pretty cards slowly, the children peeping eagerly over her shoulder.

'There they are; there's the swallows,' they both exclaimed, recognizing their friends in a moment.

Mamma drew out the card. It was very pretty. Three little swallows flying together, the blue sky behind and above, and below, in what Mab had called funny letters, were the three words –

'Wir kommen wieder.'

'"WIR",' began Mab. 'What does it mean, mamma?'

'Just what I've been telling you. "We shall come back again," or rather, "We *come* back again." You may have the card, Mab; put it up on the wall in your room to remind you not to be so easily cast down.'

'Thank you, mamma – thank you *very* much. But it *is* rather sad, isn't it, not to be able to look out of the window at the swallows, and at *our* swallow, any more – isn't it, mamma?' she repeated; and the tears would make their way into her eyes again.

'Yes, dear, it is,' said her mother. And there was a look in her eyes as if she understood how sad it was, even better than the child herself.

'Mamma, are *you* unhappy about anything? Is there anything the matter?' asked Mab, with a quick instinct of misgiving.

'Nothing that I can tell you about,' said Mamma, who never said 'no' when it wasn't 'no'. 'I am troubled, but one has often troubles, little Mab, and sometimes they clear off in ways one could never have expected. Be glad, dear, that you had no worse trouble just now than saying good-bye to your little feathered friends.'

'If we *could* have said good-bye, I wouldn't have minded so much; would you, Clem?' said Mab, as they trotted upstairs again.

'I'd have liked to see them all flying away,' said Clem. 'It must be very nice to fly, fly like that – mustn't it, Mab?'

'Yes, I daresay; but, Clem, I'm sure *our* bird was sorry to go away. I think he was saying good-night last night when he kept flying and fluttering about such a long time. Dear Birdie, we won't forget you, anyway.'

3

Nor did they. The days passed on into weeks, and still night and morning, morning and night, the curly heads chattered about their little friend. And when it grew really cold, and they heard talk of the severe winter it was going to be, they were glad to think Birdie was safe and warm in some sunny southern land.

But something of their home-brightness seemed to Mab to have gone with him. Mamma had never looked quite as happy as usual since 'that morning', the child said to herself. What could it be? One day she was sure mamma had been crying, and that was a thing Mab could scarcely remember ever to have seen before. She tried not to think about it, for mamma had said there was a trouble that could not be explained to her, and therefore Mab felt that it was better for her to put it out of her mind, unless, or till, mamma told her more about it. But still, it is not always so easy to put things out of our heads – is it? – however conscientiously we try. And there were times when Mab felt strange and anxious, as if something she could not understand was hanging over her.

And before long it was explained to her. One day there came a telegram, which did not happen very often in the quiet country place. The children were in the garden when the messenger brought it.

'What can it be?' thought Mab at once.

But Clem, who was only six, never thought of anything being the matter. He was only amused at the sight of the messenger on horseback, and wanted Mab to explain to him if the horse *and* the man *and* the letter had come by telegraph, or only the letter. But Mab could scarcely listen to him. She felt somehow so frightened. And as soon as she thought she might do so without teasing, she crept upstairs and tapped at her mother's door.

'Come in,' was the answer, but the voice did not sound as usual.

The reason was soon explained. Mamma was crying, and did not attempt to hide it.

'What is the matter, darling little mother?' cried Mab, jumping into her mother's arms, her own tears ready to spring forth. 'Oh, I am big enough to understand! Is it about the telegram?'

'Yes,' said mamma. 'It is the telegram; at least the telegram has decided it. It is from your father. You know he went away yesterday to your uncle's. Well, he promised to send me a telegram this morning which would decide something we have been anxious about for a long time. I will show you the telegram, and then I will explain it.'

She opened the pink paper. The writing was straggly and in pencil. Mab could not have read it well alone. It was very short. This was all it said:

'No help for it. Better prepare at once. Home tonight.'

Mab looked up in bewilderment.

'What does it mean?' she said.

Then her mother explained.

'You remember, Mab, the day you were so sorry about the swallows going? Well, that day you heard something I said, and you could not understand. That morning I had had a letter about one of your aunts being very ill, and that she was ordered by the doctors to go to a milder climate for the winter – like the swallows, you know, Mab. And your father and I were sorry about it, and were talking about how sad it was for her to have to go, and whether I should go to see her before she left – you remember.'

'Yes, mamma,' said Mab, 'and did she go? and did she get worse, mamma? and have you had a letter to say she was *dead*, perhaps?' the child went on, dropping her voice. 'Which of my aunts is it? – there are so many; it isn't dear Aunt Flossie is it?'

'No – oh no! It isn't Flossie. It is an aunt you have not seen since you were a baby – she is not very young. Indeed, she is my aunt as well as yours. She did go, and she has got much worse. But she is not *dead*.'

'Then why are you so *very* unhappy, mamma? You haven't seen her for a long time, and perhaps she'll still get better,' went on Mab, with a child's inconsequence.

'Yes, dear, perhaps. But, Mab, she is all alone there, and *very* ill, and she has no sister, no daughter who can go to her – ' and Mab's mother stopped and looked at her little girl.

Mab's breath came short and fast. She could hardly speak.

'Mamma,' she said at last, 'you don't mean that *you* are going away from us, mamma – away from Mab and Clem! Oh, it's

274

worse than Birdie going, twenty million times. Oh, mamma, you *can't* go away from us!'

'I must go, Mab. It is my duty,' was all her mother could answer.

'Then take us with you,' pleaded Mab.

'I cannot, dear. Your aunt is too ill and too feeble to have children near her, and I could not be with you while I was taking care of her. I must leave you here to keep your father company, and to take care of Clem. Think how useful you will be! And remember that *I* shall be like the swallows, Mab. When the winter is over, and your aunt is better, I shall fly home again.'

But at first Mab would not be comforted.

'Do you love our aunt so very much, then, mamma?' she sobbed. 'Better than us?'

'Of course not better than you,' said her mother. Then she hesitated.

'You must love her very much, though,' said Mab, who seemed growing cross with sorrow.

'Mab,' said her mother, 'it is not only those we love very much that we have to be kind to. I *do* love your aunt, for she was good to me when I was a child. But she has *not* been so kind to me since I grew up. She did not learn when she was young to think more of others than of herself, and so now that she is old she has no one to be kind to her. That is the reason why I feel that I must go.'

Mab stopped crying, and looked at her mother.

'Mamma,' she said, 'am I like that? Am I thinking of myself more than of others, mamma? I will try not. I will try to be good about your going; but oh, I wouldn't have cried so when our bird went away if I had thought our big *mother* swallow was going too.'

4

Up in the north the winter came on quickly, and, as the weather-wise folk had predicted, it turned out a very severe one. Many birds died of cold and hunger that year, and not birds only, but many poor people; little children especially suffered terribly.

But down in the south it was bright and sunny. The sea and the sky were blue and clear – and even the snow-capped mountains looked so shining and bright that it was difficult to think of them as bleak and dreary like the hills in winter in our own land. The swallows had found a pleasant southern home, and needed not to think of cold or hunger. Our young swallow was growing wiser as well as stronger. What had once seemed hard and sad to him had become right and good, and as he darted and skimmed about in the balmy air he thought of his northern home with cheerful hope. He had not forgotten the curly-heads, but he no longer feared that he would not see them again, and he thought to himself of the greeting they would give him when he should once more flutter round the well-known window.

'There,' said he to himself, 'when I have chosen a mate in the spring, shall we in our turn make our nest and rear our little ones as I was reared. They shall learn to know the pretty children, and to greet them night and morning. And oh, if I had but voice to tell to their human ears, or if they had but ears to understand our bird-language, what tales could I tell them of this glorious land of the south – of the sunshine and the flowers and the orange-groves, of the glowing sea and the gleaming mountains!'

He little knew that near him, leaning out of a window close by on which he had for a moment alighted, was one whose heart was full of the same thoughts as his, – whose eyes, while gazing on the beauty before them, yet grew dim with slowly-coming tears, and saw no more the sunshine and the brilliance, but instead the greyer, colder skies of the north, the leafless trees of the garden at home – most clearly of all, the nursery-window and two curly heads pressed against the panes.

'If *they* were here it would be beautiful to me,' she said to herself. 'But without them there is no brightness in the sunshine, no sweetness in the air. And still so many weeks to wait!'

But as she was thinking thus, so sadly, the swallow flew across in front of her, then stopped an instant and skimmed off again. It was enough; he had taught his lesson.

'I could believe it was the children's swallow,' said their mother to herself, smiling at her own fancy. 'How could I tell *them* to have more trust and hope when I am myself so faithless! Yes, little swallow, I will not be so fearful – "Wir kommen wieder." I am sure that God will take me back to my darlings.'

And through the months of absence that still remained, whenever the curly-heads' mother felt sad or hopeless – for there was much to try her – nothing so raised her flagging spirits as the sight of the swallows. They seemed to her a sort of rainbow of trust and hope.

And the winter wore through at last. One spring morning the children woke with a feeling that something *most* joyful was about to happen.

'Clem, wake up; have you forgotten that today is *the* day?'

And Clem, rubbing sleepy eyes, declared he had been awake all night thinking of it – he had only *just* fallen asleep.

'Can you believe it, Mab,' he went on; '*can* you believe that mamma is coming today? Doesn't it seem *too* beautiful?'

But it *was* true. A few hours more, and they were clasped in her arms, and which was the happiest of the three it would be difficult to say.

'Oh, mamma, mamma,' was all they could say at first.

'Wasn't it almost worth while for me to go away for the happiness of coming back?' mamma whispered.

'And poor aunt has got better?' they said in a little while.

'Yes, she is much better,' said their mother.

'It is all *you* that helped to make her better,' said Mab caressingly. 'Mamma,' she whispered, 'does she love you very much *now*?'

'I think so; yes I do think so,' said her mother in the same tone. 'And oh, children,' she went on aloud, 'do you know I really sometimes could have fancied *your* swallow came to see me? There was one that used to fly round about my window, and –' She stopped suddenly and pointed upwards.

'Why, there is a flight of swallows returning now.'

'Yes,' said the children's father; 'I have seen two or three in the last few days.'

'They're the first *we've* seen,' said Mab and Clem. 'I do believe they are *our* swallows, and that we shall have Birdie at the nursery window again,' said Mab. 'It *would* be nice, though now we've got our mother-swallow back, we don't seem as if we could ever want anything more in the world.'

MRS MOLESWORTH

Follow my Bangalorey Man

Follow my Bangalorey Man,
Follow my Bangalorey Man;
I'll do all that ever I can
To follow my Bangalorey Man;
We'll borrow a horse and steal a gig,
And round the world we'll do a jig,
And I'll do all that ever I can
To follow my Bangalorey Man!

The Thunder, the Elephant
and Dorobo

THE people of Africa say that if you go to the end of a tree (they
mean the top), you find more branches than a man can count, but
if you go to the beginning (they mean the bottom), you just find
two or three, and that is much easier. Nowadays, they say, we are
at the end, and there are so many people and so many things that a
man doesn't know where to turn for the clutter the world is in,
but that in the beginning things were simpler, and fewer, and a
man could see between them. For in the beginning there was only
the Earth, and on the Earth were just three important things.

The Earth was much as it is now except that there was nothing
on it which had been *made*. Only the things that *grow*. If you go

into a corner of a forest very early on a warm misty morning, then you might get some idea of what the world was like then. Everything very still and vague round the edges, just growing, quietly.

And in this kind of world were three important things.

First there was an Elephant. He was very shiny and black because it was a rather wet world, and he lived in the forest where it is always wet. The mist collected on his cold white tusks and dripped slowly off the tips. Sometimes he trampled slowly through the forest finding leaves and bark and elephant-grass and wild figs and wild olives to eat, and sometimes he stood, very tall, very secret, just thinking and listening to the deep dignified noises in his stomach. When he flapped his great ears, it was a gesture, no more. There were no flies.

Then there was the Thunder. He was much bigger than the Elephant. He was black also, but not a shiny black like the Elephant. Sometimes there were streaks of white about him, the kind of white that you get on the belly of a fish. And he had no *shape*. Or rather, one moment he had one shape, and the next another shape. He was always collecting himself in and spreading himself out like a huge jelly-fish. And he didn't walk, he rolled along. He was noisy. Sometimes his voice was very far away, and then it was not so much a sound as a shaking, which Elephant could feel coming up from the ground. It made the drops of mist fall off the leaves and patter on his broad back. But sometimes, when the Thunder was in his tight shape, his voice cracked high and angrily, and then the Elephant would start and snort and wheel away deeper into the forest. Not because he was frightened, but because it hurt his ears.

And last there was a Dorobo.

A Dorobo is a man, and if you want to see a Dorobo you have to go to Africa, because he lives there still. Even then you won't see him very often because he keeps on the edges of places, and most people like to stay in the middle. He lives where the gardens begin to fade out and the forests begin, he lives where the plains stop and the mountains begin, where the grass dries up and the deserts take over. If you want to see him you had better come quickly, because as more and more things are made there is less and less room for Dorobo. He likes to keep himself to himself, and he's almost over the edge.

He is a small man but very stocky. He is the kind of brown that is almost yellow, and he borrows other people's languages to save himself the bother of making up one of his own. He is always looking steadily for small things that are good at hiding, and because of this the skin round his eyes is crinkled. He makes fire by twirling a pointed stick between the palms of his hands, and then he bends his face sideways and just breathes on a pinch of dried leaf powder, and it burns. Fire is about the only thing he does make.

He is very simple and wise, and he was wise too then, when the world was beginning, and he shared it with the Elephant and the Thunder.

Now these three things were young and new in those days, not quite certain of themselves and rather suspicious of the others because they very seldom met. There was so much room.

One day the Thunder came to see the Elephant, and after he had rumbled and swelled, he settled into the shape that soothed him most, and said, 'It's about Dorobo.'

The Elephant shifted his weight delicately from one foot to the other and said nothing. His ears flapped encouragingly.

'This Dorobo,' went on the Thunder, 'is a strange creature. In fact, so strange that . . . I am leaving the earth, because I am afraid of him.'

The Elephant stopped rocking and gurgled with surprise.

'Why?' he asked. 'He seems harmless enough to me.'

'Listen, Elephant,' said the Thunder. 'When you are sleeping and you get uncomfortable, and need to turn upon your other side, what do you do?'

The Elephant pondered this.

'I stand up,' he said at last. 'I stand up, and then I lie down again on my other side.'

'Well, Dorobo doesn't,' said the Thunder. 'I know. I've watched him. He rolls over without waking up. It's ugly and very strange, and it makes me uncomfortable. The sky, I think, will be a safer home for me.'

And the Thunder went there. He went straight up, and he's been there ever since. The Elephant heard his grumbling die away, and he sucked in his cheeks with astonishment. Then he went to find Dorobo.

It took him three days, but he found him at last, asleep beneath a thorn-tree with the grass curled beneath him like the form of a hare. Elephant rolled slowly forwards until he stood right over the sleeping man, and Dorobo lay in his gigantic shadow. Elephant watched him and pondered over all that the Thunder had said.

Presently Dorobo stirred and shivered in his sleep. Then he sighed and then he rolled over and curled himself tighter. It was precisely as the Thunder had described.

The Elephant had never noticed it before. It was strange indeed, but not, he thought, dangerous.

The Dorobo opened his eyes and stared up at the Elephant and smiled.

'You are clever, Elephant,' he said. 'I didn't hear you come. You move so silently.'

The Elephant said nothing.

Dorobo sat up and put his arms round his knees.

'I'm glad you came,' he went on. 'I've been wanting to speak to you. Do you know that Thunder has left us?'

'I had heard that he had gone,' replied the Elephant.

'Yes,' said Dorobo. 'I heard him yesterday in the sky. I'm glad and grateful that he's gone, for, to tell you the truth, I was afraid of Thunder. So big, so loud; and you never knew where he might bob up next. Or in what shape. I like things definite.'

'He *was* noisy,' said the Elephant.

'Now you, Elephant, you're quite different. So quiet and kind. Just think, Elephant, now in the whole world there is just you and me, and we shall get on well together because we understand each other.'

Then Elephant laughed. He didn't mean to. It rumbled up inside him and took him by surprise. He threw up his trunk and trumpeted.

'This ridiculous little creature!'

Then he was ashamed of his bad manners, and he wheeled ponderously and smashed off into the forest, shaking his great head, shaken by enormous bellows of laughter.

'Yes,' he shouted back over his shoulder, 'we understand ...
ha ha! ... understand one another ... very ... well!'

He was a good-natured animal, and he didn't want Dorobo to
see that he was laughing at him.

But Dorobo had seen, and although the smile stayed on his face,
his eyes were very cold and hard and black, like wet pebbles.

Presently he too slipped into the forest, but he walked slowly
and looked carefully about him, and after a while he saw the tree
he wanted. It was an old white olive tree, a twisted, slow-growing
thing, with a very hard tough wood. Dorobo searched that tree,
and after a long time he found a branch that was straight enough
and he bent and twisted it until it broke off. Then he skinned it
with his teeth and trimmed it and laid it in the shade to dry. Then
he found thin, strong vines hanging from tall trees like rope from

a mast, and he tore them down and trailed them behind him to the river. There he soaked them and beat them into cords against the river rocks, and plaited them very tightly together. When his cord was long enough, he took his wild olive branch, which was dry now, and strung the first bow. And he bent the bow almost double and let it go, and it sang for him. Next he found straight stiff sticks, and he made a fire and burned the end of his sticks a little, and rubbed the charred wood off in the sand. This gave them very hard, sharp points.

Taking his bow and his arrows, he ran to the edge of the desert and found the candelabra tree. The candelabra is a strange tree. It has thick, dull green branches which bear no leaves. And the branches stick up in bunches, a little bent, like the fingers of an old man's hand. And when a branch breaks, and it does very easily, it bleeds a white sticky sap, that drips slowly on the sand. You must never shelter beneath a candelabra tree, because if the sap drips in your eyes you go blind.

Dorobo broke a branch and dipped his arrows into the thick milky sap, and twisted them like a spoon in syrup. Then he laid each carefully against a stone to dry.

When everything was ready, he went in search of the Elephant.

Elephant was asleep under a fig-tree, but he woke up when he heard Dorobo's footsteps in the undergrowth. There was something in the way Dorobo walked – something secret and unfriendly which the Elephant did not like. For the first time in his life he felt afraid. As quickly as he could he got to his feet and made off through the forest. Dorobo grasped his bow and arrows more firmly and began to follow. Elephant trumpeted to the sky for help. But the Thunder growled back, 'It is useless to ask for help now. I warned you and you did nothing. You can't tell what a man is thinking by what he *says*, you can only tell by what he *does*. It is too late.' From that time to this Dorobo has always hunted the Elephant, and so have all men that have come after him.

As for Elephant, he has never again laughed at Dorobo, and has kept as far away from him as he can.

HUMPHREY HARMAN

The Pumpkin

You may not believe it, for hardly could I:
I was cutting a pumpkin to put in a pie,
And on it was written in letters most plain
'You may hack me in slices, but I'll grow again.'

I seized it and sliced it and made no mistake
As, with dough rounded over, I put it to bake:
But soon in the garden as I chanced to walk,
Why, there was that pumpkin entire on his stalk!

ROBERT GRAVES

The Magic Ball

A COLD-EYED witch lived in the Cordilleras and when the first
snow commenced to fall she was always full of glee, standing on a
rock, screaming like a wind-gale and rubbing her hands. For it
pleased her to see the winter moon, the green country blotted out,
the valleys white, the trees snow-laden, and the waters ice-bound
and black. Winter was her hunting time and her eating time, and
in the summer she slept. So she was full of a kind of savage joy
when there were leaden clouds and drifting gales, and she waited
and watched, waited and watched, ever ready to spring upon frost-
stiffened creatures, that went wandering down to the warmer
lowlands.

This witch was a wrinkled creature, hard of eye, thin-lipped,
with hands that looked like roots of trees, and so tough was her
skin that knife could not cut nor arrow pierce it. In the country
that swept down to the sea she was greatly feared, and hated, too.
The hate came because by some strange magic she was able to
draw children to her one by one, and how she did it no man knew.
But the truth is that she had a bright and shining magic ball, and
this she left in places where children played, but never where man
or woman could see it.

One day, near the lake called Oretta, a brother and sister were at
play and saw the magic ball at the foot of a little hill. Pleased with
its brightness and beauty Natalia ran to it, intending to pick it up
and take it home, but, to her surprise, as she drew near to it the ball
rolled away; then, a little way off, came to rest again. Again she
ran to it and almost had her hand on it when it escaped, exactly as
a piece of thistle-down does, just as she was about to grasp it. So
she followed it, always seeming to be on the point of catching it

but never doing so, and as she ran her brother Luis followed, careful lest she should come to harm. The strange part of it was that every time the ball stopped it rested close to some berry bush or by the edge of a crystal-clear spring, so that she, like all who were thus led away, always found at the moment of resting something to eat or to drink or to refresh herself. Nor, strangely enough, did she tire, but because of the magic went skipping and running and jumping just as long as she followed the ball. Nor did any one under the spell of that magic note the passing of time, for days were like hours and a night like the shadow of a swiftly flying cloud.

At last, chasing the ball, Natalia and Luis came to a place in the valley where the Rio Chico runs between great hills, and it was dark and gloomy and swept by heavy grey clouds. The land was strewn with mighty broken rocks and here and there were patches of snow, and soon great snow flakes appeared in the air. Then boy and girl were terror-struck, for they knew, with all the wandering and twisting and turning they had lost their way. But the ball still rolled on, though slower now, and the children followed. But the air grew keener and colder and the sun weaker, so that they were very glad indeed when they came to a black rock where, at last, the ball stopped.

Natalia picked it up, and for a moment gazed at its beauty, but for a moment only. For no sooner had she gazed at it and opened her lips to speak than it vanished as a soap bubble does, at which her grief was great. Luis tried to cheer her and finding that her hands were icy cold led her to the north side of the rock where it was warmer, and there he found a niche like a lap between two great arms, and in the moss-grown cranny Natalia coiled herself up and was asleep in a minute. As for Luis, knowing that as soon as his sister had rested they must set out about finding a way home, he sat down intending to watch. But not very long did he keep his eyes open, for he was weary and sad at heart. He tried hard to keep awake, even holding his eyelids open with his fingers, and he stared hard at a sunlit hilltop across the valley, but even that seemed to make him sleepy. Then, too, there were slowly nodding pine trees and the whispering of leaves, coming in a faint murmur from the mountainside. So, soon, Luis slept.

Natalia, being out of the blustering wind, was very comfortable in the little niche between the great stone arms, and she dreamed that she was at home. Her mother, she thought, was combing her hair and singing as she did so. So she forgot her hunger and weariness, and in her dreamland knew nothing of the bare, black rocks and snow-patched hills. Instead, she seemed to be at home where the warm firelight danced on the walls and lighted her father's brown face to a lively red as he mended his horse gear. She saw her brother, too, with his jet-black hair and cherry-red lips. But her mother, she thought, grew rough and careless and pulled her hair, so that she gave a little cry of pain and awoke. Then in a flash she knew where she was and was chilled to the bone with the piercing wind that swept down from the mountain top. Worse still, in front of her stood the old witch of the hills, pointing, pointing, pointing with knotty forefinger, and there were nails on her hands and feet that looked like claws.

Natalia tried to rise, but could not, and her heart was like stone when she found what had happened. It was this: while she slept, the witch had stroked and combed her hair, and meanwhile wrought magic, so that the girl's hair was grown into the rock so very close that she could not as much as turn her head. All that she could do was to stretch forth her arms, and when she saw Luis a little way off she called to him most piteously. But good Luis made no move. Instead, he stood with arms wide apart like one who feels a wall in the dark, moving his hands this way and that. Then Natalia wept, not understanding and little knowing that the witch

had bound Luis with a spell, so that there seemed to be an invisible wall around the rock through which he could not pass, try as he would. But he heard the witch singing in her high and cracked voice, and this is what she sang:

> 'Valley all pebble-sown,
> Valley where wild winds moan!
> Come, mortals, come.

> 'Valley so cool and white,
> Valley of winter night,
> Come, children, come.

> 'Straight like a shaft to mark,
> Come they to cold and dark,
> Children of men!'

Then she ceased and stood with her root-like finger upraised, and from near by came the voice of a great white owl, which took up the song, saying:

> 'Things of the dark and things without name,
> Save us from light and the torch's red flame.'

Now all this was by starlight, but the moment the owl had ceased, from over the hill came a glint of light as the pale moon rose, and with a sound like a thunderclap the witch melted into the great rock and the owl flapped away heavily.

'Brother,' whispered the girl, 'you heard what the owl said?'

'Yes, sister, I heard,' he answered.

'Brother, come to me. I am afraid,' said Natalia, and commenced to cry a little.

'Sister,' he said, 'I try but I cannot. There is something through which I cannot pass. I can see but I cannot press through.'

'Can you not climb over, dear Luis?' asked Natalia.

'No, Natalia. I have reached high as I can, but the wall that I cannot see goes up and up.'

'Is there no way to get in on the other side of the rock, dear, dear Luis? I am very cold and afraid, being here alone.'

'Sister, I have walked around. I have felt high and low. But it is always the same. I cannot get through, I cannot climb over, I cannot crawl under. But I shall stay here with you, so fear not.'

At that Natalia put her hands to her face and wept a little, but very quietly, and it pained Luis to see the tears roll down her cheeks and turn to little ice pearls as they fell. After a while Natalia spoke again, but through sobs.

'Brother mine, you heard what the owl said?'

'Yes, sister.'

'Does it mean nothing to you?' she asked.

'Nothing,' he replied.

'But listen,' said Natalia. 'These were the words: "Save us from light and the torch's red flame."'

'I heard that, Natalia. What does it mean?'

'It means, brother, that the things in this horrible valley fear fire. So go, brother. Leave me a while but find fire, and come back with it swiftly. There will be sickening loneliness, so haste, haste.'

Hearing that, Luis was sad, for he was in no mood to leave his sister in that plight. Still she urged him, saying: 'Speed, brother, speed.'

Even then he hesitated, until with a great swoop there passed over the rock a condor wheeling low, and it said as it passed: 'Fire will conquer frosted death.'

'You hear, brother,' said Natalia. 'So speed and find fire and return before night.'

Then Luis stayed no longer, but waved his sister a farewell and set off down the valley, following the condor that hovered in the air, now darting away and now returning. So Luis knew that the great bird led him, and he ran, presently finding the river and following it until he reached the great vega where the waters met.

At the meeting of the waters he came to a house, a poor thing made of earth and stones snuggled in a warm fold of the hills. No one was about there, but as the condor flew high and, circling in the air, became a small speck, Luis knew that it would be well to stay a while and see what might befall. Pushing open the door he saw by the ashes in the fireplace that someone lived there, for there were red embers well covered to keep the fire alive. So seeing that the owner of the house would return soon he made himself free of the place, which was the way of that country, and brought fresh water from the spring. Then he gathered wood and piled it neatly by the fireside. Next he blew upon the embers and added twigs and sticks until a bright fire glowed, after which he took the broom of twigs and swept the earth floor clean.

How the man of the house came into the room Luis never knew, but there he was, sitting by the fire on a stool. He looked at things but said nothing to Luis, only nodding his head. Then he brought bread and yerba and offered some to Luis. After they had eaten the old man spoke, and this is what he said:

'Wicked is the white witch, and there is but one way to defeat her. What, lad, is the manner of her defeat? Tell me that.'

Then Luis, remembering what the condor had said, repeated the words: '"Fire will conquer frosted death."'

'True,' said the man slowly, nodding his head. 'And your sister is there. Now here comes our friend the condor, who sees far and knows much.'

'Now with cold grows faint her breath,
Fire will conquer frosted death.'

Having said that the great bird wheeled up sharply.

But no sooner was it out of sight than a turkey came running and stood a moment, gobbling. To it the old man gave a lighted brand, repeating the words the condor had spoken.

Off sped the turkey with the blazing stick, running through marsh and swamp in a straight line, and Luis and the old man watched. Soon the bird came to a shallow lagoon, yet made no halt. Straight through the water it sped, and so swiftly that the spray dashed up on either side. High the turkey held the stick, but not high enough, for the splashing water quenched the fire, and seeing that, the bird returned, dropping the blackened stick at the old man's feet.

'Give me another, for the maiden is quivering cold,' said the turkey. 'This time I will run round the lake.'

'No. No,' answered the man. 'You must know that when the water spirit kisses the fire king, the fire king dies. So, that you may remember, from now and for ever you will carry on your feathers the marks of rippling water.'

Down again swooped the condor and a little behind him came a goose, flying heavily. As before, the condor cried:

'Now with cold grows faint her breath,
Fire will conquer frosted death,'

and then he flew away once again toward the witch mountain.

To the goose the old man gave a blazing stick and at once the brave bird set off, flying straight in the direction the condor had taken. Over vega and over lagoon she went, pausing only at a snowclad hilltop, because the stick had burned close to her beak. So she dropped it in the snow to get a better hold, and when she picked it up again there was but a charred thing. Sad enough the goose returned to the house, bearing the blackened stick, and begged to be given another chance.

'No. No,' said the old man. 'The silver snow queen's kiss is death to the fire king. That is something you must remember. From now on and for ever you must carry feathers of grey like the ashes. But here comes the condor and we must hear his message.'

Sadly then the goose went away, her feathers ash grey, and the condor wheeled low again, calling:

'Fainter grows the maiden's breath,
Night must bring the frosted death,'

and having said this, like an arrow he set off.

No sooner had he gone than the long-legged, long-billed flamingo dropped to the ground.

'Your beak is long,' said the old man, 'but fly swiftly, for the stick is short.'

The flamingo took the burning stick by the end and made straight for the mountain, racing with all possible speed. As for Luis, he made up his mind to tarry no longer and set off, running like a deer. But an ostrich, seeing him, spread her wings like sails

and ran by his side. On her back Luis placed his hand, and with that help sped as fast as the flamingo. In the air the flamingo went like an arrow, resting not, although the blazing fire burned her neck and breast until it became pink and red. But that she heeded not. Straight up the valley and to the rock where Natalia was bound went she, and into a heap of dried moss on the south side of the rock she dropped the blazing stick. Up leaped the dancing flames, and with a tremendous noise the rock flew into a thousand pieces and the power of the witch was gone for ever. As for Natalia, she was at once freed, and with her gentle, cool hand stroked the breast of the flamingo so that the burns were healed, but as a sign of its bravery the bird has carried a crimson breast from that day to this.

As for Natalia and Luis, they lived for many, many years in the valley, and about them birds of many kinds played and lived and reared their young, and the magic ball of the witch lived only in the memory of men.

CHARLES J. FINGER

Giacco and His Bean

ONCE upon a time there was a little boy named Giacco who had no father or mother. The only food he had was a cup of beans. Each day he ate a bean, until finally there was only one left. So he put this bean into his pocket and walked until night. He saw a little house under a mulberry tree. Giacco knocked at the door. An old man came out and asked what he wanted.

'I have no father or mother,' said Giacco. 'And I have no food except this one bean.'

'Poor boy,' said the kind old man. He gave Giacco four mulberries to eat and let him sleep by the fire. During the night the bean rolled out of Giacco's pocket and the cat ate it up. When Giacco awoke, he cried, 'Kind old man, your cat has eaten my bean. What shall I do?'

'You may take the cat,' said the kind old man. 'I do not want to keep such a wicked animal.'

So Giacco took the cat and walked all day, until he came to a little house under a walnut tree. He knocked at the door. An old man came out and asked what he wanted.

'I have no father or mother,' said Giacco. 'And I have only this cat that ate the bean.'

'*Too* bad!' said the kind old man. He gave Giacco three walnuts to eat and let him sleep in the dog kennel. During the night the dog ate up the cat, and when Giacco awoke, he cried, 'Kind old man, your dog has eaten my cat!'

'You may take the dog,' said the kind old man. 'I do not want to keep such a mean brute.'

So Giacco took the dog, and walked all day until he came to a

298

little house under a fig-tree. He knocked at the door. An old man came out and asked what he wanted.

'I have no father or mother,' said Giacco. 'I have only this dog that ate the cat that ate the bean.'

'How very sad!' said the kind old man, and gave Giacco two figs to eat and let him sleep in the pigsty.

That night the pig ate up the dog, and when Giacco awoke he cried, 'Kind old man, your pig has eaten up my dog!'

'You may take the pig,' said the kind old man. 'I do not care to keep such a disgusting creature.'

So Giacco took the pig and walked all day until he came to a little house under a chestnut tree. He knocked at the door. An old man came out and asked what he wanted.

'I have no father or mother and only this pig that ate the dog that ate the cat that ate the bean,' said Giacco.

'How pitiful!' said the kind old man, and gave Giacco one chestnut to eat, and let him sleep in the stable. During the night the horse ate up the pig and when Giacco awoke he cried, 'Kind old man, your horse has eaten up my pig!'

'You may take the horse,' said the kind old man. 'I do not want to keep such a worthless beast.' So Giacco rode away on the horse.

He rode all day until he came to a castle. He knocked at the gate and a voice cried, 'Who is there?'

'It is Giacco. I have no father or mother and I have only this horse that ate the pig that ate the dog that ate the cat that ate the bean.'

'Ha! Ha! Ha!' laughed the Soldier. 'I will tell the King.'

'Ha! Ha! Ho! Ho!' laughed the King. 'Whoever heard of a bean that ate the cat that ate the dog that ate the pig that ate the horse.'

'Excuse me, Your Majesty, it is just the other way around,' said

Giacco. 'It was the horse that ate the pig that ate the dog that ate the cat that ate the bean.'

'Ha! Ha! Ho! Ho!' laughed the King. 'My mistake! Of course, it was the bean that ate the horse; no, I mean the horse that ate the bean; no, I mean – Ha! Ha Ho! Ho!' laughed the King, and the knights began to laugh, and the ladies began to laugh, and the maids began to laugh, and the cooks began to laugh, and the bells began to ring, and the birds began to sing, and all the people in the kingdom laughed and sang, and the King came to the gate and said,

'Giacco, if you will tell me every day about the bean that ate the horse; I mean the horse that ate the bean; no, I mean the horse that ate the pig that ate the dog that ate the cat that ate the bean – Ha! Ha! Ha! Ha! Ho! Ho! Ho! Ho! you shall sit on the throne beside me!'

So Giacco put on a golden crown and sat upon the throne, and every day he told about the horse that ate the pig that ate the dog that ate the cat that ate the bean, and everybody laughed and sang and lived happily ever after.

FLORENCE BOTSFORD

Snow and Sun

White bird, featherless,
Flew from Paradise,
Pitched on the castle wall;
Along came Lord Landless,
Took it up handless,
And rode away horseless
To the King's white hall.

The Wind in a Frolic

The wind one morning sprang up from sleep,
Saying, 'Now for a frolic! now for a leap!
Now for a madcap galloping chase!
I'll make a commotion in every place!'

So it swept with a bustle right through a great town,
Cracking the signs and scattering down
Shutters; and whisking with merciless squalls,
Old women's bonnets and gingerbread stalls.

There never was heard a much lustier shout,
As the apples and oranges trundled about;
And the urchins that stand, with their thievish eyes
For ever on watch, ran off each with a prize.

Then away to the fields it went blustering and humming,
And the cattle all wondered what monster was coming.
It plucked by the tails the grave matronly cows,
And tossed the colts' manes all over their brows;
Till, offended at such an unusual salute,
They all turned their backs and stood sulky and mute.

So on it went, capering and playing its pranks, –
Whistling with reeds on the broad river's banks.
Puffing the birds as they sat on the spray,
Or the traveller grave on the King's highway.
It was not too nice to hustle the bags
Of the beggar, and flutter his dirty rags;
'Twas so bold that it feared not to play its joke
With the doctor's wig or the gentleman's cloak.

Through the forest it roared, and cried gaily, 'Now,
You sturdy old oaks, I'll make you bow!'

And it made them bow without more ado,
For it cracked their great branches through and through.

Then it rushed like a monster on cottage and farm,
Striking their dwellers with sudden alarm;
And they ran out like bees in a mid-summer swarm:
There were dames with their kerchiefs tied over their caps,
To see if their poultry were free from mishaps;
The turkeys they gobbled, the geese screamed aloud,
And the hens crept to roost in a terrified crowd;
There was rearing of ladders, and logs were laid on,
Where the thatch from the roof threatened soon to be gone.

But the wind had swept on, and had met in a lane
With a schoolboy, who panted and struggled in vain;
For it tossed him and twirled him, then passed – and he stood
With his hat in a pool, and his shoes in the mud!
Then away went the wind in its holiday glee,
And now it was far on the billowy sea:
And the lordly ships felt its staggering blow,
And the little boats darted to and fro.

But, lo! it was night, and it sank to rest
On the sea-bird's rock in the gleaming west,
Laughing to think, in its frolicsome fun,
How little of mischief it really had done.

WILLIAM HOWITT
Illustrated by PEGGY FORTNUM

The Ogre Courting

In days when ogres were still the terror of certain districts, there was one who had long kept a whole neighbourhood in fear without anyone daring to dispute his tyranny.

By thefts and exactions, by heavy ransoms from merchants too old and tough to be eaten, in one way and another, the Ogre had become very rich; and although those who knew could tell of huge cellars full of gold and jewels, and yards and barns groaning with the weight of stolen goods, the richer he grew the more anxious and covetous he became. Moreover, day by day, he added to his stores; for though (like most ogres) he was as stupid as he was strong, no one had ever been found, by force or fraud, to get the better of him.

What he took from the people was not their heaviest grievance. Even to be killed and eaten by him was not the chance they thought of most. A man can die but once; and if he is a sailor, a shark may eat him, which is not so much better than being devoured by an ogre. No, that was not the worst. The worst was this – he would keep getting married. And as he liked little wives, all the short women lived in fear and dread. And as his wives always died very soon, he was constantly courting fresh ones.

Some said he ate his wives; some said he tormented, and others, that he only worked them to death. Everybody knew it was not a desirable match, and yet there was not a father who dare refuse his daughter if she were asked for. The Ogre only cared for two things in a woman – he liked her to be little, and a good housewife.

Now it was when the Ogre had just lost his twenty-fourth wife (within the memory of man) that these two qualities were eminently united in the person of the smallest and most notable woman of the district, the daughter of a certain poor farmer. He was so poor that he could not afford properly to dower his daughter, who had in consequence remained single beyond her first youth. Everybody felt sure that Managing Molly must now be married to the Ogre. The tall girls stretched themselves till they looked like maypoles and said: 'Poor thing!' The slatterns gossiped from house to house, the heels of their shoes clacking as they went, and cried that this was what came of being too thrifty.

And sure enough, in due time, the giant widower came to the farmer as he was in the field looking over his crops, and proposed for Molly there and then. The farmer was so much put out that he did not know what he said in reply, either when he was saying it, or afterwards, when his friends asked about it. But he remembered that the Ogre had invited himself to sup at the farm that day week.

Managing Molly did not distress herself at the news.

'Do what I bid you, and say as I say,' said she to her father; 'and if the Ogre does not change his mind, at any rate you shall not come empty-handed out of the business.'

By his daughter's desire the farmer now procured a large number of hares, and a barrel of white wine, which expenses completely emptied his slender stocking. Molly herself went round to all her neighbours, and borrowed a lot of new household linen, with which she filled the kitchen shelves. On the day of the Ogre's visit, she made a delicious and savoury stew with the hares in the biggest pickling tub, and the wine-barrel was set on a bench near the table.

When the Ogre came, Molly served up the stew, and the Ogre sat down to sup, his head just touching the kitchen rafters. The stew was perfect, and there was plenty of it. For what Molly and her father ate was hardly to be counted in the tub-full. The Ogre was very much pleased, and said politely:

'I'm afraid, my dear, that you have been put to great trouble

and expense on my account. I have a large appetite, and like to sup
well.'

'Don't mention it, sir,' said Molly. 'The fewer rats the more
corn. How do *you* cook them?'

'Not one of all the extravagant hussies I have had as wives ever
cooked them at all,' said the Ogre; and he thought to himself,
'Such a stew out of rats! What frugality! What a housewife!'
'I suppose you spin?' he inquired.

Molly held out her hand, in which was a linen towel made from the last month's spinnings, and said: 'All that came off my wheel last month.'

But as her hand was towards the shelves, the Ogre thought that all the linen he saw there was from thread of her spinning; and his admiration grew every moment.

When he broached the wine, he was no less pleased, for it was of the best.

'This, at any rate, must have cost you a great deal, neighbour,' said he, drinking the farmer's health as Molly left the room.

'I don't know that rotten apples could be better used,' said the farmer; 'But I leave all that to Molly. Do you brew at home?'

'We give *our* rotten apples to the pigs,' growled the Ogre. 'But things will be better ordered when she is my wife.'

The Ogre was now in great haste to conclude the match, and asked what dowry the farmer would give his daughter.

'I should never dream of giving a dowry with Molly,' said the farmer boldly. 'Whoever gets her gets dowry enough. On the contrary, I shall expect a good round sum from the man who deprives me of her. Our wealthiest farmer is just widowed, and therefore sure to be in a hurry for marriage. He has an eye to the main chance, and would not grudge to pay well for such a wife, I'll warrant.'

'I'm no churl myself,' said the Ogre, who was anxious to secure his thrifty bride at any price; and he named a large sum of money, thinking: 'We shall live on rats henceforward, and the beef and mutton will soon cover the dowry.'

'Double that, and we'll see,' said the farmer stoutly.

But the Ogre became angry, and cried:

'What are you thinking of, man? Who is to hinder my carrying your lass off, without "with your leave" or "by your leave", dowry or none?'

'How little you know her!' said the farmer. 'She is so firm that she would be cut to pieces sooner than give you any benefit of her thrift, unless you dealt fairly in the matter.'

'Well, well,' said the Ogre, 'let us meet each other.' And he named a sum larger than he at first proposed, and less than the farmer had asked. This the farmer agreed to, as it was enough to make him prosperous for life.

'Bring it in a sack tomorrow morning,' said he to the Ogre, 'and then you can speak to Molly; she's gone to bed now.'

The next morning, accordingly, the Ogre appeared, carrying the dowry in a sack, and Molly came to meet him.

'There are two things,' said she, 'I would ask of any lover of mine: a new farmhouse, built as I should direct, with a view to economy; and a feather-bed of fresh goose feathers, filled when the old woman plucks her geese. If I don't sleep well, I cannot work well.'

'That is better than asking for finery,' thought the Ogre; 'and after all, the house will be my own.' So to save the expense of labour he built it himself, and worked hard, day after day, under Molly's orders, till winter came. Then it was finished.

'Now for the feather-bed,' said Molly. 'I'll make the ticking, and when the old woman plucks her geese, I'll let you know.'

When it snows, they say the old woman up yonder is plucking geese; so at the first snowstorm Molly sent for the Ogre.

'Now you see the feathers falling,' said she, 'so fill up the bed.'

'How am I to catch them?' cried the Ogre.

'Stupid! don't you see them lying there in a heap?' cried Molly; 'get a shovel, and set to work.'

The Ogre accordingly carried in shovelfuls of snow to the bed, but as it melted as fast as he put it in, his labour never seemed done. Towards night the room got so cold that the snow would not melt, and now the bed was soon filled.

Molly hastily covered it with sheets and blankets, and said:

'Pray rest here tonight, and tell me if the bed is not comfort itself. Tomorrow we will be married.'

So the tired Ogre lay down on the bed he had filled, but do what he could, he could not get warm.

'The sheets must be damp,' said he, and in the morning he woke with such horrible pains in his bones that he could hardly move, and half the bed had melted away. 'It's no use,' he groaned, 'she's a very managing woman, but to sleep on such a bed would be the death of me.' And he went off home as quickly as he could, before Managing Molly could call upon him to be married; for she was so managing, that he was more than half afraid of her already.

When Molly found that he had gone, she sent the farmer after him.

'What does he want?' cried the Ogre, when they told him the farmer was at the door.

'He says the bride is waiting for you,' was the reply.

'Tell him I'm too ill to be married,' said the Ogre.

But the messenger soon returned:

'He says she wants to know what you will give her to make up for the disappointment.'

'She's got the dowry, and the farm, and the feather-bed,' groaned the Ogre; 'what more is there she can possibly want?'

But again the messenger returned:

'She says you've pressed the feather-bed flat, and she wants some more goose feathers.'

'There are geese enough in the yard,' yelled the Ogre. 'Let him drive them home, and if he has another word to say, put him down to roast.'

The farmer, who overheard this order, lost no time in taking his leave, and as he passed through the yard he drove home as fine a flock of geese as you will see on a common.

It is said that the Ogre never recovered from the effects of sleeping on the old woman's feathers, and was less powerful than before.

As for Managing Molly, being now well dowered, she had no lack of offers of marriage, and was soon mated to her mind.

JULIANA HORATIA EWING

Mima

Jemima is my name,
But oh, I have another;
My father always calls me Meg,
And so do Bob and mother;
Only my sister, jealous of
The strands of my bright hair,
'Jemima – Mima – Mima!'
Calls, mocking, up the stair.

WALTER DE LA MARE

Nicholas and the Fast Moving Diesel

ONCE upon a time there was a small boy called Nicholas. He had a dog called Jock and a great friend called Peter Perkins who lived at Rose Cottage near the railway line.

Now Peter's father was very sick and could not go out and earn any money, so Peter and his father and mother were very poor.

Nicholas was a kind boy and hated to see them so poor, so he often brought them big baskets of food and sometimes gave them whole piles of money.

One day Nicholas had a good idea. He got an extra big basket and put in it an extra lot of food. Then he stuffed his pockets full of money and with his dog Jock went to Mrs Perkins at Rose Cottage and said; 'Oh Mrs Perkins may I come and stay with you?'

'Nicholas I am afraid we can't have you,' said Mrs Perkins with a tear in her eye. 'You see we are much too poor.'

'That's all right,' said Nicholas. 'I have brought an extra big basket of food and lots of money.' Mrs Perkins smiled and said he was a darling boy and of course he could stay.

Peter was pleased and Jock was pleased too and wagged his tail so hard that it nearly came off.

Nicholas stayed a long time and he and Peter enjoyed themselves together; but there came a day when they arrived down to breakfast and found Mrs Perkins crying by the kitchen table.

'Why are you crying Mrs Perkins?' said Nicholas. 'Oh please don't be sad.'

'I can't help it,' sobbed Mrs Perkins. 'Mr Perkins is so ill and the doctor has ordered extra expensive medicine. I have spent all the money you gave me. There is only dry bread for breakfast. The butcher, the grocer, and the baker will not give us any food and now there is not even any water. Oh dear, what shall we do?'

'Cheer up,' said Nicholas, trying to be big and brave. 'Peter and I will have a good think. We are sure to find some way of making money. Anyhow, I will get you some water right away.'

Nicholas then took a large jug and filled it at the pump across the road and tried to be as cheerful as possible when he got back.

All the same they were rather sad munching their dry bread. Jock however was particularly gruff and muttered between his whiskers – 'Well dash my wig. This is a dog's life. I have a good mind to steal a leg of mutton from the butcher's.'

'No, you mustn't steal,' said Nicholas, who had heard him. 'That would never do.'

After they had eaten enough dry bread and had a good drink of cool clear crystal water, Nicholas, Peter and Jock walked up and down the garden path thinking and thinking.

'I wish I could be an engine driver,' said Peter 'and earn a lot of money.'

'I would like to, too,' said Nicholas, 'but we must think of something possible, like helping Farmer Giles.'

Then something exciting happened. A train came along the railway line at the bottom of the garden and stopped dead and an old lady put her head out of a carriage window to see what was wrong.

At that moment a puff of wind blew off her hat and spectacles and she was so upset she dropped her bag too. They all rolled down the embankment.

'Oh dear, oh dear, what shall I do?' she cried, and then she saw the boys and called to them to help her.

Nicholas picked up the spectacles, Peter the hat, and Jock the bag, and they clambered up the embankment and on to the train and gave them to her, but no sooner had they done so, than the train started and went too fast for them to get off. To make matters worse, the carriage door was locked and they could not get in.

The train went faster and faster till it rushed along. Jock looked very funny with his hair blown out straight by the wind.

'Are you both all right?' shouted Nicholas through his teeth.

Peter said 'Yes', and Jock went 'Wuff wuff!' as if to say 'Of course I am don't be silly.'

'Good,' said Nicholas, 'I have an idea. We will go and see the engine driver; perhaps he will give us a job. He might even teach us how to drive an engine.'

Then, with Nicholas leading the way, they all climbed along

the carriage, on to the engine tender, over the coals, and jumped with a great big clang into the cab of the engine.

You can just imagine how surprised were the engine driver and the fireman. The engine driver was very cross and said, 'Well dash my wig. Boys, boys, and a dog in the cab of my engine. Can't have them here. Impossible. Against Company regulations. Go away at once.'

'Oh please, please sir,' said Nicholas, 'do let us stay. Peter's father is so ill and we are very poor and only had dry bread for breakfast. We want to stay and learn to be engine drivers and earn lots of money.'

But the engine driver still said, 'Impossible, go away.'

Now the fireman was a kind man and said to the engine driver, 'Steady, Mate, you can't turn those boys off now. The train is going too fast. I have an idea, let's put the boys to work. I will pay them for it, and you and I can sit down and have a nice cup of tea.'

'Oh all right,' said the engine driver rather grumpily. 'They can stay, but it is against Company regulations you know.'

Soon Peter was shovelling coal on to the fire while Jock helped him by pushing lumps of coal along the floor with his nose and Nicholas was busy leaning with his head out of the cab watching the railway line very carefully to see if the signals were up or down. The fireman poured out two cups of tea, one for the driver and one for himself, BUT – they had only taken one large swig when they fell to the floor making the most horrible groans. 'Ooh, aah, what a pain, the tea is poisoned.' And so it was. There must have been something wrong with the milk.

'Good Heavens!' said Nicholas. 'What are we to do now? The train is rushing along and we must stop it at the next station.' No sooner had he said this than they dashed through a small station and roared through a long dark tunnel.

'Oh dear, oh dear, this is awful. Do you know how to stop trains, Peter?'

'No,' said Peter, 'and I am frightened.'

Then Nicholas looked up the line and went cold with horror. He saw a signal ahead. It was up, and beyond the signal was a train standing still on the line. He realized that if they did not stop they would dash into the other train and there would be a terrible accident.

'Quickly Peter and Jock, turn those little handles,' shouted Nicholas, but Peter and Jock turned and turned and the train only went faster than ever.

Then Nicholas noticed the big lever and decided to pull it;

perhaps that would stop the train, but he pulled and pulled and it would not come down. He shouted to Peter to help him, and they both pulled and still it would not come down. Finally, Jock jumped up and caught it in his teeth and they all gave a big tug together and down it came, and the train stopped just in time.

'Phew,' said Nicholas, 'what a relief. We have saved the train from a terrible accident.'

Nicholas decided to run up to the engine of the other train and ask its engine driver to help them, and he jumped out of the cab to do so, only to find that the signal was down and the other train puffing away into the distance.

They were in a fix. The engine driver and fireman were still moaning and groaning on the floor, and do you think Nicholas, Peter and Jock could push up the lever to start the train again? No, they could not, though they pushed and pulled as hard as they could.

Then Nicholas heard a sound which made him go colder with horror than before. It was the sound of a fast moving diesel coming up the line behind them. It was the express. The signal was down and it would come crashing into them from behind.

There was only one thing to do and Nicholas did it. He jumped out of the cab, ran to the end of the train, stood between the lines, pulled off his red coat and waved and waved while Jock stood beside him and barked as loudly as he could.

The diesel came rushing towards them. It seemed to go faster than ever. Would its driver see them in time to stop another terrible accident?

Nearer and nearer it came, then there was a great grinding of brakes and it stopped just in front of Nicholas and a very angry driver jumped out.

Nicholas told him the sad story and took him to the cab of his engine. There they found the engine driver and fireman still groaning and moaning as before, though they both seemed a little better.

'Here's a pretty kettle of fish,' said the diesel driver. 'This train must be started at once. My train is the express and I am late already.'

'Sorry, Mate,' said the engine driver. 'Poisoned tea – very ill – awful pain – brave boys – saved train – terrible accident – Oh! Oh! – more pain – but better now.'

'I'm better too,' said the fireman. 'Pain – still – bad – but – think we – can – start.'

'Good, then be off as quickly as you can,' said the diesel driver, 'but be sure that you stop at the next station and see the station master.'

The diesel driver went back to his train, while Nicholas, Peter, Jock, and the engine driver and fireman, still groaning, all pulled up the lever and off they went.

They soon came to a station, where they stopped, and Nicholas and Peter helped the engine driver and fireman across the platform. They found the station master in his office. The engine driver and the fireman asked to sit down, because they still felt ill; then they began their story.

At first the station master looked cross, but soon he began to smile and when the story was done he turned to Nicholas and Peter and said, 'Boys, I was cross at first because children and dogs are not allowed in the cabs of engines, but as you were very brave and saved the train from two terrible accidents, I can't help feeling pleased. Now I am going to give you some money and send you home in a car.' Then he gave them each some money and to Jock he gave a nice juicy bone, patting him on the head and calling him a fine fellow as he did so.

The station master next turned to the engine driver and fireman and said, 'You could not help having the boys in the cab of your engine, but you drank tea while on duty, which, as you know, is strictly against Company regulations. However, all's well that ends well, so we will forget it.'

Nicholas and Peter felt very pleased with themselves and enjoyed their ride in the car.

Jock ate his bone on the mat and made such a mess that Nicholas had to shake the mat out of the window in case the driver should see it and be angry.

Mrs Perkins was delighted to see them and when they gave her the money the station master had given to them, she said, 'You clever darlings, now I can buy some food.'

Then she put on her hat, picked up a big basket and went to the village. First she bought some extra strong and expensive medicine for Mr Perkins, and then she bought –

meat	milk	flour
bread	tea	eggs
potatoes	coffee	jam
cabbage	sugar	treacle
onions	cream	and lots of
carrots	salt	strawberries

When she came back she gave Mr Perkins a dose of the medicine, then she cooked a lovely dinner. The medicine did Mr

Perkins so much good and the smell of the dinner was so delicious that he felt quite hungry and asked if he could come down in his dressing gown and have dinner with them.

They all shouted 'Hurray, yes do,' and they all had a lovely time.

The next morning there was a terrific rattatat at the door. It was the postman. He had two fat envelopes, one for Nicholas and one for Peter, and a small parcel addressed to 'The Dog Jock. Rose Cottage'. In each envelope was a large sum of money and a letter from the railway company.

The letter to Nicholas read –

THE SOUTH MIDLAND RAILWAY CO.

8th Sept, 45.

Master Nicholas,
Rose Cottage.
Sir,

I wish to thank you on behalf of the Railway Co. for saving our train from two terrible accidents.

I enclose a large sum of money as a reward.

If you want to become an engine driver, either diesel, electric or steam, come and see us.

Yours faithfully,
D. Jones,
Director.

Peter's letter was just the same.

Inside the parcel for Jock was a beautiful blue collar with a gold medal hanging from it.

On one side of the medal was written – 'To Jock for helping to save our train.' On the other side – 'In gratitude from the S.M.R.'

The very next day Nicholas, Peter and Jock set off for the railway company.

Nicholas said, 'I want to be a diesel engine driver.' Peter said,

'I want to be an electric train driver.' Jock said 'Wuff Wuff. I want to be a steam engine driver,' but Nicholas said 'Don't be silly, you had better come with me.'

Nicholas and Jock became very clever at driving and soon were given to drive the fastest train in England – The Midland Flyer – a diesel.

Written and illustrated by EDWARD ARDIZZONE

I Had a Little Nut-Tree

I had a little nut-tree,
   Nothing would it bear
But a silver nut-meg
   And a golden pear.

The King of Spain's daughter
   Came to visit me,
All for the sake
   Of my little nut-tree.

I skipped over water,
   I danced over sea,
And all the birds in the air
   Couldn't catch me.

The Owl and the Pussy-Cat

The Owl and the Pussy-cat went to sea
In a beautiful pea-green boat;
They took some honey, and plenty of money,
Wrapped up in a five-pound note.
The Owl looked up to the stars above,
And sang to a small guitar,
'O lovely Pussy! O Pussy, my love,
What a beautiful Pussy you are,
        You are,
        You are!
What a beautiful Pussy you are!'

Pussy said to the Owl, 'You elegant fowl!
How charmingly sweet you sing!
O let us be married! too long we have tarried:
But what shall we do for a ring?'
They sailed away for a year and a day,
To the land where the Bong-tree grows,

And there in a wood a Piggy-wig stood,
With a ring at the end of his nose.
       His nose
       His nose,
With a ring at the end of his nose.

'Dear Pig, are you willing to sell for one shilling
Your ring?' Said the Piggy, 'I will.'
So they took it away, and were married next day
By the Turkey who lives on the hill.
They dinèd on mince, and slices of quince,
Which they ate with a runcible spoon;
And hand in hand, on the edge of the sand,
They danced by the light of the moon,
       The moon
       The moon,
They danced by the light of the moon.

Written and illustrated by EDWARD LEAR

Whence is This Fragrance?

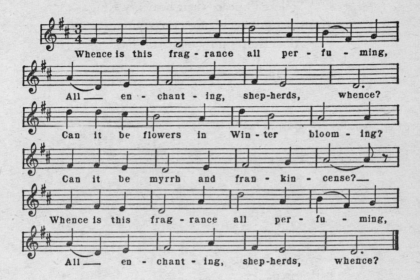

Whence is this frag - rance all per - fu - ming,
All __ en - chant - ing, shep-herds, whence?
Can it be flowers in Win - ter bloom - ing?
Can it be myrrh and fran - kin - cense?__
Whence is this frag - rance all per - fu - ming,
All __ en - chant - ing, shep-herds, whence?

Whence is this fragrance all perfuming,
    All enchanting, Shepherds, whence?
Can it be flowers in winter blooming?
    Can it be myrrh and frankincense?
Whence is this fragrance all perfuming,
    All enchanting, Shepherds, whence?

At Bethlehem in manger lowly
    Unto us a King is born.
Let us adore this infant holy,
    Let us rejoice this Christmas morn.
At Bethlehem in manger lowly
    Unto us a King is born.

Come let us kneel before the saviour,
    All creatures now on earth may sing.
Lion and lamb with mild behaviour
    Follow in peace their heav'nly King.
Come let us kneel before the saviour,
    All creatures now on earth may sing.

Cobwebs

I

TWINETTE the Spider was young, hungry and industrious. 'Weave yourself a web, my dear,' said her mother, 'as you know how, without teaching, and catch flies for yourself; only don't weave near me in the corner here. I am old, and stay in corners; but you are young, and needn't. Besides, you would be in my way. Scramble along the rafters to a little distance off, and spin. But mind! just see there's nothing there – below you, I mean – before you begin. You won't catch anything to eat, if there isn't empty space about you for the flies to fly in.'

Twinette was dutiful, and obeyed. She scrambled along the woodwork of the groined roof of the church – for it was there her mother lived – till she had gone what she thought might fairly be called a little distance off, and then she stopped to look round, which, considering she had eight eyes to do it with, was not difficult. But she was not so sure of what there might be below.

'I wonder whether mother would say there was nothing here – below me, I mean – but empty space for flies to fly in?' said she.

But she might have stood wondering there for ever. So she went back to her mother, and asked what she thought.

'Oh, dear, Oh dear!' said her mother, 'how can I think about what I don't see? There usen't to be anything there in my young days, I'm sure. But everybody must find out things for themselves. Let yourself down by the family rope, as you know how, without teaching, and see for yourself if there's anything there or not.'

Twinette was a very intelligent young spider, quite worthy of the age she was born in; so she thanked her mother for her advice, and was just starting afresh, when another thought struck her. 'How shall I know if there's anything there when I get there?' asked she.

'Dear me, if there's anything there, how can you help seeing it?' cried the mother, rather teased by her daughter's inquiring spirit, 'you with at least eight eyes in your head!'

'Thank you. Now I quite understand,' said Twinette; and scuttling back to the end of the rafter, she began to prepare the family rope.

It was the most exquisite thing in the world – so fine, you could scarcely see it; so elastic, it could be blown about without breaking; such a perfect grey that it looked white against black things, and black against white; so manageable that Twinette could both make it, and slide down by it at once; and when she wished to get back, could slip up by it, and roll it up at the same time!

It was a wonderful rope for anybody to make without teaching. But Twinette was not conceited. Rope-making came as natural to her as eating and fighting do to intelligent little boys, so she thought no more about it than we do of chewing our food.

How she did it is another question, and one not easily answered, however intelligent we may be. Thus much may be hinted: Out of four little spinning-machines near the tail came four little threads, and the rope was a four-twist of these. But as each separate thread was itself a many-twist of a great many others, still finer, I do not pretend to tell the number of strands (as rope-threads are called) in Twinette's family rope. Enough, that as she made it now, it has been from generation to generation, and there seems to be no immediate prospect of a change.

The plan was for the spinner to glue the ends to the rafter, and then start off. Then, out came the threads from the spinning-machines, and twist went the rope; and the further the spinner travelled, the longer the rope became.

And Twinette made ready accordingly, and turning on her back, let herself fairly off.

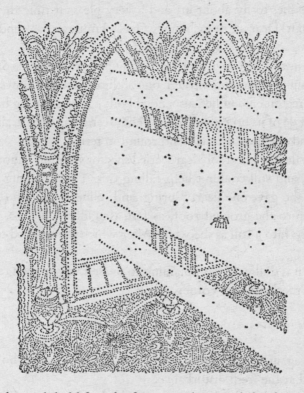

The glue ends held fast, the four strands twined closely together, and down went the family rope, with Twinette at the end, guiding it. Down into the middle of the chancel, where there were carved oaken screens on three sides, and carved oaken seats below, with carved oaken figures at each end of each.

Twinette was about half-way down to the stone-flagged floor, when she shut up the spinning-machines, and stopped to rest and look round. Then, balancing herself at the end of her rope, with her legs crumpled up round her, she made her remarks.

'This is charming!' cried she. 'One had need to travel and see the world. And all's so nice in the middle here. Nice empty space for the flies to fly about in; and a very pleasant time they must have of it! Dear me, how hungry I feel – I must go back and weave at once.'

But just as she was preparing to roll up the rope and be off, a ray of sunshine, streaming through one of the chancel windows, struck in a direct line upon her suspended body, quite startling her with the dazzle of its brightness. Everything seemed in a blaze all round her, and she turned round and round in terror.

'Oh dear, oh dear, oh dear!' cried she, for she didn't know what to say, and still couldn't help calling out. Then, making a great effort, she gave one hearty spring, and, blinded though she was, shot up to the groined roof, as fast as spider could go, rolling the rope into a ball as she went. After which she stopped to complain.

But it is dull work complaining to oneself, so she soon ran back to her mother in the corner.

2

'Back again so soon, my dear?' asked the old lady, not over-pleased at the fresh disturbance.

'Back again at all is the wonder,' whimpered Twinette. 'There's something down there, after all, besides empty space.'

'Why, what did you see?' asked her mother.

'Nothing; that was just it,' answered Twinette. 'I could see nothing for dazzle and blaze; but I did see dazzle and blaze.'

'Young people of the present day are very troublesome with their observations,' remarked the mother; 'however, if one rule will not do, here is another. Did dazzle and blaze shove you out of your place, my dear?'

Twinette said, 'Certainly not – she had come away of herself.'

'Then how could they be anything?' asked her mother. 'Two things could not be in one place at the same time. Let Twinette try to get into her place, while she was there herself, and see if she could.'

Twinette did not try, because she knew she couldn't, but she sat very silent, wondering what dazzle and blaze could be, if they were nothing at all! a puzzle which might have lasted for ever. Fortunately her mother interrupted her, by advising her to go and get something to do. She really couldn't afford to feed her out of *her* web any longer, she said.

'If dazzle and blaze kill me, you'll be sorry, mother,' said Twinette, in a pet.

'Nonsense, about dazzle and blaze,' cried the old Spider, now thoroughly roused. 'I dare say they're only a little more light than usual. There's more or less light up here in the corners even, at times. You talk nonsense, my dear.'

So Twinette scuttled off in silence; for she dared not ask what light was, though she wanted to know.

But she felt too cross to begin to spin. She preferred a search after truth to her dinner, which showed she was no common-place spider. So she resolved to go down below in another place and see if she could find a really empty space; and accordingly prepared the family rope.

When she came down, it was about half a foot further east in the chancel, and a very prosperous journey she made. 'Come! all's safe so far,' said she, her good nature returning. 'I do believe I've found nothing at last. How jolly it is!' As she spoke, she hung dangling at the end of her rope, back downwards, her legs tucked up round her as before, in perfect enjoyment, when, suddenly, the south door of the church was thrown open, and a strong gust set in. It was a windy evening, and the draught that poured into the chancel blew the family rope, with Twinette at the end of it, backwards and forwards through the air, till she turned quite giddy.

'Oh dear, oh dear!' cried she, puffing. 'What shall I do! How

could they say there was nothing here – oh dear! – but empty space for flies – oh dear – to fly in?' But at last, in despair, she made an effort of resistance, and, in the very teeth of the wind, succeeded in coiling up the family rope, and so got back to the rafters.

It was a piece of rare good fortune for her that a lazy, half-alive fly happened to be creeping along it just at the moment. As she landed from her air-dive she pounced on the stroller, killed him, and sucked his juices before he knew where he was, as people say.

Then, throwing down his carcase, she scrambled back to her mother, and told her what she thought, though not in plain words. For what she thought was that the old lady didn't know what she was saying, when she talked about empty space with nothing in it.

'Dazzle and blaze were nothing,' cried she at last, 'though they blinded me because they and I were in one place together, which couldn't be if they'd been anything; and now this is nothing, though it blows me out of my place twenty times in a minute, because I can't see it. What's the use of rules one can't go by, mother? I don't believe you know a quarter of what's down below there.'

The old Spider's head turned as giddy with Twinette's argument as Twinette's had done while swinging in the wind.

'I don't see what it can matter what's there,' whimpered she, 'if there's room for flies to fly about in. I wish you'd go back and spin.'

'That's another part of the question,' remarked Twinette, in answer to the first half of her mother's sentence. In answer to the second she scuttled back to the rafter, intending to be obedient and spin. But she dawdled and thought, and thought and dawdled, till the day was nearly over.

'I will take one more turn down below,' said she to herself at last, 'and look round me again.'

And so she did, but went further down than before; then stopped to rest as usual. Presently, as she hung dangling in the air by her line, she grew venturesome. 'I will sift the matter to the bottom,' thought she. 'I will see how far empty space goes.' So saying she re-opened her spinning-machines and started afresh.

3

It was a wonderful rope, certainly, or it would not have gone on to such a length without breaking. In a few seconds Twinette was on the cold stone pavement. But she didn't like the feel of it at all, so took to running as fast as she could go, and luckily met with a step of woodwork on one side. Up this she hurried at once, and crept into a corner close by, where she stopped to take breath. 'One doesn't know what to expect in such queer outlandish places,' observed she; 'when I've rested I'll go back, but I must wait till I can see a little better.'

Seeing a little better was out of the question, however, for night was coming on, and when, weary of waiting, she stepped out of her hiding-place to look round, the whole church was in darkness.

Now it is one thing to be snug in bed when it is dark, and another to be a long way from home and have lost your way, and not know what may happen to you next minute. Twinette had often been in the dark corner with her mother, and thought nothing of it. Now she shook all over with fright, and wondered what dreadful thing darkness could be.

Then she thought of her mother's rules, and felt quite angry.

'I can't see anything, and I don't feel anything,' murmured she, 'and yet here's something that frightens me out of my wits.'

At last her very fright made her bold. She felt about for the family rope; it was there safe and sound, and she made a spring. Roll went the rope, and up went its owner; higher, higher, higher, through the dark night air; seeing nothing, hearing nothing, feeling nothing but the desperate fear within. By the time she touched the rafter, she was half-exhausted; and as soon as she was safely landed upon it, she fell asleep.

It must have been late next morning when she woke, for the sound of organ music was pealing through the church, and the air vibrations swept pleasantly over her frame; rising and falling like gusts of night, swelling and sinking like waves of the sea, gathering and dispersing like mists of the sky.

She went down by the family rope to observe, but nothing was to be seen to account for her sensations. Fresh ones, however, stole round her, as she hung suspended, for it was a harvest-festival, and large white lilies were grouped with evergreens round the slender pillars of the screens, and filled the air with their powerful scent. Still, nothing disturbed her from her place. Sunshine streamed in through the windows – she even felt it warm on her body – but it interfered with nothing else; and, meanwhile, in such sort as spiders hear, she heard music and prayer. A door opened, and a breeze caught her rope; but still she held fast. So music and prayer and sunshine and breeze and scent were all there together; and Twinette was among them, and saw flies flying about overhead.

This was enough; she went back to the rafter, chose a home, and began to spin. Before evening, her web was completed, and her first prey caught and feasted on. Then she cleared the remains out of her chamber, and sat down in state to think; for Twinette was now a philosopher. It came to her while she was spinning her web. As she crossed and twisted the threads, her ideas grew clearer and clearer, or she fancied so, which did almost as well. Each line she fastened brought its own reflection; and this was the way they went on:

'Empty space is an old wife's tale' – she fixed that very tight. 'Sight and touch are very imperfect guides' – this crossed the other at an angle. 'Two or three things can easily be in one place at the very same time' – this seemed very loose till she tightened it by a second. 'Sunshine and wind and scent and sound don't drive each other out of their places' – that held firm. 'When one has sensations there is something to cause them, whether one sees it, or feels it, or finds it out, or not' – this was a wonderful thread, it went right round the web and was fastened down in several places. 'Light and darkness, and sunshine and wind, and sound and sensation, and fright and pleasure, don't keep away flies' – the little interlacing threads looked quite pretty as she placed them. 'How many things I know of that I don't know much about' – the web got thicker every minute. 'And perhaps there may be ever so many more beyond – ever so many more – ever so many more – beyond.' Those were her very last words. She kept repeating them till she finished her web; and when she sat up in state, after supper, to think, she began to repeat them again; for she could think of nothing better to say. But this was no wonder, for all her thoughts put together made nothing but a cobweb, after all!

MARGARET GATTY

From a Railway Carriage

Faster than fairies, faster than witches,
Bridges and houses, hedges and ditches,
And charging along like troops in a battle,
All through the meadows the horses and cattle:
All of the sights of the hill and the plain
Fly as thick as driving rain;
And ever again, in the wink of an eye,
Painted stations whistle by.

Here is a child who clambers and scrambles,
All by himself and gathering brambles;
Here is a tramp who stands and gazes;
And there is the green for stringing the daisies!

FROM A RAILWAY CARRIAGE

Here is a cart run away in the road,
Lumping along with man and load;
And here is a mill, and there is a river;
Each a glimpse and gone for ever!

ROBERT LOUIS STEVENSON
Illustrated by JOAN MILROY

There was a Crooked Man

There was a crooked man,
    And he went a crooked mile;
He found a crooked sixpence
    Upon a crooked stile:

He bought a crooked cat,
    Which caught a crooked mouse,
And they all lived together
    In a little crooked house.

The Constant Tin Soldier

THERE were once five and twenty tin soldiers, all brothers, for they had all been made out of one old tin spoon. They carried muskets in their arms, and held themselves very upright, and their uniforms were red and blue – very gay indeed. The first words they heard in this world, when the lid was taken off the box wherein they lay, were, 'Tin soldiers!' It was a little boy who made this exclamation, clapping his hands at the same time. They had been given to him because it was his birthday. He now set them out on the table.

The soldiers resembled each other to a hair. One only was rather different from the rest; he had but one leg, for he had been made last, when there was not quite enough tin left. He stood as firmly, however, upon his one leg as the others did upon their two; and this very tin soldier it is whose fortunes seem to us worthy of being told.

On the table where the tin soldiers were set out were several other playthings, but the most charming of them all was a pretty pasteboard castle. Through its little windows one could look into the rooms. In front of the castle stood some tiny trees, clustering round a little mirror intended to represent a lake. Some waxen swans swam in the lake and were reflected on its surface.

All this was very pretty, but prettiest of all was a little damsel standing in the open doorway of the castle. She, too, was cut out of pasteboard, but she had on a frock of the clearest muslin, a little sky-blue riband was flung across her shoulders like a scarf, and in the midst of this scarf was set a bright gold wing. The little lady stretched out both her arms, for she was a dancer, and raised one of her legs so high in the air that the tin soldier could not see it, and fancied she had, like him, only one leg.

'That would be just the wife for me,' thought he, 'but then she is of rather too high a rank. She lives in a castle, I have only a box. Besides, the box is not my own; there are all our five and twenty men in it; it is no place for her! However, there will be no harm in my making acquaintance with her,' and so he stationed himself behind a snuff-box that stood on the table. From this place he had a full view of the delicate little lady, who still remained standing on one leg, yet without losing her balance.

When evening came, all the other tin soldiers were put away into the box, and the people of the house went to bed. The play-things now began to play in their turn. They pretended to visit, to fight battles, and give balls. The tin soldiers rattled in the box, for they wanted to play too, but the lid would not come off. The nut-crackers cut capers, and the slate-pencil played at buying and selling on the slate. There was such a racket that the canary-bird woke up, and began to talk too; but he always talked in verse. The only two who did not move from their places were the little tin soldier and the beautiful dancer. She constantly remained in her graceful position, standing on the very tip of her toe, with out-stretched arms; and, as for him, he stood just as firmly on his one leg, never for a single moment turning his eyes away from her.

Twelve o'clock struck. Crash! Open sprang the lid of the snuff-box, but there was no snuff inside it; no, out jumped a little black conjurer, in fact it was a Jack-in-the-box. 'Tin soldier!' said the conjurer, 'please keep your eyes to yourself!'

But the tin soldier pretended not to hear.

'Well, only wait till tomorrow!' said the conjurer.

When the morrow had come, and the children were out of bed, the tin soldier was placed on the window-ledge, and, whether the conjurer or the wind caused it, all at once the window flew open, and out fell the tin soldier, head foremost, from the third storey to the ground. A dreadful fall was that! His one leg turned over and over in the air, and at last he rested, poised on his soldier's cap, with his bayonet between the paving-stones.

The maid-servant and the little boy immediately came down to look for him; but although they very nearly trod on him they could not see him. If the tin soldier had but called out, 'Here I am!' they might easily have found him; but he thought it would not be becoming for him to cry out, as he was in uniform.

It now began to rain; every drop fell heavier than the last; there was a soaking shower. When it was over, two boys came by.

'Look,' said one, 'here is a tin soldier; he shall have a sail for once in his life.'

So they made a boat out of an old newspaper, and put the tin soldier in it. Away he sailed down the gutter, both the boys running along by the side and clapping their hands. The paper boat rocked to and fro, and every now and then veered round so quickly that the tin soldier became quite giddy; still he moved not a muscle, looked straight before him, and held his bayonet tightly clasped.

All at once the boat sailed under a long gutter-board. He found it as dark here as at home in his own box.

'Where shall I get to next?' thought he. 'Yes, to be sure, it is all that conjurer's doing! Ah, if the little maiden were but sailing with me in the boat I would not mind its being twice as dark!'

Just then a great water-rat that lived under the gutter-board darted out from its nest.

'Have you a passport?' asked the rat. 'Where is your passport?'

But the tin soldier was silent, and held his weapon with a still firmer grasp. The boat sailed on, and the rat followed. Oh! how furiously he showed his teeth, and cried out to sticks and straws: 'Stop him, stop him! he has not paid the toll; he has not shown his

passport!' But the stream grew stronger and stronger. The tin soldier could already catch a glimpse of the bright daylight before the boat came from under the tunnel, but at the same time he heard a roaring noise, at which the boldest heart might well have trembled. Where the tunnel ended, the water of the gutter fell into a great canal. This was as dangerous for the tin soldier as sailing down a mighty waterfall would be for us.

He was now so close to the fall that he could no longer stand upright. The boat darted forwards, the poor tin soldier held himself stiff and immovable as possible; no one could accuse him of having even blinked. The boat span round and round three, nay, four times, and was filled with water to the brim; it must sink.

The tin soldier stood up to his neck in water; deeper and deeper sank the boat, softer and softer grew the paper; the water went over the soldier's head. He thought of the pretty little dancer whom he should never see again, and these words ran in his ears:

> Wild adventure, mortal danger,
> Be thy portion, valiant stranger!

The paper now tore asunder, the tin soldier fell through the rent; but at that moment he was swallowed up by a large fish. Oh, how dark it was! worse even than under the gutter-board, and so narrow too! But the tin soldier was as constant as ever; there he lay, at full length, still shouldering his arms.

The fish turned and twisted about, and made the strangest movements. At last he became quite still; a flash of lightning, as it were, darted through him. The daylight shone brightly, and some one exclaimed, 'Tin soldier!' The fish had been caught, taken to the market, sold, and brought home into the kitchen, where the servant-girl was cutting him up with a large knife. She seized the tin soldier by the middle with two of her fingers, and took him into the next room, where everyone was eager to see the wonderful man who had travelled in the maw of a fish. Our little warrior, however, was by no means proud.

They set him on the table, and there – no, how could anything so extraordinary happen in this world? – the tin soldier was in the very room in which he had been before. He saw the same children, the same playthings on the table – among them the beautiful castle with the pretty little dancing maiden, who was still standing upon

one leg, while she held the other high in the air; she too was
constant. It quite affected the tin soldier; he could have found it in
his heart to weep tin tears, but such weakness would have been
unbecoming in a soldier. He looked at her and she looked at him,
but neither spoke a word.

And now one of the little boys took the soldier and threw him

without ceremony into the stove. He did not give any reason for so doing, but no doubt the conjurer in the snuff-box must have had a hand in it.

The tin soldier now stood in a blaze of red light. He felt extremely hot. Whether this heat were the result of the actual fire or of the flames of love within him he knew not. He looked upon the little damsel, she looked upon him, and he felt that he was melting; but, constant as ever, he still stood shouldering his arms. A door opened, the wind seized the dancer, and, like a sylph, she flew straightway into the stove, to the tin soldier; they both flamed up into a blaze, and were gone. The soldier was melted and dripped down among the ashes, and when the maid cleaned out the fireplace the next day she found his remains in the shape of a little tin heart; of the dancer all that was left was the gold wing, and that was burnt black as coal.

HANS ANDERSEN

O Little Town of Bethlehem

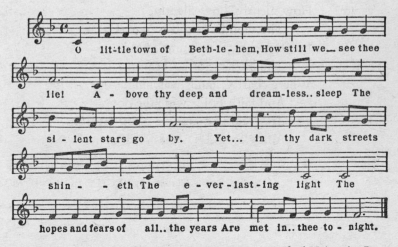

O lit-tle town of Beth-le - hem, How still we — see thee lie! A - bove thy deep and dream-less.. sleep The si - lent stars go by. Yet... in thy dark streets shin — eth The e - ver-last-ing light The hopes and fears of all.. the years Are met in.. thee to - night.

Melody from *The English Hymnal* (Oxford University Press

O little town of Bethlehem,
　　How still we see thee lie!
Above thy deep and dreamless sleep
　　The silent stars go by.
Yet in thy dark streets shineth
　　The everlasting light;
The hopes and fears of all the years
　　Are met in thee tonight.

O morning stars, together
　　Proclaim the holy birth,
And praises sing to God the King,
　　And peace to men on earth;
For Christ is born of Mary;
　　And, gathered all above,
While mortals sleep, the angels keep
　　Their watch of wondering love.

How silently, how silently,
　　The wondrous gift is given!
So God imparts to human hearts
　　The blessing of his heaven,
Where charity stands watching
　　And faith holds wide the door,
The dark night wakes, the glory breaks,
　　And Christmas comes once more.

BISHOP PHILLIPS BROOKS
Illustrated by PEGGY FORTNUM

Spells

I dance and dance without any feet –
This is the spell of the ripening wheat.

With never a tongue I've a tale to tell –
This is the meadow-grass's spell.

I give you health without any fee –
This is the spell of the apple tree.

I rhyme and riddle without any book –
This is the spell of the bubbling brook.

Without any legs I run for ever –
This is the spell of the mighty river.

I fall for ever and not at all –
This is the spell of the waterfall.

Without a voice I roar aloud –
This is the spell of the thunder-cloud.

No button or seam has my white coat –
This is the spell of the leaping goat.

I can cheat strangers with never a word –
This is the spell of the cuckoo-bird.

We have tongues in plenty but speak no names –
This is the spell of the fiery flames.

The creaking door has a spell to riddle –
I play a tune without any fiddle.

JAMES REEVES
Illustrated by JANE PATON

Here are two of the many stories which Uncle Remus, an old Negro servant, used to tell to a little boy on a plantation in the southern part of North America many years ago. The first is called 'The Wonderful Tar-Baby', and tells how the Fox got the better of the Rabbit.

The Wonderful Tar-Baby

ONE day Brer Fox went to work and got him some tar, and mixed it wid some turpentine, and fix up a contraption what he called a Tar-Baby, and he took this here Tar-Baby and set her in the big road; and then he lay off in the bushes for to see what the news

was going to be. And he didn't have to wait long, neither, 'cause by and by here comes Brer Rabbit, pacing down the road – lippity-clippity, clippity-lippity – just as saucy as a jay-bird. Brer Fox, he lay low. Brer Rabbit came prancing along till he spy the Tar-Baby, and then he fetched up on his behind legs like he was 'stonished. The Tar-Baby, she sat there, she did, and Brer Fox, he lay low.

'Morning!' says Brer Rabbit, says he – 'Nice weather, this morning,' says he.

Tar-Baby ain't saying nothing, and Brer Fox, he lay low.

'How are your symptoms this morning?' says Brer Rabbit, says he.

Brer Fox, he wink his eye slow, and lay low, and the Tar-Baby, she ain't saying nothing.

'How you come on then? Is you deaf?' says Brer Rabbit, says he. ''Cause if you is, I can holler louder,' says he.

Tar-Baby stay still, and Brer Fox, he lay low.

'You're stuck up, that's what you is,' says Brer Rabbit, says he, 'and I'm going to cure you, that's what I'm a-going to do,' says he.

Brer Fox, he sort of chuckle in his stomach, but Tar-Baby ain't saying nothing.

'I'm going to learn you how to talk to 'spectable folks, if it's the last act I do,' says Brer Rabbit, says he. 'If you don't take off that hat and tell me howdy, I'm going to bust you wide open,' says he.

Tar-Baby stay still, and Brer Fox, he lay low.

Brer Rabbit keep on asking him, and the Tar-Baby, she keep on saying nothing, till presently Brer Rabbit draw back with his fist, he did, and blip! he took her on the side of the head. His fist stuck and he can't pull loose. The tar held him. But Tar-Baby, she stay still, and Brer Fox, he lay low.

'If you don't let me loose, I'll knock you again,' says Brer Rabbit, says he, and with that he fetch her a wipe with the other hand, and that stuck. Tar-Baby, she ain't saying nothing, and Brer Fox, he lay low.

'Turn me loose, before I kick the natural stuffing out of you,' says Brer Rabbit, says he, but the Tar-Baby, she ain't saying nothing. She just held on, and then Brer Rabbit lose the use of his feet in the same way. Brer Fox, he lay low. Then Brer Rabbit squall out that if the Tar-Baby don't turn him loose, he butt her lop-sided. And then he butted, and his head got stuck. Then Brer

Fox, he sauntered forth, looking just as innocent as a mocking-bird.

'Howdy, Brer Rabbit,' says Brer Fox, says he. 'You look sort of stuck-up this morning,' says he, and then he rolled on the ground, and laughed and laughed until he couldn't laugh no more.

And that's how Brer Fox got the better of Brer Rabbit. Now in the second story you will hear how Brer Rabbit got his revenge. The story is called:

Brer Rabbit, He's a Good Fisherman

ONE day, when Brer Rabbit, and Brer Fox, and Brer Coon, and Brer Bear and a whole lot of them was clearing a new ground for to plant a roasting-pear patch, the sun began to get sort of hot, and Brer Rabbit, he got tired; but he didn't let on, 'cause he feared the others would call him lazy, and he keep on carrying away rubbish and piling it up, till by and by he holler out that he got a thorn in his hand, and then he take and slip off, and hunt for a cool place for to rest. After a while he come across a well with a bucket hanging in it.

'That looks cool,' says Brer Rabbit, says he. 'And cool I 'specs she is. I'll just about get in there and take a nap,' and with that, in he jump, he did, and he ain't no sooner fix himself than the bucket begin to go down. Brer Rabbit, he was mighty scared. He know where he come from, but he don't know where he's going. Suddenly he feel the bucket hit the water, and there she sat, but Brer Rabbit, he keep mighty still, 'cause he don't know what minute's going to be the next. He just lay there and shook and shiver.

Brer Fox always got one eye on Brer Rabbit, and when he slip off from the new ground, Brer Fox, he sneak after him. He knew Brer Rabbit was after some project or another, and he took and crope off, he did, and watch him. Brer Fox see Brer Rabbit come to the top of the well and stop, and then he see him jump in the bucket, and then, lo and behold! he see him go down out of sight. Brer Fox was the most 'stonished fox that you ever laid eyes on. He sat down in the bushes and thought and thought, but he don't make no head nor tails of this kind of business. Then he say to himself, says he:

'Well, if this don't beat everything!' says he. 'Right down there

in that well Brer Rabbit keep his money hid, and if it ain't that, he done gone and 'scovered a gold mine, and if it ain't that, then I'm a-going to see what's in there,' says he.

Brer Fox crope up a little nearer, he did, and listen, but he don't hear no fuss, and he keep on getting nearer, and yet he don't hear nothing. By and by he get up close and peep down, but he don't see nothing, and he don't hear nothing. All this time Brer Rabbit was mighty near scared out of his skin, and he feared for to move 'cause the bucket might keel over and spill him out in the water. While he saying his prayers over and over, old Brer Fox holler out:

'Heyo, Brer Rabbit! Who you visitin' down there?' says he.

'Who? Me? Oh, I'm just a-fishing, Brer Fox,' says Brer Rabbit, says he. 'I just say to myself that I'd sort of s'prise you all with a mess of fishes, and so here I is, and there's the fishes. I'm a-fishing for supper, Brer Fox,' says Brer Rabbit, says he.

'Is there many of them down there, Brer Rabbit?' says Brer Fox, says he.

'Lots of them, Brer Fox; scores and scores of them. The water is naturally alive with them. Come down and help me haul them in, Brer Fox,' says Brer Rabbit, says he.

'How I going to get down, Brer Rabbit?'

'Jump into the other bucket, Brer Fox. It'll fetch you down all safe and sound.'

Brer Rabbit talked so happy and talked so sweet that Brer Fox he jump in the bucket, he did, and so he went down, 'cause his weight pulled Brer Rabbit up. When they pass one another on the half-way ground, Brer Rabbit he sing out:

'Good-bye, Brer Fox, take care o' your clothes,
For this is the way the world goes;
Some goes up and some goes down,
You'll get to the bottom all safe and soun'.'

When Brer Rabbit got out, he gallop off and told the folks what the well belonged to, that Brer Fox was down there muddying up the drinking water, and then he gallop back to the well, and holler down to Brer Fox:

'Here come a man with a great big gun –
When he haul you up, you jump and run.'

Well, soon enough Brer Fox was out of the well, and in just about half an hour both of them was back on the new ground working just as if they'd never heard of no well. But every now and then Brer Rabbit would burst out laughing, and old Brer Fox would scowl and say nothing.

JOEL CHANDLER HARRIS
Illustrated by CONSTANCE MARSHALL

The Fairies

Up the airy mountain,
   Down the rushy glen,
We daren't go a-hunting
   For fear of little men;
Wee folk, good folk,
   Trooping all together;
Green jacket, red cap,
   And white owl's feather!

Down along the rocky shore
   Some make their home,
They live on crispy pancakes
   Of yellow-tide foam;
Some in the reeds
   Of the black mountain lake,
With frogs for their watch-dogs
   All night awake.

High on the hill-top
   The old King sits;
He is now so old and grey
   He's nigh lost his wits.
With a bridge of white mist
   Columbkill he crosses,
On his stately journeys
   From Slieveleague to Rosses;
Or going up with music
   On cold starry nights,
To sup with the Queen
   Of the gay Northern Lights.

They stole little Bridget
   For seven years long;
When she came down again
   Her friends were all gone.
They took her lightly back,
   Between the night and morrow,
They thought that she was fast asleep,
   But she was dead with sorrow.
They have kept her ever since
   Deep within the lakes,
On a bed of flag-leaves,
   Watching till she wakes.

By the craggy hill-side,
   Through the mosses bare,
They have planted thorn-trees
   For pleasure here and there.

Is any man so daring
   As dig them up in spite,
He shall find their sharpest thorns
   In his bed at night.

Up the airy mountain,
   Down the rushy glen,
We daren't go a-hunting
   For fear of little men;
Wee folk, good folk,
   Trooping all together;
Green jacket, red cap,
   And white owl's feather!

WILLIAM ALLINGHAM
Illustrated by PEGGY FORTNUM

Mary Indoors

Aren't you coming out, Mary?
   Come out: your eyes will tire –
Oh, let me be, please, please, said she,
   I want to read by the fire.

What are you reading, Mary,
   That keeps you, keeps you in? –
Oh, wonderful things of knights and kings,
   With their heart's desire to win.

Look out of the window, Mary!
   The blustering day is bright.
Come fight the wind with us, and find
   The sun on the hilly height.

Come on out of it, Mary,
   And win your heart's desire! –
Oh, let me be, please, *please*, said she,
   I want to read by the fire.

ELEANOR FARJEON
Illustrated by HOLLY BOURNE

The Hero of Haarlem

MANY years ago there lived in Haarlem, one of the principal cities of Holland, a sunny-haired boy of gentle disposition. His father was a *sluicer*, that is, a man whose business it was to open and close the sluices, or large oaken gates that are placed at regular distances across the entrances of the canals, to regulate the amount of water that shall flow into them.

The sluicer raises the gates more or less according to the quantity of water required, and closes them carefully at night, in order to avoid all possible danger of an over supply running into the canal, or the water would soon overflow it and inundate the surrounding country. As a great portion of Holland is lower than the level of the sea, the waters are kept from flooding the land only by means of strong dikes, or barriers, and by means of these sluices, which are often strained to the utmost by the pressure of the rising tides. Even the little children in Holland know that constant watchfulness is required to keep the rivers and ocean from overwhelming the country, and that a moment's neglect of the sluicer's duty may bring ruin and death to all.

One lovely afternoon, when the boy was about eight years old, he obtained his parents' consent to carry some cakes to a blind man who lived out in the country, on the other side of the dike. The little fellow started on his errand with a light heart, and having spent an hour with his grateful old friend, he bade him farewell and started on his homeward walk.

Trudging stoutly along by the canal, he noticed how the autumn rains had swollen the waters. Even while humming his careless, childish song, he thought of his father's brave old gates and felt glad of their strength, for, thought he, 'if *they* gave way,

where would father and mother be? These pretty fields would be all covered with the angry waters – father always calls them the *angry* waters; I suppose he thinks they are mad at him for keeping them out so long.' And with these thoughts just flitting across his brain, the boy stooped to pick the pretty blue flowers that grew along his way. Sometimes he stopped to throw some feathery seed-ball in the air, and watch it as it floated away; sometimes he listened to the stealthy rustling of a rabbit, speeding through the grass, but oftener he smiled as he recalled the happy light he had seen arise on the weary, listening face of his blind old friend.

Suddenly the boy looked around him in dismay. He had not noticed that the sun was setting: now he saw that his long shadow on the grass had vanished. It was growing dark, he was still some distance from home, and in a lonely ravine, where even the blue flowers had turned to grey. He quickened his footsteps; and with a beating heart recalled many a nursery tale of children lost in dreary forests. Just as he was bracing himself for a run, he was startled by the sound of trickling water. Whence did it come? He looked up and saw a small hole in the dike through which a tiny stream was flowing. Any child in Holland will shudder at the thought of a *leak in the dike*! The boy understood the danger at a glance. That little hole, if the water were allowed to trickle through, would soon be a large one, and a terrible inundation would be the result.

Quick as a flash, he saw his duty. Throwing away his flowers, the boy clambered up the heights, until he reached the hole. His chubby little finger was thrust in, almost before he knew it. The flowing was stopped! 'Ah!' he thought, with a chuckle of boyish delight, 'the angry waters must stay back now! Haarlem shall not be drowned while *I* am here!'

This was all very well at first, but the night was falling rapidly; chill mists filled the air. The boy began to tremble with cold and dread. He shouted loudly; he screamed, 'Come here! come here!'

but no one came. The cold grew more intense, a numbness, commencing in the tired little finger, crept over his hand and arm, and soon his whole body was filled with pain. He shouted again, 'Will no one come? Mother! Mother!' Alas, his mother, good practical soul, had already locked the doors, and had fully resolved to scold him on the morrow, for spending the night with blind Jansen without her permission. He tried to whistle, perhaps some straggling boy might heed the signal; but his teeth chattered so, it was impossible. Then he called on God for help; and the answer came, through a holy resolution – 'I will stay here till morning.'

The midnight moon looked down upon that small solitary form, sitting upon a stone, half-way up the dike. His head was bent, but he was not asleep, for every now and then one restless hand rubbed feebly the outstretched arm that seemed fastened to the dike – and often the pale, tearful face turned quickly at some real or fancied sound.

How can we know the sufferings of that long and fearful watch – what falterings of purpose, what childish terrors came over the boy as he thought of the warm little bed at home, of his parents, his brothers and sisters, then looked into the cold, dreary night! If he drew away that tiny finger, the angry waters, grown angrier still, would rush forth, and never stop until they had swept over the town. No, he would hold it there till daylight – if he lived! He was not very sure of living. What did this strange buzzing mean? And then the knives that seemed pricking and piercing him from head to foot? He was not sure now that he could draw his finger away, even if he wished to.

At daybreak a clergyman, returning from the bedside of a sick parishioner, thought he heard groans as he walked along on the top of the dike. Bending, he saw, far down on the side, a child apparently writhing with pain.

'In the name of wonder, boy,' he exclaimed, 'what are you doing there?'

'I am keeping the water from running out,' was the simple answer. 'Tell them to come quick.'

It is needless to add that they did come quickly and that the dike was repaired before further damage occurred. As for the boy who saved Haarlem, he was taken home and soon recovered his strength. Ever since that time, the people of Holland have remembered him as one of the heroes of their country.

MARY MAPES DODGE

Row, Row, Row your Boat

ROUND FOR FOUR VOICES

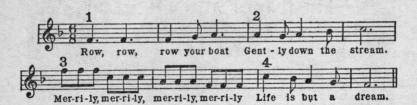

Row, row, row your boat
Gently down the stream.
Merrily, merrily, merrily, merrily
Life is but a dream.

The Tailor and the Crow

A carrion crow sat on an oak,
    Fol-de-riddle, lol-de-riddle, hi ding do,
Watching a tailor shape his cloak;
    Sing hey no, the carrion crow,
    Fol-de-riddle, lol-de-riddle, hi ding do!

'Wife, bring me my old bent bow,
    Fol-de-riddle, lol-de-riddle, hi ding do,
That I may shoot yon carrion crow';
    Sing hey ho, the carrion crow,
    Fol-de-riddle, lol-de-riddle, hi ding do!

The tailor he shot and missed his mark,
    Fol-de-riddle, lol-de-riddle, hi ding do,

And shot his own sow quite through the heart;
    Sing hey ho, the carrion crow,
    Fol-de-riddle, lol-de-riddle, hi ding do!

'Wife, bring brandy in a spoon,
    Fol-de-riddle, lol-de-riddle, hi ding do,
For our old sow is in a swoon';
    Sing hey ho, the carrion crow,
    Fol-de-riddle, lol-de-riddle, hi ding do!

Lilliput-Land

Where does Pinafore Palace stand?
Right in the middle of Lilliput-land!
There the Queen eats bread-and-honey,
There the King counts up his money!

Oh, the Glorious Revolution!
Oh, the Provisional Constitution!
Now that the Children, clever bold folks,
Have turned the tables upon the Old Folks!

Easily the thing was done,
For the Children were more than two to one;
Brave as lions, quick as foxes,
With hoards of wealth in their money-boxes!

They seized the keys, they patrolled the street,
They drove the policeman off his beat,
They built barricades, they stationed sentries –
You must give the word, when you come to the entries!

They dressed themselves in the Rifleman's clothes,
They had pea-shooters, they had arrows and bows,
So as to put resistance down –
Order reigns in Lilliput-town!

They went to the school-room and tore the books,
They munched the puffs at the pastrycooks.
They sucked the jam, they lost the spoons,
They sent up several fire-balloons.

They split or burnt the canes off-hand,
They made new laws in Lilliput-land.
Late to bed and late to rise,
Was one of the laws they did devise.

Nail up the door, slide down the stairs,
Saw off the legs of the parlour-chairs –
That was the way in Lilliput-land,
The Children having the upper hand.

They made the Old Folks come to school,
All in pinafores – that was the rule, –
They kept them in, they sent them down
In class, in school, in Lilliput-town.

Oh but they gave them tit-for-tat!
Thick bread-and-butter, and all that;
Stick-jaw pudding that tires your chin
With the marmalade spread ever so thin!

WILLIAM BRIGHTY RANDS

London Sparrow

Sparrow, you little brown gutter-mouse,
How can I tempt you into the house?
I scatter my crumbs on the window-sill
But down in the gutter you're hopping still:
I strew my cake at the open door,
But you don't seem to know what cake is for!
I drop my cherries where you can see,
I bring you water, I whistle, ' *Twee!* ' –
But nothing I offer, and nothing I utter
Fetches the sparrow out of the gutter.
What is it makes the road so nice
For sparrows, the little brown gutter-mice?

ELEANOR FARJEON
Illustrated by CONSTANCE MARSHALL

Lazy Jack

JACK lived with his mother in a cottage beside a common. He was the laziest boy in the world. His mother earned a living for them both by spinning, and when she wasn't spinning she was washing or mending, and when she wasn't washing or mending she was getting a meal ready. But all Jack would do was to sit under the apple-tree in summer sucking grasses, and in the chimney corner in winter keeping his toes warm.

At last his mother could put up with it no longer.

'Out you go,' said she one fine Monday morning. 'Out you go, and earn yourself a living or you shan't stay here any more. You're old enough to get work for yourself now, so don't come back till you've made some money to help pay for the food you eat!'

Slowly Jack got up from his seat by the fire and went out. He hired himself to a Farmer, and by the end of the day he had earned sixpence. Holding it in his hand, he started for home; but crossing over a brook, he slipped on a wet stone and dropped the sixpence. It was nowhere to be found. There was nothing for it but to go home and tell his mother what had happened.

'Why, you stupid boy!' said his mother. 'I could have done with sixpence, but now you've lost it. You should have put it in your pocket. Then you'd have kept it safe and sound. See if you can do better tomorrow.'

Well, on Tuesday morning Jack went off once more, though he would rather have sat by the fire all day. This time he hired himself to a Dairyman, and at the end of the day he was given a pail of milk for wages. So remembering what his mother had said, he emptied the pail into the pocket of his coat and began to jog along home. Of course the milk was all wasted, and his clothes were soaked into the bargain.

'Why, you silly, good-for-nothing scamp!' cried his mother, when he told her what had happened. 'We could have done with some nice new milk for supper, but now there's none – thanks to your foolishness. You should have carried the pail on your head, then you would have brought it home safe and sound.'

On Wednesday morning Jack went off again to work for the Farmer, and for his day's work the Farmer gave him a fine pat of butter.

'Now what did she tell me to do with it?' thought Jack. Then he remembered. He clapped the butter on top of his head and started for home. But it was a warm evening, and soon the butter got stuck in his hair and ran down behind his ears, and some of it fell to the ground, and all of it was spoilt.

Jack's mother was angrier than ever.

'It's too bad!' she said. 'I could have done with some good dairy butter if you hadn't gone and spoilt it all. What a donkey you are! Whatever did you put it on your head for? You should have carried it in your hand.'

Well, on Thursday morning Jack set off once more, trudging away across the common to see a Baker in the village; and all day he worked for the Baker, and the Baker gave him nothing but a black cat for his day's work. He had too many cats in the bakery and was glad to get rid of one.

When he got home, he had nothing at all to show for his day's work except a pair of hands covered all over with bites and scratches.

'What did you get today?' asked Jack's mother.

'Why, the Baker gave me a black cat, mother,' said Jack, 'and I carried her in my hands like you told me yesterday, and she scratched me till I had to let her go.'

'Deary me, deary me!' said his mother. 'Aren't you the stupidest ninny ever born? You shouldn't have tried to carry a cat home in your hands. You should have tied a string round her neck and pulled her along after you. It's very vexing,' she went on. 'We could have done with a good cat to keep the mice from the larder!'

On Friday morning Jack went off to the Butcher's Shop and hired himself to the Butcher for the day. Now the Butcher was a kind man and knew that Jack's mother was poor, so at the end of the day he gave Jack a leg of good lean mutton. Jack thanked the Butcher and left the shop. He thought very carefully about what his mother had told him the day before, and this time he was determined to make no mistake. So he took a piece of string from his pocket and pulled the meat along behind him in the road.

When she saw the meat, all dirty and spoilt, Jack's mother was more annoyed than ever.

'Oh, you dunderhead!' she cried. 'When *will* you learn sense? We could have done with a fine lean leg of mutton for dinner tomorrow and you've as good as thrown it away! Fancy bringing it home like that!'

'But what *should* I have done, mother?' Jack asked.

'If you'd had two penn'orth of common sense, you'd have lifted it on to your shoulder and carried it home like that. Be off to bed with you, for there's not a bite of supper in the house. The way you're going on, we shall both starve, and that's the truth!'

Well, next morning was Saturday, and once more Jack set out to see what he could earn. He hired himself to a Cowman that he knew, and at the end of the day the Cowman gave him a donkey. So remembering once more what his mother had told him, Jack hoisted the donkey on to his shoulders, and staggered off home. The animal gave poor Jack a great deal of trouble, for it did not like being carried upside down on his shoulders. However,

Jack was determined to get home safely *this* time, and not lose his day's wages. So he grasped the donkey's legs with all his strength and took no notice of its braying and kicking.

Now it so happened that in a great house beside the highroad lived a rich man, and he had one beautiful daughter who was both deaf and dumb. She had never heard nor spoken a word in all her life. But the doctor had told her father that if the girl could be made to laugh, she might be cured. And the rich man had spent years and years trying to make his beautiful daughter laugh, but the harder he tried the sadder she looked, till everyone gave up hope of ever having her cured.

As Jack was passing the house with the donkey upside down on his back, it happened that the girl was looking out of an upstairs window. Never had she seen such a thing in all her life! There must surely be nothing funnier in the world than to see a great country lad staggering along the road with a donkey kicking and braying upside down on his back: at first the girl could not believe her eyes, and then she began to smile, and then her smile grew broader and broader until she laughed out loud; she laughed so loud and long that the tears came to her eyes, and scarcely knowing what she was doing, she called out to everyone in the house:

'Oh, c-come and look! J-just come and look! Did you ever see such a thing? It's the funniest thing you ever saw!'

Well, the girl's father and all their friends were delighted that at last the girl had spoken, and they were so pleased that they ran out into the road and called Jack inside. So in he went, donkey and all, and the girl was so pleased with him that she wouldn't let him go.

Nothing would please the rich man's daughter but that she should marry Jack and have him to live with for always. And very happy they were in a great house which the rich man bought for them. They kept the donkey in a field at the back of the house, and Jack's mother came to live with them for the rest of her life. Jack became a fine gentleman and had servants to wait on him and see that he never did any more work from that time on.

If All the Seas

If all the seas were one sea,
What a great sea that would be!
If all the trees were one tree,
What a great tree that would be!
And if all the axes were one axe,
What a great axe that would be!
And if all the men were one man,
What a great man that would be!
And if the great man took the great axe
And cut down the great tree,
And let it fall into the great sea,
What a splish-splash that would be!

The Fairies of the Caldon Low

'And where have you been, my Mary,
    And where have you been from me?'
'I've been to the top of the Caldon Low,
    The midsummer night to see!'

'And what did you see, my Mary,
    All up on the Caldon Low?'
'I saw the glad sunshine come down,
    And I saw the merry winds blow.'

'And what did you hear, my Mary,
    All up on the Caldon Hill?'
'I heard the drops of the waters made,
    And the ears of the green corn fill.'

'Oh! tell me all, my Mary,
    All, all that ever you know;
For you must have seen the fairies
    Last night on the Caldon Low.'

'Then take me on your knee, mother;
    And listen, mother of mine.
A hundred fairies danced last night,
    And the harpers they were nine.

'And their harp-strings rang so merrily
    To their dancing feet so small;
But oh! the words of their talking
    Were merrier far than all.'

'And what were the words, my Mary,
    That then you heard them say?'
'I'll tell you all, my mother;
    But let me have my way.

'Some of them played with the water,
    And rolled it down the hill.
"And this," they said, "shall speedily turn
    The poor old miller's mill:

'"For there has been no water
    Ever since the first of May;
And a busy man will the miller be
    At the dawning of the day.

'"Oh! the miller, how he will laugh
    When he sees the mill dam rise!

The jolly old miller, how he will laugh,
   Till the tears fill both his eyes!"

'And some they seized the little winds
   That sounded over the hill;
And each put a horn into his mouth,
   And blew both loud and shrill.

'"And there," they said, "the merry winds go
   Away from every horn;
And they shall clear the mildew dank
   From the blind old widow's corn.

'"Oh! the poor blind widow,
   Though she has been blind so long,
She'll be blithe enough when the mildew's gone,
   And the corn stands tall and strong."

'And some they brought the brown lintseed,
  And flung it down from the Low;
"And this," they said, "by the sunrise
  In the weaver's croft shall grow.

'"Oh! the poor lame weaver,
  How he will laugh outright,
When he sees his dwindling flax-field
  All full of flowers by night!"

'And then out spoke a brownie,
  With a long beard on his chin;
"I have spun up all the tow," said he,
  "And I want some more to spin.

'"I've spun a piece of hempen cloth,
  And I want to spin another;
A little sheet for Mary's bed,
  And an apron for her mother."

'With that I could not help but laugh,
  And I laughed out loud and free;
And then on the top of the Caldon Low
  There was no one left but me.

'And all on the top of the Caldon Low
  The mists were cold and grey,
And nothing I saw but the mossy stones
  That round about me lay.

'But coming down from the hill-top,
  I heard afar below

How busy the jolly miller was
    And how the wheel did go.

'And I peeped into the widow's field,
    And, sure enough, were seen
The yellow ears of the mildewed corn,
    All standing stout and green.

'And down to the weaver's croft I stole,
    To see if the flax were sprung;
But I met the weaver at his gate,
    With the good news on his tongue.

'Now this is all I heard, mother,
    And all that I did see;
So, prithee make my bed, mother,
    For I'm tired as I can be.'

MARY HOWITT
Illustrated by PEGGY FORTNUM

A Kitten

He's nothing much but fur
And two round eyes of blue,
He has a giant purr
And a midget mew.

He darts and pats the air,
He starts and pricks his ear,
When there is nothing there
For him to see and hear.

He runs around in rings,
But why we cannot tell;
With sideways leaps he springs
At things invisible –

Then half-way through a leap
His startled eyeballs close,
And he drops off to sleep
With one paw on his nose.

ELEANOR FARJEON
Illustrated by CONSTANCE MARSHALL

The Well of the World's End

ONCE upon a time, and a very long time ago it was, there was a girl called Rosemary. She was a good girl but not very clever, and a merry girl but not too pretty; and all would have been well with her but that she had a cruel step-mother. So instead of having pretty dresses to wear and sweet cakes to eat and idle friends to play with, as all girls should, she was made to do the housework: to go down on her knees and scrub the stone floors, and roll up her sleeves to the elbows and do the washing. And the better she did the work, the worse her step-mother hated her. If she got up early in the morning, it was not early enough; if she cooked the dinner, it was not cooked right. Poor Rosemary! She worked all the day, yet everything she did was wrong.

Well, one day her step-mother decided to be rid of her.

'Child,' said she, 'take this sieve and go to the Well of the World's End; and when you have found it, fill the sieve with water and bring it back to me. Mind now, and see that you don't spill a drop. Be off with you!'

So Rosemary, who never dared answer her step-mother back, nor even ask her a question hardly, took the sieve and went out to look for the Well of the World's End.

Presently she met a carter, who had stopped to tighten his horse's reins.

'Where are you off to?' asked he. 'And what have you got in your hand?'

'I am trying to find the Well of the World's End,' she answered, 'and this is a sieve that I must fill with water.'

The carter laughed heartily and said she was a foolish girl and that he had no idea where the well was. So saying, he jumped back upon his cart, whipped up the horse, and left poor Rosemary standing in the road.

She walked on a while, and soon she saw three little boys bowling their hoops in the yard before an inn.

'Where are you off to?' one of them shouted. 'And what have you got in your hand?'

'I am trying to find the Well of the World's End,' she answered, 'and this is a sieve that I have to fill with water.'

All the three boys laughed aloud at this and told her she was stupid and that there was no such well in the world.

So Rosemary trudged on, asking everybody she met if they could tell her where the well was; but no one knew. Some were rude, some laughed at her, and others said they would have helped her if they could, but they knew not how.

At last she spied an old ragged woman, bent nearly double, looking for something in a cart-rut. She had a torn bonnet, very nearly no teeth at all, and a crooked stick. With this she was poking about in the mud.

'What are you looking for?' asked Rosemary.

'I had two groats that I was going to buy bread with, and if I don't find them I shall have nothing to eat tonight.'

So Rosemary helped her look for the two groats, and presently her sharp eyes caught sight of them.

'Thank you,' said the old woman in her creaky voice. 'I should never have found them by myself, I do declare. Now tell me where you are going and what you are doing with that sieve.'

'I am going to the Well of the World's End,' said Rosemary, 'but I am afraid there is no such place in the world. When I get there, I must fill the sieve with water and take it home to my step-mother.'

'Why, indeed,' said the old woman, 'there is a Well of the

World's End, and I will tell you how to find it. As for what you are going to do when you get there, that is another matter.'

So, pointing with her stick, she showed Rosemary the way.

'Through the gap in that hedge,' she said, 'over the far hill, up the stony path along the hazel wood, and along the valley – that

will take you there. God speed you, and may the way seem short.'

Rosemary thanked her, and the old woman hobbled off, clutching her stick in one bony hand and her two groats in the other.

Through the gap in the hedge went Rosemary with her sieve, up the hill, along the stony path by the hazel wood, until she came to a deep valley, all wet underfoot, and very green and lonesome. And at the very end of the valley was a well. It was so overgrown with ivy and moss that she nearly missed it. But there it was, sure enough: and this was the Well of the World's End.

Rosemary knelt down on the bank beside the well, and dipped her sieve into the water. Many times she dipped it, but each time the water ran out through the holes in the sieve, so that not a drop was left to take home to her step-mother. She sat down and cried.

'I shall never do it,' she sobbed. 'I shall never have a sieve-full of water to take home.'

Just as she was beginning to think that her misery would never end, something croaked, and a fat green frog hopped out from under a fern-leaf.

'What's the matter?' asked the frog.

Rosemary told him.

'If you promise,' said the frog, 'to do everything I ask for a whole night, I can help you.'

'Yes, of course I will,' said Rosemary eagerly. 'I'll promise whatever you like – only *do* help me, *please*.'

The frog considered for a moment or two, gulped once or twice, and spoke:

> 'Stop it with moss, and daub it with clay,
> And then it will carry the water away.'

Quickly Rosemary gathered soft, green moss from the mouth of the well and covered the bottom of the sieve with it. Then she scooped up some damp clay from the bank and spread it on top of the moss, pressing it down until all the holes in the sieve were filled. Next, she dipped the sieve into the water, and this time not a drop ran out.

'I must get home as quickly as I can,' she said, turning to go. 'Thank you, thank you, dear frog, for helping me. I should never have thought of that for myself.'

'No, I don't suppose you would,' croaked the frog. 'Carry the water carefully – and don't forget your promise.'

Rosemary remembered that she had promised the frog to do anything he wanted for a whole night. She didn't suppose that any harm would come of a promise made to a frog, so she told him she would not forget, and went gratefully on her way.

You can imagine how surprised her step-mother was to see her when she got home. She had hoped to get rid of the girl for good and all. But here she was, none the worse for her journey, carrying a sieve full of water, just as she had been told. The step-mother didn't say much, because she was too angry. Instead, she made her get the supper for them both and wash the dishes afterwards, just as if nothing had happened.

As night was falling, they were surprised to hear the sound of knocking at the door.

'Who can it be?' asked the step-mother.

Rosemary went to the door and called out:

'Who's there, and what do you want at this time of day?'

There was a little croaking noise, and a voice said:

> 'Open the door and let me in,
> Let me in, my heart of gold;
> Remember the words we spoke so true
> Down by the water green and cold.'

It was the frog. Rosemary had almost forgotten him. Her step-mother asked her who it was at the door, and Rosemary told her all about the frog and the promise she had made him.

'Well, let him in,' said the step-mother, 'and do as he tells you. Girls must keep their promises.'

She rather liked the idea of her step-daughter's having to obey the commands of a frog. So Rosemary opened the door, and the frog hopped in. He looked at her, and then he spoke again. This is what he said:

> 'Lift me, lift me up to your knee,
> Up to your knee, my heart of gold;
> Remember the words we spoke so true
> Down by the water green and cold.'

Rosemary did not much like the idea of having a damp frog sitting on her knee, but her step-mother said:

'Do as he tells you. Girls must keep their promises.'

So the girl lifted the frog up, and he sat perched on her knee. Then once more he spoke to her.

> 'Give me, O give me meat and drink,
> Meat and drink, my heart of gold;
> Remember the words we spoke so true
> Down by the water green and cold.'

'Do as he tells you,' ordered the step-mother. 'Girls must keep their promises.'

Rosemary fetched from the larder the food that had been left from supper and put it on a plate in front of the frog, and he bent his head down and ate every scrap of it. Then once more he spoke:

> 'Take me, take me into your bed,
> Into your bed, my heart of gold;
> Remember the words we spoke so true
> Down by the water green and cold.'

'No,' said Rosemary, 'I will never have such a cold, clammy creature in bed with me. Get away, you nasty animal!'

At this the step-mother almost screamed with laughter.

'Go on!' she cried. 'Do as the frog bids. Remember your promise. Young girls must keep their promises.'

With that she went off to her room, and Rosemary was left with the frog. Well, she got into bed, took the frog in beside her, but kept him as far away as she could. After a while she slept soundly.

In the morning, before the break of day, she was awakened by a croaking sound close to her ear.

'Everything I have asked, you have done,' said the frog. 'One more thing I ask, then you will have kept your promise. Take an axe and chop off my head!'

Rosemary looked at the frog, and her heart went cold.

'Dear frog,' she said, 'don't ask me to do that. You have been so kind to me. Don't ask me to kill you.'

'Do as I ask,' said the frog. 'Remember your promise. The night is not yet over. Fetch an axe, and cut off my head.'

So very sadly Rosemary went into the kitchen and fetched the chopper that was used to cut up logs for the fire. She could scarcely bear to look at the poor frog, but somehow she managed to raise the chopper and cut off his head.

Then she had the greatest surprise of her life. For the frog was no more: in his place stood a young and handsome man. She stepped back in amazement, dropping the chopper to the floor. The young man was smiling at her.

'Don't be afraid,' he said in a soft and musical voice. 'I am not here to hurt or alarm you. Once I was a prince, but a foul enchantress turned me into a frog; and her wicked spell could not be unspelled until a young girl should do my bidding for a whole night.'

At these words the step-mother, who had been woken by the sound of voices, came into the room. Great was her astonishment to see the young Prince there, instead of the slimy frog.

'Madam,' said the Prince, 'your daughter has had the kindness to unspell the spell that made me a frog; for that I am going to marry her. I am a powerful prince, and you shall not deny me. You wanted to get rid of your step-daughter. Well, you have done so, for now I am going to take her away to be my wife.'

For once the step-mother had nothing to say. She looked at the Prince and opened her mouth, but no words came; then she looked at Rosemary and opened her mouth, but still no words came. So she turned away and began to get some breakfast for them all. It was the only thing she could do.

Not long afterwards the Prince and Rosemary were married, and very happy they were. As for the step-mother, she had tried to get rid of her daughter, so that she had the pleasure of knowing that by this means she had caused her to rescue the Prince from enchantment and find herself a kind and loving husband.

JAMES REEVES

Written in March

The cock is crowing,
The stream is flowing,
Small birds twitter,
The lake doth glitter,
The green fields sleep in the sun;
The oldest and youngest
Are at work with the strongest;
The cattle are grazing,
Their heads never raising;
There are forty feeding like one!

Like an army defeated
The snow hath retreated,
And now doth fare ill
On the top of the bare hill;
The ploughboy is whooping – anon – anon:
There's joy in the mountains;
There's life in the fountains;
Small clouds are sailing,
Blue sky prevailing;
The rain is over and gone!

WILLIAM WORDSWORTH
Illustrated by JANE PATON

396

Six o'Clock Bells

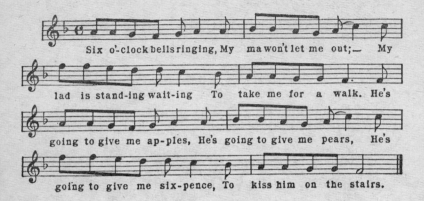

Six o'clock bells ringing,
My ma won't let me out;
My lad is standing waiting
To take me for a walk.
He's going to give me apples,
He's going to give me pears,
He's going to give me sixpence,
To kiss him on the stairs.

La Hormiguita and Perez the Mouse

LA HORMIGUITA was a little black ant – very enchanting, very agreeable, very industrious. She could not have been more charming if she had been a fairy.

One day as she was sweeping behind the door of her little house she found an *ochavito*. An *ochavito* is almost the smallest piece of money in the world, but it filled the little black claw of La Hormiguita and she drew her breath in an ecstasy as she looked at it.

'What luck! What shall I do with this ochavito? Shall I buy pine-nuts? No, for I have nothing to crack them with. Shall I buy meringues? No, that would make me a glutton. Let me think harder.'

She leaned her dainty head on her claw and thought very, very hard. '*Por Dios*, now I know. I will go to the store and buy me a pot of rouge.'

She washed herself all over. She combed her hair. She dressed herself in a new, red, ruffled dress and put on her high comb and black mantilla. On each cheek she put a touch of the rouge; and a touch of powder on her very distinguished nose. She was then content. She sat herself down in the balcony to watch all of God's world pass by.

Now, it happened that she was so exquisite, so beautiful, so wholly desirable, that all who passed fell at once in love with her.

There passed a handsome bull. 'Marry me, Hormiguita?'

'And if I do, how will you make love to me?'

'Like this!' And the bull roared handsomely.

So terrible was the sound that La Hormiguita clapped her claws over her ears and said in distress: 'Continue your way, Señor Bull. I could never live to be loved that way.'

There passed a dog who was a dandy. 'Marry me, Hormiguita?'

'And if I do, how will you make love to me?'

'Like this!' And the dandy opened his mouth and barked.

'I do not like your wooing. Keep on your way,' said La Hormiguita.

There passed a mincing cat – all grace and sleekness. 'Marry me, Hormiguita?'

'And if I do, how will you woo me?'

'Like this!' And the cat caterwauled until the little black ant shook in her balcony with fear. 'Señor Cat, I beg you to stop. Go also on your way.'

There passed a pig who grunted his love. There passed a cock who crowed his to the sky. But none of them pleased La Hormiguita. She turned her head sadly and rested it on her little claw in despair. But by and by there passed Perez the Mouse; so gallant, so beseeching.

'Marry me, Hormiguita *mia*.'

'And if I do, how will you woo me?'

'Like this!' And he laid his grey paw to his cheek as if it had been her black one; and he caressed it so gently. Then he looked up at her with his soft, engaging eyes.

'I will marry you, Señor Ratonperez,' said La Hormiguita. 'Come right in.'

They lived together in the little house very, very contented. All the things that La Hormiguita wanted to cook were the very things Perez the Mouse wanted to eat. The way La Hormiguita wanted to pass the day was precisely the way Perez the Mouse

wanted to pass it. Time went through from their front door to their back door on soft, slippered feet.

At last there came a day of misfortune. La Hormiguita went alone to mass. But first she put the *olla* over the fire, filled with rice and cabbage and sausage and garlic, to make a good dinner for them. And she said to Perez the Mouse, 'You must stir this with the great spoon and not with the small one; then you will be quite safe.'

But Perez the Mouse did not listen well – or at all. When the time came to stir the *olla*, he took the small spoon. He had to stand on his toes to reach the rim of the *olla*; he had to climb on the rim to reach the bottom of the *olla*. The steam and the smell made him giddy and in he fell. Alas! – there was no little black ant there to pull him out.

La Hormiguita returned. She called from the street: 'Perez the Mouse, I am here.' She called from the patio, but no answer came. She went into the kitchen. She looked into the *olla*; and what did she see? What misfortune! What sorrow!

She drew a rocking-chair into the patio. She sat down in it, all in the little black dress that she had worn to mass. She drew her mantilla over her face and she rocked and she wept for Perez the Mouse, who had wooed her more enchantingly than had all of God's world, passing by. She rocked and she wept; '*Ay de mi . . . ay de mi!*'

A small bird came to the patio, flying:
'Hormiguita . . . Hormiguita . . . why are you crying?'

'Perez the Mouse in the *olla* lies dead –
So I rock and I weep and I cover my head.'

'I will cut my small bill, then,' the little bird said.

A white dove perched on the patio sill:
'Small bird . . . oh, small bird . . . why cut your bill?'

'Perez the Mouse in the *olla* lies dead,
La Hormiguita has covered her head.'

'I will clip my long tail,' the white pigeon said.

The dove-house on high gave a pitiful wail:
'White pigeon . . . white pigeon . . . why clip your long
     tail?'

'Perez the Mouse in the *olla* lies dead,
La Hormiguita has covered her head.'

'I will shake myself, break myself up,' the house said.

The clear, happy fountain shed tears in her sorrow.
The little Infanta kept a fast till the morrow.
La Hormiguita still covers her head,
Perez the Mouse in the *olla* lies dead.

RUTH SAWYER
Illustrated by FAITH JAQUES

Turtle Soup

Beautiful soup, so rich and green,
Waiting in a hot tureen!
Who for such dainties would not stoop?
Soup of the evening, beautiful soup!
Soup of the evening, beautiful soup!
    Beau – ootiful soo – oop!
    Beau – ootiful soo – oop!
Soo – oop of the e – e – evening,
    Beautiful, beautiful soup!

Beautiful soup! Who cares for fish,
Game, or any other dish?
Who would not give all else for two p
ennyworth only of beautiful soup?
Pennyworth only of beautiful soup?
    Beau – ootiful soo – oop!
    Beau – ootiful soo – oop!
Soo – oop of the e – e – evening,
    Beautiful, beauti – FUL SOUP!

LEWIS CARROLL

A Naughty Boy

There was a naughty boy,
    And a naughty boy was he
He ran away to Scotland,
    The people there to see –
    Then he found
    That the ground
    Was as hard,
    That a yard
    Was as long,
    That a song
    Was as merry,
    That a cherry
    Was as red,
    That lead
    Was as weighty,
    That fourscore
    Was as eighty,
    That a door
    Was as wooden
    As in England –
So he stood in his shoes
    And he wondered,
    He wondered,
He stood in his shoes
    And he wondered.

JOHN KEATS

The Fool of the World and
the Flying Ship

THERE were, once upon a time, an old peasant and his wife, and they had three sons. Two of them were clever young men who could borrow money without being cheated, but the third was the Fool of the World. He was as simple as a child, simpler than some children, and he never did any one a harm in his life.

Well, it always happens like that. The father and mother thought a lot of the two smart young men; but the Fool of the World was lucky if he got enough to eat, because they always forgot him unless they happened to be looking at him, and sometimes even then.

But, however it was with his father and mother, this is a story that shows that God loves simple folk, and turns things to their advantage in the end.

For it happened that the Tsar of that country sent out messengers along the highroads and the rivers, even to huts in the forest like ours, to say that he would give his daughter, the Princess, in marriage to any one who could bring him a flying ship – ay, a ship with wings, that should sail this way and that through the blue sky, like a ship sailing on the sea.

'This is a chance for us,' said the two clever brothers; and that same day they set off together, to see if one of them could not build the flying ship and marry the Tsar's daughter, and so be a great man indeed.

And their father blessed them, and gave them finer clothes than ever he wore himself. And their mother made them up hampers of food for the road, soft white rolls, and several kinds of cooked meats, and bottles of corn brandy. She went with them as far as the highroad, and waved her hand to them till they were out of sight. And so the two clever brothers set merrily off on their adventure, to see what could be done with their cleverness. And what happened to them I do not know, for they were never heard of again.

The Fool of the World saw them set off, with their fine parcels of food, and their fine clothes, and their bottles of corn brandy.

'I'd like to go too,' says he, 'and eat good meat, with soft white rolls, and drink corn brandy, and marry the Tsar's daughter.'

'Stupid fellow,' says his mother, 'what's the good of your going? Why, if you were to stir from the house you would walk into the arms of a bear; and if not that, then the wolves would eat you before you had finished staring at them.'

But the Fool of the World would not be held back by words. 'I am going,' says he. 'I am going. I am going. I am going.'

He went on saying this over and over again, till the old woman his mother saw there was nothing to be done, and was glad to get him out of the house so as to be quit of the sound of his voice. So she put some food in a bag for him to eat by the way. She put in the bag some crusts of dry black bread and a flask of water. She did not even bother to go as far as the footpath to see him on his way. She saw the last of him at the door of the hut, and he had not taken two steps before she had gone back into the hut to see to more important business.

No matter. The Fool of the World set off with his bag over his shoulder, singing as he went, for he was off to seek his fortune and marry the Tsar's daughter. He was sorry his mother had not given him any corn brandy; but he sang merrily for all that. He would have liked white rolls instead of the dry black

crusts; but, after all, the main thing on a journey is to have
something to eat. So he trudged merrily along the road, and sang
because the trees were green and there was a blue sky overhead.

He had not gone very far when he met an ancient old man
with a bent back, and a long beard, and eyes hidden under his
bushy eyebrows.

'Good day, young fellow,' says the ancient old man.

'Good day, grandfather,' says the Fool of the World.

'And where are you off to?' says the ancient old man.

'What!' says the Fool; 'haven't you heard? The Tsar is going to give his daughter to anyone who can bring him a flying ship.'

'And you can really make a flying ship?' says the ancient old man.

'No, I do not know how.'

'Then what are you going to do?'

'God knows,' says the Fool of the World.

'Well,' says the ancient, 'if things are like that, sit you down here. We will rest together and have a bite of food. Bring out what you have in your bag.'

'I am ashamed to offer you what I have here. It is good enough for me, but it is not the sort of meal to which one can ask guests.'

'Never mind that. Out with it. Let us eat what God has given.'

The Fool of the World opened his bag, and could hardly believe his eyes. Instead of black crusts he saw fresh white rolls and cooked meats. He handed them out to the ancient, who said, 'You see how God loves simple folk. Although your own mother does not love you, you have not been done out of your share of the good things. Let's have a sip at the corn brandy . . .'

The Fool of the World opened his flask, and instead of water there came out corn brandy, and that of the best. So the Fool and the ancient made merry, eating and drinking; and when they had done, and sung a song or two together, the ancient says to the Fool,

'Listen to me. Off with you into the forest. Go up to the first big tree you see. Make the sacred sign of the cross three times before it. Strike it a blow with your little hatchet. Fall backwards on the ground, and lie there, full length on your back, until somebody wakes you up. Then you will find the ship made, all ready to fly. Sit you down in it, and fly off whither you want to go. But be sure on the way to give a lift to every one you meet.'

The Fool of the World thanked the ancient old man, said good-bye to him, and went off to the forest. He walked up to a tree, the first big tree he saw, made the sign of the cross three times before it, swung his hatchet round his head, struck a mighty blow on the trunk of the tree, instantly fell backwards flat on the ground, closed his eyes, and went to sleep.

A little time went by, and it seemed to the Fool as he slept that somebody was jogging his elbow. He woke up and opened his eyes. His hatchet, worn out, lay beside him. The big tree was gone, and in its place there stood a little ship, ready and finished. The Fool did not stop to think. He jumped into the ship, seized the tiller, and sat down. Instantly the ship leapt up into the air, and sailed away over the tops of the trees.

The little ship answered the tiller as readily as if she were sailing in water, and the Fool steered for the highroad, and sailed along above it, for he was afraid of losing his way if he tried to steer a course across the open country.

He flew on and on, and looked down, and saw a man lying in the road below him with his ear on the damp ground.

'Good day to you, uncle,' cried the Fool.

'Good day to you, Sky-fellow,' cried the man.

'What are you doing down there?' says the Fool.

'I am listening to all that is being done in the world.'

'Take your place in the ship with me.'

The man was willing enough, and sat down in the ship with the Fool, and they flew on together singing songs.

They flew on and on, and looked down, and there was a man on one leg, with the other tied up to his head.

'Good day, uncle,' says the Fool, bringing the ship to the ground. 'Why are you hopping along on one foot?'

'If I were to untie the other I should move too fast. I should be stepping across the world in a single stride.'

'Sit down with us,' says the Fool.

The man sat down with them in the ship, and they flew on together singing songs.

They flew on and on, and looked down, and there was a man with a gun, and he was taking aim, but what he was aiming at they could not see.

'Good health to you, uncle,' says the Fool. 'But what are you shooting at? There isn't a bird to be seen.'

'What!' says the man. 'If there were a bird that you could see, I should not shoot at it. A bird or a beast a thousand versts away, that's the sort of mark for me.'

'Take your seat with us,' says the Fool.

The man sat down with them in the ship, and they flew on together. Louder and louder rose their songs.

They flew on and on, and looked down, and there was a man carrying a sack full of bread on his back.

'Good health to you, uncle,' says the Fool, sailing down. 'And where are you off to?'

'I am going to get bread for my dinner.'

'But you've got a full sack on your back.'

'That – that little scrap! Why, that's not enough for a single mouthful.'

'Take your seat with us,' says the Fool.

The Eater sat down with them in the ship, and they flew on together, singing louder than ever.

They flew on and on, and looked down, and there was a man walking round and round a lake.

'Good health to you, uncle,' says the Fool. 'What are you looking for?'

'I want a drink, and I can't find any water.'

'But there's a whole lake in front of your eyes. Why can't you take a drink from that?'

'That little drop!' says the man. 'Why, there's not enough water there to wet the back of my throat if I were to drink it at one gulp.'

'Take your seat with us,' says the Fool.

The Drinker sat down with them, and again they flew on, singing in chorus.

They flew on and on, and looked down, and there was a man walking towards the forest, with a faggot of wood on his shoulders.

'Good day to you, uncle,' says the Fool. 'Why are you taking wood to the forest?'

'This isn't simple wood,' says the man.

'What is it, then?' says the Fool.

'If it is scattered about, a whole army of soldiers leaps up.'

'There's a place for you with us,' says the Fool.

The man sat down with them, and the ship rose up into the air, and flew on, carrying its singing crew.

They flew on and on, and looked down, and there was a man carrying a sack of straw.

'Good health to you, uncle,' says the Fool; 'and where are you taking your straw?'

'To the village.'

'Why, are they short of straw in your village?'

'No; but this is such straw that if you scatter it abroad in the very hottest of the summer, instantly the weather turns cold, and there is snow and frost.'

'There's a place here for you too,' says the Fool.

'Very kind of you,' says the man, and steps in and sits down, and away they all sail together, singing like to burst their lungs.

They did not meet anyone else, and presently came flying

up to the palace of the Tsar. They flew down and cast anchor in the courtyard.

Just then the Tsar was eating his dinner. He heard their loud singing, and looked out of the window and saw the ship come sailing down into his courtyard. He sent his servant out to ask who was the great prince who had brought him the flying ship, and had come sailing down with such a merry noise of singing.

The servant came up to the ship, and saw the Fool of the

World and his companions sitting there cracking jokes. He saw they were all moujiks, simple peasants, sitting in the ship; so he did not stop to ask questions, but came back quietly and told the Tsar that there were no gentlemen in the ship at all, but only a lot of dirty peasants.

Now the Tsar was not at all pleased with the idea of giving his only daughter in marriage to a simple peasant, and he began to think how he could get out of his bargain. Thinks he to himself, 'I'll set them such tasks that they will not be able to perform, and they'll be glad to get off with their lives, and I shall get the ship for nothing.'

So he told his servant to go to the Fool and tell him that before the Tsar had finished his dinner the Fool was to bring him some of the magical water of life.

Now, while the Tsar was giving this order to his servant, the Listener, the first of the Fool's companions, was listening, and heard the words of the Tsar and repeated them to the Fool.

'What am I to do now?' says the Fool, stopping short in his jokes. 'In a year, in a whole century, I could never find that water. And he wants it before he has finished his dinner.'

'Don't you worry about that,' says the Swift-goer, 'I'll deal with that for you.'

The servant came and announced the Tzar's command.

'Tell him he shall have it,' says the Fool.

His companion, the Swift-goer, untied his foot from beside his head, put it to the ground, wriggled it a little to get the stiffness out of it, ran off, and was out of sight almost before he had stepped from the ship. Quicker than I can tell it you in words he had come to the water of life, and put some of it in a bottle.

'I shall have plenty of time to get back,' thinks he, and down he sits under a windmill and goes off to sleep.

The royal dinner was coming to an end, and there wasn't a

sign of him. There were no songs and no jokes in the flying ship. Everybody was watching for the Swift-goer, and thinking he would not be in time.

The Listener jumped out and laid his right ear to the damp ground, listened a moment, and said, 'What a fellow! He has gone to sleep under the windmill. I can hear him snoring. And there is a fly buzzing with its wings, perched on the windmill close above his head.'

'This is my affair,' says the Far-shooter, and he picked up his gun from between his knees, aimed at the fly on the windmill, and woke the Swift-goer with the thud of the bullet on the wood of the mill close by his head. The Swift-goer leapt up and ran, and in less than a second had brought the magic water of life and given it to the Fool. The Fool gave it to the servant, who took it to the Tsar. The Tsar had not yet left the table, so his command had been fulfilled as exactly as ever could be.

'What fellows these peasants are,' thought the Tsar. 'There is nothing for it but to set them another task.' So the Tsar said to his servant, 'Go to the captain of the flying ship and give him this message: "If you are such a cunning fellow, you must have a good appetite. Let you and your companions eat at a single meal twelve oxen roasted whole, and as much bread as can be baked in forty ovens!"'

The Listener heard the message, and told the Fool what was coming. The Fool was terrified, and said, 'I can't get through even a single loaf at a sitting.'

'Don't worry about that,' said the Eater. 'It won't be more than a mouthful for me, and I shall be glad to have a little snack in place of my dinner.'

The servant came, and announced the Tsar's command.

'Good,' says the Fool. 'Send the food along, and we'll know what to do with it.'

So they brought twelve oxen roasted whole, and as much bread as could be baked in forty ovens, and the companions had scarcely sat down to eat before the Eater had finished the lot.

'Why,' said the Eater, 'what a little! They might have given us a decent meal while they were about it.'

The Tsar told his servant to tell the Fool that he and his companions were to drink forty barrels of wine, with forty bucketfuls in every barrel.

The Listener told the Fool what message was coming.

'Why,' says the Fool, 'I never in my life drank more than one bucket at a time.'

'Don't worry,' says the Drinker. 'You forget that I am thirsty. It'll be nothing of a drink for me.'

They brought the forty barrels of wine, and tapped them, and the Drinker tossed them down one after another, one gulp for each barrel. 'Little enough,' says he. 'Why, I am thirsty still.'

'Very good,' says the Tsar to his servant, when he heard that they had eaten all the food and drunk all the wine. 'Tell the fellow to get ready for the wedding, and let him go and bathe himself in the bath-house. But let the bath-house be made so hot that the man will stifle and frizzle as soon as he sets foot inside. It is an iron bath-house. Let it be made red hot.'

The Listener heard all this and told the Fool, who stopped short with his mouth open in the middle of a joke.

'Don't you worry,' says the moujik with the straw.

Well, they made the bath-house red hot, and called the Fool, and the Fool went along to the bath-house to wash himself, and with him went the moujik with the straw.

They shut them both into the bath-house, and thought that that was the end of them. But the moujik scattered his straw before them as they went in, and it became so cold in there that the Fool of the World had scarcely time to wash himself before the water in the cauldrons froze to solid ice. They lay down on the very stove itself, and spent the night there, shivering.

In the morning the servants opened the bath-house, and there were the Fool of the World and the moujik, alive and well, lying on the stove and singing songs.

They told the Tsar, and the Tsar raged with anger. 'There is no getting rid of this fellow,' says he. 'But go and tell him that I send him this message: "If you are to marry my daughter, you must show that you are able to defend her. Let me see that you have at least a regiment of soldiers."' Thinks he to himself, 'How can a simple peasant raise a troop? He will find it hard enough to raise a single soldier.'

The Listener told the Fool of the World, and the Fool began to lament. 'This time,' says he, 'I am done indeed. You, my brothers, have saved me from misfortune more than once, but this time, alas, there is nothing to be done.'

'Oh, what a fellow you are!' says the peasant with the faggot of wood. 'I suppose you've forgotten about me. Remember that I am the man for this little affair, and don't you worry about it at all.'

The Tsar's servant came along and gave his message.

'Very good,' says the Fool; 'but tell the Tsar that if after this he puts me off again, I'll make war on his country, and take the Princess by force.'

And then, as the servant went back with the message, the whole crew on the flying ship set to their singing again, and sang and laughed and made jokes as if they had not a care in the world.

During the night, while the others slept, the peasant with the faggot of wood went hither and thither, scattering his sticks. Instantly where they fell there appeared a gigantic army. No-body could count the number of soldiers in it – cavalry, foot soldiers, yes, and guns, and all the guns new and bright, and the men in the finest uniforms that ever were seen.

In the morning, as the Tsar woke and looked from the windows of the Palace, he found himself surrounded by troops upon troops of soldiers, and generals in cocked hats bowing in the courtyard and taking orders from the Fool of the World, who sat there joking with his companions in the flying ship. Now it was the Tsar's turn to be afraid. As quickly as he could he sent his servants to the Fool with presents of rich jewels and fine clothes, invited him to come to the palace, and begged him to marry the Princess.

The Fool of the World put on the fine clothes, and stood there as handsome a young man as a princess could wish for a husband. He presented himself before the Tsar, fell in love with the Princess and she with him, married her the same day, received with her a rich dowry, and became so clever that all the court repeated everything he said. The Tsar and the Tsaritza liked him very much, and as for the Princess, she loved him to distraction.

ARTHUR RANSOME

Topsyturvey-World

If the butterfly courted the bee,
    And the owl the porcupine;
If churches were built in the sea,
    And three times one was nine;
If the pony rode his master,
    If the buttercups ate the cows;
If the cat had the dire disaster
    To be worried, sir, by the mouse;
If mamma, sir, sold the baby
    To a gipsy for half a crown;
If a gentleman, sir, was a lady, –
    The world would be Upside-Down!
If any or all of these wonders
    Should ever come about,
I should not consider them blunders,
    For I should be Inside-Out!

(*Chorus*)
    Ba–ba, black wool,
        Have you any sheep?
    Yes, sir, a pack-full,
        Creep, mouse, creep!
    Four-and-twenty little maids
        Hanging out the pie,
    Out jumped the honey-pot,
        Guy-Fawkes, Guy!
    Cross-latch, cross-latch,
        Sit and spin the fire,
    When the pie was opened,
        The bird was on the briar!

WILLIAM BRIGHTY RANDS

Birthdays

Monday's child is fair of face,
Tuesday's child is full of grace,
Wednesday's child is full of woe,
Thursday's child has far to go,
Friday's child is loving and giving,
Saturday's child works hard for its living;
But the child who is born on the Sabbath day
Is bonny and blithe and good and gay.

The Small Brown Mouse

You might not think that smells would travel round the corners in a mousehole, but you would be wrong. The small brown mouse knows at exactly what angle in the hole to sit so that all the smells from the room beyond are reflected to him, accurately and deliciously. He is safe there, with the roof of the mousehole just above his head, and the sides of it sitting snugly to his shoulders, so that nothing can jump at him suddenly from any direction, and he can see the light from the room shining up the tunnel which generations of his family have polished with their furry flanks. Whichever of his ancestors it was who had been the architect for that mousehole, he had known his business well, and each evening the small brown mouse takes up his position, and his quivering nose-tip explores all the smells that reach him.

In the winter evenings the most exciting of the smells are of cocoa and digestive biscuits. And when he smells those the small brown mouse knows that soon there will be a stir in the room, chairs will be pushed back, someone will say, 'Come on, puss – time you were out', doors will open and shut again, feet will sound on the stairs, light feet first, then heavier feet, and at last the room will be left in the quiet dark, but for the glimmer from what is left of the fire.

This is the moment that the mouse has been waiting for. He comes out of the mousehole and across the floor like the flicker of a shadow, and he has his supper from the crumbs on the carpet, and he is thankful that digestive biscuits are so very brittle, and that the family make so many crumbs.

One evening in the middle of winter, the small brown mouse was sitting just round his particular angle in the mousehole, waiting for his supper. It was cold and frosty outside, and he was hungry, and he hoped the biscuits had been rather more brittle than usual, and the family more careless. He waited and he waited, growing hungrier and hungrier, but also more and more puzzled. For mixed up with the smell of cocoa and digestive biscuits he smelt other, unfamiliar smells, which greatly puzzled even so wise a mouse as he. There was cigarette smoke, of course, and the smell of the fire, and he rather thought someone had been sucking peppermints. But there was a very unusual smell – unusual, that is, for a drawing-room – a fresh keen outdoor smell, a smell that didn't belong to a house at all, and there were other sweeter smells that were foreign to him, and most exciting.

The small feet had gone up to bed a long time ago. The other, heavier feet should have been on their way, but still the light burned and there came the continued sound of voices. What with hunger and curiosity the small brown mouse crept another inch towards the room – and then crept an inch back again, for the cat was still there, the silent presence that turned your legs to water and made your heart sick, the dreadful and inescapable cat.

The mouse was beginning to think he should go back up the mousehole and take his supper off the piece of cheeserind he had stored there, in case of emergencies, when at last he heard the familiar sounds that he had been waiting for. Chairs scraped across the floor, the cat was called, the front door opened and closed again, the light was extinguished and feet – slow, tired feet – went up the stairs.

The small brown mouse came out of the mousehole and looked around him. And he forgot all about the digestive biscuits, but sat back on his little haunches, and with bright unwinking eyes he stared his fill.

It was a tree, a tall strong tree, set in a tub at the further end of the room. That was the outdoor smell, though what a tree was doing inside a house the mouse did not know. But he breathed in the sharp sweet smell of its branches, and it reminded him of the wood where, in the sunny summertime, he had sometimes wandered. But this tree was different from all other trees. Its dark green branches were hung and spattered from tip to toe. It burned and glittered and sparkled. It was alive with bright colours that were not fruit nor blossom. And at the top was a figure, half child, half bird, and he knew that it was an angel.

Forgetting how hungry he was the mouse crept forward to investigate this unexpected tree. He climbed carefully over the tub and up among the branches, nosing around backward and forward, smelling and feeling and looking at all the things that he found there. There was a bottle of French perfume, and though it was tightly wrapped and stoppered, his nose discovered it, and it made him feel very romantic and sentimental so that he nearly ran away home up the mousehole, to tell his wife about it right away. But a little higher up there was a cigar, and although there was only a breath of it coming through its silvery case, it was enough to make our mouse feel bold and manly, so that he went higher up still, examining everything as he went.

There were boxes of chocolates and trumpets, balls and

oranges, candles, wisps of tinsel, cotton wool snow, tiny shining birds that dipped on the branches as his small weight came on to them, and flaunted bright glittering tails. There were books and boxes of handkerchiefs, and many other things which baffled the mouse completely, so strange and unusual they were. But what he most admired were the large bright balls, red and blue, green and gold, in which, by the light of the fire, he could see his own reflection looking out at him – a warlike red mouse in the red ball, a romantic blue mouse, a mermaid mouse of cool translucent green. Best of all was an amber ball which reflected a tawny benevolent lion of a mouse, a mouse as truly golden as the cheese that mice dream about when they are happiest.

Soon he had been all over the tree, except for the highest branches, where there was little foothold, and where even his feather weight might find little enough support. It was only then that he remembered how hungry he was, and he went down to the carpet again, and ate up the crumbs of the digestive biscuits, and as he chewed he never took his eyes off the splendid tree.

His supper gave him courage, and he decided that after all he would attempt the last perilous inches to the top, where on the slender stem the angel was poised.

So up he went again, scrambling and sliding, and he paused only to look just once more at his golden self, reflected in the amber glass ball. And at last there was only a slim six inches between him and the small white feet of the angel.

But just at the base of the final pinnacle was something that the mouse had not seen in his first excursion, something as small as himself, something in fact very like himself – three chocolate mice. They lay side by side on the very last branch, just beneath the angel, and our mouse looked at them, first with curiosity and then with pity, for they were clumsy things com-

pared with his own exquisite shape. Their ears were no more than humps on either side of their thick heads; their eyes were just spots of white sugar on the chocolate – set on unevenly at that; there wasn't a whisker between them; and their tails were poor things of limp string that hung down behind them. Our mouse looked back at his own elegant tapered tail that kept the balance of his body, and he looked again at the dangling bits of string, and he felt rather ashamed. But he also felt extremely interested, for the smell of the chocolate had reached him so suddenly and so magnificently that he almost lost his balance and fell from his precarious perch.

It was like the smell of cocoa, of course, but so much better, so much richer, that there was really little comparison. The shock of its sweetness paralysed him for a moment, and then he came a little closer, delaying – just for the pure pleasure of delaying – the lovely moment when his tongue should slide up the shining sides of the first mouse.

'No,' said the angel suddenly – so suddenly that the small brown mouse once more had difficulty in keeping his footing – 'No. Not now – not yet – not for you.'

She wasn't scolding, she was just telling him, and she smiled at him as she spoke so that the mouse was at once ashamed of himself. 'Yes ma'am,' he said, and because the chocolate mice still smelt so overpoweringly beautiful – so much so that he could not keep his whiskers from vibrating – he came down off the tree, where the smell of them was mixed up with a lot of other smells, and he finished up a few crumbs of biscuit that he had previously overlooked.

He should then have gone back into the safety of his mouse-hole, but he could not bring himself to leave the enchanted tree, and all night he sat in front of the fire, watching it.

Even when the last flicker of the fire had burned itself out, and the coals sighed and fell together in white ash on the hearth, the mouse still sat on, for of course a mouse can see in the dark, and this mouse had never seen anything like this before. He forgot his wife who was waiting for him, he forgot to count the hours striking on the big clock in the hall, he forgot everything except the tree. That was why, when morning had come he was still sitting there when the mistress of the house opened the door – and the cat walked in! Before he knew it the great cat was coming softly and steadily across the hearth towards him, and the mouse knew that he was lost indeed.

The cat sat down placidly, a few feet away, and made no spring. The mouse watched him, sick with fear, unable to move. He wished the cat would be quick and spring, and make a finish to it.

'Hallo, nipper,' said the great animal, and the mouse saw his strong white pointed teeth as he spoke, 'don't be in a hurry to move. You needn't mind me.'

And still he didn't spring.

'I'm not going to chase you,' the cat said. And for some reason that he could not explain the mouse believed the cat, just as he had believed the angel.

'Why not?' he asked, trying to keep the wobble out of his voice.

'I don't know exactly,' the cat replied, blinking a mild yellow eye, 'but it's a thing we always do at this time of year. Traditional, you know.'

The mouse didn't know, but a warm gratitude made it impossible for him to speak.

'Mind you,' the cat went on, 'I shall chase you tomorrow, and every other day that I get the chance. Like as not I shall catch you too. But not today.' And he busied himself licking the pads of his great paws, keeping the claws politely hooded.

The mouse believed this too. He knew that the cat would indeed chase him tomorrow and every other day, but he also knew that after this it would always be different. He would be able to run away from the cat now, because he knew that the cat was just another animal, as he himself was an animal – a much stronger animal of course, but just an animal: not a horror that turned your legs to water and made your heart sick. Oh yes, he could run away from the cat now. Out of sheer bravado he crept across the few feet that lay between the cat and himself, and he leaned for a small daring moment against the cat's side, and felt the warmth and power of his great body. That would be something to tell his wife about when he got home.

Then the house began to stir, there were laughter and voices, people came and went, the cat was called for his breakfast – and the small brown mouse, who was by this time so excited that he hardly knew what he was doing, instead of running to his mousehole and safety, streaked for the tree, and lay hidden among its branches and saw all that was going on.

There was plenty to see. Visitors arrived all day long. They greeted each other, and laughed, and opened parcels, and kissed, and sang. And in the evening they drew the curtains across the windows, and they lighted the candles on the tree.

This was something so alarming that the mouse, between the striking of one match and the next, fled up the tree where there were no candles, and found himself lying once again beside his chocolate cousins.

When all the candles were lit, the parcels were untied from the tree, and handed down into small excited hands, and the mouse, from his point of vantage, looked down on the children's up-turned faces. Then it was the turn for the grown-up people to receive their parcels, and at last each pair of hands was filled.

There was nothing left on the tree now, except the angel and the candles and the bright balls – oh, and the chocolate mice. 'I'd forgotten about these,' someone said, and a hand reached up and up, among the branches.

There was no hope for it – he would be discovered. But just as the fingers fumbled for the chocolate mice, the angel's golden wing tilted ever so slightly, and the small brown mouse was safely sheltered behind it. There he lay, hidden and safe, until the party was over, until people had said good-bye, until the door had opened many times and shut again, until the candles were blown out and the light extinguished, and until the last of the feet had once more gone up the stairs and the house was quiet.

Suddenly it all seemed rather sad. Even the tree looked a little sad. The mouse thought of all the hands that had gone home full of treasures, and he felt sad, too – sad, and also tremendously tired.

'I'll go now,' he said to the angel, 'and thank you, ma'am, for helping me.'

And he got slowly down off the tree – he was stiff with lying so long in one position – and he crossed the room to the mousehole. Just before he went home he turned to the tree, for one last look.

'You are sad,' the angel said. 'What is the matter?'

He found it difficult to explain. 'You said "Not yet – not now",' he faltered, 'but the party is over.'

Just then the amber ball slid off the twig that held it, softly down from one branch to another, gently to the ground, and it rolled to his feet and stopped there.

The mouse looked up at the angel questioningly. 'For me?' And the angel smiled and nodded.

You might not think that a bright ball from a Christmas tree would travel round the corners in a mousehole. But you would be wrong.

JANET McNEILL
Illustrated by ROWEL FRIERS

Nicholas Nye

THISTLE and darnel and dock grew there,
　　And a bush, in the corner, of may;
On the orchard wall I used to sprawl
　　In the blazing heat of the day:
Half asleep and half awake,
　　While the birds went twittering by,
And nobody there my lone to share
　　　But Nicholas Nye.

Nicholas Nye was lean and grey,
　　Lame of a leg and old,
More than a score of donkey's years
　　He had seen since he was foaled;
He munched the thistles, purple and spiked,
　　Would sometimes stoop and sigh,
And turn his head, as if he said,
　　　'Poor Nicholas Nye!'

Alone with his shadow he'd drowse in the meadow,
　　Lazily swinging his tail;
At break of day he used to bray –
　　Not much too hearty and hale.
But a wonderful gumption was under his skin,
　　And a clear calm light in his eye;
And once in a while he would smile a smile,
　　Would Nicholas Nye.

Seem to be smiling at me, he would,
   From his bush, in the corner, of may –
Bony and ownerless, widowed and worn,
   Knobble-kneed, lonely, and grey;
And over the grass would seem to pass,
   'Neath the deep dark blue of the sky,
Something much better than words between me
    And Nicholas Nye.

But dusk would come in the apple boughs,
   The green of the glow-worm shine,
The birds in nest would crouch to rest,
   And home I'd trudge to mine;
And there, in the moonlight, dark with dew,
   Asking not wherefore nor why,
Would brood like a ghost, and as still as a post,
    Old Nicholas Nye.

WALTER DE LA MARE

A Norwegian Childhood

I

EDWIN was his name and he cried when he was born. But as soon as he sat on his mother's lap he laughed, and when they lit the lamps in the evening the room rang with his laughter but he cried when he could not get at them.

'Something odd will come of that boy,' said his mother.

A barren crag, though not very high, hung over the house he was born in; birches and firs looked down on it and gean blossom lay strewn upon its roof. And on that roof was a little goat of Edwin's, kept there so that it should not stray, and Edwin took grass and leaves up to it. One fine day the goat jumped down and ran away up the crag; up it went till it came to a place where it had never been before. Edwin could not see the goat when he went out in the afternoon and he thought at once of the fox. He went hot all over, looked all round and cried,

'Killy, killy, killy goat.'

'Ba-a-a,' said the goat up on the edge of the cliff, putting its head on one side and looking down.

But by the side of the goat there knelt a little girl.

'Is this goat yours?' she asked.

Edwin stood with his eyes and mouth agape, thrust his hands into his pockets and said,

'Who are you?'

'I am Marit, mother's little one, father's darling and grand-daughter to Ola Nordistuen of Hejde Farm. I shall be four in the autumn two days after the frost comes.'

'You are, are you,' said Edwin and drew breath, for he had not dared to breathe while she was speaking.

'Is this goat yours?' said the girl.

'Yes it is,' said he, looking at her.

'I should so like to have it. Won't you give it me?'

'No I won't.'

She lay kicking her heels in the air and looked down at him.

'Now if, for the goat, I gave you a cake can I have it then?'

Edwin came from a poor house: only once in his life had he ever eaten cake and that was when his grandfather came. Never till then and never since had he eaten anything as good. He looked up at the girl.

'Let me see the cake first,' he said.

She quickly held out a large cake she had in her hand.

'Here it is,' she said, and threw it down to him.

'Oh! it has broken to bits,' said the boy.

He picked each bit up very carefully. He thought he could eat the tiniest bit of all, and it was so good he had to eat just one more, and before he knew it he had eaten up the whole cake.

'Now the goat's mine,' said the girl.

The boy stopped with the last piece of cake in his mouth; the girl lay there laughing with the goat standing by her side, white under its chin, brown on its back, looking down sideways at him.

'Couldn't you wait a little?' asked the boy; his heart began to throb. Then the girl laughed even louder and got up on to her knees.

'No, it's my goat now,' she said throwing her arms round its neck. Then she took off her hair ribbon and tied it round it. Edwin looked on. Then she stood up and began to pull the goat, but it did not want to go with her and stretched its head out towards Edwin.

'Ba-a-a,' it said.

But she took its hair in one hand and the ribbon in the other and said to it coaxingly,

'Come along, goat, you shall go into the house and eat out of mother's plate and my apron.' And she sang:

'Come, boy's goat,
Come, mother's calf,
Come, mewing cat
In snow-white shoes.
Come, yellow ducks,
Come out of your hiding-place;
Come, little chickens,
Who can hardly run;
Come, my doves
With soft feathers;
See, the grass is wet,
But the sun does you good;
And early, early is it in summer,
But call for the autumn and it will come.'

There stood the boy. He had taken care of the goat ever since it was born last winter and it had never entered his head that he could lose it. And now it was gone all at once and he would never see it again.

His mother came tripping up from the beach with some pans she had been scouring. She saw the boy sitting cross-legged on the grass, crying, and she went over to him.

'What are you crying for?'

'The goat! The goat!'

'Well, where is the goat?' asked his mother looking up at the roof.

'It will never come back again,' said the boy.

'Darling, how can that be?'

He would not own up at first.

'Did the fox get it?'

'I wish it had been the fox.'

'Don't be so silly,' said his mother. 'What has happened to the goat?'

'Oh! Oh! Oh! I had hard luck and I – I sold it for a cake.'

As he uttered the words he saw what it really meant to sell the goat for a cake, for he had not thought about it before. His mother said, 'What do you suppose the little goat thinks of you, when you could sell it for a cake?'

And the boy thought it out for himself and came to the conclusion that he could never again be happy in this world, nor in heaven either.

He was so sad at heart that he made up his mind never again to do anything wrong: not to cut the cord of the spinning wheel, not to let the sheep loose, not to go down to the sea alone. He fell asleep where he lay and dreamed that the goat went up into heaven, that Our Lord was sitting there with a great beard as in the pictures in the prayer book, that the goat stood there cropping leaves off a tree – but Edwin sat by himself on the roof and could not get there.

Then he felt something wet touching his ear and he jumped up.

'Ba-a-a,' it said and it was his goat come back again.

'Well, you've come back!' He leapt up, took both its paws and danced it up and down; he caught it by its beard and was just going to take it in to his mother when he heard someone behind him and there was the girl sitting near him on the grass. Then he understood everything and he let go of the goat.

'Did you bring it over?'

She sat tearing up the grass in her hands and said, 'I wasn't allowed to keep it; grandfather is sitting waiting for me up there.'

While the boy stood looking at her he heard a sharp voice calling from the path at the top.

'Come on!'

Then she remembered what it was she had to do; she got up, went over to Edwin, put one of her grubby hands into his and said, looking into the distance,

'I'm sorry!'

After that she could not keep herself in, and flinging her arms round the goat she burst into tears.

'I think you'd better keep the goat,' said Edwin weakly.

'Hurry up now!' said grandfather from the crag. And Marit got up and went with faltering steps towards him.

'You've forgotten your hair ribbon!' Edwin cried after her.

She turned round and looked first at the ribbon, then at him. At last she plucked up courage and said to him with a choke in her voice,

'You can keep it.'

He went up to her and took both her hands in his.

'Thank you so much,' he said.

'But there's nothing to thank me for,' she answered and drawing a long sigh she hurried away.

He sat down on the grass again with the goat at his side, but he was not so fond of it now as he had been before.

2

The goat lay tethered near the house, but Edwin went out and looked up at the mountain. His mother came out and sat down by him. He wanted to hear stories of things far away, for the goat was no longer enough for him. So he heard how once upon a time everything could talk; the mountain talked to the stream and the stream talked to the river and the river to the sea and the sea to the sky; and then he asked if the sky didn't talk to anyone, and the sky talked to the clouds and the clouds to the trees and the trees to the grass and the grass to the birds and the birds to the beasts and the beasts to the children and the children to the grown ups, and so it went on till it went all round and no one knew who began. Edwin looked at the mountain and the trees and the lake and the sky and felt he had never really seen them before. The cat came out just then and lay down on the door-step in the sun.

'What is the cat saying?' asked Edwin, pointing at it. So his mother sang:

'At evening softly shines the sun,
The cat lies lazy on the stone.
Two small mice,
Cream thick and nice,
Four bits of fish,
I stole from the dish,
And am lazy and tired
Because so well I've fared.'

Then the cock came with all its hens.

'What is the cock saying?' asked Edwin, clapping his hands.

'The hen upon her wings doth sink,
The cock stands on one leg to think;
That grey goose
Steers high her course;
But sure am I that never she
As clever as a cock can be.
Run home, you hens, stay in today,
For the sun has leave to be away.'

Then two little birds sat singing on the roof.

'And what are the birds saying?' asked Edwin laughing.

And so he heard what every one of them was saying, down to the very ant crawling in the grass and the worm gnawing the bark.

That same summer his mother began to teach him to read. He had had books of his own for a long time and often thought how it would be when they began to talk too. Then the letters turned into animals, birds and all kinds of things and soon they began to go about together two and two: A stood about under a tree called B and C came and did the same, but when three or four of them got together they began to quarrel with each other and nothing went right. And the further he went on the less he remembered who they all were; the one that stayed longest in his head was A because he liked him best, but soon he forgot him too and there were no stories left in the book, but only lessons.

One day his mother came in and said to him, 'School begins again tomorrow and you must go up to the farm.'

Edwin had heard that a school was a place a lot of boys played about in, and he had nothing against that. He was very pleased at the idea. He had often been to the farm but never when the school was there, and he walked faster than his mother up the hill in his eagerness to be there. As they reached the old people's

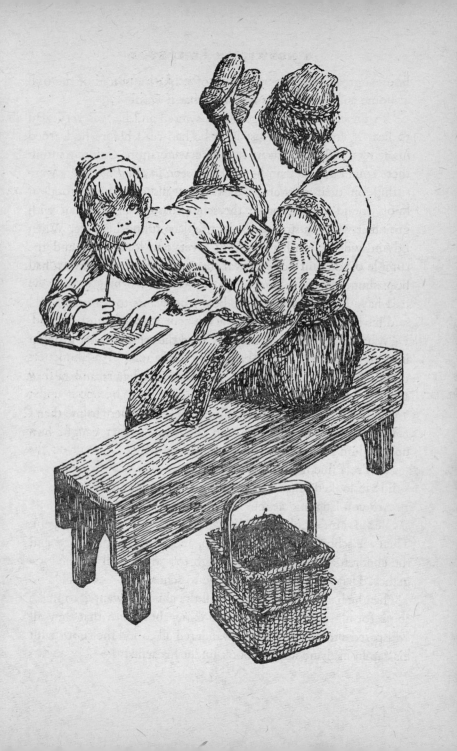

house a great rumbling came out of it like the sound of the mill at home and he asked his mother what it was.

'It's the children reading,' she answered and he was very glad to hear it, for that was just how he had read before he learned his letters. When he went in, there were more children sitting there round a table than he had ever seen in church; others were sitting on their satchels against the walls and some stood in knots round a blackboard; the schoolmaster, an old man with grey hair, sat on a stool near the fireplace filling his pipe. When Edwin and his mother came in, everyone looked up and the rumble of the mill stopped as if the sluice of the mill stream had been shut down.

'I have brought you a little boy who wants to learn to read,' said his mother.

'What is the little chap's name?' said the schoolmaster groping into his pouch for more tobacco.

'Edwin,' said his mother. 'He knows his letters and he can spell.'

'Can he now?' said the schoolmaster. 'Come here to me then.'

Edwin went over to him and the schoolmaster caught him up, put him on his knee and took his cap off.

'You're a fine fellow,' he said.

Edwin looked him straight in the eye and laughed.

'Are you laughing at me?' he asked, frowning.

'Yes, I am,' replied Edwin and burst out laughing again. Then the schoolmaster laughed too, and his mother laughed and the children all felt they could laugh too so they all laughed together. That was how Edwin came to school.

Then he had to find a seat and all the children wanted to make room for him; he stood so long looking about him that they all whispered and pointed but he wandered all round the room with his cap in his hand and his book under his arm.

'What's all this about?' asked the schoolmaster, busy with his pipe again.

Just as the boy turned towards him, he saw close by his side, sitting on a little red box near the fireplace, Marit of the many names. She had hidden her face behind her hands and sat there peeping through at him.

'This is where I'm going to sit,' said Edwin quickly jumping across to her and seating himself by her side. She raised the arm that was nearest to him and peered out at him under her elbow; he too covered up his face with his hands and peered out at her under his elbow. They sat playing like this until she laughed and he laughed too and the other children saw what was going on and they joined in the laughter. Then a loud voice broke in, gruff at first but milder almost at once.

'Be quiet you little devils! You wretched little monkeys, be quiet and behave yourselves.'

It was the schoolmaster, who had a way of flaring up at first and then dying down again before he had got very far. The school was quiet at once, the mills began to turn again and they all read aloud each from his own book; discords arose as voices grew louder and shriller as they struggled to be heard. Edwin had never had such fun in all his life.

'Is it like this always?' he whispered to Marit.

'Yes,' she said. 'It's always like this.'

After a while they had to go up to the schoolmaster and read to him; then another little boy was put to read with them, but after that they were allowed to go off and sit quietly by themselves.

'I've got a goat of my own now,' said Marit.

'Have you?'

'Yes, but it isn't such a pretty one as yours.'

'Why don't you come up on to the cliff any more?'

'Grandfather is afraid I should fall over it.'

'But it isn't so high as all that.'

'All the same, Grandfather won't let me.'

'Mother knows such a lot of songs,' said Edwin.

'So does Grandfather.'

'But not so many as Mother knows.'

'Grandfather knows one about a dance. Would you like to hear it?'

'Yes, I'd love to.'

'But you must come nearer so that the schoolmaster can't hear what we are saying.'

He moved towards her and she went four or five times through her little song till the boy had learned it by heart. It was the first thing he learned at school.

'Up children!' cried the schoolmaster. 'Today is your first day and you can go off early, but first we must say a prayer and sing.'

The whole school burst into life: they leapt from the benches, ran across the floor and all began talking at once.

'Be quiet, you little brutes! Gently, children, gently!' said the schoolmaster, and then there was silence. He stood in front of them and said a short prayer. Then they sang, the schoolmaster starting off in his deep bass and all the children stood with their hands folded and joined in. Edwin stood next to the door with Marit and looked on; they folded their hands but they could not sing. That was the first day at school.

BJÖRNSTERNE BJÖRNSEN
Translated by GERALD ELVEY
Illustrated by CHRISTOPHER BROOKER

The Fly

How large unto the tiny fly
Must little things appear! –
A rosebud like a feather bed,
Its prickle like a spear;

A dewdrop like a looking-glass,
A hair like golden wire;
The smallest grain of mustard-seed
As fierce as coals of fire;

A loaf of bread, a lofty hill;
A wasp, a cruel leopard;
And specks of salt as bright to see
As lambkins to a shepherd.

WALTER DE LA MARE

Rilloby-Rill

Grasshoppers four a-fiddling went,
   Heigh-ho! never be still!
They earned but little towards their rent
But all day long with their elbows bent
   They fiddled a tune called Rilloby-rilloby,
   Fiddled a tune called Rilloby-rill.

Grasshoppers soon on fairies came,
   Heigh-ho! never be still!
Fairies asked with a manner of blame,
'Where do you come from, what is your name,
   What do you want with your Rilloby-rilloby,
   What do you want with your Rilloby-rill?'

'Madam, you see before you stand,
   Heigh-ho! never be still!
The Old Original Favourite Grand

Grasshoppers' Green Herbarian Band,
 And the tune we play is Rilloby-rilloby,
 Madam, the tune is Rilloby-rill.'

Fairies hadn't a word to say,
 Heigh-ho! never be still!
Fairies seldom are sweet by day,
But the grasshoppers merrily fiddled away,
 Oh, but they played with a willoby-rilloby,
 Oh, but they played with a willoby-will!

Fairies slumber and sulk at noon,
 Heigh-ho! never be still!
But at last the kind old motherly moon
Brought them dew in a silver spoon,
 And they turned to ask for Rilloby-rilloby,
 One more round of Rilloby-rill.

Ah, but nobody now replied,
  Heigh-ho! never be still!
When day went down the music died,
Grasshoppers four lay side by side.
  And there was an end of their Rilloby-rilloby,
  And there was an end of their Rilloby-rill.

HENRY NEWBOLT
Illustrated by JANE PATON

The Old Woman in the Basket

There was an old woman tossed up in a basket,
    Ninety times as high as the moon;
And where she was going, I couldn't but ask it,
    For in her hand she carried a broom.

'Old woman, old woman, old woman,' quoth I,
'O whither, O whither, O whither so high?'
'To sweep the cobwebs off the sky!'
'Shall I go with you?'
                   'Ay, by and by.'

The Cat That Walked by Himself

HEAR and attend and listen; for this befell and behappened and became and was, O my Best Beloved, when the Tame animals were wild. The Dog was wild, and the Horse was wild, and the Cow was wild, and the Sheep was wild, and the Pig was wild – as wild as wild could be – and they walked in the Wet Wild Woods by their wild lones. But the wildest of all the wild animals was the Cat. He walked by himself, and all places were alike to him.

Of course the Man was wild too. He was dreadfully wild. He didn't even begin to be tame till he met the Woman, and she told him that she did not like living in his Wild ways. She picked out a nice dry Cave, instead of a heap of wet leaves, to lie down in; and she strewed clean sand on the floor; and she lit a nice fire of wood at the back of the Cave; and she hung a dried wild-horse skin, tail-down, across the opening of the Cave; and she said, 'Wipe your feet, dear, when you come in, and now we'll keep house.'

That night, Best Beloved, they ate wild sheep roasted on the hot stones, and flavoured with wild garlic and wild pepper; and wild duck stuffed with wild rice and wild fenugreek and wild coriander; and marrow-bones of wild oxen; and wild cherries, and wild grenadillas. Then the Man went to sleep in front of the fire ever so happy; but the Woman sat up, combing her hair. She took the bone of the shoulder of mutton – the big flat blade-bone – and she looked at the wonderful marks on it, and she threw more wood on the fire, and she made a Magic. She made the First Singing Magic in the world.

Out in the Wet Wild Woods all the wild animals gathered

together where they could see the light of the fire a long way off, and they wondered what it meant.

Then Wild Horse stamped with his wild foot and said, 'O my Friends and O my Enemies, why have the Man and the Woman made that great light in that great Cave, and what harm will it do us?'

Wild Dog lifted up his wild nose and smelled the smell of the roast mutton, and said, 'I will go up and see and look, and say; for I think it is good. Cat, come with me.'

'Nenni!' said the Cat. 'I am the Cat who walks by himself, and all places are alike to me. I will not come.'

'Then we can never be friends again,' said Wild Dog, and he trotted off to the Cave. But when he had gone a little way the Cat said to himself, 'All places are alike to me. Why should I not go too and see and look and come away at my own liking?' So he slipped after Wild Dog softly, very softly, and hid himself where he could hear everything.

When Wild Dog reached the mouth of the Cave he lifted up the dried horse-skin with his nose and sniffed the beautiful smell of the roast mutton, and the Woman, looking at the blade-bone, heard him, and laughed, and said, 'Here comes the first. Wild Thing out of the Wild Woods, what do you want?'

Wild Dog said, 'O my Enemy and Wife of my Enemy, what is this that smells so good in the Wild Woods?'

Then the Woman picked up a roasted mutton-bone and threw it to Wild Dog, and said, 'Wild Thing out of the Wild Woods, taste and try.' Wild Dog gnawed the bone, and it was more delicious than anything he had ever tasted, and he said, 'O my Enemy and Wife of my Enemy, give me another.'

The Woman said, 'Wild Thing out of the Wild Woods, help my Man to hunt through the day and guard this Cave at night and I will give you as many roast bones as you need.'

'Ah!' said the Cat, listening. 'This is a very wise Woman, but she is not so wise as I am.'

Wild Dog crawled into the Cave and laid his head on the Woman's lap, and said, 'O my Friend and Wife of my Friend, I will help your Man to hunt through the day, and at night I will guard your Cave.'

'Ah!' said the Cat, listening. 'That is a very foolish Dog.' And he went back through the Wet Wild Woods waving his wild tail, and walking by his wild lone. But he never told anybody.

When the Man woke up he said, 'What is Wild Dog doing here?' and the Woman said, 'His name is not Wild Dog any more, but the First Friend, because he will be our friend for always and always and always. Take him with you when you go hunting.'

Next night the Woman cut great green armfuls of fresh grass from the water-meadows, and dried it before the fire, so that it smelt like new-mown hay, and she sat at the mouth of the Cave and plaited a halter out of horse-hide, and she looked at the shoulder-of-mutton bone – at the big broad blade-bone – and she made a Magic. She made the Second Singing Magic in the world.

Out in the Wild Woods all the wild animals wondered what had happened to Wild Dog, and at last Wild Horse stamped with his foot and said, 'I will go and see and say why Wild Dog has not returned. Cat, come with me.'

'Nenni!' said the Cat. 'I am the Cat who walks by himself, and all places are alike to me. I will not come.' But all the same he followed Wild Horse softly, very softly, and hid himself where he could hear everything.

When the Woman heard Wild Horse, tripping and stumbling on his long mane, she laughed and said, 'Here comes the second Wild Thing out of the Wild Woods, what do you want?'

Wild Horse said, 'O my Enemy and Wife of my Enemy, where is Wild Dog?'

The Woman laughed, and picked up the blade-bone and looked at it, and said, 'Wild Thing out of the Wild Woods, you did not come here for Wild Dog, but for the sake of this good grass.'

And Wild Horse, tripping and stumbling on his long mane, said, 'That is true; give it me to eat.'

The Woman said, 'Wild Thing out of the Wild Woods, bend your head and wear what I give you, and you shall eat the wonderful grass three times a day.'

'Ah!' said the Cat, listening. 'This is a clever Woman, but she is not so clever as I am.'

Wild Horse bent his wild head, and the Woman slipped the plaited-hide halter over it, and Wild Horse breathed on the Woman's feet and said, 'O my Mistress, and Wife of my Master, I will be your servant for the sake of the wonderful grass.'

'Ah!' said the Cat, listening. 'That is a very foolish Horse.' And he went back through the Wet Wild Woods, waving his wild tail and walking by his wild lone. But he never told anybody.

When the Man and the Dog came back from hunting, the Man said, 'What is Wild Horse doing here?' And the Woman said, 'His name is not Wild Horse any more, but the First Servant, because he will carry us from place to place for always and always and always. Ride on his back when you go hunting.'

Next day, holding her wild head high that her wild horns should not catch in the wild trees, Wild Cow came up to the Cave, and the Cat followed, and hid himself just the same as before; and everything happened just the same as before; and the cat said the same things as before; and when Wild Cow had promised to give her milk to the Woman every day in exchange

for the wonderful grass, the Cat went back through the Wet Wild Woods waving his wild tail and walking by his wild lone, just the same as before. But he never told anybody. And when the Man and the Horse and the Dog came home from hunting and asked the same questions same as before, the Woman said, 'Her name is not Wild Cow any more, but the Giver of Good Food. She will give us the warm white milk for always and always and always, and I will take care of her while you and the First Friend and the First Servant go hunting.'

Next day the Cat waited to see if any other Wild Thing would go up to the Cave, but no one moved in the Wet Wild Woods, so the Cat walked there by himself; and he saw the Woman milking the Cow, and he saw the light of the fire in the Cave, and he smelt the smell of the warm white milk.

Cat said, 'O my Enemy and Wife of my Enemy, where did Wild Cow go?'

The Woman laughed and said, 'Wild Thing out of the Wild Woods, go back to the Woods again, for I have braided up my hair, and I have put away the magic blade-bone, and we have no more need of either friends or servants in our Cave.'

Cat said, 'I am not a friend, and I am not a servant. I am the Cat who walks by himself, and I wish to come into your Cave.'

Woman said, 'Then why did you not come with First Friend on the first night?'

Cat grew very angry and said, 'Has Wild Dog told tales of me?'

Then the Woman laughed and said, 'You are the Cat who walks by himself, and all places are alike to you. You are neither a friend nor a servant. You have said it yourself. Go away and walk by yourself in all places alike.'

Then Cat pretended to be sorry and said, 'Must I never come into the Cave? Must I never sit by the warm fire? Must I never drink the warm white milk? You are very wise and very beautiful. You should not be cruel even to a Cat.'

Woman said, 'I knew I was wise, but I did not know I was beautiful. So I will make a bargain with you. If ever I say one word in your praise, you may come into the Cave.'

'And if you say two words in my praise?' said the Cat.

'I never shall,' said the Woman, 'but if I say two words in your praise, you may sit by the fire in the Cave.'

'And if you say three words?' said the Cat.

'I never shall,' said the Woman, 'but if I say three words in your praise, you may drink the warm white milk three times a day for always and always and always.'

Then the Cat arched his back and said, 'Now let the Curtain at the mouth of the Cave, and the Fire at the back of the Cave, and the Milk-pots that stand beside the Fire, remember what my Enemy and the Wife of my Enemy has said.' And he went away through the Wet Wild Woods waving his wild tail and walking by his wild lone.

That night when the Man and the Horse and the Dog came home from hunting, the Woman did not tell them of the bargain that she had made with the Cat, because she was afraid that they might not like it. Cat went far and far away and hid himself in the Wet Wild Woods by his wild lone for a long time till the Woman forgot all about him. Only the Bat – the little upside-down Bat – that hung inside the Cave knew where Cat hid; and every evening Bat would fly to Cat with news of what was happening.

One evening Bat said, 'There is a Baby in the Cave. He is new and pink and fat, and the Woman is very fond of him.'

'Ah,' said the Cat, listening, 'but what is the Baby fond of?'

'He is fond of things that are soft and tickle,' said the Bat.

'He is fond of warm things to hold in his arms when he goes to sleep. He is fond of being played with. He is fond of all those things.'

'Ah,' said the Cat, listening, 'then my time has come.'

Next night Cat walked through the Wet Wild Woods and hid very near the Cave till morning-time, and Man and Dog and Horse went hunting. The Woman was busy cooking that morning, and the Baby cried and interrupted. So she carried him outside the Cave and gave him a handful of pebbles to play with. But still the Baby cried.

Then the Cat put out his paddy paw and patted the Baby on the cheek, and it cooed: and the Cat rubbed against its fat knees and tickled it under its fat chin with his tail. And the Baby laughed; and the Woman heard him and smiled.

Then the Bat – the little upside-down Bat – that hung in the mouth of the Cave said, 'O my Hostess and Wife of my Host and Mother of my Host's Son, a Wild Thing from the Wild Woods is most beautifully playing with your Baby.'

'A blessing on that Wild Thing whoever he may be,' said the Woman, straightening her back, 'for I was a busy woman this morning and he has done me a service.'

That very minute and second, Best Beloved, the dried horse-skin Curtain that was stretched tail-down at the mouth of the Cave fell down – *woosh!* – because it remembered the bargain she had made with the Cat; and when the Woman went to pick it up – lo and behold! – the Cat was sitting quite comfy inside the Cave.

'O my Enemy and Wife of my Enemy and Mother of my Enemy,' said the Cat, 'it is I: for you have spoken a word in my praise, and now I can sit within the Cave for always and always and always. But still I am the Cat who walks by himself, and all places are alike to me.'

The Woman was very angry, and shut her lips tight and took up her spinning-wheel and began to spin.

But the Baby cried because the Cat had gone away, and the Woman could not hush it, for it struggled and kicked and grew black in the face.

'O my Enemy and Wife of my Enemy and Mother of my Enemy,' said the Cat, 'take a strand of the thread that you are spinning and tie it to your spinning-whorl and drag it along the floor, and I will show you a Magic that shall make your Baby laugh as loudly as he is now crying.'

'I will do so,' said the Woman, 'because I am at my wits' end; but I will not thank you for it.'

She tied the thread to the little clay spindle-whorl and drew it across the floor, and the Cat ran after it and patted it with his paws and rolled head over heels, and tossed it backward over his shoulder and chased it between his hind-legs and pretended to lose it, and pounced down upon it again, till the Baby laughed as loudly as it had been crying, and scrambled after the Cat and frolicked all over the Cave till it grew tired and settled down to sleep with the Cat in its arms.

'Now,' said Cat, 'I will sing the Baby a song that shall keep him asleep for an hour.' And he began to purr, loud and low, low and loud, till the Baby fell fast asleep. The Woman smiled as she looked down upon the two of them, and said, 'That was wonderfully done. No question but you are clever, O Cat.'

That very minute and second, Best Beloved, the smoke of the Fire at the back of the Cave came down in clouds from the roof – *puff!* – because it remembered the bargain she had made with the Cat; and when it had cleared away — lo and behold! – the Cat was sitting quite comfy close to the fire.

'O my Enemy and Wife of my Enemy and Mother of my Enemy,' said the Cat, 'it is I: for you have spoken a second word in my praise, and now I can sit by the warm fire at the back of the Cave for always and always and always. But still I am the Cat who walks by himself, and all places are alike to me.'

Then the Woman was very very angry, and let down her hair and put more wood on the fire and brought out the broad blade-bone of the shoulder of mutton and began to make a Magic that should prevent her from saying a third word in praise of the Cat. It was not a Singing Magic, Best Beloved, it was a Still Magic; and by and by the Cave grew so still that a little wee-wee mouse crept out of a corner and ran across the floor.

'O my Enemy and Wife of my Enemy and Mother of my Enemy,' said the Cat, 'is that little mouse part of your Magic?'

'Ouh! Chee! No indeed!' said the Woman, and she dropped the blade-bone and jumped upon the footstool in front of the fire and braided up her hair very quick for fear that the mouse should run up it.

'Ah,' said the Cat, watching, 'then the mouse will do me no harm if I eat it?'

'No,' said the Woman, braiding up her hair, 'eat it quickly and I will ever be grateful to you.'

Cat made one jump and caught the little mouse, and the Woman said, 'A hundred thanks. Even the First Friend is not quick enough to catch little mice as you have done. You must be very wise.'

That very moment and second, O Best Beloved, the Milk-pot that stood by the fire cracked in two pieces – *ffft!* – because it remembered the bargain she had made with the Cat; and when the Woman jumped down from the footstool – lo and behold! – the Cat was lapping up the warm white milk that lay in one of the broken pieces.

'O my Enemy and Wife of my Enemy and Mother of my Enemy,' said the Cat, 'it is I: for you have spoken three words in my praise, and now I can drink the warm white milk three times a day for always and always and always. But *still* I am the Cat who walks by himself, and all places are alike to me.'

Then the Woman laughed and set the Cat a bowl of the warm white milk and said, 'O Cat, you are as clever as a man, but remember that your bargain was not made with the Man or the Dog, and I do not know what they will do when they come home.'

'What is that to me?' said the Cat. 'If I have my place in the Cave by the fire and my warm white milk three times a day I do not care what the Man or the Dog can do.'

That evening when the Man and the Dog came into the Cave, the Woman told them all the story of the bargain, while the cat sat by the fire and smiled. Then the Man said, 'Yes, but he has not made a bargain, with *me* or with all proper Men after me.' Then he took off his two leather boots and he took up his little stone axe (that makes three) and he fetched a piece of wood and a hatchet (that is five altogether), and he set them out in a row and he said, 'Now we will make *our* bargain. If you do not catch mice when you are in the Cave for always and always and always, I will throw these five things at you whenever I see you, and so shall all proper Men do after me.'

'Ah,' said the Woman, listening, 'this is a very clever Cat, but he is not so clever as my Man.'

The Cat counted the five things (and they looked very knobbly) and he said, 'I will catch mice when I am in the Cave for always and always and always; but *still* I am the Cat who walks by himself, and all places are alike to me.'

'Not when I am near,' said the Man. 'If you had not said that last I would have put all these things away for always and always and always; but now I am going to throw my two boots and my little stone axe (that makes three) at you whenever I meet you. And so shall all proper Men do after me!'

Then the Dog said, 'Wait a minute. He has not made a bargain with *me* or with all proper Dogs after me.' And he showed his teeth and said, 'If you are not kind to the Baby while I am in the Cave for always and always and always, I will hunt you till I catch you, and when I catch you I will bite you. And so shall all proper Dogs do after me.'

'Ah,' said the Woman, listening, 'this is a very clever Cat, but he is not so clever as the Dog.'

Cat counted the Dog's teeth (and they looked very pointed) and he said, 'I will be kind to the Baby while I am in the Cave, as long as he does not pull my tail too hard, for always and always and always. But *still* I am the Cat that walks by himself, and all places are alike to me.'

'Not when I am near,' said the Dog. 'If you had not said that last I would have shut my mouth for always and always and always; but *now* I am going to hunt you up a tree whenever I meet you. And so shall all proper Dogs do after me.'

Then the Man threw his two boots and his little stone axe (that makes three) at the Cat, and the Cat ran out of the Cave and the Dog chased him up a tree; and from that day to this, Best Beloved, three proper Men out of five will always throw things at a Cat whenever they meet him, and all proper Dogs will chase him up a tree. But the Cat keeps his side of the bargain too. He will kill mice, and he will be kind to Babies when he is in the house, just as long as they do not pull his tail too hard. But when he has done that, and between times, and when the moon gets up and night comes, he is the Cat that walks by himself, and all places are alike to him. Then he goes out to the Wet Wild Woods or up the Wet Wild Trees or on the Wet Wild Roofs, waving his wild tail and walking by his wild lone.

Written and illustrated by RUDYARD KIPLING

Night

The sun descending in the west,
    The evening star does shine;
The birds are silent in their nest,
    And I must seek for mine.
The moon, like a flower,
In heaven's high bower,
With silent delight
Sits and smiles on the night.

WILLIAM BLAKE

The Fable of the Old Man, the Boy and the Donkey

Hobbled to market an old man and his boy
Hobbledehoy
Their donkey to sell.
  'Well, well,' said a dairymaid,
'What fools you are to walk
When one of you might ride!'
  'Jump on Neddy's back, boy,'
The old man cried.

The sun struck hard and the old man sighed.
A ploughman peered at him over the hedge.
  'Hey, gaffer!
In less than a week you'll be dead
Unless you ride. The donkey's back is wide
And there's room for two.'
  'Of course,' said the old man.
He jumped up beside.

The donkey staggered. He groaned and he whined.
His back was curved as a slice of melon rind.

A passing priest for pity of the beast
Cried out on the cruel pair:
  'Oh, shame to treat him so!
To think these days a Christian dare!
Sirs, you shall pay
For your sins.' He threw up his hands in despair
And dropped to his knees.

To please the priest
They carried the beast.
The little boy limped for the load on their backs;
The old man tottered, he creaked and he cracked,
While Neddy nibbled his silk top-hat.

So they toiled to town.
A crowd had gathered by the market stall.
　'What ninnies, what clowns
To lug a donkey along like that!'
And they laughed loud
To see them stumble and fall.
The old man was angry. He muttered and cursed,
　'I try to please all and I please not a soul.
What a fool
I've been! I couldn't do worse.'
And tipping the donkey into a pool
He stumped off home with the boy,
Not a penny in his purse . . .
Hobbledehoy . . . hobbledehoy.

But Neddy was free to frolic and splash
In the cool of the pool,
Then scamper away to the fields.
He was no fool.

IAN SERRAILLIER

How Still the Bells

How still the bells in steeples stand
Till, swollen with the sky,
They leap upon their silver feet
In frantic melody.

EMILY DICKINSON
Illustrated by ROBERT HODGSON

Pooh and Piglet Go Hunting

THE Piglet lived in a very grand house in the middle of a beech-tree, and the beech-tree was in the middle of the forest, and the Piglet lived in the middle of the house. Next to his house was a piece of broken board which had: 'TRESPASSERS W' on it. When Christopher Robin asked the Piglet what it meant, he said it was his grandfather's name, and had been in the family for a long time. Christopher Robin said you *couldn't* be called Trespassers W., and Piglet said yes, you could, because his grandfather was, and it was short for Trespassers Will, which was short for Trespassers William. And his grandfather had had two names in case he lost one – Trespassers after an uncle, and William after Trespassers.

'I've got two names,' said Christopher Robin carelessly.

'Well, there you are, that proves it,' said Piglet.

One fine winter's day when Piglet was brushing away the snow in front of his house, he happened to look up, and there was Winnie-the-Pooh. Pooh was walking round and round in a circle, thinking of something else, and when Piglet called to him, he just went on walking.

'Hallo!' said Piglet, 'what are *you* doing?'

'Hunting,' said Pooh.

'Hunting what?'

'Tracking something,' said Winnie-the-Pooh very mysteriously.

'Tracking what?' said Piglet, coming closer.

'That's just what I ask myself. I ask myself, What?'

'What do you think you'll answer?'

'I shall have to wait until I catch up with it,' said Winnie-the-

Pooh. 'Now, look there.' He pointed to the ground in front of him. 'What do you see there?'

'Tracks,' said Piglet. 'Paw-marks.' He gave a little squeak of excitement. 'Oh, Pooh! Do you think it's a – a – a Woozle?'

'It may be,' said Pooh. 'Sometimes it is, and sometimes it isn't. You never can tell with paw-marks.'

With these few words he went on tracking, and Piglet, after watching him for a minute or two, ran after him. Winnie-the-Pooh had come to a sudden stop, and was bending over the tracks in a puzzled sort of way.

'What's the matter?' asked Piglet.

'It's a very funny thing,' said Bear, 'but there seem to be *two* animals now. This – whatever-it-was – has been joined by another – whatever-it-is – and the two of them are now proceeding in company. Would you mind coming with me, Piglet, in case they turn out to be Hostile Animals?'

Piglet scratched his ear in a nice sort of way, and said that he had nothing to do until Friday, and would be delighted to come, in case it really *was* a Woozle.

'You mean, in case it really is two Woozles,' said Winnie-the-Pooh, and Piglet said that anyhow he had nothing to do until Friday. So off they went together.

There was a small spinney of larch trees just here, and it seemed as if the two Woozles, if that is what they were, had been going round this spinney; so round this spinney went Pooh and Piglet after them; Piglet passing the time by telling Pooh what his Grandfather Trespassers W. had done to Remove Stiffness after Tracking, and how his Grandfather Trespassers W. had suffered in his later years from Shortness of Breath, and other matters of interest, and Pooh wondering what a Grandfather was like, and if perhaps this was Two Grandfathers they were after now, and, if so, whether he would be allowed to take one home and keep it,

and what Christopher Robin would say. And still the tracks went on in front of them . . .

Suddenly Winnie-the-Pooh stopped, and pointed excitedly in front of him. '*Look!*'

'*What?*' said Piglet, with a jump. And then, to show that he hadn't been frightened, he jumped up and down once or twice more in an exercising sort of way.

'The tracks!' said Pooh. '*A third animal has joined the other two!*'

'Pooh!' cried Piglet. 'Do you think it is another Woozle?'

'No,' said Pooh, 'because it makes different marks. It is either Two Woozles and one, as it might be, Wizzle, or Two as it might be, Wizzles and one, if so it is, Woozle. Let us continue to follow them.'

So they went on, feeling just a little anxious now, in case the three animals in front of them were of Hostile Intent. And Piglet wished very much that his Grandfather T. W. were there, instead of elsewhere, and Pooh thought how nice it would be if they met Christopher Robin suddenly but quite accidentally, and only because he liked Christopher Robin so much. And then, all of a sudden, Winnie-the-Pooh stopped again, and licked the tip of his nose in a cooling manner, for he was feeling more hot and anxious than ever in his life before. *There were four animals in front of them!*

'Do you see, Piglet? Look at their tracks! Three, as it were, Woozles, and one, as it was, Wizzle. *Another Woozle has joined them!*'

And so it seemed to be. There were the tracks; crossing over each other here, getting muddled up with each other there; but, quite plainly every now and then, the tracks of four sets of paws.

'I *think*,' said Piglet, when he had licked the tip of his nose too, and found it brought very little comfort. 'I *think* that I have just remembered something. I have just remembered something that I forgot to do yesterday and shan't be able to do tomorrow. So I suppose I really ought to go back and do it now.'

'We'll do it this afternoon, and I'll come with you,' said Pooh.

'It isn't the sort of thing you can do in the afternoon,' said Piglet quickly. 'It's a very particular morning thing, that has to be done in the morning, and, if possible, between the hours of – What would you say the time was?'

'About twelve,' said Winnie-the-Pooh, looking at the sun.

'Between, as I was saying, the hours of twelve and twelve five. So, really, dear old Pooh, if you'll excuse me – *What's that?*'

Pooh looked up at the sky, and then, as he heard the whistle again, he looked up into the branches of a big oak tree, and then he saw a friend of his.

'It's Christopher Robin,' he said.

'Ah, then you'll be all right,' said Piglet. 'You'll be quite safe with *him*. Good-bye,' and he trotted off home as quickly as he could, very glad to be Out of All Danger again.

Christopher Robin came slowly down his tree.

'Silly old Bear,' he said, 'what *were* you doing? First you went round the spinney twice by yourself, and then Piglet ran after you and you went round again together, and then you were going round a fourth time –'

'Wait a moment,' said Winnie-the-Pooh, holding up his paw.

He sat down and thought, in the most thoughtful way he could think. Then he fitted his paw into one of the Tracks . . . and then he scratched his nose twice, and stood up.

'Yes,' said Winnie-the-Pooh.

'I see now,' said Winnie-the-Pooh.

'I have been Foolish and Deluded,' said he, 'and I am a Bear of No Brain at All.'

'You're the Best Bear in All the World,' said Christopher Robin soothingly.

'Am I?' said Pooh hopefully. And then he brightened up suddenly.

'Anyhow,' he said, 'it is nearly Luncheon Time.'

So he went home for it.

A. A. MILNE
Illustrated by E. H. SHEPARD

Bells

Hard as crystal,
   Clear as an icicle,
Is the tinkling sound
   Of a bell on a bicycle.

The bell in the clock
   That stands on the shelf
Slowly, sleepily
   Talks to itself.

The school bell is noisy
   And bangs like brass.
'Hurry up! Hurry up!
   Late for class!'

But deep and distant
   And peaceful to me
Are the bells I hear
   Below the sea.

Lying by the sea-shore
   On a calm day
Sometimes I hear them
   Far, far away.

With solemn tune
   In stately time
Under the water
   I hear them chime.

Why do the bells
  So stately sound?
For a sea-king dead,
  A sailor drowned?

Hark, how they peal
  Far, far away!
Is it a mermaid's
  Marriage-day?

Do they ring for joy
  Or weeping or war,
Those bells I hear
  As I lie by the shore?

But merry or mournful
  So sweet to me
Are those dreamy bells
  Below the sea.

JAMES REEVES

Then

Twenty, forty, sixty, eighty,
A hundred years ago,
All through the night with lantern bright
The Watch trudged to and fro.
And little boys tucked snug abed
Would wake from dreams to hear –
'Two o'the morning by the clock,
And the stars a-shining clear!'
Or, when across the chimney-tops
Screamed shrill a north-east gale,
A faint and shaken voice would shout,
'Three! and a storm of hail!'

WALTER DE LA MARE

A Hymn for Saturday

Now's the time for mirth and play,
Saturday's an holiday:
Praise to Heaven unceasing yield,
I've found a lark's nest in the field.

A lark's nest, then your playmate begs
You'd spare herself and speckled eggs;
Soon she shall ascend and sing
Your praises to the eternal King.

CHRISTOPHER SMART

Rapunzel

I

THERE was once a poor couple who lived in a cottage at the edge of a wood. At the back of the cottage was a little window which looked out over a high stone wall. Beyond the wall was a most beautiful garden, where grew all manner of flowers and herbs. In the trees the birds sang sweetly all day long, and in the middle of a green lawn a sparkling fountain played. The couple had never seen a garden like this. But they had not been inside it, for it belonged to a cruel witch named Gothel.

Now in that garden there grew a herb called rampion, which is used for making salads. In that country it was known as rapunzel.

'Ah, husband,' sighed the poor woman one day as she looked out of the window. 'I don't feel well, but I believe I would get better if only I had some of that rampion to eat.'

472

The poor man was distressed to see his wife ill, and he determined to get her some of the herb, cost what it might. So that evening, when the witch was not to be seen in her garden, he climbed over the wall and seized a handful of the rampion. Then he scrambled back and gave it to his wife. When she had eaten it, she felt better.

But next day it was just the same.

'Oh, I shall die,' said she, 'if I can't have more of that herb.'

And indeed she looked so pale and ill that her husband went once more into the garden and took a bunch of the rampion. He was just going to climb back over the wall when the witch came and saw him.

'Aha!' she cried. 'What are you doing in my garden? Why do you come here in the dark and steal my magic herbs?'

'Oh madam,' said the poor man, 'my wife is very ill. She says that if she can't get this herb to make into a salad she will die. Please, I beg you, let me keep it.'

At this the witch seemed to take pity on the man.

'Very well,' she said, 'you may keep it. You have no children yet, but soon your wife is to have a daughter. In payment for the rampion, you must allow me to have the child when it is born!'

What could the poor man do but agree? For he thought that otherwise his wife would die, and he would have no one left in the world.

So every evening he went into the witch's garden for a bunch of the herb his wife so much desired. She seemed to get better every day, and at last her little girl was born.

Almost immediately the cruel witch appeared at her bedside and demanded the baby. So the poor couple were obliged to give up their only child. Gothel laughed with glee and took the baby away, to bring up as her own. She named her Rapunzel after the name of the herb as it was called in those parts. Every

day the child grew stronger, until she could be seen playing in the witch's beautiful garden. Sometimes her parents caught a glimpse of her running amid the flower-beds, chasing a butterfly or calling to the birds, while her golden hair waved behind her in the breeze. And it seemed to the poor couple that their daughter was more beautiful than any of the flowers in the garden.

But when Rapunzel was twelve years old, the cruel witch took her away from the garden and shut her in a tall, dark tower in the middle of a forest. Now this tower was built of stone, and had no door and no stairs, but only a window at the top. Hour after hour Rapunzel would sit at the window looking out on the forest or singing to herself. And when the witch wanted to get to her, she would call, 'Rapunzel, Rapunzel, let down your long hair.' The girl's hair was so long and fine, like spun gold, that it came nearly to the ground, and was as strong as a cord. She would twist it round one of the bars of the window, and the witch would climb up it like a ladder. Then, when she had finished with Rapunzel and given her her food, she would climb down again by the strands of gold hair, which Rapunzel would then draw up again into her room at the top of the tower. It was a lonely life, but the girl sang to keep herself happy.

So the years passed. Rapunzel grew into a fair and graceful maiden, and the witch hated her beauty and vowed she would keep her in the high tower for ever.

2

One day, some years later, it happened that the king's son, who had strayed from his companions while hunting, passed by the stone tower when Rapunzel was singing to herself in her lonely room. He stopped and listened, for never had he heard so beautiful a voice. This is what the voice was singing.

Bird of the air, bird in the tree,
Sing your happiest song to me.
Bird in the tree, bird of the air,
Sing me a song of love or care.
Sing your best,
And I will give you a golden hair,
To line your nest.

The young prince longed to know who it was who sang with such a clear, lovely voice, and he rode up to the tower, but nowhere could he find a door; and even if he had found a door, he could not have climbed up the tower, for there were no stairs. So cunningly had the cruel witch Gothel imprisoned the girl. The prince could do nothing but turn his horse's head and ride home.

Next day he came again, so enchanted was he by the sound of Rapunzel's voice; and every day he came, but never could he find a way into the tall tower.

Then one day he was just approaching it when he saw the witch a little way ahead of him. He hid behind a tree to see what she did.

'Rapunzel, Rapunzel,' called the witch, 'let down your long hair!'

Then the prince was astonished to see a long rope of spun gold being twisted round one of the bars of the window and let down to the ground. Next, he saw Gothel grasp it with her two bony hands and climb nimbly to the window and squeeze through.

'Aha!' thought he. 'That is how to get into the tower where the lady sings!'

So he rode home, and next day he came again towards evening, when he thought the witch would be out of sight. He stood below the window and called softly, 'Rapunzel, Rapunzel, let down your long hair.'

He waited a moment, then the same thing happened as he had seen the day before. The long coil of gold hair fell almost to his feet; so, looking round to see that the witch was nowhere near, he climbed swiftly to the top of the tower and got in through the window.

At first Rapunzel was frightened to see the strange young man instead of the old witch. But he spoke to her in friendly tones, and she thought he was kinder and gentler than Gothel.

'Don't be afraid, sweet maiden,' said the king's son. 'I do not come to harm you. For many days I have listened to the sound of your voice as you sing at the window, and at last I have come to see you.'

So he sat down, and they talked, and the prince told Rapunzel of the world outside the tower, and of the great country over which his father the king ruled.

He came to see her every evening until one day he said to her:

'Rapunzel, I am a prince, and I wish no one but yourself to be my princess. Will you marry me?'

Rapunzel, who loved him dearly, answered, 'Yes,' and put her hand in his. Then he told her that as soon as he could get her out of the stone tower, he would make her his wife.

'Every day when you come to see me,' said Rapunzel, 'bring me a skein of silk. Then I shall weave a ladder, and with this I shall escape out of the window and get safely to the ground.'

The prince did as she said. Every evening, when the witch was nowhere to be seen, he came to the tower and climbed up to Rapunzel and gave her a skein of silk, so that before long she had almost woven the ladder for her escape.

The witch Gothel knew nothing of this until one unlucky day Rapunzel said to her: 'Tell me, Gothel, how is it that when you climb up my hair, you are so much heavier than the young prince who visits me? Why, he seems to fly up in no time.'

Now this was a foolish thing to say, but Rapunzel did not know how angry the witch would be.

'Oh, you wicked girl!' screamed Gothel. 'So you have visitors, have you? It was not for that that I shut you in this tower. Well, I shall put an end to your tricks, you deceitful child!'

So she took out her sharp scissors and snip-snap! in a moment she had cut off all Rapunzel's beautiful hair. Next, she spirited her from the tower and led her away to a wild and dreary wilderness where there was nothing but dead trees and scrub growing amidst the dry stones. And she left Rapunzel there to wander about looking for roots and berries to keep herself from starving.

Then Gothel returned to the tower and fixed Rapunzel's long coil of hair to the bar of the window, and waited. When the prince came and called, 'Rapunzel, Rapunzel, let down your long hair,' she threw down the golden coil at his feet. Lightly he climbed to the window, expecting to see the sweet face of his loved Rapunzel. Instead, he saw the cruel mocking eyes of the witch Gothel.

'So you are the prince who comes sneaking through the forest to see the little bird in the stone cage!' cried the witch in triumph. 'Well, the bird has flown, my beauty, and you will never see her again! Instead, the old cat will scratch out your eyes, you meddling thief!'

'Never!' cried the prince in anger and despair.

So saying, he leapt from the window and fell upon the ground. But he was not killed, only bruised and shaken, for he had fallen into some thorn bushes. Alas! the thorns stuck in his eyes and, blinded, he wandered away, almost mad with grief.

For days he stumbled through the woods, calling upon his lost Rapunzel, blundering here, there and everywhere in his blindness; but no one heard him, and he believed he must soon die from hunger and weariness.

Rapunzel, meanwhile, struggled on through the stony desert that Gothel had banished her to. She seemed to go round and round in circles, for there was no way out. There was scarcely anything to eat or drink, and no birds sang to cheer her. She almost ceased to think of her prince whom she would never see again. Her hair, which the cruel Gothel had snipped off, began to grow again, but her clothes were ragged, and her body thin and starved, so that anyone who had seen her before would no longer recognize her.

One day, when the sun shone, she tried to cheer herself by singing in a voice now small and shaking, and yet with something of its old sweetness:

> 'Bird of the air, bird in the tree,
> Sing your happiest song to me.
> Bird in the tree, bird of the air,
> Sing me a song of love or care.'

The wind carried the notes of her song across the wilderness to the ears of the prince, who, almost dead from weakness and despair, had at last reached the place where Rapunzel wandered.

'What is that sound?' he cried feebly. 'Surely that is her voice – or do I imagine it?'

Blindly he stumbled towards the place where the sound seemed to be, calling out as best he could, 'Rapunzel, Rapunzel, where are you?'

Then she saw him. She ran towards him, crying, 'My prince, is it you? Have you found me at last?'

Then she saw that he was blind. She ran to him and put her arms about him; and the prince, so overcome with joy and faint from thirst and hunger, dropped at her feet. The girl wept to see him in such a sorry state; and as she looked down at his tired, thin face, the tears fell from her eyes on to his. Rapunzel's tears entered his eyes, and he received his sight back again. He looked up at her face and saw her almost as clearly as he had seen her when first he climbed up her golden hair to the window in the high tower.

Somehow they found their way out of the dreary wilderness, and the first thing they did was to go to the king's palace; and the king knew all about Rapunzel's mother and father, and how they had to give up their only child to the cruel witch. So the poor man and his wife were sent for; and there was great rejoicing. Afterwards, the prince and Rapunzel were married, and a great and solemn feast was held.

As for Gothel, they shut her up in her own high tower and kept her there. But the tower was struck by lightning in a great storm and crashed to the ground. The witch vanished, to be seen no more. Some say she was destroyed by lightning; others, that she had flown away on a black cloud. So her garden was deserted, and after a time it was given to the poor man and woman, Rapunzel's parents, who walked in it whenever they wished without fear or hindrance.

THE BROTHERS GRIMM adapted by James Reeves
Illustrated by PEGGY FORTNUM

Foo the Potter

I

LONG ago, in the land of Chen, which is far away in the eastern half of the world, there lived a Princess called Lo-Yen. She was young, beautiful, and passionately fond of music. Now in those days – so long ago it was – the people of Chen did not have music like ours, music on instruments and on bells, and the music of voices. They did not have tunes made up of a series of notes, now high, now low, now soft and now loud. No, their music was made on vases, and each tune consisted of one note only, or at most two or three, made by tapping the side of a vase with a little hammer. The hammer was a wooden ball on the end of a short bamboo stick, and the ball was covered with a piece of kid-skin, so that it did not crack the vase.

It was the object of all the potters in the land of Chen to make a vase more beautiful and of a purer tone than any that had been made before. Each year, in the fifth month, all the makers of vases throughout the land would go up to the palace of the Princess Lo-Yen and take their vases. There was a solemn contest or competition, and the maker of the most beautiful vase would be rewarded with the present of a gold ornament or silver money, and he would be given a special title which would make him highly honoured for the rest of his life.

There was one potter called Foo, who desired most eagerly to make a vase so beautiful that he would be rewarded by the Princess. This was not so much because he wanted a gold ornament or silver coins, as because he wished to please Lo-Yen and see her smile in gratitude. For her beauty was known throughout the land, and her smile was considered to be so gracious that once you beheld it you remembered it for the rest of your days.

So Foo worked in his shed in a poor part of the city, moulding and turning from morning till night. But although he was so hard-working a potter, the truth is that he was clumsy. Sometimes his clay was too dry and broke in the firing. Sometimes it was too thick, so that his vases would not ring to the touch. Sometimes the shapes were ugly, or the glaze was too thick, or the bottom uneven, so that the vase would not stand straight. All the same, he cared little for failure, and worked away diligently, confident that one day he would make the vase which would win him the Princess's bright smile. He had little to live on, but he needed little; the vases that turned out to be failures – and there were plenty of those – were sold in the market as common water-pots, so that Foo was never without the means to live.

Well, the fifth month had come round again, and Foo was resolved to try his luck. So wrapping up his best vase in an old shawl, he walked up to the Palace. He found a great crowd of people assembled. There were musicians and scholars, as well as soldiers to keep the crowd in order, fine ladies and gentlemen who had come to see the contest, and of course a throng of potters who had brought their vases from all over the kingdom.

On a throne in the great hall of state sat the Princess, magnificently clothed in silken robes, with jewelled combs in her hair. Yet for all her splendour, she looked simple and kind as she waited for the competitors to enter. The judges sat beneath the throne at a long table covered with paper and ink and brushes for them to make notes. In front of them was a smaller table spread with a soft cloth on which the vases would be placed. Down the sides of the hall were seats for the audience – silk-covered chairs and couches for the nobles, rough benches for the ordinary people. At the door of the hall stood the first competitor, an old white-haired potter from the far south, who had tried for fifty years to win the prize. Beside him stood a marshal – that is, a man whose business it was to lead him forward and place his vase on the table ready for the chief musician to strike it with the little hammer.

Foo took his place among the other potters. The Princess nodded her head to the chief steward for silence, and the steward struck a great brass gong, and everybody was suddenly hushed. Then the marshal stepped forward and announced the name of the old potter, and the province from which he came. Slowly the old man carried his vase to the table in the centre, placed it on the soft covering, and stood aside. The chief musician examined it for a moment, then struck one, two, three notes on its rounded side. There was a murmur of approval. The note was a fine one – soft, but very pure and sweet. The judges made marks on their papers, for not only was the beauty of the tone considered, but also the shape of the vase, its colour, and its general appearance.

For several hours the contest went on. Some of the vases were tall and slender, some squat and round; some were as white and soft-looking as a summer cloud, others were brightly coloured – jade-green, sky-blue, flame-red, or lemon-yellow. All were different, and all had different notes. To hear some of them, you might have supposed that the note came up from the depths of a tranquil sea; others suggested a sunlit stream in the mountains; one recalled the note of a wood-pigeon on a June afternoon, another was sharp and clear like the noise of a pebble dropping into water. Some notes were long and died away slowly; others were loud and hollow and sharp, and lasted only for the twentieth part of a second.

The day was warm, and the contest went on as if it would never end. The judges covered sheets and sheets of paper with their figures. No one knew who would win. Poor Foo, squatting on the floor just inside the great hall, several times nearly went to sleep. But at last it was his turn. The marshal called out his name and the name of his province, and Foo stepped forward, nearly tripping over the end of the old shawl which had come loose from his precious vase. He reached the table without dropping it, and handed it to the marshal, who placed it on the centre of the table – not without a faint smile, for it was a clumsy-looking object after all the elegant productions that had been seen that day. Its shape was roundish but not very regular; its colour was a dull grey, with an uneven glaze; and it did not stand any too steadily. The people of Chen are very polite, and no one said anything about the appearance of Foo's vase, but most of them thought how clumsy and ill-contrived it was. The court musician took a step forward and struck it with his hammer. It gave no note at all, but a hollow, dead sound, like the sound made by an old cracked jar when a boy kicks a stone against it. Unable to believe his ears, the musician struck it again more loudly. It sounded even worse than before. He tried a third time, more softly, and on the other side of the vase. It was no better. There was a pained silence among the onlookers, except for one little girl who was unable to keep herself from uttering a high-pitched laugh of sheer amusement. Her parents quickly silenced her, but they could scarcely help laughing. Afterwards everybody told each other that it was probably the worst vase that had ever been brought into the presence of the Princess. As for Lo-Yen herself, she said nothing, but looked a little sad.

There were no more vases, and the judges, after talking and comparing notes for some time, finally awarded first place to the old potter whose vase had been tried at the beginning. Everyone was pleased, for he had tried for many years, and now at last the Princess had smiled upon him and given him a tiny golden vase in exchange for his own vase of shapely white porcelain whose note was like the sound of the sea on the rocks in a little bay surrounded by tall cliffs. Then everyone went home, and Foo took up his clay pot, wrapped it in its shawl, and went back to his shed.

He wasted no time feeling sorry about his failure, but the very next day began all over again. A year went by, and he had made no less than a hundred and fifty more pots, of all shapes and sizes. He had little ear for music, but when the fifth month came round again, he chose the one that seemed to him the best, and once more set off for the Palace.

Once more the Princess sat on her throne surrounded by the nobles, the musicians, and the judges; once more the marshals called out the names of the potters, and the chief musician tried out the music of every vase that was brought.

When it was Foo's turn, he came forward with his new vase wrapped in the same ancient shawl that he had used the year before. Some people recognized him, and could not help smiling

to remember what a fool he had made of himself. This time he was a little nervous, for he did so want to please the Princess. Even if he did not win the first prize, he hoped that at least she would keep his vase in her collection, and when she was tired of all her other music, would request her musicians to play on his vase.

Well, sad to say, the noise made by the new one was even worse than that made by the old one.

'It is like the last cluck of a dying hen,' said one listener, and almost half the people could not help laughing out loud.

Without waiting for the end of the contest, Foo, covered with shame and blushing deeply, took up his vase and ran from the hall.

'At least I gave them a good laugh,' he said to himself. But he had noticed that the Princess did not even smile. She was too polite to do that, but she could not keep a certain look of pity from her face.

'Why does such a fool as that come a second time?' asked the chief musician, but no one could answer him. As for the judges, they did not even bother to put a single mark against Foo's name.

2

'Third time lucky,' said the clumsy potter to himself next morning, beginning all over again with a new barrel of clay. But somehow he seemed to make no progress at all. Some of his pots cracked before he could bake them; some fell to pieces in the oven; others were so mis-shapen that even Foo could see they were no good and would not even fetch a single small coin in the market.

It was as if he had lost heart. In the winter, he fell ill and had to spend much of his time keeping warm beside his wretched fire, and making soup from dried herbs to keep himself alive. When at last he felt better, he had scarcely enough spirit in him to begin work again. But one day spring came all in a rush. The sun shone clear and bright, the birds sang joyously, and flowers appeared on the trees in the city square. Foo sat down at his wheel and was soon turning away with a lighter heart than he had had for many months. But he could not think of making a vase for the contest. His landlord came for the rent, and the shopkeepers asked him for money for rice and other things he needed for his scanty meals. He had to work for a living, in order to make up for the time he had lost during his illness. When the fifth month came, Foo had not a single vase on his shelf – no, not so much as a flat dish he could take to the Palace. But on the day before the contest he decided he must have one last try. He remembered the smile of the Princess two years before, when she had handed the old potter his reward, passing to him the little gold vase in a hand more white, more slim and shapely than anything he had ever seen. So with the image of the Princess in his mind, he seized a great lump of red clay and slapped it on to his wheel. He began to turn and shape and mould, until at last he could do no more. He had scarcely time to bake the pot hard before the contest began. He made the oven as hot as he dared and put the pot inside. He knew that he was firing it too fast, but he would have to risk that. All night long he sat beside the oven, keeping it hot by putting pieces of charcoal on the fire beneath. Then as dawn came, he let the fire die down, and when the oven was cool enough he opened the door. By this time the contest was due to begin, so as soon as the vase was cool enough he wrapped it in the old shawl without even troubling to look at it, and carried it to the Palace.

Now there was a new law about this contest, that if any potter tried for a third time, and utterly failed to satisfy the judges, he was to be thrown in prison until it was decided whether he would be kept there for the rest of his life, sent out of the country, or even put to death. It was a cruel law, and few potters dared risk a third attempt unless they had shown themselves reasonably competent in earlier contests.

No one supposed that Foo would have a third try. It would mean certain imprisonment, and several people, who felt kindly towards Foo, clumsy and pig-headed as he seemed, warned him of his danger.

'What do I care about prison?' he said. 'I've never been there before. I'm willing to try it.'

It was no use arguing. Foo was determined to make a fool of himself for the third time. As he looked through the door of the great hall towards where Lo-Yen was sitting, he cared for nothing else. Yet, as the contest went on, he could not help becoming dreadfully nervous, not because of the thought of going to prison, but because he seemed to have lost all hope of pleasing the Princess. Still, he had come to have a last try, and nothing would stop him now. By the time his name was called, poor Foo was trembling all over with fear.

He stepped forward, letting the shawl slip from his vase; and as he did so, he stumbled towards the centre of the hall, tripped over, and fell to the ground. He managed to hold his vase on high just long enough for everyone to see that it was even more monstrous and clumsy than the ones he had brought before. It really was a hideous affair – squat, pot-bellied, and with two rounded handles that were meant to be alike but which anyone could see didn't match. A great roar of laughter filled the hall, and in the middle of it could be heard the crash of Foo's jar as it fell on the marble floor and was smashed to pieces. Indeed, some even said it fell to pieces before it hit the floor.

'Take him away!' shouted the judges, and the chief musician

put his hands to his ears because he could not stand the up-roar.

The Princess said nothing. Instantly, two or three guards ran forward, picked Foo up from the floor, and hurried him out of the hall. He was dragged from the Palace and put in a dark dun-geon, where he lay on the floor and wept from misery and weariness. Apart from his gaoler, who came at sundown and brought him a little rice and some water, everybody in the world soon forgot about him.

Meanwhile, a servant had come forward and swept up the pieces of Foo's wretched vase, and the contest went on. The prize was awarded to a young potter from the eastern province, on whom the Princess smiled enchantingly as she gave him a purse of white leather full of silver pieces in exchange for the exquisitely musical vase which he had brought.

Days passed, then weeks. Nobody thought about Foo, and even the gaoler almost forgot to bring him food and water. Nobody at the Palace bothered to think what to do with him. As for Foo, he no longer cared whether he lived or died.

But a kitchen-boy, a mere youngster who ran errands for the Palace cook, was fond of toys and loved playing about with odds and ends. He didn't care a rush if the cook called him a lazy rascal, so long as he had a length of string to make into a cat's cradle, or a piece of paper to turn into a boat and send down the stream when he had the afternoon off. At the time of the contest, he had seen the servant, who swept up Foo's pot, drop the bits into a rubbish bin in the back yard. He noticed that as the bits of pottery dropped into the bin, they made a pleasant tink-ling sound, rather like the rippling of a stream over the pebbles in some gravelly hillside. The boy picked the pieces out of the bin and took them away. He noticed that, as he tapped each piece, or dropped it on a stone floor, it made a different sound.

So to amuse himself, he chipped a hole in each piece and threaded it on a string. Then he made a frame of bamboo sticks and hung the strings from it in a row. Next, he took a good-sized chicken-bone from the rubbish bin and, using it as a hammer, began to fashion a little tune on the different bits of pottery. He found that the little pieces made high, tinkling sounds, and the bigger ones gave deeper notes.

Now the kitchen-boy, when he was not working, lived in a tiny room at the very top of the Palace, just under the roof, and setting up his bamboo frame in the window, he spent hours tapping out little tunes on the broken crocks. You must remember that nothing like a tune had ever been heard before in the land of Chen, so this was something entirely new. The kitchen-boy had a good ear for music, and it seemed to him that this new kind of sound, hopping up and down from low notes to high, and back, was a merrier, more amusing kind of sound than just single notes.

Well, one afternoon the Princess was walking on a terrace of flowering trees far below the kitchen-boy's window, and so quiet and still was the air that she heard the notes of the pottery instrument quite clearly. And so bright and merry was the kitchen-boy's tune that she gave a little laugh and almost danced for pleasure. At once she sent one of her maids upstairs to tell the boy to come down and bring with him whatever was making this strange new sound. Very shyly the boy came into the presence of the Princess and played his instrument for her until he could think of no more tunes, and it was long past the time when he should have been helping the cook in the kitchen.

The Princess was delighted. She made the boy tell her how he had invented the instrument, and when he said he had got the pieces of crockery from the rubbish-bin, she wanted to know how they had come there. The boy could not remember, so the

servants were sent for and questioned. At last the one who had
swept up Foo's broken vase on the day of the contest remembered
what had happened, and told the Princess.

'Yes, yes,' she cried, 'I remember! Poor fellow. I wonder
what became of him.'

Well, to make a long tale shorter, the Palace guards went to
the prison where Foo was shut up, and brought him out. He
staggered out, hardly able to walk for weakness and hardly able
to see because the light was so strong after his dark cell. So he
was carried to the presence of Lo-Yen, who thanked him most
graciously for having made the pieces of crockery which had

been turned into so delightful an instrument. Then he was given food and clean clothing, and afterwards was allowed to use a little shed in the Palace yard, where he could go on making pieces of crockery for musical instruments. For soon this new music became the fashion, and the noble ladies and gentlemen all wanted sets of pieces strung on a bamboo frame. And the Palace musicians came and learned the new music from the kitchen-boy, and invented different and complicated tunes of their own. And that was the beginning of true music in the land of Chen.

As for Foo, he got strong and well again, and worked happily at his trade in the Palace yard. The Princess came and talked with him sometimes and smiled upon him; but to Foo she never smiled more sweetly than when she first spoke to him after he had left prison, and thanked him for making the vase that had broken in pieces.

JOHN PENDRY

A Spell for Sleeping

Sweet william, silverweed, sally-my-handsome.
Dimity darkens the pittering water.
On gloomed lawns wanders a king's daughter.
Curtains are clouding the casement windows.
A moon-glade smurrs the lake with light.
Doves cover the tower with quiet.

Three owls whit-whit in the withies.
Seven fish in a deep pool shimmer.
The princess moves to the spiral stair.

Slowly the sickle moon mounts up.
Frogs hump under moss and mushroom.
The princess climbs to her high hushed room,

Step by step to her shadowed tower.
Water laps the white lake shore.
A ghost opens the princess' door.

Seven fish in the sway of the water.
Six candles for a king's daughter.
Five sighs for a drooping head.
Four ghosts to gentle her bed.
Three owls in the dusk falling.
Two tales to be telling.
One spell for sleeping.

Tamarisk, trefoil, tormentil.
Sleep rolls down from the clouded hill.
A princess dreams of a silver pool.

The moonlight spreads, the soft ferns flitter.
Stilled in a shimmering drift of water,
Seven fish dream of a lost king's daughter.

ALASTAIR REID

INDEX OF TITLES

Ah Poor Bird!, 164

Baker's Daughter, The, 165
Before the Paling of the Stars, 172
Bells, 469
Birthdays, 420
Blunder, 90
Bobby Shaftoe, 245
Boy, The, 202
Brer Rabbit, He's a Good Fisherman, 357

Calico Pie, 109
Caliph Stork, The Story of, 54
Can Men be Such Fools as All That?, 203
Cat That Walked by Himself, The, 448
Cherry, A, 219
Christmas Tree, The, 41
Cobwebs, 329
Constant Tin Soldier, The, 342
Cripple Creek, 220

Dobbin and the Silver Shoes, The Tale of, 112
Dutch Cheese, The, 7

Elizabeth, 219

Fable of the Old Man, the Boy and the Donkey, The, 461
Fairies, The, 361

Fairies of the Caldon Low, The, 381
Father Sparrow's Tug-of-War, 240
Fly, The, 443
Flying Postman, The, 246
Follow my Bangalorey Man, 279
Foo the Potter, 481
Fool of the World and the Flying Ship, The, 403
Frog and the Crow, The, 52
From a Railway Carriage, 339

Gather ye Rosebuds, 208
Giacco and His Bean, 298
Golden Touch, The, 135
Grand Panjandrum, The, 53
Green Broom, 146

Hare and Tortoise, 98
Hero of Haarlem, The, 365
Hole in Your Stocking, A, 236
Hopping Frog, 40
How Still the Bells, 463
Hymn for Saturday, A, 471

I Had a Little Nut-Tree, 324
If All the Seas, 380

John Cook's Mare, 78
Johnny Crow's Garden, 68
Jumblies, The, 198

Kind Visitor, The, 120
Kitten, A, 386

Lady Greensleeves, 221
La Hormiguita and Perez the Mouse, 399
Lazy Jack, 375
Lilliput-Land, 372
Lion and Mouse, 143
London Sparrow, 374
Lory Who Longed for Honey, The, 82

Magic Ball, The, 288
Mary Indoors, 364
Mima, 312
My Delight, 171

Naughty Boy, A, 404
Needle and Thread, A, 201
Nicholas and the Fast Moving Diesel, 313
Nicholas Nye, 430
Night, 460
Norwegian Childhood, A, 432

O Little Town of Bethlehem, 349
Ogre Courting, The, 306
Old Grey Goose, The, 15
Old Man, the Boy and the Donkey, The Fable of the, 461
Old Shellover, 67
Old Woman and Her Pig, The, 79
Old Woman in the Basket, The, 447
Owl and the Pussy-Cat, The, 325

Paul, the Hero of the Fire, 24
Paul's Tale, 209
Pavilion in the Laurels, The, 148

Pooh and Piglet Go Hunting, 464
Poor Old Horse, 23
Poringer, 174
Prickety Prackety, 16
Pumpkin, The, 287

Queen Mab, 239

Rapunzel, 472
Rilloby-Rill, 444
Robin Goodfellow, 37
Robin Redbreast's Thanksgiving, 191
Roddy and the Red Indians, 175
Row, Row, Row your Boat, 370

Simple Simon, 174
Six Badgers, The, 261
Six o'Clock Bells, 398
Small Brown Mouse, The, 421
Sneezing, 108
Snow and Sun, 301
Spell for Sleeping, A, 494
Spells, 351
Statue, The, 207
Story of Caliph Stork, The, 54
Swallows, The, 262

Tailor and the Crow, The, 371
Tale of Dobbin and the Silver Shoes, The, 112
Then, 471
There was a Crooked Man, 341
Theseus and the Minotaur, 102
Thunder, the Elephant and Dorobo, The, 280
Tim Rabbit, 1
Topsyturvey-world, 419

Turn Again Whittington, 89
Turtle Soup, 403

W, 197
Well of the World's End, The, 387
Whence is This Fragrance?, 327

Where Arthur Sleeps, 72
Wind in a Frolic, The, 302
Wonderful Tar-Baby, The, 354
Written in March, 396

York, York for my Money, 259

INDEX OF AUTHORS

AESOP
Hare and Tortoise, 98
Lion and Mouse, 143
ALLINGHAM, William
The Fairies, 361
ANDERSEN, Hans
The Constant Tin Soldier, 342
ARDIZZONE, Edward
Nicholas and the Fast Moving
Diesel, 313
Paul, the Hero of the Fire, 24

BERG, Leila
The Lory Who Longed for
Honey, 82
BIANCO, Margery Williams
The Baker's Daughter, 165
BJÖRNSEN, Björnsterne
A Norwegian Childhood, 432
BLAKE, William
Night, 460
BOTSFORD, Florence
Giacco and His Bean, 298
BROOKE, L. Leslie
Johnny Crow's Garden, 68
BROOKS, Bishop Phillips
O Little Town of Bethlehem, 349
BROWNE, Frances
Lady Greensleeves, 221

CARROLL, Lewis
Turtle Soup, 403
CHOLLET, Louise E.
Blunder, 90

CLARK, Elizabeth
Father Sparrow's Tug-of-War,
240
Robin Redbreast's Thanksgiving,
191
The Tale of Dobbin and the
Silver Shoes, 112

DE LA MARE, Walter
The Dutch Cheese, 7
The Fly, 443
Mima, 312
Nicholas Nye, 430
Old Shellover, 67
Then, 471
DICKINSON, Emily
How Still the Bells, 463
DODGE, Mary Mapes
The Hero of Haarlem, 365
DRUMMOND, V. H.
The Flying Postman, 246

ELDERTON, William
York, York for my Money, 259
ELVEY, Gerald (translator)
A Norwegian Childhood by
Björnsterne Björnsen, 432
EWING, Juliana Horatia
The Ogre Courting, 306

FARJEON, Eleanor
The Boy, 202
Can Men be Such Fools as All
That?, 203

FARJEON, Eleanor – *contd*
  A Kitten, 386
  London Sparrow, 374
  Mary Indoors, 364
FINGER, Charles J.
  The Magic Ball, 288
FOOTE, Samuel
  The Grand Panjandrum, 53

GARNETT, Eve
  The Kind Visitor, 120
GATTY, Margaret
  Cobwebs, 329
GRAVES, Robert
  The Pumpkin, 287
  The Six Badgers, 261
GRIMM, The Brothers
  Rapunzel, 472

HARMAN, Humphrey
  The Thunder, the Elephant and
    Dorobo, 280
HARRIS, Joel Chandler
  The Wonderful Tar-Baby, 354
  Brer Rabbit, He's a Good
    Fisherman, 357
HERRICK, Robert
  Gather ye Rosebuds, 208
  Queen Mab, 239
HOWITT, Mary
  The Fairies of the Caldon Low,
    381
HOWITT, William
  The Wind in a Frolic, 302

JANSSON, Tove
  The Christmas Tree, 41

JONES, Gwyn
  Where Arthur Sleeps, 72
JONSON, Ben
  Robin Goodfellow, 37

KEATS, John
  A Naughty Boy, 404
KINGSLEY, Charles
  Theseus and the Minotaur, 102
KIPLING, Rudyard
  The Cat That Walked by
    Himself, 448

LANG, Andrew
  The Story of Caliph Stork, 54
LANG, E. H.
  Roddy and the Red Indians, 175
LEAR, Edward
  Calico Pie, 109
  The Jumblies, 198
  The Owl and the Pussy-Cat, 325

McNEILL, Janet
  The Small Brown Mouse, 421
MILNE, A. A.
  Pooh and Piglet Go Hunting,
    464
MOLESWORTH, Mrs
  The Swallows, 262

NEWBOLT, Henry
  Rilloby-Rill, 444
NORTON, Mary
  Paul's Tale, 209

PENDRY, John
  Foo the Potter, 481

PICARD, Barbara Leonie
  The Pavilion in the Laurels, 148

RANDS, William Brighty
  Lilliput-Land, 372
  Topsyturvey-World, 419
RANSOME, Arthur
  The Fool of the World and the
    Flying Ship, 405
REEVES, James
  Bells, 469
  Spells, 351
  The Statue, 207
  W, 197
  The Well of the World's End,
    387
REID, Alastair
  A Spell for Sleeping, 494
ROSS, Diana
  A Hole in Your Stocking, 236
  Prickety Prackety, 16
ROSSETTI, Christina
  Before the Paling of the Stars, 172
  Hopping Frog, 40

SAWYER, Ruth
  La Hormiguita and Perez the
    Mouse, 403
SERRAILLIER, Ian
  The Fable of the Old Man, the
    Boy and the Donkey, 461
SHARP, Cecil J. (collector and arranger)
  Cripple Creek, 220
SMART, Christopher
  A Hymn for Saturday, 471
STEVENSON, Robert Louis
  From a Railway Carriage, 339

TURNER, Marianne (translator)
  The Christmas Tree by Tove
    Jansson, 41

UTTLEY, Alison
  Tim Rabbit, 1

WORDSWORTH, William
  Written in March, 396
WYATT, Honor
  The Golden Touch, 135

INDEX OF FIRST LINES OF VERSE

A carrion crow sat on an oak, 371

A jolly fat frog did in the river swim, O, 52

Ah poor bird!, 164

And where have you been, my Mary, 381

Aren't you coming out, Mary?, 364

As I was a-hoeing my lands, 261

As I went through the garden gap, 219

As I went through the North country, 259

Beautiful soup, so rich and green, 403

Before the paling of the stars, 172

Bobby Shaftoe's gone to sea, 245

Calico Pie, 109

'Come!' said Old Shellover, 67

Cripple Creek girls don't you want to go to Somerset?, 220

Elizabeth, Elspeth, Betty and Bess, 219

Faster than fairies, faster than witches, 339

Follow my Bangalorey Man, 279

From Oberon in Fairyland, 37

Gather ye rosebuds while ye may, 208

Go and tell Aunt Nancy, 15

Grasshoppers four a-fiddling went, 444

Hard as crystal, 469

He's nothing much but fur, 386

Hobbled to market an old man and his boy, 461

Hopping frog, hop here and be seen, 40

How large unto the tiny fly, 443

How still the bells in steeples stand, 463

I dance and dance without any feet, 351

I had a little nut-tree, 324

If all the seas were one sea, 380

If the butterfly courted the bee, 419

If ye will with Mab find grace, 239

Is it, I wonder, a rum thing, 202

Jemima is my name, 312

John Cook he had a little grey mare, 78

Johnny Crow, 68

Monday's child is fair of face, 420

My clothing was once of the linsey woolsey fine, 23

My delight's in pansies-o, 171

Now's the time for mirth and play, 471

O little town of Bethlehem, 349
Old Mother Twitchett had but one
    eye, 201
On a stone chair in the market-
    place, 207

Row, row, row your boat, 370

Simple Simon met a pieman, 174
Six o'clock bells ringing, 398
Sneeze on Monday, sneeze for
    danger, 108
Sparrow, you little brown gutter-
    mouse, 374
Sweet william, silverweed, sally-
    my-handsome, 494

The cock is crowing, 396
The King sent for his wise men all,
    197
The Owl and the Pussy-cat went to
    sea, 325
The sun descending in the west, 460
The wind one morning sprang up
    from sleep, 302

There was a crooked man, 341
There was a naughty boy, 404
There was an old man lived out in
    the wood, 146
There was an old woman tossed up
    in a basket, 447
They went to sea in a sieve, they
    did, 198
Thistle and darnel and dock grew
    there, 430
Turn again Whittington, 89
Twenty, forty, sixty, eighty, 471

Up the airy mountain, 361

What is the rhyme for poringer?,
    174
Whence is this fragrance all
    perfuming, 327
Where does Pinafore Palace stand?,
    372
White bird, featherless, 301

You may not believe it, for hardly
    could I, 287

INDEX OF ARTISTS

ARDIZZONE, Edward, 24, 26, 28, 30, 32–3, 35, 313, 316, 318, 321

BOURNE, Holly, 202, 364
BROOKE, L. Leslie, 68, 71
BROOKER, Christopher, 434, 439

CALDECOTT, Randolph, 89
CONWAY, Gillian, 55, 62; 76; 79, 81, 82, 87, 95; 102, 107; 137, 141; 147; 151, 152–3, 159; 169, 193; 204–5, 206; 227, 232; 240; 264, 270; 280, 284, 285; 308; 324; 331, 334; 341; 345, 347; 366, 369; 371; 378; 389, 393, 394; 407, 411, 413; 447; 481, 486, 492

DRUMMOND, V. H., 246, 247, 248, 249, 251, 255, 256, 257, 258

FORTNUM, Peggy, 37; 172, 173; 302, 303, 304, 305; 349; 361, 362, 363; 381, 383; 472, 474
FRIERS, Rowel, 421, 425

GARNETT, Eve, 120, 122, 127, 129, 133

HAWKINS, Irene, 9
HODGSON, Robert, 259; 463

JANSSON, Tove, 44, 45, 47, 51
JAQUES, Faith, 236, 238; 399, 401

KIPLING, Rudyard, 452

LEAR, Edward, 109, 110, 111; 198; 325, 326

MARSHALL, Constance, 99, 100; 143, 145; 261; 354, 356, 358, 359; 374; 386
MILES, Jennifer, 1, 3, 6; 16, 19, 22
MILROY, Joan, 220, 339
MERMAGEN, Ismena, 112, 114, 118

PATON, Jane, 351, 352; 396, 397; 444, 445

SHEPARD, E. H., 466
SPENCE, Geraldine, 208, 211, 215, 217

WALKER, Audrey, 175, 178–9, 181, 182, 186, 187, 189

THE STORIES CLASSIFIED

*The following classified list has been contributed by a librarian as a
help to parents, teachers, and other librarians*

STORIES FOR THE YOUNGEST READER

TIM RABBIT *by Alison Uttley* 1
PRICKETY PRACKETY *by Diana Ross* 16
THE OLD WOMAN AND HER PIG 79
THE TALE OF DOBBIN AND THE SILVER SHOES *by Elizabeth Clark* 112
THE BAKER'S DAUGHTER *by Margery Williams Bianco* 165
A HOLE IN YOUR STOCKING *by Diana Ross* 236
THE FLYING POSTMAN *by V. H. Drummond* 246
GIACCO AND HIS BEAN *by Florence Botsford* 298
LAZY JACK 375
POOH AND PIGLET GO HUNTING *by A. A. Milne* 464

STORIES OF THE SUPERNATURAL

THE DUTCH CHEESE *by Walter de la Mare* 7
THE STORY OF CALIPH STORK *by Andrew Lang* 54
BLUNDER *by Louise E. Chollet* 90
THE PAVILION IN THE LAURELS *by Barbara Leonie Picard* 148
LADY GREENSLEEVES *by Frances Browne* 221
THE MAGIC BALL *by Charles J. Finger* 288
THE OGRE COURTING *by Juliana Horatia Ewing* 306
THE CONSTANT TIN SOLDIER *by Hans Andersen* 342
THE WELL OF THE WORLD'S END *by James Reeves* 387
THE FOOL OF THE WORLD AND THE FLYING SHIP
   by Arthur Ransome 405
RAPUNZEL *by the Brothers Grimm* 472

STORIES FROM HISTORY AND MYTH

WHERE ARTHUR SLEEPS *by Gwyn Jones* 72
THESEUS AND THE MINOTAUR *by Charles Kingsley* 102

THE STORIES CLASSIFIED

THE GOLDEN TOUCH *by Honor Wyatt*   135
THE HERO OF HAARLEM *by Mary Mapes Dodge*   365

STORIES OF YESTERDAY

THE LORY WHO LONGED FOR HONEY *by Leila Berg*   82
CAN MEN BE SUCH FOOLS AS ALL THAT? *by Eleanor Farjeon*   203
THE SWALLOWS *by Mrs Molesworth*   262
A NORWEGIAN CHILDHOOD *by Björnsterne Björnsen;*   432
FOO THE POTTER *by John Pendry*   481

STORIES OF TODAY

PAUL, THE HERO OF THE FIRE *by Edward Ardizzone*   24
THE KIND VISITOR *by Eve Garnett*   120
RODDY AND THE RED INDIANS *by E. H. Lang*   175
PAUL'S TALE *by Mary Norton*   209
NICHOLAS AND THE FAST MOVING DIESEL *by Edward Ardizzone*   313

FABLES AND ANIMAL STORIES

HARE AND TORTOISE *by Aesop*   98
LION AND MOUSE *by Aesop*   143
ROBIN REDBREAST'S THANKSGIVING *by Elizabeth Clark*   191
FATHER SPARROW'S TUG-OF-WAR *by Elizabeth Clark*   240
THE THUNDER, THE ELEPHANT, AND DOROBO
     by Humphrey Harman   280
COBWEBS *by Margaret Gatty*   329
THE WONDERFUL TAR-BABY *by Joel Chandler Harris*   354
BRER RABBIT, HE'S A GOOD FISHERMAN *by Joel Chandler Harris*   357
LA HORMIGUITA AND PEREZ THE MOUSE *by Ruth Sawyer*   399
THE CAT THAT WALKED BY HIMSELF *by Rudyard Kipling*   448

STORIES AND CAROLS FOR CHRISTMAS

THE CHRISTMAS TREE *by Tove Jansson;*   41
BEFORE THE PALING OF THE STARS *by Christina Rossetti*   172
WHENCE IS THIS FRAGRANCE?   327
O LITTLE TOWN OF BETHLEHEM *by Bishop Phillips Brooks*   349
THE SMALL BROWN MOUSE *by Janet McNeill*   421

THE INVISIBLE WOMBLE AND OTHER STORIES

Elisabeth Beresford

Fresh from their television appearance, here are the Wimbledon Wombles, led by Great Uncle Bulgaria, cared for by Tobermory and entertained, as ever, by Bungo and Orinoco. These five stories are re-tellings of some of the television adventures and reveal the Wombles at their funniest and best and will certainly ensure their place in the family long after they have left the studios and bolted the door of their burrow behind them.

BAD BOYS

compiled by Eileen Colwell

Twelve splendid stories about naughty boys, by favourite authors like Charlotte Hough, Helen Cresswell, Barbara Softly and Ursula Moray Williams. (*Original*)

FATTYPUFFS AND THINIFERS

Andre Maurois

Edmund Double loved food and was plump, but his brother Terry was very thin, and when they took a moving staircase to the Country Under the Earth, they found themselves split up and in the midst of the dispute between the Fattypuffs and the Thinifers.

TALES OF OLGA DA POLGA

Michael Bond

Michael Bond's latest heroine is an enchantingly independent guinea-pig with a zest for adventure, but amongst her tall stories there is a lot of practical advice on how to keep guinea-pigs healthy and happy. (*Original*)

OLGA MEETS HER MATCH

Michael Bond

More stories about Olga, her friends Noel, Fangio and Graham, and a fascinating new suitor, a Russian guinea-pig prince named Boris. (*Original*)

CHARLIE AND THE CHOCOLATE FACTORY

Roald Dahl

When Charlie won the fifth Golden Ticket which allowed him to inspect the wonders of Mr Wonka's Chocolate Factory, he entered a 'world of mystic and marvellous surprises', and so will all newcomers to this entrancing and astonishing book which has already sold half a million copies all over the world and is now published in paperback for the first time. Guaranteed pleasure for anyone old or young enough to enjoy Hot Ice Cream, Eatable Marshmallow Pillows or Mr Wonka's Three Course Dinner chewing gum.